FOR KILLERS WITH LOVE

Arrie G. Weiss

The country and the city mentioned in this novel
are fictitious. Instead of giving them made-up names, the
author has decided to leave them nameless because they have
many real-world prototypes.

CHAPTER ONE

I have named myself Miro Kazimirski, but the name I was born with, sadly, is Zomirovan Lavrovrodinski. As you can see, I've taken the "Miro" from Zo-miro-van, while from Lavrovrodinski I have used only the suffix "ski," which I have attached to Kazimir, who is my favorite physicist, because he was the first to discover the power of the vacuum or, in other words, of nothingness. As a child, I used to think of myself as nothingness—as an absolute nobody, that is—but that time is over now. I began discovering my strength while just a teenager, and now, on my thirtieth birthday, I can say openly that I am one hell of a specimen—strong like a Bengal tiger and almost as handsome. My childhood traumas, however, continue their sorry existence in me in a dangerous union, with the tendency for taking risks I've inherited from both my father and mother. A pathological tendency for taking risks that are huge and mostly physical.

Actually, I have never seen my father, and the last time I saw my mother, I was a one-month-old baby. I don't know where they are today or if they are alive, which I strongly doubt, considering the aforementioned reckless tendencies of theirs. My grandfather also doubts that. He's the man who raised me after his wacky daughter took off for the unknown on her motorcycle.

I must say that my grandfather stands out sharply, with his unkind character and main flaws of groundless short-temperedness, uncontrollable avariciousness, and, first and foremost, uncalled-for, untimely frankness. I've suffered from these flaws of his many times, but it was his frankness that was too much for me and far too much than I deserved. I was only six when he told me, "Your mother and father are two idiots," and drove home the point with the following story.

They met on a minefield in Afghanistan, where they were in their capacity as volunteers. They liked each other at first sight, and while defusing a land mine, they started a casual flirtation that later grew into passionate love or probably passionate hate. It doesn't matter. What matters is that their relationship became more and more strained, and this process included not only quarreling in the face of death but also fighting in the most inappropriate places—close to the enemy while on a reconnaissance mission, for example, or up in the clouds during parachute jumps.

But the tension between them reached its peak when they were least expecting it or, in other words, when, in the form of an embryo, I came from the void. Actually, whether there was an "I" during those first months is a question no one can answer. Probably we would never know the exact moment an embryo becomes a human. It's a fact, however, that my parents neither planned me as an embryo nor wanted me as a human. This is what my grandfather told me during one of his bursts of uncalled-for frankness. A burst that unfortunately coincided with my sixth birthday.

Well, is it any wonder then that from that day on I hated my birthdays? It's not, right? And is it any wonder that my grandfather, a man of such bad temper, is a psychotherapist? Why, yes, it is a wonder, and when you add his professional success to this, the wonder becomes even greater. But that's how things are. The world is full of mysteries, as people say.

What's also a mystery, at least to me, is my mother's behavior thirty years ago. First she told my father that she was going to get rid of the "little bun"—meaning me—and when he agreed with her, she suddenly became stubborn about it and didn't get rid of it. I was born out of wedlock, of course. After that it was my father's turn to act stubborn, so he acknowledged me as his son without even seeing me. I've been asking myself why did he do it, and the only explanation that comes to mind is that he acknowledged me only to get back at her by forcing on her his ridiculous family name: Lavrovrodinski. While my mother's revenge for this was to stitch together my name, Zomirovan, using syllables from the names of two or three of her previous lovers.

Alas! I am at a loss for words to express my outrage at this parental disgrace. The only consolation I have is that both he and she have disappeared from my life during my earliest years, so at least now I am not plagued by firsthand memories of them. It's the secondhand ones that I cannot get rid of, because, besides imposing a bunch of those on me, my grandfather never misses an opportunity to refresh them. I have the feeling that he would somehow manage not to miss it even today, on my thirtieth birthday, even though I've turned my phone off and the distance between us is almost three hundred miles.

So, it has always been crystal clear to me that I wasn't born under a lucky star. Recently, however, my situation has deteriorated drastically, and now I am a broke and fired cop, headed for the bottom not only figuratively but also literally. Yes, literally, because I started a new job today—I'll be tagging sharks with satellite trackers in their natural environment. I hope the job is interesting. After idling away an entire month feeling depressed, I need some excitement in my life.

In fact, the process of my failure began a little over a month ago when Harry, my closest friend, hit me with the news that his wife was in the hospital. Fulminant lung cancer—such was the diagnosis—and only an emergency and extremely expensive surgery could save her. I knew that there was no way for him to collect such a sum in so little time, so I decided to help him. I transferred all my savings to his account and also gave him the money from the sale of my car, an almost new Audi A8, for which I quickly found a buyer. His eyes filled with tears, Harry thanked me and hurried away to arrange his wife's deliverance, but on the very next morning, I got a phone call from her—and she sounded perfectly well and mad with anger. Last week, it turned out that she went to her mother's for a week. She came back to a ransacked apartment and, as she found out later, depleted bank accounts. "I'm starting a new life with a new woman in a new place," Harry's angry message said.

"I hope you and Miro forgive me. And not follow me!" Well, we didn't forgive him, and we didn't follow him. I give him a year or so to come back, to his wife—a lot less than that.

But it seems true that evil never comes alone. On that morning, I went to work an hour later and, of course, in a nasty mood, and my boss, the way he is, instantly jumped on me, this time for being late. I reminded him that for the three years in the Criminal Investigation Department, I'd accumulated hundreds and hundreds of extra—and unpaid—hours. Absolutely unabashed, he started fuming and even called me a slacker. I endured that too. I suggested he shut up, but he didn't listen, so I shut his mouth with a fist. And although it really wasn't my goal to break his jaw, that's what happened.

This is how my boss got his orthopedic braces and I an instant dismissal. He could have pressed charges against me but was wise enough not to do it. Otherwise, the media would've made the incident public, thus turning him into a laughing stock: "The Beaten Boss," "Punch-Bag Boss," and so on.

CHAPTER TWO

As soon as my feet touched the ocean floor, all thoughts of past troubles left my head and shot up to the surface. My intention was to survive, and in order to do this, I had to focus only on the present. I kneeled for better stability, took a salmon from the basket, and waved it at the white shark swimming not far from where I stood. Naturally, the twelve-feet-long creature instantly showed gastronomical interest, but whether it was for the salmon or me, I could not tell. Having taken a comfortable position in his cage, the cameraman was already filming and probably hoping for the second option. It's nothing personal. That's his job.

I focused my attention back on the shark. Just as I thought, I didn't have to wait long. After a few exploratory rounds, it came closer to me, opened a mouth as big as a politician's during an election campaign, and…swallowed the salmon without even touching my hand! An agile animal, and, at least at this point, friendly. I guess some stories about the ferocity of the white sharks are greatly exaggerated. I took another salmon from the basket, and it was swallowed in the same fashion. I changed the tactics for the next portions—I would not let go of the treat right away so that the shark would have to pull it from my hand. I used the opportunity to take a closer look at its face. I wanted to try a technique applied by some famous divers who, by rubbing the receptors around the nose and the mouth of these dangerous predators, manage to bring them into a trance.

It was not an easy task, especially as I had no past experience whatsoever, but then again if I had, the thrill would not have been so strong. My adrenaline was rushing madly. I felt charged with energy, with emotion, and I no longer regretted refusing to put on the protective suit. I slowly reached my hand—which appeared frighteningly vulnerable in its thin glove—over its toothy snout. Time seemed to stretch indefinitely in this short moment that could have been my last. *I love you, life!* I thought. *I also love myself! I love that shark too…*

I began rubbing its nose and gradually moved to around the mouth. I felt its body of a killer relax and continued on. I caressed it like I have never caressed any of my lovers. I watched its eyes, and it was watching me too. We were swaying on the ocean floor in rhythm, trusting each other, and the trance was no longer the beast's alone; to some degree, it was mine also.

As usual, though, the human partner, in this case me, was about to prove his treacherousness. I overcame my sentimental scruples without any difficulty. I slid my hand down toward the pliers with the satellite tracker, and as soon as I unhooked it from my belt, I abandoned my caresses. I swam by the dazed fish, and reaching for its dorsal fin, I squeezed it with the pliers, turning on the drill.

I don't know if the shark felt pain or was just startled, but in any case, it came out of the trance. It bolted forward, pulling me with it because the vaunted special pliers locked. I had to either let go of them and leave the shark to carry the pliers on its fin to the end of its days or...keep my grip.

I pressed close to its body; waited for it to slow down; and, still clutching at the pair of pliers, managed to climb on its back. The ride was short but effective. I opened the pliers with a sudden movement that pushed me backward, but the shark reacted to this by taking a turn and heading straight for me. It passed me by! The satellite tracker on its fin flashed before my eyes—it looked firmly attached, although right now that was no cause for joy.

I searched for the cameraman's cage and found it not far off. I started swimming toward it. The shark rushed in my direction once again but sped past me a second time. I reached the cage, but the cameraman didn't seem to remember to open it. He was filming like a madman. I thrust my hand through the bars and pushed the button myself so that despite the delay, I was safe inside during the shark's next round. The cage closed automatically. I gave a signal to pull us up and shoved my knee into the cameraman's stomach, but due to the water's resistance, the result was far from what I had intended.

CHAPTER THREE

Back on the yacht, everything swam before my eyes from anger because of the blocked pliers and the insufferable operator. The moment I took off my mask, though, I started seeing red, even though the woman who approached me was all in white.

"A fabulous spectacle!" She applauded. "I was watching in real time, but I'm definitely buying the film..." She turned toward the cameraman but saw only his back while he was reasonably walking away from me, scuttling on the deck.

I glowered at my employer, the ichthyologist-environmentalist.

"I didn't invite her here!" He hurried to deny. "I, too, had no idea she was on board!"

I nodded at him; got rid of the diving tank; and, kicking my flippers to the side, made for the captain's cabin. I stormed inside.

"Congratulations!" the captain greeted me, looking embarrassed. "Everything's fine. The satellite is already sending—"

I cut him off. "Who is she? And why is she here?"

"She's here because of you, but she's been hiding until now…from you."

"You've sold me out!" I said, through clenched teeth. "You've made a spectacle out of me!"

"Well, yes," he admitted. "The lady was very insistent…and generous."

"I'll be generous toward you too!" She entered with a smile. "Now I have no doubts that you are the man I need."

I didn't say anything. I was shocked by this stranger who had sneaked onboard for some unclear reason and who was now talking to me in such an unceremonious tone. I mean, what the hell was that attitude? Did she take me for a gigolo? I pulled down the zipper of the diving suit. I was sweating, almost suffocating, but suddenly realized that she might interpret this for something implying agreement—as if I was saying, *There! I'm ready to take everything off, madam*—and quickly pulled the zipper back up.

The captain used the moment to sneak out, and she took his seat and smiled again. Her face— a cocreation between Mother Nature and plastic surgery—was cleaned from even the tiniest mimic wrinkles, but I could tell she was getting closer to forty, unless she had already passed fifty...or was only thirty. Due to some strange coincidence, her eyes were big, round, and glass blue, just like the shark's. But her mouth was small, which unfortunately did not stop her from dealing a serious verbal blow to me: "Your grandpa directed me to you."

"But he doesn't know where I am!" I exclaimed. "He's not supposed to know—"

"You're wrong," she objected. "Immediately after you were fired from the police, he sent two private investigators after you, whose daily reports pushed him to 'the edge of despair,' as he himself called it. 'My grandson would've made a great detective had he not inherited the idiocy of his mother and father, who—'"

"And so on!" I stopped her rudely. "This is old news, madam."

"You're wrong," she objected again. "The news is that, according to your grandpa, it's about time you took at least one intellectual risk, not only physical ones. That's why he directed me to you. And he told me to tell you that I am your birthday present from him."

"Is that so?"

"Yes. Because the job I will hire you for involves all kinds of risk, plus a hefty sum of money in exchange."

"I'm not interested," I said and headed for the door.

"You're wrong," she objected a third time. "After I explain, I'm sure you'll be interested. Also, your grandpa insists—"

I left the cabin. Anger was urging me to find the captain or at least the cameraman immediately, but I managed to contain it. A month ago I got off lightly with discharge only for battery, but a second offense would surely put me behind bars.

CHAPTER FOUR

I took a shower, not caring how much water I used, and after that poured myself whiskey, not caring how much I used of that either. I put some decent clothes on, because I was almost sure that my grandfather's "gift" was going to pay me another visit soon, and lay back on the uncomfortable bunk, glass in hand. The cabin I was given was tiny and not cozy, but that was not bothering me. I had just escaped a visit to the shark's belly, so this place looked great to me.

I sipped the whiskey and waited. My anger had calmed down, giving way to curiosity. Of course, out of pure stubbornness, I declined the job offer, no matter the size of the paycheck and the dangers it promised, but I was nevertheless excited by the fact that my grandfather had personally made an effort to take care of me—and went to such extent as to hire detectives! A true feat, considering his fanatical avariciousness.

Presently someone knocked at the door and opened it immediately, without waiting for an invitation to come in. I turned, put out by such insolence, but the moment I saw the visitor, I was dumb with surprise. An unpleasant surprise, that is, because compared to him, I—with my solid build and height of over six feet—felt like a dwarf.

I stood up immediately. The uninvited guest stepped in, and the cabin darkened, from his enormous size, black clothes, and the dark-brown color of his skin. My trained eye easily guessed that he was born with a face with regular features. Not that it was ugly now, but I wouldn't call it handsome either, what with its repeatedly broken nose, badly healed eyebrow arch, and the botched stitch job across the cheekbone and all the way to the drooping right ear.

"Valdo," he said.

"No," I told him. "I'm Miro."

"But I am Valdo," he clarified.

I shrugged. "So?"

"So?" I saw a flash of irritation in the darkness of his eyes. "So what?"

"Hmm. What are you saying?"

We stared at each other with a primal hostility that stopped us from overcoming in a civilized manner the awkward start of our conversation. Neither of us would avert his eyes first, and even though we were silent, the air around us seemed to vibrate from some telepathic snarls.

"What's happening? Did you start playing cards?" someone called from outside. A moment later another guy, a blond, but also dressed in black and of a size as impressive as Valdo's, showed up at the frame of the open door. Unlike Valdo, this one didn't look like a professional wrestler, only like a body builder on steroids.

"Dammit!" I lost it. "How many of you are there? How many of you boars have been hiding from me on this shit boat?"

"Move it!" Valdo said. "We have to take you to the lady."

"What if I don't want to?"

"Call me Sirius," the blond suggested. "But if you don't want to walk, we can carry you."

The idea of those two carrying me away was something I did not like at all. I salvaged some of my dignity by slowly finishing the whiskey before their envious eyes and then urged them on with a strict gesture as if the decision to take them to the "lady" was mine, not theirs.

Still dressed in white but with her hat missing, the lady was sitting comfortably in one of the chaise longues sheltered by the upper deck. Beside her was a table covered with sandwiches and all kinds of fancy biscuits—an abundance, in the midst of which stood out a solitary and relatively small pitcher filled with orange juice.

I relaxed in the chaise longue on the other side of the table and grabbed a sandwich right away. Not so much out of hunger, really, but because I felt I had to answer to these threes' lack of manners with a demonstration of the same. I yawned and did not cover my mouth and then scarfed half the sandwich in a single bite.

"Pour me some of that juice," I mumbled, chewing.

The lady nodded at Valdo, who took the pitcher in a way that made me think that he was going to pour it over my head. But he just filled a glass and pushed it gently toward me, using only an index finger, which looked like a sausage.

"You can go, boys," the lady said, and after they disappeared, she turned her shark eyes toward me. "I chose this place so that no one could eavesdrop on us. It's time I introduced myself to you, don't you think?"

"No," I replied. "You're free not to."

"You're right," she agreed surprisingly. "That won't be necessary, if I decide not to use your services."

"I don't remember offering any service to you," I remarked with annoyance. "Whatever it is that Grandfather has offered you does not concern me. I no longer live with him, and he is no longer my master!"

"Yes, yes, I know about that." She smiled. "Honestly, Miro, I know you quite well. I've been visiting your grandfather for years, and you've been a frequent topic in our conversations."

"That's a weird approach," I said, puzzled.

"Why? What do you mean 'weird'?"

"Well, talking about me being part of your psychotherapy sessions."

"Oh no!" She stopped smiling and started laughing. "I personally don't need therapy. Your grandfather and I, we're helping each other as colleagues."

"Don't tell me you're a therapist too."

"Yes. I'm also a psychiatrist. Although I no longer practice. Or more precisely, I practice but only using experimental methods."

I was losing my patience. "Listen, lady—"

"Graziella," she said. "Graziella Prond."

"Fine. Listen, Graziella Prond! Try to make yourself clear; otherwise, I'll be off."

"It's all very messed up," she sighed. "I mean, it's not. Not messed up; it's quite ordered, actually, but it's complicated. I don't know…I wonder where to start."

"Start from the end by saying *good-bye*," I advised her, standing up.

She reached out; took my hand; and, pulling me closer to her, raised her perfectly smooth white face. Her hair, the color of lemon, was neatly drawn back. So spurred by curiosity, I searched for the traces of sutures around her temples. I couldn't find any, but I saw her lips moving, and mixed with the gentle splash of the ocean, an indistinct murmur reached my ears.

"What?" I asked. "I didn't hear that."

There was a pause, during which she held my hand, as if mustering the courage to make a life-changing decision. Finally, she shook her head, squinting her eyes at me, and said, "I live under the same roof with six serial killers."

CHAPTER FIVE

I stood by the table like a shaken tree until Graziella started treating me like one: With one hand she grabbed my belt and with the other my elbow and slowly stood up.

"My back hurts these days," she informed me and started pacing back and forth along the deck.

I sat down again and stared at her. She didn't look like someone in pain—she walked gracefully, in absolute harmony not only with her name but also with her slender body, now showing clearly beneath the sheer dress, which reached her ankles. She looked like a white bird, and the ocean breeze was blowing the wide sleeves covering her arms to the wrist, as if urging her to fly…

I frowned. A short while ago, I had compared this woman to a shark; now I was seeing her as a bird, and I don't think I was wrong in either case. Yes, nothing about her was unambiguous. She looked equally vulnerable and dangerous, equally young and old, equally attractive and repulsive. But what worried me most was that she did not look crazy, although some of her statements were pointing to the contrary.

"Well, Graziella," I began gently, after she had returned to her chaise longue, "what makes you think that you're living with serial killers? And how do you think so many of them have come together? After all, *six* is an impressive number when it comes to such freaks."

"There were seven of them," she told me, "but one fell victim to cold-blooded murder."

"Oh?" I didn't know how to react to that, so I just blurted out, "That's more than deserved! That's what they deserve for being serial killers."

"It's true, but I covered the murder up. I made it look like an accident."

"Yep. Not a wise move, Graziella. Now, you'll have to excuse me. I need to go back to my cabin and lie down for a couple of hours after my encounter with that shark."

She waved a hand as if instead of saying words I had just spewed out a cloud of flies.

"I wanted you to act naturally for the camera," she said, staring into the distance behind me. "If you had known that your behavior would determine whether I'd hire you or not, then you probably would have demonstrated how brave you are. That's why I monitored you secretly and realized that I would probably never find someone more suitable than you."

"Suitable for what, dammit?" I grabbed my glass and drank the insipid juice in a single gulp. Just as I expected, Valdo had soured it with his look. "What do you want from me?"

"I want you to carry out an investigation. It is certain that one of the six is the killer, but the question is who? *Who?*" Pressing a palm to her brow, she successfully drew a simple logical conclusion: "But you won't understand me. Not before I've told you about the events that led to this…" She waited for me to nod and continued, "About two years ago, I inherited a large sum of money. Large is an understatement, actually. I stopped working as a psychotherapist and last year bought a small, isolated island, the location of which I shall not divulge. I shall also remain silent, for the moment, on the actions I was forced to carry out in order to realize my daring professional idea. Bribery, forgery, evidence destruction, blackmail, protected database hacking, political racketeering, double games with judges, prosecutors, police officers, psychiatrists—"

"Wow! If that's your way of remaining silent, I can't imagine what it would be when you start talking! But let's move straight to the end result. If I understand correctly, by the said *criminal* actions, you've isolated those serial killers from the justice system. And then you gathered the motley crew on the island you've bought."

"Exactly. From the first year at university, I've been interested in forensic psychiatry, and I've always dreamed of conducting such an experiment. I want to write a book with my direct observations of their psyche. Imagine the discussions this would provoke! A best seller, the echo of which would resonate powerfully!"

I put my hands over my head. "That's insane! Sneaking out of prison six—I mean, seven—psychos only to write a best seller!"

"No, no. Only Valdo was in prison. The rest, with the exception of Sirius and a girl, I helped get out of the psychiatric ward. They were pronounced mentally irresponsible for their actions, so after some pressure from my side, I was allowed to continue with their treatment on an island that no one can escape from."

"What about Sirius and the girl?" I asked. "Where did you take them from?"

"Nowhere. Sirius was imprisoned for life, but they released him after fourteen years for good conduct. He's part of the experiment voluntarily, with a salary; plus, I trust him as my bodyguard. The girl's case was a more complicated one, because she was saved from a guilty verdict only after the main evidence disappeared."

"A disappearance arranged by you," I added, without any claims to quick-wittedness. "So, let's summarize, Graziella: You're collecting psychopaths, yet you have no doubts about your mental health!"

"Well, you think of yourself as a psychohealthy, too, don't you? And you don't care that for some of your thoughtless and risky actions you should've been admitted to the psychiatric ward, do you?"

"You're quoting my grandfather's bullshit," I pointed out, with insincere contempt. "Anyway. Whatever I might be like, I don't think it's appropriate to compare yourself to me."

"Yes, not appropriate at all! You're after extreme adventures because otherwise you feel *hollow*. You risk your life only to add some temporary value to it, while I am a woman of science. People like me pave the roads for progress! By the way, I bet you're an admirer of Roger Smith and Jacques Ponto, for example. Am I right?"

"You might be," I mumbled, blushing.

"Ahaaa!" She pointed an accusing finger at me. "You don't even know who these famous medics are. Here, listen: Roger Smith studied the properties of curare by injecting himself with that powerful poison. He was paralyzed, and his colleagues barely saved him after emergency resuscitation. His risk, however, was not in vain, because thanks to him, now strictly standardized doses of curare are being used in the field of surgery. Jacques Ponto created an antivenom serum, and in order to test it, he let himself be bitten by three vipers! And later, based on his experiments, were manufactured antidotes counteracting poisoning from other species of snake."

"OK," I agreed, "these men deserve admiration. But what do they have to do with—"

"Shut up! Don't you realize what they and I have in common? They poisoned their bodies in the name of science, and I...I am poisoning my soul! I've been living for five months with those murderers, listening to their stories, trying to understand them, to analyze them. And on top of that, I have to overcome my indescribable fear day after day! Because I know that I could meet the same horrific fate as their victims at any moment."

"Hold on! Haven't you taken any measures to prevent that?"

"No, none. I am alone with them on the island. It's my home now. *Our* home, mine and theirs. And mind you, I don't dull their brains with any sort of medication. I'm not trying to turn them into puppets drenched in sedatives. No! My patients are authentic, and so are my therapeutic methods. I am doing everything I can to reach the healthy core of their psyche."

"Fine. But what if there is no healthy core?"

"There has to be. No one is born a killer! My experiment will prove this. This, and much more, of course. My goal is much more ambitious, Miro. And the advice coming from your grandfather is priceless. He really is an exceptionally talented psychiatrist! I keep him informed about everything that is happening on the island. I share with him every problem I face. Then we both try to find the best approach to each of the seven—"

"Who are now six," I reminded her.

"Yes." She wrinkled her nose. "But at least now you see why I covered the murder, don't you? The whole experiment would've gone to hell!"

"Where it belongs," I added coldly. "And you can count me out. The job I'm doing now seems more meaningful to me. I am sure that sharks deserve conservation attempts more than serial killers."

"But children deserve safety and security more than anyone, Miro! *Children!*" she exclaimed dramatically. Then she took a deep breath and continued in a calmer voice, "Almost every serial killer has suffered childhood abuse. Some from their natural parents; others by adoptive parents, teachers, coaches, classmates, and so on. The question is, why is this allowed to happen? There are child-protection laws. Why do people break them? Very simple: because the state does not have the resources to enforce them effectively. That's the argument, Miro, we're going to use in court in an unprecedented lawsuit if the experiment turns out to be successful. It will be a public suit, a *megasuit*, in which the six serial killers will sue the state for allowing their transformation into serial killers!"

I could feel a dumb expression taking over my features, but I had no idea what to counter its progress with, so I just laughed. Graziella ignored me.

"You heard me!" She seemed to be nodding to herself. "I am going to prove that they wouldn't have turned into murderers if the state had taken care of them in their childhood years. I am going to turn the media to our side. I'm going to start a campaign that's both large scale and scandalous. A campaign with the following goal: Make the state the default principle defendant in every trial against a serial killer!"

"I see!" This time it was easier to laugh. "And are you going to send the state to…prison? Or administer the deadly injection right away?"

"Take this more seriously!" she scolded me. "Focus and think about it!"

"I am thinking. And I'm asking, what do you think you'll achieve with such a campaign?"

"More effective tools for child protection, that's what. Like setting up a large number of teams with three types of specialists in each: a psychologist, a psychiatrist, and a psychoanalyst. And arranging compulsory sessions with every child every six months. Holding extensive conversations with the child that include a lie detector in case the child decides to hide his abuser out of fear or for other reasons. Since these teams will function as representatives of the state, if at a later stage it is found out that they had not done their job properly, they shall be prosecuted...and so on. The project needs more specificity, but I have hired several distinguished lawyers, as well as a significant number of politicians, of course."

"Hmm, there is some sense to this," I mumbled.

"Of course there is," she said. "But at this stage, everything depends on the success of the experiment, which depends on me. And I, Miro, depend on the person who has committed the murder on the island! I even received a threatening note from them: *You don't know who I am, but I know what you have done.* Dear Lord! I'm in such a grotesque situation. I am now in the hands of the killer because only he or she knows that I've masked as an accident their crime."

"But wouldn't everyone on the island know that it wasn't an accident the moment I start with the investigation?"

"No, no!" She waved her hands. "No one should know anything! You're going to investigate in secret, and I will introduce you to the group as a replacement for the dead man."

"So…you're asking me to play the killer there? A serial killer! And constantly come up with all kinds of psycho stories?"

"Oh, don't worry about the stories. I'll have them prepared for you. You've heard of the Merry Maker, haven't you?"

It was a rhetorical question. By now probably everyone knew about that freak and his way of making his victims "feel merry" with the help of laughing gas.

"What?" I said, through clenched teeth. "You want me to pass myself off as him?"

"Yes. We'll tell them you almost got caught, but that I found you first, with some help from people I know in the police, and gave you an ultimatum: the island or prison!"

"What if they do catch him in the meantime?"

"Highly unlikely. But if they do, I'll make sure no one on the island finds out about it. I'm sure I'll be informed about his arrest in due time, because the truth is, I have people everywhere."

Well, I did not doubt her final statement, although instead of "people I trust," she should've said "people I pay." But no matter how deep my personal financial crisis was, I had no wish to join their ranks. Yet I asked, "When and how was the murder done? Tell me—"

"Not now. We'll discuss it on the island."

My eyebrows jumped in sincere surprise. Her behavior has been bordering on pure insolence from the start, but I wasn't prepared for such high brazenness.

"I'm afraid I'll have to disappoint you, madam," I said politely. "My grandfather has painted you a rather misleading picture of me. I am not so crazy as to take unquestioningly the road to hell."

"'Hell' is an appropriate word." She approved the metaphor. "But since you mentioned your grandfather, I'll just say that he was fully engaged in some of my criminal deeds. And these deeds could creep out of the shadows at any moment if we, together, fail to make sure that the fact of the death being 'an accident' is undeniable. Because, Miro, if the police start suspecting murder, the investigation will be much wider. Its tentacles will spread in all directions, one of which will doubtlessly be him. Your grandfather! Do you understand?"

There was no need for an answer. I threw her a gloomy look, and she replied to it with her usual smile.

"In this wonderful weather," she said, "we'll be at the harbor in about an hour. We'll take a twenty-minute ride and then take off."

CHAPTER SIX

The ichthyologist-environmentalist was still sulking from my refusal to meet the shark dressed in a protective suit, but when I told him that we were parting ways, his mood lightened. He paid me the daily wage in cash, we wished each other all the best, and I went back to my cabin. I took my phone out, turned it on, and thought about my grandfather again.

Should I call him or not? The question pushed me into another cycle of hesitation and conflicting emotions. On the one hand, I was touched by his, albeit veiled, seeking out my help. But on the other, such clumsy veiling was chewing on my nerves much more than his usual frankness. Of course!

He's knee-deep in his colleague's criminal machinations, and now he's counting on me to pull him out, but instead of admitting it, he believes he's making me a gift by sending me away on an island full of psychopaths.

I stopped midthought. What if he never believed such a thing and never was part of her schemes? What if she lied to me to make me do the dirty work for her and believe that this way I'm saving my grandfather, who actually doesn't need to be saved? On the surface, these questions seemed logical, but then I heard his cantankerous voice in my head: *Ah, will you ever learn to think? Isn't it close to the mind that she didn't lie to you if you have the opportunity to ask me whether she lied or not? Otherwise she would've stopped you—one way or another—from contacting me.*

I stopped hesitating and didn't call him. I could see the outline of the nearby shore, and it was time I did something useful. I put my jacket on, although I was feeling hot without it, stepped out of my cabin, and made for the captain's. I found him there, a pipe in his mouth and spade-shaped feet resting on the tiny desk.

"I came to say good-bye!" I growled at him, and he suddenly remembered he had important work to do.

"Yes, yes, good-bye, but, see, I have to take over the steering," he mumbled, jumping on his feet. "I don't trust my mate—"

"You're not going anywhere!" I shouted, though at the same time, I stepped away from the door to make way for him. "Stop!" I said, but he slipped past me and flew out.

Just as I hoped, he left his phone on the desk. I turned it off and put it in my jacket pocket. I found the charger in one of the drawers. Luckily, it turned out to be universal. I took it with me. I went back to my cabin, turned my phone off, wrapped it in a towel with the charger, poured some shampoo over the towel, and stuffed it into a polyethylene bag, which I then stuffed into my sports bag. I sat down by the hatch and sunk into gloomy thoughts.

Upon nearing the harbor, Valdo came into my cabin, while Sirius stopped at the door and said with a sneer, "I knew you'd choose the island. Just in time for the *fun*."

"Yeah, right!" I grunted, taking on the role of that Merry Maker freak that was imposed on me. "I'm always good fun, *deadly* some might say."

Valdo picked up my bag and shook out its contents on the bunk. He quickly ran through the stuff and shoved his hand into the polyethylene bag, but the moment his fingers felt the slimy towel, he drew it back with disgust.

"Easy there!" I said playfully.

"Shut your mouth and collect your stuff!" he ordered spitefully.

I was not going to step back from my initial positions.

"You took everything out, and you're going to put it back," I said and folded my arms.

Swearing violently, he stuffed my belongings back into the bag and handed it to me. I zipped it and slung it over my shoulder. The three of us headed for the deck, and the first thing I saw when we got there was my own familiarly tattered suitcase.

Perched next to it, dressed in white, Graziella winked at me in secret and explained, "The hotel you're staying at must be besieged by now. But I sent Valdo to get everything from your room that morning. The moment you stepped out of there."

I looked sternly at Valdo. "I hope you didn't forget something."

"I did!" He bared his teeth. "Very kind of you to remind me. Give me your phone!"

"Why? Don't you have one of your own?"

"Give it to him," Graziella said. "We'll turn it off so no one can track you and give it back to you when the time comes."

"Oh, no!" I objected with indignance. "I'm not giving my personal phone to anyone! There's some… very dear stuff on it."

Finally, out of patience, Valdo reached for my jacket pocket, but I jumped back. I took out the captain's phone and threw it overboard. I followed its flight toward the water with a sad face and turned to Graziella, my brows knitted together.

"I'm sorry." She threw her arms out. "I'm the only one on the island who can use a satellite connection anyway."

Presently, we heard the splash of the anchor hitting the water. We waited for the drawbridge to fall, and Graziella set off, a bodyguard or serial killer on each side. It was a contrasting and impressive image—the innocent white dove flanked by two giant black ravens. She seemed to have a penchant for good special effects, especially when they showed her in a false light.

CHAPTER SEVEN

We took a road that wasn't going through the city, which meant that the citizens had a chance of survival, because, apparently, Graziella did not know how to use the brakes. The car—a rented Mercedes SL—yielded to her frantic driving style without problems, but the signals of distress Valdo and Sirius were sending from the back seat made me think they didn't go on many rides with her, or at least not rides like this one. Maybe she was showing me what ironclad nerves she had. Or maybe she was consciously recreating a scene from an action movie, intensifying it by tense glances at the rearview mirror as if we were being chased by a horde of cops on bikes.

"Jesus!" she said, after a particularly dangerous turn. "I won't rest until we're firm on the ground."

"You think we'd be better off in the ground?" I asked her, and Sirius groaned nervously from the back seat.

"Idiot!" Valdo chimed in. "We're risking jail because of you!"

"I'm the only one risking anything, boys," I heard her controlled voice. "If there's an ambush at the airport too, we're strictly sticking to the story that neither of you have any idea who he is."

"Did you hear that, Merry Maker?" Valdo yelled in my ear. "We have no idea who you are!"

"Then how come you call me by my sobriquet?" I replied, with a question that made him shut up.

The airport, where, of course, we were not ambushed, turned out to be someone's private property—it was a small one, but it was enough for the only plane there to take off. The plane turned out to be Graziella's.

Waiting by the plane, looking relaxed, were a man and a woman, both dressed in matching pilot suits. We stopped there and got out of the Mercedes.

"Take the bags, and have the car returned," Graziella commanded. She walked with quick steps toward the airstair and asked over her shoulder, "Did you do everything on the list?"

"Almost," the woman answered. "The only thing we didn't find was cutting deck for the mower."

Sirius snorted next to me like a startled horse, and Graziella froze, hand on the airstair railing.

"You should've bought a new machine!" she moaned.

"Tell them to buy it first thing in the morning!" Valdo begged her. "I still can't fix the old one!"

"Yes, first thing tomorrow, of course! I want it delivered before noon!"

The pilots nodded, unmoved by the story of the broken lawn-mower part. We left them to do their job and climbed one after the other on the plane, but once we got inside, a commotion broke out. Sirius suddenly pushed me in the back, and I, staggering, almost pushed Graziella to the ground. I turned sharply toward him—I expected such boorish behavior from Valdo, but now he was showing me the cloven foot too.

"I'll put you on different seat rows!" Graziella decided on the instant. "But you'll have to become friends on the island."

The plane had two passenger cabins—both were tiny but luxuriously furnished and well isolated from each other. Graziella and I took seats in the one closer to the cockpit, leaving her bodyguards in the other.

"Alone with the cruel Merry Maker!" I joked while we were fastening the seat belts.

"I'm fine with that. I'm used to being alone with all kinds of...ah!" She twitched as if waking from deep sleep. "Pardon me, Miro! I'm getting too caught up in this fiction."

"No wonder, if you've started from early morning. But tell me, what would you have ordered those two to do if I had refused to come with you? To kidnap me? Or throw me overboard with my suitcase?"

"Nonsense! After our conversation on the deck, I would've just told them that you're not the one we're looking for. That I'd read the wrong info. But your grandfather was sure you wouldn't refuse. Oh, by the way! He's very disappointed in you."

"Again? Why? What for now?"

"What with the current situation, he was hoping for a phone call from you, despite your relationship being 'below freezing,' as he put it."

"That's an adequate description," I said.

"I had a talk with him," she said. "I told him you're on the case now, just as he had expected. Isn't it wonderful that he believes in you with his whole soul? An old man who *knows* that his grandson would do anything to help him in such a delicate time when deadly fateful danger is about?"

"Let's not exaggerate, Graziella. Neither am I one to do anything nor is he in deadly fateful danger."

She shook her head pointedly, and the plane took off and quickly gained height. An expensive machine, capable of almost vertical takeoff.

"Not quite the frugal type, are you?" I remarked.

"No," she sighed. "The amount of money I put into the experiment's realization is truly exorbitant. And everything comes from what I've inherited from my father. If he'd known what I'd undertake after his death…"

"He probably would've cut you out of his will," I guessed.

"For sure, not probably. He was a good man. And he loved me."

Until now I had only seen coldness and subdued fierceness in her eyes, but now there was a somewhat sentimental glow in them. Sadness for her father, I guess, or for her own self—if he was the only one unwise enough to love her.

"I achieved a lot for the past five months," she said, changing the topic. "But in order to produce evidential proof, the experiment has to continue for at least half a year, and—"

"There would be enough time for more murders during the next month," I suggested tactlessly.

"I doubt that." She waved a hand. "I expect blackmail, not new murders. I think that someone has set a trap for me on the island. They had foreseen that I'd cover the murder, and that's why they did it."

"OK, but could they blackmail you without revealing who they are?"

"I don't know. Even if they did reveal themselves, this wouldn't change anything. Their message is already clear: 'If you reveal me as the murderer,

I would not only sabotage your experiment but also bring you to trial for covering a criminal homicide!'"

"Well, I hope you're wrong," I said. "Otherwise, my investigation would be of no help whatsoever."

"Let's hope, yes...I mean, it will help." She looked confused. "It will help, but...you don't have to think about the killer for the next few days. Forget about them!"

I tried to take this nonsense as a joke.

"And how am I supposed to find out who they are if I don't remember them?" I grinned. "You're suggesting an unusual approach."

She looked at me askance, unfastened her seat belt, and went to the fridge. She took two sealed cups with iced coffee, handed one to me, and began in a reproachful tone, "Miro, it's true that our situation has some comic aspects. But I assure you that the nightmarish ones prevail. And the greatest nightmare will come if the people on the island find out that your persona is nothing but a bluff. Then I'd lose their trust, and the consequences for the experiment would be fatal, probably for me and you too. That's why you *must* get into the role of the Merry Maker convincingly."

"Get into?" I said, disgusted. "I will fail, Graziella. I'm not a good actor, and I hate all murderers, especially the serial ones. How can I hide that?"

"Don't worry." She smiled a little. "I am sure that once you get there, your hate will disappear. As you've probably guessed already, your grandfather and I chose these killers after a very careful selection, guided by the idea of the particular positive impression they will make during the public trial. There are no outright monsters among them. No fools also, Miro. All of them are as sly as foxes, and always on guard, always suspicious. It's impossible to make them believe using only lies; that's why you'll have to add some true stories to your repertoire and be completely honest sometimes."

"And how would I pull that off? Play the Merry Maker and be honest at the same time?"

"The most convincing lies are those that are thick with truths." Graziella held up an instructive finger. "That's what you're going to do. You'll dip Merry Maker's image into your real life."

"How convenient," I said, through teeth.

"It really is. You were kicked out of the police about a month ago, and only two days later, Merry Maker commits his first murder. The calendar proximity would give you the opportunity to make a connection between the two events without mixing them. Do you understand? You've got one life before the discharge, and you'll speak about it sincerely from your own point of view, and then you've got another life—the one after the discharge, about which you'll speak from Merry Maker's point of view. The idea is that the discharge itself was the trigger. Before it all your pathologies were latent, and you didn't even suspect about their existence, or maybe you did, but you somehow managed to suppress them with your extreme way of life—"

"Stop!" I could feel my face turning white with indignation. "That schizoid idea is my grandfather's, isn't it?"

"No," Graziella denied, looking me in the eyes. "It's my idea, and your grandfather is against it."

"And why is he against it?"

"He's afraid of you, Miro. He thinks that because you're psychologically unbalanced, you might distance yourself from…yourself and identify with…" She stopped, embarrassed.

"Identify with the serial killer? With the sadist!"

The question remained in the air, as ridiculous as it was needless. Of course, my grandfather would think that! Damn him and his obsession for constantly analyzing, depressing, embarrassing, traumatizing me…

My breathing had quickened, and my hands were twitching. I clumsily took the lid of the iced coffee cup off and sipped a few times. I needed something to cool me off, but at this moment, a block of ice on my head would have done a better job.

"We're getting closer," Graziella said under her breath. She tilted her head toward the window and added, staring at the abyss below us, "We'll get there before sunset."

CHAPTER EIGHT

B efore landing, I caught a glimpse of the island from above—it was almost circular in shape and looked like a magnificent bouquet thrown into the golden waters of the ocean. Under different circumstances, I would have been happy to have the chance to live for a while in such an exotic place, but now I felt like a man who was headed for paradise only to meet a bunch of infernal demons there.

The smooth landing was followed by a sudden speed decrease and an even more sudden stop at the end of the runway, which was no longer than a third of a mile. We got off the plane, and Sirius made straight for the pickup truck parked nearby.

He drove it to the now-open cargo hold, and the pilots started pushing cardboard boxes, trucks, and large packages from inside. Valdo took each item and handed it over to Sirius, who deftly placed them in the pickup-truck cargo bed. My suitcase and sports bag ended up there, too, and the cargo hold was emptied except for a package tied with a pink bow and two cardboard boxes, on which was written "FATA" with a red felt-tip pen.

"See you," Graziella said curtly and got into the pickup truck and drove off somewhere.

"Here!" Valdo nudged me while I was watching in bewilderment her driving away. As soon as I turned toward him, he shoved the package with the bow into my hands. Then he and Sirius took a "FATA" box each and headed for the magnolia grove in the vicinity.

I followed them, but when we stepped into the grove, they moved aside and urged me to go ahead. I walked further in down a narrow path winding through the richly blossomed trees, whose scent was so strong that it almost made me sick. Large insects buzzed, droned, and whizzed past us; thousands of birds chirped, squeaked, squawked, and cawed from the branches; lizards, mice, and spiders ran under my feet; and at some point, a rather long snake slid its canelike body. Well, if biblical Eden was something like this, I'm not surprised that Adam and Eve made everything possible to be cast out of it. To think that everything looked so alluring from above...

The roar of the plane came from the runway blended with the avian commotion, which only grew louder. The grove's dwellers seemed used to hearing it so frequently as not to be frightened by it; however, I was frightened. Especially when the roar died into the distance. That's it! I was here and would most likely remain here forever—in the form of a corpse, for example, masterfully mutilated by some psychopath. I turned my head and saw only a few steps away the huge body of Valdo, who looked back at me with malice in his eyes.

After zigzagging for about half a mile, we reached a small meadow, in the middle of which was a small wooden house. In front of it was a wooden bench, and on the bench was a tiny old woman, a wooden staff, perfect for pole jumping, propped next to her.

"Hello, Fata," Valdo greeted her kindly.

"We're bringing everything you ordered," Sirius said obsequiously.

"Now snuff it, both of you!" she replied. She looked at me, and after a prolonged pause, she said curtly, "They, not you!"

"But why?" Valdo protested, albeit meekly. "Why not him too?"

"'Cause she says so," Sirius mumbled, placing the cardboard box carefully on the grass by the bench. Valdo followed his example, and I put the package on top of the boxes.

"Of course I say so," the old lady agreed, after another pause that was even longer. "If you were telling me who to curse, there would be no people left in the world by now."

I laughed, and she lifted her head toward me again. Her face was an inharmonious mixture of Asiatic and European features, and her eyes were the color of ripe blueberries and carried a heavy look, devoid of kindness.

"Kuber used to laugh like that," she told me.

She stood up with surprising agility; grabbed the staff; and, dragging it behind her, went to one of the magnolia trees surrounding the meadow. She raised the staff and began beating the branches. Star-shaped white flowers rained down, and I suddenly realized that the branches of most of the other trees were naked. *What's the point of this?* I wondered but then realized something else: The insects here were many fewer than in the grove.

I ran to Valdo and Sirius, who were turning behind the house.

"Who is Kuber?" I asked.

"No...no...no...*one!*" Sirius sang, out of tune. "Because he died. She pinned him!"

"Who is *she*? Fata?"

"Yes. But Graziella refuses to believe that. She thinks it was an accident."

"Are you sure it wasn't an accident?"

"No, Merry Maker," Valdo snorted. "If there's anything we're sure about, it's that Fata herself is a huge accident on this island."

"Well said!" Sirius approved his dumb line, rendering the questions I was going to ask pointless.

The path we came by crossed the meadow and went on past the house. Further down the way, it became narrower, winding through more trees. We went in, in single file, accompanied by the sound of the ceaseless beating the old woman was giving the branches. Did she really *pin* that Kuber guy? If she did, why is Graziella saying that she has no idea who the murderer is?

We soon got out of the grove and went up a gentle slope, which was divided into two almost equally long sides—one was covered with a beautiful diversity of wild flowers, and the other was so closely mown that it looked naked. Yes, someone had done their best to ruin the landscape here and, as a result, had also broken the only available mower.

"Are you out of drugs, sirs?" I asked them, feigning concern. "Do I see a cannabis field in the making?"

Their answers came in the form of a harmonious swearing and quickening of the pace.

"Why the long face?" I called after them. "You'll get a new mower tomorrow. You'll catch up—"

Sirius stopped and turned around.

"You have no idea what you're joking with," he said in a low voice. "And I hope I'm not around when you find out."

An ominous tone crept into his words and soured my mood even more. We followed Valdo, whose tempo could make every race walker envious; reached the crest of the slope, breathing heavily; and then climbed down and ended up in the shadows of tall umbrellalike palm trees. We walked past an ugly bungalow with a single, barred window and reached a large meadow full of elegantly trimmed yellow, orange, violet, pink, and red hibiscus shrubs.

On the opposite end of the lawn was a picturesque two-story house built with sparkling red stones and lightwood with mirror-glass windows. We went to it, staggering through the thick grass, and stopped at the door, where I saw my suitcase and sports bag. I reached out to take them, but Sirius gestured me to wait and followed Valdo inside the house, slamming the door in my face.

I got angry and pressed the handle down—to no avail. The door was locked. I listened for any sounds but heard nothing, as if those two were hiding inside, ears pricked up for sound too. I walked around the house not because I wanted to take a good look at it but because I didn't like the idea of waiting at the door like a homeless dog. When I got to the back of the house, I saw that it was built on a rock cliff high above the ocean. There was a closed porch on this side, its French windows with mirror-glass shut. I couldn't see if anyone was watching me, and I didn't care.

I continued walking for about ninety feet and reached the edge of the cliff. Here one could watch both the sunrise and the sunset. Now the ocean looked like liquid lead to the east while the sun was immersing into the purple waves, and in the sky above it, scattered clouds swam, merging and dividing into all kinds of strange shapes.

The rocks at the edge of the cliff descended almost vertically and had the same reddish color as the stones of the house. They looked like a giant horseshoe, whose two ends cut into the coastal waters creating a bay, which right now was so shadowed by them as to look almost black.

CHAPTER NINE

"You bastard!" The whisper whizzed right behind me, and I was still at the edge of the cliff, much too close to the abyss.

I clenched fists and turned as if I was wound up, after which, instead of relaxing, I got even more agitated. Female beauty has always a source of positive emotions for me, but this time it was a source of shock. I was stricken by it, unable to explain why.

The woman before me was about twenty-three, of medium height, and although truly beautiful, there was nothing really striking about her. Many women in the world have the same fair, smooth skin; the same auburn, long, thick hair; the same exquisite features; the same sensual lips; and the same deep and dark eyes…expressive eyes from which now poured out something unbelievably powerful. Hatred!

Who wouldn't be shocked by that? I was used to being liked by women, but this one here…

"I want to kill you," she said.

"What's stopping you?" I asked.

"Five million. Although I'm not sure it will stop me."

After this mysterious reply, she moved her hand hesitatingly, and I saw that she was holding a ballistic knife. Her thumb was on the trigger, and the distance between us was no more than two steps. She didn't need to take a good aim at me to hit me. She could do it with her eyes shut.

"I haven't slept all night!" she said in anger. "I've never felt such desire. To kill! To kill *you*!"

"But why?" I faltered. "Why me?"

"So that I can watch you die!" She bared her perfect teeth. "Watch you die while telling you, 'Come on, laugh now! Laugh now!'"

I nodded—I could see what she meant. I could see so clearly that it instantly made me feel better. Yes, her hatred wasn't for me but for Merry Maker, whom Graziella must have introduced me as…yesterday! And horrified by his laughing-gas atrocities, the beauty before me lost her sleep and then flew into a rage. She was still holding her thumb on the trigger, probably kissing her final inhibitions good-bye.

I was out of time. I looked beyond her shoulder and said a quick, "Oh, hi!" As soon as she turned her head, I grabbed her by the arm and twisted it, but I was a bit late—the blade shot out, and before disappearing into the abyss, it zoomed past me, cutting my shirt and then the skin on the left side of my waist. There was a short struggle, during which she bit me, and I took the knife from her. I looked at it, happy that I had received such essential for this place, a gift from fate. It had a spare ballistic blade and an automatic one. I blocked both, tucked the handle under my belt, and shrugged at its previous owner.

"You're going to tell on me, aren't you?" she mumbled and lowered her eyes toward my wound.

I looked down too. My shirt was light blue, and I could see the growing red spot.

"No, I'm not," I replied. "Your act was…natural. I would've killed him gladly too."

"Who?"

"Merry Maker. I mean…myself. So that I can ask my victims for forgiveness."

"Screw the victims!" Once more anger reared its head behind her exquisite features. "Death, though, deserves *respect*. She is serious and has dignity. And you've bothered her with their pathetic dying cackle!"

I tried to look guilty and hurried to change the topic. "I'm not going to tell on you, but someone might have seen us from the house."

"Impossible. They would've done something. By the way, my name is Roxanna," she announced snappily, and quickly she added, "Come on! Graziella sent me to take you to your bungalow."

I set off behind her so as to be able to feel my wound without her noticing me. It was a shallow one and didn't hurt much. I wiped my fingers with the end of the shirt and matched my pace to unfriendly Roxanna's. We reached the housedoor in silence, where now a dappled, well-fed cat was sitting and meowing. My suitcase and sports bag were still there. I picked them up and only then remembered to ask, "What bungalow? Graziella told me you all live under the same roof."

"Yes," Roxanna said, "we do, but only during the second half of the month. We sleep in our bungalows during the first. It's all part of the therapy."

We crossed the lawn and entered the dusk among the umbrellalike palm trees, under one of which stood the bungalow prepared for me. A concrete cube with a barred window and a huge number "4" nailed to the knotty wooden door: this was going to be my home for the next thirteen days—if I lived that long, that is.

"Kuber used to live here." Roxanna infused some strength into my fatalism. She unlocked the door and turned the lights on.

The inside looked like something very close to a relatively squalid prison cell. The only significant difference was that this place had a separate bathroom and a toilet—both the size of a phone booth.

"As you can see"—Roxanna made a welcoming gesture—"the idea is to make us feel like we're in prison. Especially during the night, because we never stay inside in the day." She pointed at a piece of paper on the nightstand. On top of it was written, "Daily Schedule," and below was its description in items. I left it for later.

"Where is Kuber now?" I asked absent-mindedly.

"I don't want to talk about him," she said. "Take your shirt off. I'll wash it tomorrow and sew it."

"Thank you, but you don't have to."

"Take it off!" She was already rummaging through the medicine cabinet on the wall. "And sit down!"

I obeyed without further objections, and a moment later she took to cleaning my wound. She wasn't trying to be careful, taking her time probably on purpose, as if to enjoy longer the pain she was causing me. I endured her sadistic performance with clenched teeth, but in the end, when instead of taping the wound she pressed her fingers into it, I pushed her hand away.

"My kindness has boundaries," I warned her. "Control yourself."

"I can't!" she yelled at me. "I showed what a coward I am! You insulted her...I was obliged to avenge her. I still am!"

I patted the knife under my belt.

"Obliged or not, now is not the time for revenge. So calm down and explain to me what you're talking about. Death again?"

"Of course!" She moved away from me and sat on the bed. "I am alive, thanks to her and no one else. She would save me every time one of those freaks tried to kill me!"

"And how would she do this? By giving *you* the opportunity to kill them, right?"

"Me? That's ridiculous! I would always freeze in such moment. I would lie like a corpse and wait for Death. But she would come only for them. Them and not me! She would look at them and...drill holes into their hearts!"

"Would she?"

"Yes, yes! That's exactly how it would go, but no one ever believed me." There was sincere bitterness in her voice. "I know that you don't believe me either."

But she believed herself—it was obvious. Sadly, I had to admit to myself that this beautiful woman was one of the group of killers Graziella had got out of the asylum. Sad, indeed! It would've made things much easier for me if she realized what she had done, but now…I caught myself watching her with compassion. She looked so innocent and young. And humble. There was no makeup on her face, and she wore a pale-green polka-dot dress with a white collar and short sleeves with white trim. She looked like a schoolgirl.

I imagined her locked in among deranged wretches, maybe even habitually raped by lewd psychiatrists. I imagined her as a child—a fragile girl who, instead of playing with her dolls, was turned into a toy, a living doll for some child molester…

It took a lot of effort to put an end to this string of nightmarish visions. But were they completely imaginary? Alas, no. Probably there was a lot of truth in them. After all, all murderers on the island had been chosen because they had been molested in their childhood.

"I'm sorry." The words slipped out.

"I'm not," Roxanna replied. She continued in a lively manner, "I'm no longer sorry that I didn't kill you. I realized that I can show you Death in a whole new light!"

"Interesting," I muttered. "Care to elaborate? What exactly is that light?"

"It's a secret." She laughed. "A surprise. And I suspect, I am even sure, that I will help you repent before *her* sincerely and from the bottom of your heart!"

Yeah, right, I thought. *I will repent from the bottom of a deep hole in my heart.*

"I really appreciate your good intentions," I said to her, "but I'm surprised they let you have weapons on the island."

"No, no one has weapons. And no one knows about this knife. Keep it, but I'm begging you, do not tell on me! Or Fata will die!"

"Fata? Why she?"

"It's her knife. I didn't want it, but she insisted I take it. She's got into her head that since I live with murderers, I must be in constant danger..." Roxanna looked at her watch and quickly stood up. "Come to the house in exactly half an hour—"

"Wait! Isn't Fata a murderer also?"

"In half an hour exactly," she repeated. She grabbed my shirt, and before stepping out, she said to me, "No. Fata is much more than a murderer. Don't forget this!"

CHAPTER TEN

The clothes in my suitcase were so crumpled and entwined that everything looked like a ball of rags. I began taking them out, silently cursing Valdo, but the moment I saw my laptop on the bottom, I switched to singing praises. *He's not such a bad guy, after all*, I told myself and instantly knew I was wrong: the satellite modem was on the bottom, smashed as if with a hammer. Well, I had a backup plan. I took the polyethylene bag from the sports bag. My phone was still there, wrapped in the towel. I turned it on and moved closer to the barred window, where I discovered that I wouldn't be able to connect to anything or anyone here. But I was sure that tomorrow, when I took a longer walk around the island, I'd find a secluded spot with a satellite connection that was strong enough.

I returned the phone to its hiding place, put my clothes in the sorry excuse for a wardrobe, and stepped into the shower cabin. There was a tiny sink inside with a mirror hanging over it, the black frame making me feel as if I was watching the picture in my own obituary. An impressive picture, as a matter of fact. That was undeniable. Light-brown hair with golden undertones; a symmetrical face displaying the rare combination of intelligence, sensitivity, and primal...heroic masculinity, enforced by the iron glint in the gray, extraordinarily perceptive eyes. And when you add to this the perfect body with clean-cut muscles speaking of strength and flexibility and endurance...

"Too soon for an obituary," I said, in the end.

Showering was not a problem, as the Band-Aid over my wound was waterproof and covered it excellently. I returned to the cell room and once again felt angry at my grandfather. I had ended up here because of him, and because of him I would have to endure not only a bunch of psychos but also this "therapeutic" environment. Why, dammit, should *I* feel like I'm in jail? And why should I be greeted by a knife-wielding mad beauty? Why did I agree to playing the role of a freak? A degenerate freak! What has my grandfather done to deserve my selflessness?

I had no answer to the last question, the main one. I have never known what exactly are my feelings for my grandfather, and now I seemed to know even less.

I went with a sigh to the narrow, bunklike bed, on which, next to the unopened bedding set, were also two towels. I used one to dry myself, put some clothes on, and sat on the naked mattress. I took the sheet of paper with the daily schedule from the nightstand.

1. *Breakfast—whenever you want, if you want.*
2. *From 8:00 a.m. to 9:30 a.m.—everyone does their household chores.*
3. *From 9:30 a.m. to 10:30 a.m.—sharing.*
4. *From 10:30 a.m. to 1:00 p.m.—free time in the nursery.*

Nursery? My eyes moved down the list:

5. *From 1:00 p.m. to 2:00 p.m.—lunch in the common room.*
6. *From 2:00 p.m. to 4:30 p.m.—playtime or age regression again/hypnotic or not/at one's own choosing.*

"Or age regression *again*," I repeated. So, just some kind of regression therapy done in the "nursery."

I coughed; my throat had dried up. I went to the bathroom, drank some water, and went back to the psycho schedule.

7. *From 4:30 p.m. to 6:00 p.m.—a gathering at the porch. Testimony and conduct during trial rehearsal. Discussion of ideas for new details in the indictment speeches.*
8. *From 6:00 p.m. to 7:00 p.m.—compulsory walk in pairs.*
9. *From 7:00 p.m. to 8:00 p.m.—dinner in the common room.*
10. *From 8:00 p.m. on—cultural activities at one's own choosing, and sleep.*

Visits to Graziella's office IN PRIVATE. As follows:

Monday—Danko
Tuesday—Roxanna
Wednesday—Valdo

Kuber was stricken off on Thursday and replaced with *Miro Merry Maker*. Considering it was still Monday, I realized that I would have to wait for more than two days to speak in private with Graziella about the murder. I wasn't going to follow the schedule strictly, but she definitely was— after all, she was the one who told me that I should stop thinking about the murder for the next few days and start getting into the Merry Maker role.

I continued reading:

Friday—Maya
Saturday—Sirius
Sunday—Frant
Group MOTTO: Down with misanthropy! Love
        yourself so you can love the others!

"All right," I said to myself. I took my T-shirt off and grabbed the largest shirt from the wardrobe. It was also the most creased one, but that didn't matter. What mattered was that when I put it on, it completely covered the knife, which I tucked back under my jeans belt.

CHAPTER ELEVEN

I tried to enjoy the lovely evening while crossing the meadow, but the only thing I could feel was exasperation. Everything was in almost unbearable profusion—the sky seemed overstuffed with stars, the moon was enormous, various aromas fused into suffocating mixtures, and the song of the cicadas was so intrusive that I wanted to plug my ears.

I reached the brightly lit house and stopped a step away from the door. I smoothed my hair, straightened my shoulders, bucked up. *That's it. The die is cast*, I said to myself. I took one step, and the moment I rang the doorbell, I saw my task in its entire paradoxicality: I was about to start playing a murderer in order to investigate, among six murderers, the murder of another murderer.

I waited for the feeling of absurdity to kick in while also waiting for someone to open the door for me, but neither came. I rang the bell again and then opened the door myself. I stepped into a spacious lobby leading to a two-winged gate with embossed wood carvings. I headed toward it, and then everything went black. I froze. I heard a low creaking noise—it seemed to come from the sliding wings of the gate. Then I heard a rustle of cloth, constrained breathing...whispering! I reached for the knife.

"*Surpriiise!*" a choir of out-of-sync voices cried out.

The lights returned, and I saw before me a bunch of grinning faces under a poster with "HAPPY BIRTHDAY, MIRO!" written on it. My hands fell down, and my body swayed. *Please, God, don't let them start singing*, I begged. But he didn't hear me.

My eyes met Graziella's, and she winked at me, glowing with satisfaction. For a second I thought that maybe everything, absolutely everything, was a bluff, and that my grandfather would appear from somewhere, singing, "Happy birthday, you fool! Gotcha!" Terrified, I yelled, "Shut up!"

Everyone burst into laughter.

"Don't worry, buddy! You're among friends," a short, dandified man with sleek hair and a goatee tried to assure me. He came closer and extended his hand. "I am Frant!" He introduced himself, tilting his head to the side, probably expecting me to gasp in amazement.

I managed not to gasp, although I did realize who he was, which shattered my bluff theory to pieces.

"And I am Maya," a skinny, weird-looking teenager said, introducing herself to me. Her hair was short, spiky, and dyed in many colors, grass green being the most prominent. Her lipstick was dark violet, almost black, as was her nail polish. A miniature golden piercing sparkled from her left eyebrow, and yellow plastic earrings in the shape and size of pears hung from her ears.

"This one here's Danko," I heard Graziella say and saw her put her hand on the shoulder of a nice-looking guy in his midthirties with a shy expression on his face. "He barely says a word."

"But whenever he does, it's the right one," Roxanna finished the sentence, and Danko seemed to blush.

"You already know Valdo and Sirius," Graziella said, "but, of course, you are just starting to know each other truly!" She said this in an exalted voice as if our acquaintance was going to be an activity with endlessly increasing levels of happiness in both sides.

Dressed in same dappled shirts and beige long shorts, Valdo and Sirius were watching me kindly—as if they had taken off their bad feelings for me—for Merry Maker, that is—together with their black clothes.

"Let's go!" Maya took my hand and led me to the wide-open gate. The others followed, taking the poster with them.

We ended up in a cozy dining room with a long, beautifully arranged table inside. In the lively commotion, I was made to sit in the honorary seat, and Graziella and the six murderers sat on both sides of the table.

"The cake, the cake!" some of them started chanting, with enthusiasm.

"Don't rush it," Maya scolded them. "Unlike us, Miro hasn't had dinner yet."

"Oh, I don't need to; I don't want to." I blurted out something meaningless.

"I understand." Maya nodded at me. "It'd be awkward for you to eat while the rest of are watching and waiting. This is what we're going to do: I'll get you a couple of sandwiches, but I'll also bring the cake. You'll blow out the candles, and we'll leave a big, big piece for you to eat later. Is that OK?"

"Absolutely," I agreed, with fake glee, and Maya flew out of the dining room.

"Such an industrious child," Roxanna said, with love. "She didn't rest the entire day until the marvelous cake was ready!"

"Diligence and talent," Valdo added to the praises. "Ever since she started cooking for us, I have stopped doubting that the culinary is an art."

When Maya came with the cake, everyone, including me, applauded her in sincere admiration.

"Wouldn't cutting and eating this masterpiece be a crime?" Sirius wondered.

"Not eating it would be a crime," Frant replied to him and took a lighter from his pocket and started lighting the candles.

"Come on, wish something," Graziella urged me, with a smile.

I tried to think of something, but much to my regret, I came up with nothing. How long have I been like that—dreamless, ambitionless, aimless? I took a deep breath and blew out all thirty candles. I heard cheering but felt like I had just taken the light out of my whole former life, that I was now in the dark, no flame to guide me in sight.

Using a special knife, Maya cut the cake and served everyone a piece. She put two aside for me and then brought me the promised sandwiches with a glass of cold white wine. I watched her, wondering how many people she killed with those skillful hands of hers. And how old she must have been, if she was no older than seventeen now? It was obvious that she was the girl who was saved from a guilty verdict because Graziella had arranged the disappearance of the main evidence. But I doubted that the evidence was destroyed. On the contrary, I was sure that Graziella had kept it and that Maya was aware of that. Which meant that the murder I was about to investigate might have been committed for the purpose of future blackmailing: *Give me the evidence or else...*

"How's Fata?" Graziella asked, relishing in the cake.

"She's good," Valdo told her ruefully. "But she cursed us again!"

"Aaah!" Frant drawled. "It's time you got used to this."

"No!" Sirius objected. "We have to be always on guard. Kuber got used to it, took down his guard, and...she pinned him! What's stopping her from making a voodoo doll for one of us—"

"Enough with the nonsense!" Graziella raised her voice and turned to me. "Fata is just an impertinent old woman. She's capricious, grumpy for no reason, always shouting empty threats."

"How did she end up here?" I asked. "Why is she on the island if she's not...of the group?"

"It's a sad story, Merry Maker," Graziella sighed.

I got angry at her for using that nickname, but it seemed that I would have to put up with this from now on. Probably she would not miss a chance to rub it into my face. I sipped from the wine and started eating the sandwiches. I had gone through too much ordeal for the day to spend the rest of it feeling hungry.

"Three years ago," Graziella began, "Fata's brother, Ichiro Ashikawa, bought the island, built that house, and brought his wife here so they could continue with their lives among nature. They had a big family: two sons and three daughters, plus a dozen grandsons who would visit frequently. Last year, though, his wife died—"

"She drowned in the bay," Maya specified.

"Yes." Graziella looked at her tenderly and turned back to me. "She was in perfect health, and a good swimmer to boot, but she probably had one of those swim cramps and panicked and…that's why I'm always telling you to stay close to the shore!"

"Don't worry, *Mom*." Frant smiled. "Just say the word, and we'll be splashing around in floaties!"

His tease was met with general laughter. It seemed that these creeps had become close to one another here. In their group, there was openness and geniality, something rare even among normal and honest people.

"So, after the accident, Ichiro plunged into deep depression." Graziella went on with the story. "He forbade his relatives to come visit him and started living a hermit's life on the island. But after a while and against his will, Fata arrived and remained here to take care of him until his dying hour. An hour that came...because of me!" She emphasized her words with a dramatic gesture. "He committed suicide, Merry Maker! Because I offered him an unreasonably high price for the island, and he was a responsible man. He didn't want to deny his family such a large sum, but he also didn't want to leave the island—"

"So he sold it and cut his veins," Maya spoiled the ending. "You can still see stains of his blood in a nook among the rocks by the bay. And Fata says that his ghost is haunting the island since then!"

"She says other stupid things also," Frant said mockingly. "She's playing the scary voodoo witch, and our two brawny lads, Merry Maker, believe her and tremble in fear. They're big, as you can see, gorilla big, but they have the hearts of bunnies."

"That's not surprising," Danko joined in suddenly. His voice was deep and low, unexpectedly melodious. "It's a known fact that most serial killers are cowards."

"But not our Valdo!" Roxanna objected passionately.

"That's right, sweetheart!" Valdo leaned forward and kissed her on the forehead. "I know the word 'fear' only from the dictionary."

This time I joined the laughter, after which I finished the second sandwich and pulled the cake pieces closer to me. Maya began cleaning the table, and Graziella helped her. They took the empty dishes away and soon returned with trays, carrying cups with hot coffee. Sirius and Frant joined the housework by taking out of the liquor cabinet a bottle of cognac and glasses for everyone.

"It's good that we don't have alcoholics here," Sirius informed me.

"It's also good that no one here is on neuroleptics," Frant also informed me. "They used to stuff me with such every day in the loony bin. My head would become heavy like a cannonball, my tongue would dry up and turn into a shoe sole...and once one of the orderlies let me have a gulp of his vodka, and I almost died!"

"Terrible!" Roxanna flinched while filling the glasses with cognac. "But if you had mixed neuroleptics with liquor, then you were truly crazy."

"Either crazy or dumb," Valdo said.

"Crazy with dumbness," I offered my two cents' worth.

Everyone liked the joke, especially Frant.

"Well said, Merry Maker! That's how those good-for-nothings would treat me there. I had become so dull from the meds that my brain could only crow."

A short but lively discussion on the advantages and disadvantages of the various types of medication followed, and in the end, Danko said, "Cheers," and everyone raised their glasses to me. I realized that I was touched by the attention, which instantly made me angry at myself and at my grandfather, of course. Because after the string of dark and lonely birthdays I had gone through, thanks to him, I was now entering my thirtieth year in the company of psychopaths. Again thanks to him!

But the worst thing was that they did not look like psychopaths at all. They looked the opposite: balanced, affable, cordial. My grandfather and Graziella had chosen them after "a very careful selection" with precisely this purpose in mind: so that during the public trial, people like me—normal folks, in other words—would start liking them and rooting for them, forgetting all about their many victims. *Screw the victims*, as Roxanna—now intimately resting her head on the shoulder of the prematurely-released-from-prison Valdo—had said only an hour ago.

"Hey, Valdo!" I called him, not knowing why. "Tell me...hmm...tell us how you managed to take my suitcase out of the hotel this morning."

"What hotel, man? That was a crummy inn. I rented a room to be, you know, legally there and then unlocked yours with my favorite skeleton key, put your stuff into the suitcase, and threw it out the window right into the shrubs under it. You should be thankful for getting a room on the ground floor; otherwise your laptop wouldn't have survived."

"Your laptop's fine; we checked it," Sirius assured me. "But you wouldn't have been if we weren't there before the cops. And judging from their lack of love for you, you could've been shot. *Shot while trying to escape*, nonetheless."

Shaking her yellow-haired head, Graziella suddenly began to cry as if, even unrealized, the possibility of me getting shot to death filled her soul with mourning sorrow. She was overdoing it again, and this time it was completely unnecessary.

"I have to admit," she said, "that I am still in distress. We've taken some great risks today. Let's hope it's been for the best. Let's hope you won't disappoint us, Merry Maker!"

"Oh, it depends," I replied, in a moderately casual tone. "I will decide whether to disappoint you or not after you've made yourself clear what you expect from me."

"To win the five million!" Frant announced solemnly. "That's what."

"He's right," Graziella confirmed, staring at me with marked seriousness. "If the experiment ends in success, each of you shall get two million dollars plus three more after the end of the trial. That's exactly how much you'll get, too, *Miro*. This was the sum I had in mind earlier today when I told you that your paycheck would be exceptionally generous. Do you see now?"

I did but somehow in stages. First, I realized that this time she was actually speaking to me, not to Merry Maker, and then my heart began beating faster—*five...five...million...five*—and finally I got so dizzy that I resorted to the cognac in my glass to clear my head. Reaching out, Sirius was kind enough to pour me another dose, while the others were watching me with friendly smiles on their faces.

"Don't suppress your joy," Frant advised me. "Let it all out; don't be shy. We've all walked the same path, both in good and bad times."

"From bad to good," Graziella corrected him. "That's your path."

"To the path!" Danko raised a glass for another toast. "And to its end, which will be a wonderful beginning for us all!"

"Yes, yes, to its end...of the path," I mumbled, and the moment I heard my own voice, I realized that I would have to stick to silence for the rest of the evening.

CHAPTER TWELVE

I knew about Frant's case; I had even studied it in my criminology course. And if back then a clairvoyant had told me that in seven years I'd be taking a walk with him under the starry sky, well, I would've told her that she should cut down on the hallucinogenic drugs. Yet here I was, strolling across the meadow next to the nutter, in whose house the police had found the bodies of nine old people, all stuffed and dressed as if for the runway.

"Many lies were written about me back then." He broke the silence and changed direction to my bungalow. It was clear he wanted to go in there with me, but I stopped him by heading for one of the benches among the hibiscus shrubs. We sat there. "Many lies!" he repeated. He lit a cigarette and continued, "And the biggest one was the version the judge accepted and, based on it, decided to send me to a mental hospital instead of putting me to sleep forever and ever."

"You were lucky," I said, my teeth clenched. "But are you saying that you weren't really unanswerable?"

"No, what I'm saying is that I was very happy with my lawyer. He insisted on playing the sexually-molested-by-the-father card, and I was a good player. I even went through every psychiatric evaluation without a single glitch, maybe because I really was abused, though not sexually and not by my father but by my mother. She used to beat me, that bitch, every blessed day. She would stick needles into me and put out her cigarettes on my ass. Like this!" Frant moved his cigarette to the edge of the bench and put it out on it with slow twisting motions. "Like this! On the next day in school, the teacher would punish me for always fidgeting on my chair."

"What about your father?" I asked with unexpected compassion. "Did he know?"

"No. He wasn't living with us, and he was sick, and he rarely visited me."

"But you wanted to kill him, and not your mother, didn't you?"

"I did, but he got ahead of me and died quickly. Then I began murdering him in my fantasies, seeing him in every one of those old men!" Frant smirked. "Or so the story my lawyer came up with goes. And during the trial, my mother finally did one good thing by corroborating the sexually-molesting-father fabrications."

He smirked once more, and that did it for me. "You lousy bastard!" I burst out. "You sorry murderer of old men!"

I felt relieved but also scared. That was it; I had blown my cover right at the beginning!

"Don't worry," Frant said meekly. "I know about your memory loss."

"You do?"

"Yes. Graziella warned us that sometimes you forget what you've done and that in such moments you'd treat our deeds like a cop would, not like the murderer you've become."

"Would I?" I uttered dumbly.

"Yes. And you're an even bigger bastard than me, because I, unlike you, have never wanted to kill anyone."

"Aha! You never wanted to, but one day God told you to. He also told you to start living with the stuffed 'doubles' of your father under one roof."

"Stop it, buddy!" Frant reached and poked me in the ribs. "Do you still believe that they were my father's doubles?"

"Whose then?" I poked him too.

"Ugh! It's hard for me to talk about this, but I have to. We decided that each of us should tell you their true story, and Graziella insisted I go first. And she's as clever as she is rich, which is very. You have no idea!"

After this uncalled-for praise, he took some uncalled-for actions: He got a mirror and a flashlight out of his jacket pocket, lit his face with the latter, and carefully examined his face with the former. He then plucked a hair from his perfectly trimmed beard and adjusted his bow tie, which didn't need adjustment—yes, no wonder he had become disgustingly notorious by the sobriquet "Frant," some strange word for "dandy." I imagined him fussing around "his" stuffed old men, brushing their elegant suits every day, dusting their professionally painted faces with a special brush—

"They kept me in the loony bin for eight years!" he said in indignation, admiring his plain features in the reflection. "They damaged my kidneys with their pills, dulled my brain, broke my spirit. Wretches! But she—Graziella, I mean—put me back on my feet in less than a month. And not only me, mind you. Roxanna, Kuber, and Danko are also victims of such form of 'healing,' but she fixed them too. She healed them. How did she do it? That's what you're going to ask me, aren't you? Aren't you, Merry Maker?"

"Yes," I said tiredly. "I am asking you."

"And here's my answer: She did this in the most effective way! First, with the five-million-dollar contract, she gave us all equal start, some hope, and a common goal, so to say. Second, thanks to the first, we created a commune of our own, with simple rules and bearable obligations. And third, the contrast! You get half a month in the luxurious house and then…back to the cells! Meaning, 'Compare and be careful! It's up to you how you choose to live your lives: free and in opulence or confined and in the loony bin or prison, respectively.' In short, give a man money and a human touch, show him the contrast to always remember, and you've got one very successful form of therapy!"

Interesting, I thought. *How many people would become murderers only to participate in such "successful therapy"? Money and a human touch…yeah, right! I'd rather we brought back the guillotine or the good old gallows.*

"That's the effective way!" I finished my thought aloud, and, of course, Frant got the wrong impression.

He gave me several nods of approval, after which he turned off the flashlight. He put it back in his pocket with the mirror, lit a new cigarette, and said out of nowhere, "Strong as a bear and nasty like a wasp. I personally have never known a worse combination. Not for a mother, at least!"

"Yes, it's a terrible combination," I agreed.

"Well, add to this the fact that I was small as a sparrow, and you'll get a clear picture of the distribution of power in our miserable home." He threw me a challenging look. "I know what you're thinking. I know that I'm still tiny and small! That's why I dress in such a way. It's how I confront my natural plainness."

"I think you've confronted it in *nine* other ways, also."

"I wanted them to be ten. Then I would've stopped, and no one would've found me. But I didn't have luck with the last old man. He got scared when I least expected it, and instead of jumping into the car, he started shouting. He's the reason they caught me."

"Small chance," I expressed compassion on Merry Maker's behalf. "But are you sure you would've stopped if they hadn't caught you?"

"Absolutely. Stuffing corpses is a complicated, exhausting, and expensive thing to do. I was broke and couldn't go on even if I wanted to."

He drew on his cigarette so deeply that I heard his lungs wheeze. He rounded his lips and began puffing out circles, zeros of smoke that dissolved quickly in the twilight of the moon.

"It's winter. Christmas." He started talking with the drawling voice of someone immersing into their memories. "I am now sixteen years old, although I still look twelve. My mother is mad again: 'Midget, sissy, just like your father!' She had gone completely berserk because it's a holiday and we're alone again. She starts to chase me around the house, manages to wedge me in the corner by the outside door. She brings her cigarette closer to me...this time aiming for my eyes! I start to scream. Just like some sissy. She opens the door and throws me out in the stairs. I am wearing only a T-shirt and no shoes. I go down, weeping, and just when I'm about to go out of the building and lie in the snow and die, *he* comes! The neighbor. We haven't exchanged a single word until that moment. The only thing I know is that he lives up there in an attic room. We look at each other, saying nothing. But he opens his arms, and I realize—if I make a step in his direction—he will hug me! Yes, yes, he is hugging me! We start climbing the stairs together and walk past our apartment door from where loud music is coming—my mother is listening to the radio again. We get to the attic, enter the room. He turns on the heater, hands me a pair of thick socks, wraps me in a blanket. I am still shaking, though not from the cold. I can't stop thinking about his warm embrace. Dear God! I have never felt and will never feel anything lovelier than it in my entire life!"

Frant closed his eyes, smiling, but then the dying cigarette stung his fingers. Startled, he dropped it at his feet and then crushed it.

"That's all," he sighed. "I lived with him for ten days. I'm not saying I was hiding, because my mother did not look for me at all and hadn't bothered to tell the police about my disappearance. You understand why, don't you? Too many scars from her on my body."

"What about the neighbor...during these ten days, did he...?"

"Stop it; shut up! I had to leave him because of such dirty suspicions as yours. He was ready to take me with him somewhere far, to take care of me. But I thought that if they found us, they'd treat him as some pedophile! While he was...well, he was simply a good man. That's why I ran from him. I left him a note: *I will come back in ten years. And you'll be proud of me!*"

"You'll be proud; you'll be proud." He mouthed the words, and the monotone song of the cicadas seemed to echo his song: "You'll be proud, proud..."

"I traveled here and there, and until I was twenty-one, I survived mostly on stolen stuff. I had no other choice because no one would hire someone as short as me. But after that I found work; I finished school. I developed two really amazing software programs, and that is how I got rich the legal way. Just as I had planned! And just as I had planned, I went back there exactly ten years later on Christmas day. I parked my limo in front of the apartment building and got out, wearing only a T-shirt and carrying so many gifts that I barely made it to the attic. But the strangest thing is that when I reached our floor, I didn't look at the door; I didn't even remember to look at it! 'Hello! Will you get me warm?' was all I was repeating to myself, grinning with joy, imagining the surprise on *his* face, the happiness. I also imagined how I would take him from his miserable room, how I would start taking care of him in *our* house by the lake, now that he's old—"

He stopped suddenly, his shoulders drooped, and huddled like that on the bench, he really looked like a sparrow...a wretched, wingless sparrow.

"But why...what happened?" I whispered.

"He was dead! Hit by a car...in the winter I left him. I spent ten years of my life living for him while he was living only in my heart. He was dead...but you still don't know why I went mad!"

"Yes," I agreed gloomily. "I don't."

Frant stood up and waved his hands before me. "I couldn't find his grave! That's why. A poor man's funeral paid by Social Security, documents missing, and so forth. Screw them all! But my old men…I would take them all from the cold on the street and put them to sleep in a warm room. They would feel no pain. Then, instead of leaving them in *lost* graves dressed in rags, I would leave them with me…clean and dignified in our house by the lake."

Turning his back on me, he started going back across the meadow.

"Doubles!" he shouted, without looking back. "Dou-bles! Blah-blah! Even if I did think of them as such, well, I was wrong. Because *he* was like no other. Unique."

CHAPTER THIRTEEN

I remained on the bench for a long while. I wasn't in a hurry—spending a sleepless night in a prisonlike cell was not among my favorite pastimes, and the bungalow could offer me nothing else. I was exhausted; my mind was frantic, if the chaos reigning in my head right now could be called a mind. "So much emotion and no thoughts," my grandfather would say and, unfortunately, be right. Almost everything from the past day had burdened me with conflicting, even opposite, emotions. The shark was the only exception, because after our fortunate parting, I felt nothing short of sympathy for it.

Of course, the moment I thought of the shark, Graziella's face appeared on the surface of my mind. I wasn't so dumb as to be blind to her machinations. She must have set them in motion even before we met by giving me the role of Merry Maker and informing the others that I'd come here. Then she warned them about my memory "loss," thus both insuring herself from eventual misfires and denying me the possibility to refuse the role. If I were to go to them now and say, "Yes, I really am Miro, the fired cop, but no, I am not Merry Maker; I'm not a murderer like you!" they simply would not believe me.

Well, she deserves applause. She's a clever one, I thought, but that didn't make things easier. This woman had the talent of a true puppet master, and now she was trying to add another puppet to her collection—me. Trying and succeeding. I am a normal person, and as such I hate murderers, but that most natural of feelings didn't seem to be of use to her, so she came up with a plan to neutralize it.

First, she sent me with Valdo and Sirius to Fata—the old shrew, of whom every murderer here takes good care and to whom they bring boxes with food, gift packages, while she's cursing them constantly. All this only to make me a witness of a scene filled with patience and kindness of enormous scale. Then, taking her machinations to another level, Graziella choses none other than

Roxanna to take me to the bungalow—the inno-cent-looking beauty who quickly touches my heart because she is crazy and has forgotten she's a mur-derer. How could I hate such a poor thing?

But Graziella doesn't stop there. She softened me even more with another machination: Happy birthday, Miro! A cake, toasts to me, a cordial reception. And right after that came the biggest blow: Frant. She must've wanted him to be the first to tell me his story on purpose. His true story, which made me feel sympathy for him—a nutter stuffing old men!

I pressed my palm against my forehead and screwed up my eyes at the invisible-from-here house. She must be there now, probably by herself, asleep in her lush bedroom, while I was sitting here, in the night, stiff from the uncomfortable bench. Sitting here instead of going straight to her with the following questions: Why is she not sure that my grandfather's authority and the giant paycheck would be enough to motivate me for participation in her weird experiment? Why does she want to involve me emotionally in it? What's in it for her if the seeds of sympathy for the murderers here take root in my heart?

I looked at my watch; it was past midnight. Waking her up now and asking her was not a good idea. She probably wouldn't answer the door at this hour, and if I pressed on, her guards might appear from their bungalows. I was someone new here, and it was only natural for them to be on guard. Especially when *I* was actually the psychotic Merry Maker.

I realized that I was still pressing my forehead and dropped my hand tiredly. I had to get used to the paradoxical idea that I—the way I was in reality—was not here, in fact. I was not here for anyone except Graziella, who would sometimes get so carried away as to believe I was Merry Maker and no one else. Anyway. I had to be careful not to get carried away myself. And this meant that from now on I would have to treat as the lowest scum those in the group who are the kindest to me—to Merry Maker, that is. And vice versa—those who can barely stand me, thinking I'm Merry Maker, I'd consider the kindest...which meant that for now, Roxanna seemed like the friendliest of them all, because she tried to cut my throat before even saying hi.

"God!" I moaned. *How will I make it through such an absurd situation? How!*

You won't. I heard my grandfather's voice in my head the moment I felt something rubbing against my feet.

I didn't move, only looked down. It was a cat. I smiled at it, and as soon as it sensed my friendliness, it jumped up next to me on the bench. I saw that it had something in its mouth—a mouse, a dead mouse, which it dropped on my thigh. I instantly reached to take it off, but the inept thought that this might hurt the cat's feelings stopped me. It must be a big thing for a predator to give its prey to someone else, so I should be flattered.

"All right, I *am* flattered," I murmured, and the cat purred, inviting me to pet it.

Its fur was soft and fluffy, and its eyes sparkled like diamonds in the moonlight. *See, there's at least one creature on this island who likes you, the real you,* I thought, gently pulling its ears. But then the mouse moved, limped down my leg, and ended up in the grass. I tried to give it a chance by holding back the cat, but it scratched me and wrestled free of my hands.

Seconds later the small squeal of the dying critter ruptured for a moment the talentless choir of the cicadas. I stood up and headed for the bungalow. That's life. The living have to eat. The living have to sleep, also.

CHAPTER FOURTEEN

His hair had changed—it's white, not gray. White and fluffy like a cloud. I reach out to touch it but see that tens of tiny white mice are tangled in it. Barely moving, suffocating. Just born but already dying.

"Careful, Grandpa!" I shout when I see him burying fingers in his hair as he usually does.

His eyes turn to me, and...they are not his. They sparkle like diamonds. Ferocious feline eyes.

"Careful!" I plead, but it's already too late. His fingers are casually crushing the mice; red spots appear in his hair.

"I wanted laws, child-protection laws," he says to me. "But now I'll be discredited. Because you

won't make it through. You're only good for making people laugh and then killing them."

"What are you talking about? Grandpa—"

"Merry Maker, Merry Maker!" he starts whispering to me, and it's as if he's moving away from
me, but his words whistle in my ear. "Hey, *Merry
Maker!*"

"Yes?" I answered.

Yes? Everything became dark, and I realized I
had opened my eyes. Then someone turned the
night light on. Its light blinded me, but a moment
later, I was able to make out the figure leaning over
me. The sight of it woke me fully and disturbed
me: dressed in a lace nightgown, teenaged Maya
was standing by my bed, watching me in some kind
of rapture...or maybe with love?

I stood up quickly, jumped into my jeans, and
reached for my shirt.

"Wait!" She stopped me. She went to the wardrobe, took my dark-blue sweater from it, and handed it to me. "Put this on. Your shirt is too light in
color."

Her face looked quite sweet without the heavy
makeup and the tacky earrings. She had even tak-
en the piercing off her eyebrow, and if it wasn't for
her colored hair and highly inappropriate nightgown, she would have looked no less decent than a
diligent college student. The look in her eyes was

still worrying me, though—there really was something like love in it.

I decided not to argue with her the choice of clothing. I simply put the sweater on and glanced sternly at my watch.

"It's two a.m., Maya. Two *a.m.*!"

"It is." She sat on the bed. "We have enough time. But before we go, I want you to know that I'd be forever grateful to you!"

"What for?"

"Oh, come on! I'm not a fool!" She looked at me with a happy smile. "I figured it out right away."

"What?" I asked again, and then another question occurred to me: "What do you mean, right away?"

"The morning on the fifth last month. It was Friday, the day the pilots deliver the supplies...and the week's newspapers! I read what you've done *for me on the third*! But don't worry. I haven't told anyone. It's our secret."

I considered this. I got discharged on the first of the last month, and as Graziella had explained to me, Merry Maker committed his first murder only two days after that. So for some reason or as a result of some crazy fantasies, Maya had decided that he had done this for her...

"I imagined you'd be like this." Her smile lit up again. "Young, strong, and handsome!"

"I'm glad," I said, defeated.

"But now I have a big favor to ask you," she went on. "Try to distance yourself from Merry Maker for at least an hour. I need you as a cop."

Now this made me truly glad. I nodded encouragingly and sat in the chair across from her, hoping that I'd finally hear something useful for the investigation.

"It's about Kuber." She supported my hope. "I suspect his death was not an accident. But I didn't dare tell anyone here because every one of them might be the killer!"

"When?" I asked. "How long has it been?"

"It will be forty days this Saturday. Graziella said there'll be a memorial service."

"And why didn't you share your suspicions with her?"

"I decided not to worry her. I might be wrong, after all. But if you find out it was murder, we'll tell her."

"You're overestimating me, Maya. I don't think I'd be able to find anything out in circumstances like these here."

"But you can try! Promise me?"

I tried to look hesitant, and in the end, I replied to her imploring look with a sighing, "OK."

"Thanks!" She jumped from the bed. "Let's go! First, we have to inspect the body."

"Hang on! Is he buried on the island? Are you telling me you want to dig—"

"God, no! He's not buried at all. He's in the wine cellar, in cold storage. I've been meaning to take a look at him for a long time but couldn't get the key unnoticed and only last evening realized that Valdo has a skeleton key. Here it is!" She pointed at the table, and there indeed was a skeleton key on it. "I found it in his bungalow while he and Roxanna were taking a stroll at the beach. They're engaged and madly in love with each other."

"I see..." was all I offered as a comment. I grabbed my jacket from the wardrobe, put it over her shoulders, and dropped the skeleton key in its pocket.

We went outside, and she took my hand.

"Everyone's asleep by now, I guess," she whispered, "but we should walk slowly, just in case. If anyone sees us, I'll tell them I had nightmares again, and I asked you to keep me company while I calm down. Hence the nightgown. As if I had stormed out of my bungalow in terror."

"Do you have a lot of them?" I whispered too. "Night terrors, I mean?"

"What do you think?" she replied and shivered in the warm night.

We reached the western side of the house in absolute silence. We climbed down the stairs leading to a rectangular landing enclosed by three stone walls and stopped in front of the wine-cellar door. Maya took the skeleton key out and handed it to me. Her hand was shaking, her entire body was shaking, actually, and even her teeth chattered.

"No need to go in with me," I said. "Wait—"

"No, no! I want to go in. Go on, unlock it!"

"You're overestimating me again," I mumbled. "At least, you could've taken a flashlight with you."

I fiddled blindly with the lock, surprised by the ease of it all. It took me only seconds to unlock the door and thus brought upon myself the renewed excitement of the eccentric teenage murderer.

"Amazing! You're the best!" She slipped past me and went into the cellar.

I went in after her, closed the door, and felt for the light switch. I turned it on, and before the lights had gone on, Maya had moved away into one of the two opposite corridors. She was in such a hurry that she almost ran. *No, she was not afraid,* I thought, shocked. *She was shivering with impatience to see the corpse!*

There was another explanation, however, and it made me run after her too. I caught up with her just when she was about to open the door of the freezer room. I grabbed her by the elbow and pulled her back.

"Easy," I said, a severe look on my face. "You'll stay away from the body. At least two steps away. Understand?"

"But why?"

"Understand?" I repeated, with aplomb.

She shrugged and nodded. She didn't look disappointed, as she would have if she had meant to take something from here or erase a trace she had left on the body. It seemed that the only thing drawing her in was her sick curiosity, though that didn't mean I should stop keeping an eye on her. I had to take advantage of this moment in which her mind was busy with thoughts about the sight behind the door and wouldn't be able to switch quickly back to lying and distorting the facts.

"What was the evidence?" I asked.

"What evidence?" She looked perplexed.

"The evidence whose disappearance saved you from prison."

"Ah...yes. But you know...you know very well!"

"No, I know almost nothing. I want to be sure. So, tell me about it."

"It was a small vial with what's left of the mixed poisons and with my fingerprints on it."

"Where is it now? Is it still with Graziella?"

Spreading her arms, Maya suddenly swayed forward and embraced me.

"Thank you!" she said, stuttering with excitement. "No one has ever worried about me. Only you!"

"Well, yes," I muttered, slipping from her embrace. "I do worry."

"But you don't have to. Graziella insisted I participate in the experiment voluntarily, not as someone dependent on her. She even gave me the vial and asked me to break it."

I smiled at her. It wasn't hard to abandon the version that she had killed Kuber so that she could get the dangerous evidence back by blackmail. I preferred to put a thicker neck on the block: Valdo's, for example.

I opened the freezer-room door, made sure no one could lock us in from outside, and we went in. The place looked bigger than it actually was, because there was nothing else inside beside the corpse. We both stepped closer to it, Maya obediently stopping two steps from it. I also stopped. I wasn't expecting to see such blatant neglect for the death of someone who's been part of the "commune" for months. It was obvious that the body was not laid down but simply thrown here, on the naked floor. They could have covered it with something at least—the body was spread-eagled, a somewhat obscene position, and the face was staring at the ceiling, the mouth open and the eyes half-shut and covered in frost.

I turned to Maya. "Who brought it here?"

"I don't know."

I could barely hear her.

"When…the moment I saw he was dead, I ran away. And now…I'll be outside…"

She left the room, hands pressed against her stomach, body swaying like a drunkard's. I was pleasantly surprised. *There's something normal about her, after all*, I said to myself and turned back to the corpse. The body was naked to the waist, dressed in shorts, short socks, and trainers on the feet. One leg was stretched, and the other was bent in a way that was not natural and with a bruised knee. I wanted to check if it was broken, but the frozen flesh was unyielding. I did check the arms, though, and found out that the palm of the right one was bruised too. The nails were closely clipped, and I saw no fibers or pieces of someone else's skin under them. The chest was too hairy, and I couldn't see if there were scars on it. I also couldn't tell if he had lost lots of blood, because in this temperature the face and the body were bluish in color, no signs of blood clotting anywhere.

At this point, it wasn't clear what might have caused the death. I needed to turn the body over, and that wasn't going to be easy. My hands were too cold; I could barely move my fingers, and what once used to be Kuber was now a heavy mass stuck to the metal floor. He was of medium height, stocky, and broad-shouldered—one of those brawny boys who looked perfect with a farm in the background. He had rough features, low brow, strong jaw, and big teeth in the gaping—as if for its final scream—mouth.

After several unsuccessful attempts to unstick his body from the floor, I realized I should give up. If I kept on trying, I would leave no skin on his back—as if I had flayed him. I stepped back, kneeled down, and leaned to the side to see the head from a horizontal point of view. It looked crushed at the nape, as flat there as the floor was. I shuffled forward, still on my knees, and looked at the hair: it was frozen in locks, which meant that it had been wet, maybe with blood. But I couldn't tell more, because its color was the unhelpful dark brown. The only thing I saw was a grayish bird feather tangled in the locks. I moved to his feet. Tiny pebbles were stuck to the soles of the trainers, but this couldn't tell me much about his whereabouts at the moment of his death.

I stood up. I had to get out of there before becoming stiff with cold. I threw one last look at the dead man, still puzzled by his gaping mouth. If he was ambushed and murdered—with a blow from behind so strong as to crush the back of his head—would he have found the time to scream?

CHAPTER FIFTEEN

I t was foolish of me to think I could lock the door with hands stiff from the cold. I dropped the skeleton key once and then dropped it again when I tried to pick it up. It would be at least five or six minutes before my blood circulation went back to normal. I decided to use the time to ask Maya, who was probably waiting for me nearby, some of my questions. I walked to the stairs, but when I reached them, I didn't start climbing up. I was blinded by the bright light of someone's flashlight, and a second later, I heard the voice I least wanted to hear.

"How are you?" he rumbled politely.

"I'm very good; thank you," I replied immediately.

I hadn't felt this bad in years—I was at the bottom of the stairs, blinking like a rat, and Valdo was at the top, staring at me, moving the flashlight's beam from my face down my body and back to my face again. I saw him only as a huge black silhouette, but from his wheezing breathing, it was clear that he was mad with rage.

"You look very much like a buffalo," I told him candidly, and he rushed down the stairs, bellowing out curses at me.

I moved aside before he could push me down, which he no doubt intended. He flashed past me and hit the wall at the far end of the landing. The landing was narrow, by the way, allowing almost no space for maneuvering. But even if it did allow, I wouldn't have been able to do anything, because I was still stiff with cold. Alas, I had to brace myself for an unequal fight with a clear ending.

"Give it to me!" Valdo stepped toward me and reached out a hand. "The key, give me the *skeleton key*, you idiot!"

Well, I handed it to him. He waved it before my eyes, called me an idiot once more, and turned his back to me. He started locking the cellar door, taking his time deliberately, giving me the opportunity to run up the stairs, tail between legs—something as reasonable as it was humiliating. I stood firmly on my feet and expressed my "boredom" with a loud sigh, after which Valdo turned the key one last time, put it in his pocket, and pointed the flashlight at me.

"Why are you so dumb?" he asked me, amazed. "Didn't it occur to you that you could've run?"

"It did! You're like a buffalo...no! Like a bison."

He turned off the flashlight and put it in his pocket with the key, and I saw the outlines of his fists before me, much darker than the night. In the end, however, there was no fight. It seemed that my dumbness had exhausted him beforehand. Dropping his fists, he started up the stairs. I followed him. I looked around and was relieved to find out that Maya had shown the good sense to hide somewhere.

When we were past the house, Valdo started whispering. "You broke into my bungalow, rummaged in my stuff, took the skeleton key. OK, I'm not angry at you, but...why? Why the hell? What made you go to the corpse?"

"No particular reason," I replied. "I enjoy the sight of dead people."

"Are you serious...no kidding?" he stuttered.

"Of course. Don't you?"

"No. But I might if you're the dead one! Nutter! Psycho!"

"Look who's talking. The other nutter. Psycho number two."

From his silence, I assumed that his conscience had suddenly woken up, but he spoke again, and I realized I was wrong.

"No, I am not a psycho," he announced proudly. "I've only killed for revenge, and what's more natural than that?"

"Are you asking me? Or making a statement?"

"I want nothing from you except to stay away from me. And Roxanna!"

"Or else I'll meet your special form of revenge?"

"Don't think so much of yourself. I'm not going to sabotage the experiment for a wretch like you. But I will beat you black and blue...or not! I will give you such beating that would make your eyes shoot sparkles and set your hair on fire!"

Delighted by the idea, he got into such a good mood that he even wished me a good night and continued across the meadow, puffing out his chest, which was broader than the wardrobe in my cell. *He might not be a psycho*, I told myself, *but he definitely is infantile.*

I went back to my bungalow and saw that Maya had left my jacket on the bed. I pushed a chair up against the door and got into the bathroom for a hot shower. But the water was cold.

CHAPTER SIXTEEN

S unrise found me on a hill with a view of the ocean. No one could see me from the house, because I was sitting behind the trunk of the only tree here—a lonely fig tree. I sat under its low, heavy-with-unripe-fruit branches, exhausted from lack of sleep and food. I was also saddened that I seemed to have lost my ability to enjoy nature's beauty, which was in abundance in this fresh, tropical morning.

Just as I expected, the satellite connection was strong here. I had spent hours browsing the net, my eyes teary from staring at the phone screen, which was far from high quality. My fingers were numb from typing on the small keyboard. And? So far I hadn't found anything in support of Maya's conviction that Merry Maker had murdered his first victim for her.

Patrick Krenz: twenty-two years old, third-year medical student. No offenses to his name, nothing strange about him. Described by everyone as being modest, shy, ordinary. Neither the *A*-grade type nor the outsider. Born in an ordinary family that was neither poor nor rich, neither perfect nor broken. Murdered during the night in his rented apartment, found by his sister, also a medical student but in her first year.

That was all. I combed through the usual shocking articles in the papers but found nothing else about him. I rested for a while and then went back to where I had started by opening again that picture—"The Ugly Woman with the Éclairs" was its caption, and the photographed face was strikingly ugly, indeed. The two bumps on the forehead looked like horns about to break out. One eye was almost closed by a swelling, the cheeks were covered by lumps, and the chin was a shapeless potato. Yet the most terrifying thing in this absolute deformity was the good eye. There was so much pain in it—so much suffering in that wide-open brown eye—that I started to hurt from staring at it. I was hurting about Maya, about her life, destroyed in such an absurd way.

Of course, looking at that picture, I never would have guessed it was her. Now, after Graziella had taken good care of her, she had a normal and kind face. I also never would have guessed that the case I had heard so much about from my colleagues was hers. A story that had begun with several lipomas and ended with eleven dead bodies. In her typically offhand manner, Graziella had described her as a serial killer, but in fact, she was more a mass murderer. I was sure Graziella didn't make that rookie mistake while documenting the experiment.

I looked up the so-called lipomas and read that they are growths of fat cells under the skin that are usually removed by different methods, all of which are quite simple, even the surgical one, which is performed under local anesthesia and leaves no scars. This meant that Maya's lipomas could have been removed without problem in their earliest stage, but instead her parents—both criminally negligent!—let them grow. They were one of those archaeologists who would travel the world in never-ending search for the "great discovery," and Maya actually grew up with her grandmother—a hypochondriac obsessed entirely by her imaginary illnesses.

Maya's troubles started when she was about ten and became unbearable when she was a teenager. The bullying, all the mockery and humiliation at school, turned her life into hell. Before taking the fatal step, she made several attempts to soften her classmates' cruelty by bringing them all sorts of homemade cakes. Her culinary talent was truly impressive, and the days during which her torturers had something to munch on were less painless. On the next day, though, everything would go back to normal.

This went on until one morning Maya came to school with her usual plastic box stuffed with exactly thirty éclairs. She left it, as usual, in the teachers' room, because she was allowed to give the cakes to her classmates during recess, which on that day turned out to be the last for nine of them. It was also the last recess in the lives of those who would usually be the first to taste the cakes—the school principal and the vice principal. Six more pupils were poisoned, all of them saved in the local hospital, and one of them…was Maya! Whether she was playing something like Russian roulette or she simply ate one of the deadly éclairs by mistake remained unclear. And later, despite the thorough laboratory analysis, no one could make out the components in the "specific mixture of poisons." It's a fact, however, that the vial carrying this mixture was found in Maya's pocket with her fingerprints all over it.

"It's not my vial. I found it in the box with the éclairs when I took it from the teachers' room. I put it into my pocket to ask later who brought it and put it there." Those were the only words Maya said during the investigation and at the trial. She would repeat them whenever she would open her mouth to speak, but her lawyer, unlike her, demonstrated his eloquence. And his questions were absolutely logical:

If Maya had poisoned the éclairs, why would she eat one? Why would she carry the vial around with her? How could she make such a mixture of poisons?

Because of the unsuccessful lab analysis, the last question influenced much of the trial. What also influenced the trial was the lawyer's version based on the fact that the principal and vice principal were among the victims. As in every other school, this one also suffered from inner conflict, intrigue, and schemes against "those on top." So, the defense lawyer would say, it's entirely possible a teacher poisoned the éclairs while the box was in the teachers' room. Everyone knew that Maya's cakes were usually left there for the time between morning and recess, which meant that the murderer could have prepared earlier for their deed. They had the vial and a syringe for inserting the poison with them, waited for the right time, and carried out their plan, leaving the blame for everything to Maya.

Naturally, after this version the prosecution's positions were shaken. Then it was found out that the vial—the main evidence against Maya—cannot be presented in court, because it had disappeared from the evidence-storage facility.

"We all know we're dealing with a monster here," the defense lawyer said in his closing speech, "but is that poor girl the monster? Let only those who believe in her monstrosity be the first to throw a stone at her! But before doing so, I beg you: ask yourselves how much of your decision is influenced by the facts presented during the trial, and how much by her appearance. And her appearance is something she's absolutely not guilty of!"

This was followed by a mass refusal to throw stones, and Maya was released for lack of evidence. But wouldn't that be the right ruling, even if it was proved that she was the poisoner? After all, she had always been surrounded by monsters—parents, teachers, classmates—and as the saying goes, one is known by the company they keep.

CHAPTER SEVENTEEN

The door of the house was unlocked. I went in, hoping that due to the early hour I would breakfast alone, but I found Valdo and Graziella in the kitchen. They were drinking coffee, and from the expressions on their faces, I could tell that their day had started with a conversation that was unpleasant for both. Or maybe even for the three of us—if the infantile wrestler had told on me for my night visit to the frozen chamber of the dead man.

"Good morning," I greeted them, on my way to the fridge.

Graziella nodded, and Valdo snarled at me and left the kitchen, leaving his coffee unfinished.

"What's wrong with him?" I tried to look surprised.

"He's worried about the girls," Graziella replied. "Says he stood watch in front of your bungalow until the break of dawn."

More like took a nap, I thought. *Or went home just before I woke up.*

I scowled to hide the relief I felt. If Valdo had followed me to the hill, I would have said good-bye to my phone and maybe to some of my teeth.

"It's only natural for him to be suspicious of you," Graziella began justifying him. "Maya and Roxanna are so helpless, and you...don't forget who you *are!*"

"I'm trying to," I said, equivocally. I took a package of vacuum-sealed ham and a box of pineapple juice from the fridge and two baguettes from the bread box.

"Would you like me to cook you an omelet?" Graziella smiled at me.

"Yes, please!" I answered right away and sat on the table.

She started making the omelet without much fuss. She wasn't one of those prissy rich girls, wasn't trying to be all swanky and affected. I watched her with increasing curiosity, as if now was the moment to decide whether to let her in my bed or refuse her offer before she has even made it.

I approved of her slender figure but not of her rather modest bosom. Those jeans looked perfect on her, and the sleeveless shirt she wore gave me a good view of her arms—beautiful and long and leanly muscled, albeit unnaturally pale, with a strange silvery sheen to them, which I suppose was the same all over her body. It probably would be like holding a fish in your arms...or maybe a mermaid? Her hair was long and tied back, and the light lemon-yellow color seemed natural and not the result of some hairdresser's skill or lack thereof. Her eyebrows were the same color, as were her thick eyelashes, delicately framing her glassy blue eyes. Despite the early hour, there were no wrinkles or signs of swelling on her face. It was as smooth as always.

Am I attracted to her? Or repulsed by her? I asked myself, and just like yesterday, I replied with a yes to both questions. I was in two minds about her too—as if shuttling between the mind of the nasty Merry Maker and my own, between my hatred for serial killers and compassion for some of them poisoning my soul, wasn't enough.

"Hide this!" Graziella whispered, handing me something wrapped in tinfoil.

"What's this?" I asked and put it in my pants pocket.

"It's a flash drive. Everything you need to know about...about your role is on it."

I was going to say that "need" is probably not the right word, but she served me the omelet, which smelled delicious and tasted great too.

"Actually, Valdo's distrust is good for us," Graziella almost whispered in my ear. "He insisted I give everyone keys to the bungalows, and I agreed. So that, locking yourself in, you'd be able to read unperturbed every police report on the flash drive."

"OK," I said. "Now I'd really like to eat."

She ignored that and continued with her instructions. "And be careful not to mix the information! Only what's in the reports is true. Forget everything you've seen in the papers!"

"There's not much to forget, Graziella. You don't think news about Merry Maker was my favorite read, do you?"

"Of course I don't!" She raised her voice. "But don't speak of *yourself* in the third person! And stop riling Valdo up! You should be more communicatively passive with him—"

"Oh, don't give me that psychobabble crap!" I raised my voice too, ignoring her warning gestures. "Valdo has been my enemy from day one. Not that I care, but I'd like to know why. Who is he to judge me? He's a murderer just like...like me."

The door opened with a bang, and Roxanna stormed into the kitchen.

"No!" she screamed at me. "Valdo is nothing like you!"

Graziella rushed to her and hugged her. "Yes, he's not, my dear, he's not," she talked soothingly. "Of course, he's nothing like him. No one is like your Valdo, no one."

"Yes, but...I heard him!" Roxanna pointed a finger at me and started crying. "I heard you talking."

"I know, dear, I know!" Graziella looked at me with reproach.

"I heard him!" Roxanna repeated, now pointing a fist at me. "He said—"

"My dear, he only said it because he still has no idea what Valdo's been through. But now you're going to explain to him, and he will stop comparing himself to Valdo. Right, Merry Maker?"

"Right," I agreed immediately. "She doesn't have to explain. I'll stop."

I used the pause to focus back on my breakfast.

"But she has to," Graziella decided a moment later. "*She has to!*"

"Nooooo!" This time Roxanna didn't yell; she screamed.

I was so startled that I almost choked.

"I can't, nooo!" Another scream came.

"Hush!" Graziella pushed her to one of the chairs, placed hands on her shoulders, and then pushed her down. "You can; you can; you can," she began chanting.

Roxanna started shaking her head to the rhythm, and her face went blue. I leaped to the fridge and grabbed a bottle of mineral water from it.

"Don't move!" Graziella told me in a business-like manner. She leaned toward Roxanna and gave her a loud smack on the face, then another one... and another one...

"Enough!" I shouted, but she smacked her again. "There!" She sounded happy with what she had just done.

I stepped closer, dizzy with bewilderment. Now Roxanna sat on the chair in absolute stillness, like a statue. Her eyes were open but not blinking; her face was frozen in a grimace of painful resignation.

"What's wrong with her?" I turned to Graziella.

"Motor immobility with intact or reduced consciousness. In other words, this is what psychogenic stupor looks like," she answered calmly.

"Isn't that dangerous?"

"Not for her. It's been her reaction to stress and abuse and humiliation since childhood."

"Yet here you are stressing and humiliating her!"

"Yes." Graziella pulled the bottle from my hand, opened it, and took a few gulps. "I had to. So that she could gather herself together and tell you all about Valdo."

"But I don't want to…I don't want her to tell me anything."

"You don't, but we have to take advantage of the fact that you've only been here for a day. She can think logically, you know, Miro. How could I ask her to tell his story to some of the others when she knows perfectly well that they had already heard it?"

"Why do you have to ask her in the first—"

"For her own good. The end."

"The end of what?"

"Your questions," Graziella said curtly. "Come on, take her, and let's get out of here before any-one shows up."

I wondered what would deal more damage to my dignity—to follow her orders or not to. In the end, I decided that both decisions would be equal-ly damaging, so I went with the easier.

CHAPTER EIGHTEEN

Graziella's bedroom was far less splendid than I expected. It was quite modest, monastic even. A narrow bed covered with a cheap brown bedspread, a nightstand that looked more like a wooden box, a chipboard table, a wardrobe no bigger than the one in my cell, two ancient naked chairs, and a naked plank floor.

"Put her here." Graziella pointed at the bed.

Not only didn't Roxanna move while I was carrying her up the stairs but she also remained in the same sitting position. I felt terrible—as if I was walking with a stiff corpse in my arms. A living corpse I left lying on its side on the bed, and Graziella quickly closed her eyes with her hand.

"Otherwise they dry up," she explained. "She's not blinking, you see."

"Dear God!" I said in shock. "When will she go back to normal?"

"Soon, I guess. I've put her in such state only once before, and it didn't last long."

"*Put?* She is like a lab rat to you!"

"I told you already; it's for her own good." Graziella pulled me farther from the bed. "Let's wait."

We sat on the uncomfortable chairs, and while they creaked under our bodies, she said smugly, "As you can see, I also spend my nights in something like a prison cell. I am solidary with my patients. That's why I'll return to the wing with the comfortable bedrooms no earlier than the sixteenth this month, with everyone else."

"Good for you. But in order to be fully solidary, you'd have to kill at least five or six people."

Her yellowish eyebrows knotted, and her face looked so focused that I started to worry. It was as if she had taken my idea absolutely seriously and was now considering who to kill first. As it turned out, her thoughts were in a completely different direction.

"Roxanna's parents were junkies," she said, in a loud voice. "They needed money for drugs and for years would get it from three loyal clients.

Perverted creeps who began to abuse the junkies' daughter from the age of seven—"

"Enough!" I whispered in panic. "She can probably hear you!"

"She can, although I'm not sure how much she can understand. Unlike your grandfather, I believe that in such moments her mind sees reality through distorted filters."

"It doesn't matter! Stop talking about her!"

"Miro," she started patiently, "you're still not getting that this island is a place for therapy. Psychotherapy! I *work* here, and I can assure you I'm doing my job quite well. I know what I'm doing and why I'm doing it. Do you understand?"

I shrugged. The only thing I did understand was that I should not involve myself in this confusing situation.

"So," Graziella started talking again in a loud voice, "Roxanna was constantly abused and humiliated until she was fifteen, when she found the courage to tell the whole story to her aunt. Then the woman took her in her home and warned her parents that she would tell the police if they didn't disappear forever from the life of the child whom they had heartlessly turned into a commodity. Into an underage *prostitute*!"

Roxanna didn't move, although she squealed once, and her eyelids jumped, leaving her glassy eyes exposed.

"Roxanna stayed with her aunt, who would take selfless care of her." Graziella resumed her intrusive storytelling. "But her soul was beyond healing! And when she turned twenty, she decided to take her revenge on those three perverts. Within a month she managed to lure every one of them to her bedroom and shoot him with the gun she had stolen from a privately owned shooting range. But after each of the murders, she would descend into a stupor like the current one, during which her mind would twist the reality into a blend of aural and visual hallucinations. *Hallucinations* that her mind would later mistake for memories. *False* memories like those that lead even normal people to believe that they had, for example, been abducted by aliens."

"Deaaath," Roxanna said, with much effort. "Deaaath was killing them. I...I would only bury them."

Graziella swiftly stood up and went to her. "When will you stop lying to yourself, dear?" She murmured and helped her take a more comfortable position on the bed. "You know perfectly well that death can take on a human form only in the movies. Or in a person's imagination!"

"What about the shots?" I asked. "Did no one hear them?"

"No one," Graziella said. "The neighboring houses were far, the aunt was on sleeping pills, her bedroom was on the second floor, and the gun was not one of the loud ones. A point-twenty-two-caliber Colt Woodsman, right, dear? *Right?*" Head tilted in Roxanna's direction, she waited for a confirmation, and getting none at all, she went on. "But, Miro, her aunt's boyfriend had a dog, unfortunately. *A dog*! Every time he would visit, he'd leave it in the yard, and one evening it dug out and even began *eating* the corpse of…I don't remember whose corpse it was, but it doesn't matter now. What matters is that since then, Roxanna has a painful fear of *all kinds* of dogs!"

Graziella sat next to her on the bed, looked closer into her now-blinking eyes, and started repeating: "Dog, dog, dog—"

"Don't!" Roxanna joined her palms beggingly. "I will do what I promised. I'll say I murdered them."

"It was you, dear. It was really *you*! You'll have to start believing that. You also must remember where you hid the gun! Or else everyone at the trial will know that you still have amnesia, and they'll lock you up in the loony bin again. Think of Valdo! What will he do then? And tell me, why are you trying to distance yourself from him? Is it only because you think he used to be a dog? Dog, dog, dog—"

"A war dog," Roxanna said, in a surprisingly controlled voice. "But I'm not distancing myself from him."

"Then why do you deny that you both have similar fates, that you both have murdered to take your revenge on those who have abused and humiliated and destroyed you?"

"Only he has had his revenge, Graziella. Only he! And he would've respected me more if I had had mine too. But I haven't, I haven't…and I don't want to lie to him. I'm not going to lie to him!"

"I'm not asking you to lie to him, dear. I want the opposite—to tell him the truth. But first you'll have to admit it before yourself. And you're doing what now? He's your fiancé, yet you still can't accept him for what he is. You're trying to forget his story instead of continue telling it—"

"Tell it? To this bastard here?" Roxanna waved a hand in my direction. "No! You can both go to hell!"

She pushed Graziella away, stood with much difficulty from the bed, and left us, her head raised proudly.

"Too bad," Graziella sighed. "I failed again. Those murders are cemented in her memory. I keep trying to break them free but without success so far."

"But how could she remember burying the victims and not killing them?"

"Dissociative amnesia, Miro—blocked memories, in other words, related to events that have been particularly traumatic to the subject. This was the diagnosis, thanks to which Roxanna was declared mentally irresponsible. She does believe that she hasn't murdered anyone and that she had stolen the gun only for self-defense. The gun's missing, though. And she will remember where she hid it only if I make her remember the murders themselves."

"So your main goal is to find out where the gun is?"

"Yes, because it will help me prove that I had broken her amnesia down. Otherwise, there wouldn't be much left of my reputation as a psychiatrist, and this would compromise the experiment." Graziella rubbed her temples, grimacing. "God! This girl is so confused that even hypnosis was completely useless. My only hope lies in her relationship with Valdo, but as you just witnessed, my approach seems to be far too gentle."

"Interesting," I said. "If you call this gentle, I wonder what rough would be like."

"Fraught with risk. But also probably the only one left." Graziella stood up and headed for the door with what looked like desperate resolve. "I have no choice. I will show it to her!" she whispered and stepped into the corridor, leaving me or maybe forgetting I was there.

I caught up with her just when she was about to disappear into the next room, and took her hand.

"What? *What* are you going to show to her?" I asked.

"Wait until half past nine. Then you'll see for yourself."

Her hand slipped from mine. She slipped into the room—spacious, equipped with all sorts of electric machines—and shut the door and locked it from inside.

CHAPTER NINETEEN

I stopped by the kitchen to see if Maya was there. She was but with Danko. They were at the table, peeling potatoes and talking. Actually, Maya was talking about some "super restaurant," and he listened blissfully as if to a nightingale's song. They were so carried away that they didn't see me until I stood right next to them. Maya greeted me with a gleeful exclamation, and Danko only looked at me. His eyes were swampy green, and the black of his hair contrasted sharply with the paleness of his face, which in turn contrasted with the bright red of his lips. I didn't know why I had thought he was good-looking last evening. He looked like a vampire to me now.

"You'll have breakfast, won't you?" Maya moved quickly to the stove and took a whole tray with doughnuts from the oven. "I prepared them yesterday. Only baked them today. I thought you'd like them, 'cause you were a cop, you know."

I smiled. "I liked doughnuts even before I became a cop."

"Wonderful! Take a seat!"

"Thank you," I replied but did not sit down. I felt no desire to eat in the presence of the silent vampire and his swampy eyes. I wondered what his story was. How many people had he murdered? And how? I hoped that at least he would remain outside the perimeter of my foolish sympathy when I got the answers.

"I understand." Maya nodded at me. "Sometimes it's hard to be around Danko. But once you get used to his presence, you'll always seek his company. He's good, like an angel!"

Her words disturbed me far more than I expected, and a red grin jagged across Danko's pale face, revealing small white teeth. Well, I seemed to have no luck in this kitchen! I said good-bye and left.

In fact, unlike Danko, Maya did prove she was like an angel—she caught up with me just when I was crossing the vestibule and handed me a large box full of doughnuts. I was about to feel touched by this when I remembered that she was taking care not of me but of Merry Maker.

"I'm sorry for last night," Maya whispered. "I saw Valdo coming, got scared, hid, and then ran away."

"You did all the right things," I said.

"Do you think he's going to rat you out for visiting the dead man?"

"He hasn't, for now."

"Did you find anything suspicious on the body?"

I frowned. "We'll talk some other time. Now go back to the kitchen."

"OK, but—"

"Back to the kitchen, Maya!"

I was left with the impression that the commanding tone to my voice pleased her. She seemed to see in me the strict but just-older guardian brother she never had. She gently touched my arm and then headed back through the vestibule.

I left the house, divided by conflicting emotions. The pleasant vanilla smell of the doughnuts wafted from the box, and the faceless shadows of the victims poisoned by Maya's éclairs filed through my mind. The box she took to school must have been similar to this one...

Soon my attention was captured by a pastoral view, which in other circumstances would have passed for comical: Sitting in the thick grass beyond the area with the hibiscuses, Sirius—the man first sentenced to life and then released from prison for good behavior—was holding a flute with his body builder's arms and was drawing discordant, howling sounds from it. Around him, a bay stallion, two spotted cows, and three closely sheared sheep grazed lazily.

"Miro, Miro!" he shouted. "Come!"

I went to him, accompanied by a new series of howling sounds. Next to him was a green bucket with a lid, on top of which was a nickel-silver can. I was tempted to kick first the bucket and then the "flautist," but my good manners held me back.

"I'm not against having cattle around," he began, "but I'd really appreciate it if you would stop putting off and actually start doing your duty tomorrow."

"I'd appreciate it if you'd tell me what my duties are, and then I might start doing them," I said.

"I'll explain." He dropped the flute in the grass and pointed at the acacia trees nearby. "The pens and the stables are just over there. You must clean them up early in the morning and then milk the creatures and herd them here. You must leave them to graze all day and return in the evening to take them back to the pens, where you're supposed to feed them dried yeast with vitamins before milking them again. That's all."

"And why do you think that's my duty?"

"Because it used to be Kuber's, and you're taking his place now."

I did not object to that, although I didn't like his answer. "Well, let's hope I'll take his place only in the pens and not in the fridge," I said, and Sirius grinned widely in appreciation of my humor.

I thought that it was the right time to ask him a few questions about the "accident." I sat down next to him and put the box with the doughnuts between us. Then he reached out and lifted the bucket lid. He filled the can with milk and handed it to me. I took it from him, sipped, and then each of us grabbed a doughnut and relaxed in the friendly atmosphere.

"The stallion's name is Doro," he informed me. "He's mild-tempered until you try to mount him. Then he goes berserk. Becomes a murderer! We keep him only for his good looks."

"What about the cows? Are they mild-tempered too, or do I have to prepare for kicks while milking them?"

"You have to. Both are easily scared. There are no predators on the island, but we have snakes—"

"And a ghost," I added, joking. "Wasn't that what Fata was saying about her brother?"

"Damn her!"

"Yes, I can tell she's one evil lady. But is her magic responsible for Kuber's death? Sorry, but I don't believe that."

"I believe one day, and the next I don't." Sirius tapped his forehead with a finger. "That old witch will make me lose my mind! I've never been superstitious, but...let me tell you the facts: She and Kuber get into a fight, and she threatens him. She tells him, 'You'll be dead tomorrow!' waving a tiny red wax figure before his eyes. 'I'll stick some needles into it, and you'll fall. You'll fall from somewhere high!' And on the next morning...well, he fell! We found him in the rock below the house, his skull crushed."

"Yes." I nodded. "A strange coincidence. But what were they fighting for?"

"We don't know. The old witch raised her voice only at the end, and Roxanna heard only her threats."

"Was she eavesdropping on them?"

"Yes. She has had the habit since childhood. But in this case, it was not as easy as she thought."

"I see. And what did Fata say after that?"

"After? You think someone went asking her anything after this? No, we all act as if we know nothing about the fight. Or else if not her, then Valdo will take care of us, as he made it perfectly clear. And he's right! Because if Fata found out that Roxanna was eavesdropping, she would seek revenge."

"I doubt that," I said, only to provoke him. "You all seem a bit obsessed to me."

"No, we're not!" Sirius grew agitated. "I am almost sure that we're dealing with a witch here, Miro. That's why Kuber was like a zombie on that morning. There's no way a normal person would fall from there."

"And you're telling me that up to that morning, Kuber was a completely normal person? Excuse me for repeating myself, but I doubt that. Don't forget that Graziella took him from a mental institution. As she did Frant, Roxanna, and Danko."

"Dammit! It's true. He did have his fits of insanity. Much more than the other three. But he was aware of that. Yet, instead of being careful about it, he went and challenged Fata. Dammit, dammit! I'm still mad at him!"

Sirius looked really mad. So mad that his freckled face turned red and stopped being freckled for a while. He finally looked evenly tanned. So, that's who had thrown the body in the freezer room, I thought, and began hypocritically, "Sirius, I am sure that Fata can't hurt you, no matter what she is. Voodoo magic works only on people who are weak minded, and you seem like a stable guy to me."

"Well, I am." He showed no sense of self-criticism. "But Fata hates me with all her heart, which gives her more power. She thinks that of all the criminals on the island, I am the biggest one."

"And isn't she right?"

"She's not, of course! I have killed only three prostitutes in my entire life. But she doesn't believe me. She thinks I'm lying."

"Then prove her wrong. There must be some info about you on the net. Find a way to show it to her."

"I can't, Miro. Here, only Graziella has access to the Internet, and she wants us to keep my real name in secret. I have no idea why."

The murderer with the astral pseudonym looked truly devastated now—as if his only chance to escape from the evil witch had just revealed itself as nothing more than a mere mirage. But what he had just told me was a blatant lie, and I had to answer with the same. In other words, I had to play the absolute fool. I hesitated for a moment and then said, "If we keep going like this, the milk will go sour."

"You're right." His lips twisted. "It's time I took it to the house."

"And I'll take some of the doughnuts to Roxanna. Valdo asked me to do it."

"You're lying!"

"Of course I am," I agreed, with a smile. "Well? Aren't you going to point me in direction of her bungalow?"

It was a curious moment for me and an unpleasant one for him. I listened to his directions, enjoying the sight of his worried face. The poor guy was wondering what he did or said wrong, totally unaware that I was doing the same.

CHAPTER TWENTY

Roxanna's bungalow, as it turned out, was close to mine. I knocked quietly, politely on the door, and then I knocked harder and louder, but the result was always the same—no one answered. Finally, I went in, assuming Roxanna would be hiding inside, still upset by the stupor she experienced, and I was partly right. She was inside, but she wasn't hiding, and she didn't look upset. She was sitting on the bed, a big sketch pad propped against her bent knees. She was holding a black pastel pencil and was drawing, drawing like someone in trance. I stepped forward and closed the door behind me.

"Sit. I'm just finishing," she murmured. Then she looked up, saw me, and added, "Get out! I'll come to you in a moment."

"Why?" I asked. Then I elaborated. "Why would you come to me?"

"To fulfill my promise," she answered.

I couldn't recall any promise, but I nodded as if I remembered. I sat on the only chair around and observed politely, "I see that you're better now."

"Nonsense! I've been drawing her all night long; there's no way I could be better after that." She bit fiercely into the pencil. "I'm trying to recreate her image for the first time, and it's terribly hard! I don't know if I've succeeded. I don't know!"

She's been drawing death! I thought in amazement. *Yesterday she promised she'd show her to me and… here's what she meant.*

"Oh, you must've done it right," I mumbled. "But you shouldn't have bothered so much. You could've just described her to me."

"Nonsense!" she said and continued drawing.

She tilted her head now to one side and then to the other. She stuck her tongue out and then half closed her eyes. All in all, she looked as diligent as a child—she, who had never had a childhood, only "clients." So sad! Too bad she murdered them quickly and painlessly. She should have tortured them, cut them slowly piece by piece. I started imagining what I would do to perverts like them, and my mind became a scene for such cruelties that I was shocked. I was surprised I had such an inventive sadistic streak in me.

"Done!" Roxanna nervously rolled the paper, as if already terrified by the image she had recreated. She tied it with a rubber band and handed it to me. "It will work only if you're alone with *her*," she told me and pointed with an impatient gesture at the bag hanging on a nail on the door. "Go! And take your shirt on your way out. I washed and sewed it, but I didn't iron it. To keep you from idling all day long."

"Thank you for asking me about my wound," I said, somewhat spitefully. "It's hurting and itching."

"Then it's healing," she said. "But you're lucky Valdo is on the roof today. Because otherwise he could've come here and seen you bothering me—"

"On the roof? What's he doing there?"

"Some repairs. He's fixing everything around the house. He's very good with his hands!"

I tried to look disappointed. "Oh, I was hoping I'd be lucky and he'd fall from there. Kuber wasn't as skillful as him, was he?"

"Kuber?" She raised her eyebrows.

"Why, yes. He also fell, didn't he? Though not from a roof but from a rock."

Roxanna got angry. "What are you hinting at? What do you want?"

"I want you to provide short and clear answers to my questions."

"And if I refuse?"

"You'd better not. Or else I'll go to Graziella this very moment and show her both my wound and the knife you used to inflict it on me. Of course, I'll also explain that it was Fata's knife and that she gave it to you—"

"Stop it!" Her face was pale now. "I will answer your questions."

After she calmed down, I began with the interrogation, which could cost me my life if Kuber's murderer was indeed her beloved Valdo.

"When exactly was the fight between Kuber and Fata that you eavesdropped on?"

"About nine p.m. I go to her only at this hour. I tell everyone I'm going to bed early because of a headache or something like this and go to—"

"You go to her in secret?"

"Yes. Unfortunately, Fata is not one to hide her hatred for the murderers here, and she's become quite the nuisance for them. If Graziella found out about our friendship, she would definitely use that against her. She'd accuse her of influencing me to keep my 'amnesia' alive, and that would be her pretext for banishing her from the island."

"Be careful, Roxanna," I warned her. "I think you just started lying. Why would Graziella need a pretext when she can banish her without one?"

"No, she can't! Fata's brother agreed to sell the island on one condition—that she can stay here as long as she wants to. And Graziella insisted that Fata sign a declaration of noninterference in the experiment, and only then was the deal sealed. So, yes, she needs a reason to banish her. Otherwise, the lawyers of the family would take legal actions, and this would definitely not be good for the experiment."

"Hmm...and why on earth would Fata want to live on the island?"

"I have no idea. Everyone has their secrets, Miro, including her."

"And you," I added. "But if your visits to her were a secret, how did you tell the others about her fight with Kuber? How did you explain your being there?"

"I lied to them that I accidentally saw him going there and followed him."

"And when did you lie to them? Before you found the body or after?"

"Before. Right after we realized he was...gone."

"So Kuber disappears, and you, who are supposed to be Fata's friend, tell on her as soon as you can: 'I heard her threaten him. She told him he'd fall...'"

"Yes, yes! That evening I went to see her, but when I realized Kuber was with her, I didn't show up. I only listened, and I heard her. This is exactly what she told him! Then we all discovered that her threats had become reality. She is a master of voo-doo magic!"

"Good for her. And good for you. You must have very strong eyes if you were able to see through distance and dusk that the wax figure was red."

"Well…I supposed it was red because she uses such candles. Sometimes there's no electricity in her house, and the generator doesn't work every time…"

"And when it breaks down, Valdo fixes it, right?"

"Yes, but…how is this relevant?"

"In no way, probably. Because there was no fighting at all. My question is, why did you make it up?"

"You don't seem able to think!" She laughed nervously. "If I had told them about the fight after we had discovered Kuber's body, you might have been right in assuming I had made it up. But I told them before that. I quoted Fata's threats word for word, and it all corresponded with reality!"

"It corresponded because you made everything up," I replied, watching her eyes. "You saw Valdo pushing Kuber off the rock. And decided to steer the suspicions away from him and toward Fata, ascribing her those threats and magic powers."

Roxanna did not move for the next ten seconds. I worried she might be in stupor again and even started blaming myself for being so rough with her, when she threw the pencil box at me. It hit me in the shoulder, although she was aiming at my head. She screamed, "Filthy cop! Murderer! Sadist! Merry Maker!"

I stood up and stepped toward the door. I wanted her to think I was leaving.

"Wait!" She looked startled. "Where are you going?"

"To Graziella. I have to warn her that Valdo has committed a murder here."

"But that's not true!" Panicked, Roxanna took a leap and landed between me and the door. "Valdo has nothing to do with Kuber's death! And he knows nothing, absolutely nothing, about my visits with Fata or my...lies. Just like the others, he thinks I overheard the fighting."

I tried to look hesitant. "OK, but even if that's so, my question remains."

"What question?"

"The following, Roxanna: Why did you make the quarrel up?"

"All right!" She pushed me back toward the chair. "I'll explain everything. I promise!"

We went back to our seats, and her monologue started. It was unexpectedly quiet, almost like the murmur of the rain.

"The terrible accident happened to Kuber in a period when all of us lived in the house. I have insomnia; I'm usually awake all night long. I sit by the window and wait for the sun to show up. I watch it emerge from the ocean and grow into a big red ball, while the birds dart so swiftly before it that they look like scratches on its face. Fleeting black, white, and gray scratches: birds out hunting..." Roxanna shook her head sadly. "But on that morning, a person suddenly appeared in the picture. Kuber. He was naked from the waist up, walking in the direction of the eastern edge of the cliff. He stopped there, right at the edge of one of the rocks. He peeked down from it and then stepped to the side and peeked again. Then he stepped to the side again...I wondered what was wrong with him. I quickly put on some clothes and ran outside. I was at the same rock no more than three minutes later, but he was already gone from there. I looked down. And...there he was, dead."

"Did you climb down to check for sure?" I asked, puzzled by the way she had described the "terrible accident."

"No, I did not," she snapped back at me. "I went quietly back into my bedroom and waited for the others to 'wake me up.' And when they told me that Kuber has disappeared, I lied that I had overheard Fata threatening him the previous evening. Later, all were shocked by the way her threats had turned into reality!" Roxanna laughed with sincere glee.

"And?" I urged her, irritated. "Still no answer to the question *why* you lied!"

"I don't want to say good-bye to Fata. That's why! She's…like a mother to me. And the day before the tragedy, Sirius boasted to everyone that he had secretly taped some of the curses she would usually direct at him, as she considers him the lowest of all the murderers around."

"But is she right to think so?"

"I don't know, and I don't care." Roxanna laughed again. "Thing is, after my lie, Sirius became more superstitious than a savage! He now believes that voodoo magic can work from any distance and that if Fata is banished from here, she'll take her revenge on him. That's why instead of giving Graziella the recording, he destroyed it."

"And Fata continued pouring curses over him, unaware of everything." I also laughed, but Roxanna pointed at the door with a sudden gesture.

"Now leave! Go, but remember that if you tell the others what I've just told you, I will deny it. And at least Valdo will believe me. But even if he doesn't, his wrath will be directed at you anyway. Only at you, understand?"

There was no need for such warning. I had no intention to tell the story to anyone, and I wasn't surprised that she didn't intend to either.

CHAPTER TWENTY-ONE

I went back to my cell, carrying the rolled-up portrait of Death and the bag with my washed-clean-of-blood shirt. I put them all on the table, right next to the box with the doughnuts made by the poisoner, and took out of my pocket the flash drive with the police reports that were supposed to tell me every nasty detail I had to know about "myself." Could it get more idiotic than this? I asked and immediately answered myself with a yes. The tendency showed that it not only was possible but inevitable.

I checked my watch. Forty minutes to nine thirty. I had no idea what the risky thing was that Graziella was going to show us then, but I wasn't dying to see it. Usually, my curiosity is piqued by pleasant expectations, and with such absent right now, it barely flickered—just like a crushed firefly.

I walked about the narrow space, drank some water although I wasn't feeling thirsty, and took the laptop out of my suitcase. I placed it on the table, sat down before it, and did not turn it on. I was immediately gripped by hesitation: What should I look at first? *Death* or the reports? Both seemed equally repulsive to me, because the former meant me peeking, like some voyeur, into Roxanna's pathological visions, and the latter—getting to know in detail the deeds of the sadist I was pretending to be. In the end, I took the following decision: I put the flash drive back into my pocket, dropped the roll in the bag where the shirt was, and locked the bag in the wardrobe. I sat back at the table and sunk my teeth into the doughnuts, enjoying a calm breakfast at last.

Yes, if there was anything on this island not tarnished by suspicion, it was Maya's culinary talent. After washing the box so that she could fill it up with another treat tomorrow, I stretched myself on the narrow bed, comforted by the primal satisfaction of the satisfied. I was also satisfied with the advance I was making with the investigation, although I was still unable to estimate its exact proportions. I only had the vague feeling that I was in possession of some of the key pieces of the puzzle and that the moment I put them together, Sirius would take up a significant place in the picture.

A significant place, yes, but not that of the murderer. I was sure that his fear of Fata was sincere. He truly believed that Kuber had become a victim of her magic, which meant that someone else had committed the murder. It was early for questions such as who or why, but as far as how went, I had an idea:

The murderer sneaks behind Kuber, who is walking along the edge of the rock, but Kuber hears him or her, turns around to see, and that is why, when the other pushes him, he falls. That's why the back of his head was smashed and his mouth—frozen in the scream of death.

I also remembered the note Graziella had received: "You don't know who I am, but I know what you've done." What exactly had she done? When and how had she disguised the murder as an accident? It was about time I got the answer from her.

I picked up Maya's box and rushed toward the house, but the moment I stepped on the meadow, I saw Frant and walked in his direction. He was standing on his toes by one of the hibiscus bushes, trimming it carefully with a pair of long-handled pruners. I moved closer, put a sweet smile on my face to set him at ease, and said, "Hello, friend," and he lashed the pruners at me! I jumped back.

"What's gotten into you, huh?"

"Not into me, into you," he objected. "Hypocrisy, that's what. Why are you pretending to be my friend when you don't trust me? Tell me!"

"You mean I had to sit there and wait trustfully for you to stab me with these?"

"No, waiting was out of the question. I was going to tell you right away that it's a test." He closed the pruners. "Come on, relax. But let this be a lesson for you: I can see through your insincerity."

These last words were the perfect opportunity for a change of tactic.

"OK, Frant, I'll be honest with you," I began cordially. "The truth is that I've been very worried and quite stressed since last night. Despite its beauty, this island has turned out to be a truly macabre place. Three deaths so far: a drowning, a suicide, a voodoo revenge…"

"Ugh! Please, don't start with that superstitious nonsense. The Japanese guy committed suicide simply because his wife drowned. As for Fata, she has threatened each and every one of us in one way or the other, and as you see, we're all alive and doing fine. Kuber would have been alive, too, if it wasn't for his sentimentality."

"Sentimentality…in a serial killer?"

"Why not? Don't you get sentimental sometimes?"

"I…well, yes, yes, I do, sometimes."

"Well, he was like that all the time. That's why he ended up a murderer."

Frant threw the pruners in the grass, plucked a couple of blossoms from the bush, crushed them in his palms, and inhaled their fragrance, with his eyes closed.

"Dying, they emit their strongest fragrance," he mumbled and began his story. "As a child, Kuber watched his mother strangle his just-born sister. He was on the next bed, pretending to be asleep, when she grabbed his favorite pillow, with a small bird embroidered on it, and pressed it against the whimpering child's face. The girl quieted down... this time forever, and the mother, unaware that her son was awake, put the pillow back on his bed and left the room. In the morning there were screams, crying, and other simulations, but everything was over in exactly three days. The medic's conclusion was "sudden-infant-death syndrome." The family buried the little bean of a baby, and everyone returned to their normal lives. Not Kuber, though! He was only four at that time, unable to grasp what had happened. But the scene with the pillow would return to his memory every time he looked at it or rested his head on it..."

Pressing his lips together, Frant crouched and grabbed the pruners. He then turned toward the bush and started trimming it with fierce movements, making the whole thing look more like an act of mutilation.

"No need for that, Frant," I said quietly. "The plant's done nothing."

"You're right." He dropped his hands. "But I feel pity; I pity Kuber...because he, the fool, loved even the plants. I told you: too sentimental for his own good!"

"You also told me that's the reason he became a murderer," I reminded him.

"Absolutely! He developed an extreme sensitivity to babies and went completely mad when he first stepped into puberty. He started hanging around playgrounds to observe the women with babies there. He would follow to their homes those who, in his eyes, treated their children badly; murder them; and leave the babies at the door of a church or a hospital, where someone could find them right away and take care of them. In the course of about fifteen years, he managed to "save" a dozen babies, or at least that's the number he's confessed to. Yet he never told anyone about his mother—only us!"

"How did he get caught?" I asked.

"He took too much care of one of the babies. He gathered information about all of them, followed the development of their new lives, but he took it too far with one certain girl. First, he killed her mother and then her father and finally her grandmother, because they too, according to him, treated the baby poorly. And when afterward she was adopted, he attempted to kill her adoptive mother too, but a clever cop foresaw this move and got him at the right moment. Dammit! He had stopped being cautious. He had started living in the world of his dreams entirely."

"And his sentiments also?" I added futilely.

"Yes, Merry Maker, *yes!*" Frant looked at me with resentment. "Even the long years spent in the loony bin had not managed to break him. His soul remained full of...*stuffed* with love until the very end. Love for the babies, the children, the animals, the plants...for nature in its every aspect. He was going to invest the five million in building a unique, magnificent orphanage..."

"Enough! I got it." This requiem for a psychopath from another psychopath was too much. "What has all this to do with his death?"

"Because, you see, even without the voodoo magic, he was like under some spell. He was more of a scatterbrain than anyone I've seen or will ever see. He went out to watch the sunset that morning, and soon he was staring at the sun like some mad poet, lost footing, and fell.

"If it was like you say, how come he fell backward?"

"Why, it's simple: he turned around to go and lost balance."

"Yes, there's some logic to that." I nodded in agreement. "How long do you think was he alive there before Graziella found him?"

"Not a single moment, because the back of his head was smashed to pieces, the blow hammering some of them into his brain. And it wasn't Graziella who found him but me and Danko. No one would be happy to make such a discovery, though!"

"What?" I showed my surprise after a short delay. "But I thought—"

"No! Spare me what you've thought!" He shivered as if from disgust. "Seems like you and I have different ideas of making a joyful discovery."

"I thought that Graziella had found him. *That* is what I thought."

"Aha...but I don't believe you. You're feeling me out, Merry Maker! The cop in you will stick with you even in hell. You mislead me—"

"No, Frant, no—"

"Damn you!" His scream was deafening. "You duped me into talking about my dead friend's soul...as if you could understand something like that!" He waved the pruners at me again. "But you can't! Because you have a tiny soul! A tiny, dirty soul that feeds on the agony of others and drinks only their pain..."

I left him, although I didn't want to. I wanted to stay and somehow...justify myself. *What use? I am not Merry Maker; I'm not him,* not him! I kept repeating to myself. No use. I was starting to feel guilty… about everything. I realized I was still clutching Maya's box under my arm, and I threw it in the nearby shrub. It perched there among the gentle rose flowers…Nine children, God, nine children had died, writhing in pain from her éclairs, and here I was, admiring her culinary talent!

CHAPTER TWENTY-TWO

I walked along the precipice's edge, gradually stepping back into a more energetic mood. After all, I hadn't come to the island only to sulk. I had work to do here, work I was good at, and my conversation with Frant, albeit depressing, was useful, because now I could make the following conjecture:

Graziella was the first to find the body, and judging from the spot where it was lying, she determined that Kuber was pushed from above. She moved him closer to the foot of the rock, where he would have landed if he had suddenly lost balance, and that was her way of masking the murder as an accident. Then she walked away and continued her "search for the missing" until Frant and Danko, by chance or not, stumbled upon him.

I stopped, looking at the house. It had a north-facing rear, which meant that the only way one could see the sunrise was from the window farthest to the right on the second floor. So, Roxanna was behind that window when Kuber appeared at the eastern end of the plateau. I walked toward the house. It stood about ninety feet from the precipice, and there were no bushes or trees someone could hide behind anywhere around it. Provided that Roxanna had told me the whole truth, things must've gone as follows:

She sees Kuber, puts some clothes on in a hurry, and comes here in no more than three minutes, during which the murderer had succeeded not only in getting to him and pushing him but also in running behind the nearest corner of the house to hide there. Let's say that the murderer was quite nimble and that Kuber was too slow to react if he had managed only to turn around and do nothing else before letting himself be pushed. Hard to believe but not impossible, not impossible at all.

What's more interesting, however, is what was Kuber *after* right before he was murdered? According to Roxanna, he was not sauntering; he was walking straight toward the edge of one of the rocks. Upon reaching it, he looked down, took a step to the side, looked down again, and took another step to the side...as if trying to see something he was thinking was on a jut of rock right below the spot where he was standing. Yes, he most likely wasn't there to enjoy the sunrise. And why was he shirtless? Every morning he would rise early to take care of the cattle, but if he had only stopped here on his way to the pens, he would've put on at least a shirt or a T-shirt.

I made an estimation of what Roxanna's vision span from that window must have been, moved closer to the edge of the rock, and peeked down, taking a step after another to the side. So far nothing out of the ordinary down there. Or maybe there was, but my eyes were not seeing it as something out of the ordinary. The rock was about seventy feet high and almost vertical, but there were many bumps on its face, and the jagged stones at the bottom made me think of the ugly end of Kuber and of what my end would be if I were to fall on them. To cheer myself up a bit, I looked at the small beach covered with sparkling red-hued sand and the smooth ocean waters in the secluded bay, but the view only reminded me of the woman who had drowned there.

"Miro! Miro, come!"

I stepped back and looked around: Graziella was running in my direction. Oh yes, she certainly was graceful. And at the moment she also looked angry. A real tigress!

"Why are you not coming?" she yelled, stopping only a few inches from me.

I felt her hot breath, noticed the panic in her eyes undermining the rage written all over her face.

"Maybe I would've if you hadn't come here," I told her, but my logic left her unimpressed.

"It's past nine thirty!" she yelled again. "We're all waiting for you, and you…what are you looking for here?"

I put my hands on her shoulders and gently pushed her back.

"Why do you think I'm looking for something?" I asked.

"What are you looking for here?" she asked again.

I again did not answer her. "I don't remember, Graziella. You know well that I suffer from frequent memory lapses."

"Did I just sense reproach instead of gratitude? I made up those lapses so I could protect you. So that you have an excuse in case you make a mistake."

"Or in simpler words, you're worried about me and not about the mistakes you're making."

"I am making?"

"You, of course. Weren't you saying that some-one had set a trap for you? That they knew you were going to conceal the murder and that's why they did it?"

"Alas, yes. Each one of the group could easily foresee that I would do something like that to save the experiment from failing."

"Yes, but in order to conceal a murder, you have to be the first to find the body. And no one can foresee such a thing."

She looked abashed. "Oh, you're right! I should've thought of that..."

"Oh, you have. You knew from the very beginning that the 'murder followed by blackmail' version is not worth a dime, yet you tried selling it to me. What kind of game are you playing, Graziella? Hiring me to find the murderer and then doing your best to confuse and slow me down."

"You're wrong! I'll prove it but not now."

Looking at me with eyes full of tears, she repeated, "Not now, not now," and taking my hand in hers, she led me to the house. Somehow I wasn't surprised by the sudden feeling that she wasn't leading me by the hand but by the nose.

CHAPTER TWENTY-THREE

We stopped at a door on which was written, "CONFESSION ROOM," as if the six murderers were contestants on a special edition of *Big Brother.* Two Ficus plants flanked the door, their leaves shining as if polished, and from inside came the cheerful melody of a piano, although a funeral march would have suited the place more.

"Take it," Graziella said and handed me a key I could tell was for another door. "Go to your bungalow and lock yourself in as soon as we're done here and read carefully the reports on the flash drive. Believe me; it's important, *fatefully* important, that you're ready by lunchtime!"

Touching her lips with a finger, she signaled me to be quiet and sneaked into the room without a sound. I went in after her. Inside was cozy, and everything looked confession-friendly: silk wallpapers the color of old gold, thick Oriental carpets, upholstered furniture in pleasant green, a minibar displaying all kinds of soft drinks, exquisitely inlaid small tables, pots with exotic plants, a huge plasma TV...

The TV was not on, but everyone present was stretching their necks toward it as if something very interesting was happening on the screen. We used the cover of the music to get closer without them hearing us, and then Graziella clapped her hands once, and each head turned in our direction before the face could change its expression. They all looked surprisingly different. Roxanna was pale with horror; Maya looked both frightened and animated; Frant was frowning; Sirius and Valdo were impenetrable, like sphinxes; and Danko...well, his face was twitching with barely controlled excitement, which could also be seen in his madly burning eyes.

"I changed my mind," Graziella said, staring at Danko. "You, Maya, and Frant don't have to participate. You're free to go."

The three obediently left the room in single file, and she turned the music off with some kind of a multifunctional remote control and asked Valdo, "Are you ready?"

"No. I still don't get it how my past could bring hers back."

"She needs a shock, buddy," Sirius joined in. "A shock to fight amnesia! Besides, how are you going to marry her if you cannot be sure that she's going to accept you as you are?"

"I've already accepted him!" Roxanna exclaimed. "Just the way he *is*!"

"We'll see about that." Graziella shook her head in doubt. "I think that you don't realize what he's capable of."

"I agree." Valdo looked down, and Roxanna disappointed him by not objecting.

"What if I go back to…to that state of mind?" she asked, with barely concealed hope in her voice.

Graziella stepped closer to her. "Dear, if you go back there, it would mean that deep inside you're no less terrified by Valdo than by those three—"

"You've murdered, Roxy!" Sirius finished her sentence.

"You've murdered them, dear, and now *you're going to remember* doing it." Graziella put her hand on her shoulder. "I do believe that your love for Valdo shall prevail. I believe that your desire to be solidary with him would turn out strong enough to wrestle the truth about yourself from your unconscious."

"Or," Sirius took up, "you'll spend the rest of your life believing that you, *the innocent one*, have married a murderer. And just imagine what his life would be knowing this. Tell her, buddy! Tell her how hard it is for you with her amnesia!"

"It is hard, yes, but...I'd rather not risk."

"Ahaaa!" Graziella drawled. "There, you let it out! You're not sure of her love!"

Valdo cowered as if she had struck him with a whip, and his more-than-six-and-a-half-feet-tall body seemed to shrink on the chair. If I didn't find him so repellent, I probably would have felt sorry for him. Right now, however, I felt mostly bored.

"I've had enough," I said. "Is that a soap-opera rehearsal?"

"Merry Maker!" Graziella said angrily.

"Miro. The name's Miro. And I'll repeat: I've had enough! Why did you drag me here? So that I could admire your lousy skills as a theater director?"

"He's right." Roxanna backed me up. "You're *playing* with us, Graziella. Mocking our feelings!"

"Feelings? What feelings are you talking about, dear? Didn't it just become clear that everything between the two of you is an illusion?"

"An illusion this test will tear down," Sirius energetically predicted.

"What test?" I asked. "It's time you explained!"

"The test they're afraid of." Graziella explained virtually nothing. "You heard Valdo; he doesn't want to risk. He's almost sure Roxanna will leave him *afterward*."

"No!" Roxanna pushed her hand from her shoulder. "All in all...I agree."

Graziella's thin smile showed her relief. Using the same remote control, she rolled down the blinds, and a pleasant greenish half-light filled the room. I moved to one of the chairs, but Sirius gestured me to wait, pushed it a little farther from Roxanna's chair, and then nodded invitingly at me. I sat on it. Graziella sat on the chair behind Roxanna's, and Sirius finally sat down too, choosing a seat right behind Valdo.

He fixed his eyes on the back of Valdo's head, meanwhile taking a tie out of his pocket. He wound the ends of the tie around his hands and froze, ready to tighten it around Valdo's neck. That sneaky weasel! I decided that the easiest would be to kick him from the chair...

Valdo turned and saw the tie in his hands.

"Man! Again?" He snorted. "Still underrating me? You should've taken a hammer or at least a brick for a change, but no..."

"Don't worry." Graziella patted him and showed him the syringe in her hand. "This will put you down long before you've dealt with Sirius."

"Liars!" Roxanna was indignant. "This is how you *trust* him?"

"We let you be next to him," Graziella told her. "What more can you want from us?"

"Yes, that's the most trust they can place in me," Valdo said, after which Roxanna sighed and turned her attention back to the TV's dark screen.

I sighed too. These people's relations were completely beyond my understanding, so there was nothing I could do but endure them.

"Until recently," Graziella began, "only I and the wife of Femke Mahler knew about the recording I'm about to play for you. She made it with the intention of using it at a later stage to get a divorce with the best possible settlement. But as you will see, there was no divorce. And when nine years later I started fighting for Valdo's release, she got in touch with me and threatened to send the recording to the people on the committee. So I bought it from her for a huge sum—"

"A sum she paid back to you," I guessed.

"She returned more than I gave her. How did you guess?"

"I figured out what the recording is."

"Yes, it's evidence! 'You had been hiding *crucial* evidence against an extremely dangerous murderer' was what I told her right after buying the recording. 'Think about the consequences for you if I gave it to the prosecutor!' So she not only gave me double the money back but also living in fear that my threat might not be an empty one."

Sirius grinned in approval, and Roxanna groaned.

"I cannot stand this anymore!" She got up and stood before me, the beauty of her face almost entirely wiped out by a spiteful expression. "Listen to me, you freak!" she yelled, and rolling her eyes toward the ceiling, she started talking like someone reciting a lesson: "Father is unknown. The mother gives birth to twins, Valdo and Axel. She takes care of them by herself until they are six, and then she gets bitten by a rabid dog and dies. Her brother takes the children, only to turn them into rabid dogs themselves. He would starve them and then throw chunks of raw meat at them and watch them fight for a bite. He would use all kinds of ways to set them against each other, to make them ferocious. And, of course, he would keep them away from school. Valdo learned to read and write in prison. It's where he got his secondary education. He's very smart—"

"Stick to what happened *before* prison!" Graziella ordered her. "We have a deal, remember?"

"Yes, yes, of course…" Roxanna's voice broke into a whimper. "Their uncle would make them fight each other to entertain rich people. He would also make them fight other…dogs."

"But most of the time, they fought each other," Sirius added, in a voice of prompter. "That's what the spectators wanted the most. It was like watching a boy fight himself!"

"The boy...*the boy*!" Roxanna reached out and caressed Valdo's cheek.

"That's why he was always warning us," he said, somewhat pleadingly to her. "Our uncle, Roxy, was always telling us to guard our faces well, to keep them from blows, so that we could be completely... identical. But we were not absolutely alike!" Valdo took a breath and said lovingly, "My brother was stronger than me! Here, now, I'll show you..." He bared his neck and gently ran the tips of his fingers over the large scar there. "This is from his teeth...a souvenir. From my brother's teeth. Axel!"

"Why don't you tell her how he died?" Sirius opened his mouth again. "Or is your courage going to leave you once again?"

What followed lasted no longer than ten seconds. Valdo turned toward Graziella, tore the syringe from her hand, pointed it at Sirius, and as soon as the man raised a hand to protect his face, he grabbed the tie without even rising from his chair. Their eyes met only for a moment, at the end of which Sirius dropped the useless tie and jumped to his feet. Meanwhile, Graziella had jumped to hers. Whether the two of them were about to run or not remained unclear, because Valdo gave the syringe back to Graziella with a gesture full of contempt, threw the tie at Sirius, and then turned his back to both of them, while they returned to their seats.

"My brother died after I bit him," he said quietly. "He got gangrene."

"Gangrene…" echoed Roxanna.

"Yes. Truth is, I killed him. He went through a lot of suffering. Our uncle was afraid to take him to the hospital, tried to treat him at home…and failed. My brother was left to rot alive before my eyes in our kennel of a room—"

"Enough!" Roxanna screamed.

"So, Miro." Graziella seemed unperturbed. "After finally freeing himself from his uncle, Valdo managed to take his revenge on five of the aforementioned spectators over the course of a year. What's more interesting is what he was doing for a living during that period. The same as before! Bloody fights for the eyes of the rich!"

"Yes, but…but…" Roxanna stuttered and then composed herself and went on. "Fighting was the only thing he knew how to do then. And now we're going to make it without your millions!"

"How exactly, my dear? How are you going to make it? It's true that Valdo is capable of doing other things—"

"He is! He's so skillful!"

"I agree; he is skillful and smart. But look at him! Who is going to hire such a scarred face? An ex-prisoner, a serial killer? No one, dear. And he would have to return to making a living, this time for the both of you, by participating in cheap, bloody fights in rings in seedy brothels. And you know he won't always be the stronger one, right? He's almost thirty—"

"Stop it!" Roxanna looked down. "Stop it! And you..." She nudged Valdo without looking at him. "Say something!"

"It's too late." He shrugged. "Yes, I can give up the millions. I believe I can deal with everything... despite everything. But I no longer believe in you, Roxanna. You truly are incapable of accepting me or yourself as we are."

Well, after these bitter words, Roxanna gave up and took her place next to Valdo. I saw Sirius and Graziella nod at each other behind her back. Then she handed him the syringe and took out of her bag a tablet, the screen of which flickered with images. I moved my chair closer to hers and looked at the screen: the images were of Valdo and Roxanna seated before us. Yes, the secret of the confession didn't seem to have any value in this "confession room." Who knew how many electronic eyes and ears were recording everything here.

Moving her fingers deftly across the screen, Graziella used the tablet to switch the TV on. It instantly came to life, but the image on its screen was of someone else.

CHAPTER TWENTY-FOUR

The paused image showed Femke Mahler, a man of about forty, tall and thin. He had a bony face with haughty features, and his reddish hair was clumsily parted in the middle and was shining, the hairs like copper wires. He was dressed in a white suit and white shirt, the collar tightened by a bright-red bow tie. He was standing, feet apart, on the edge of an empty indoor swimming pool covered with bluish tiles. The light came from the ceiling, where there were probably many neon lamps.

A moment later the recording started playing again, but since there was no sound, what we saw took place in an unnatural silence. Femke Mahler raised his hand, thumb pointing up, and a cage that was too small for the huge dog inside slowly appeared into frame. The dog was forced to cower, to keep its head low; the cage was swaying, and the animal was snarling soundlessly—a brownish mongrel, probably a mixture of Rottweiler and wolfhound. The cage reached the edge, and we could see that it was being pushed by a large dark-skinned man with a shaved head, in camouflage overalls. He pushed a button, and the door of the cage opened toward the pool. The dog could go out only if it jumped down, so it was hesitating. The pool was a deep one, it seemed. The man shook the cage to prompt it, accomplishing nothing, so he sharply raised the end of the cage on his side, and the animal fell through the door, disappearing from the frame. Frowning, Femke Mahler peeked down—everything seemed to be fine. The other man stepped next to him and also took a look down and then stepped back, with an angry expression on his face.

The point of view changed: Now we see through a camera that was looking at the inside of the pool. We saw the dog in a deformed perspective but enough to realize that it was limping and, after we'd seen it raise its head, also whimpering. It looked as if it had twisted or broken one of its front legs.

Another change of the point of view brought back into frame the two men, who were having a heated argument. Finally, Mahler shows his consent with an impatient gesture, and the man with the shaved head's lips pouted, and he whistled. And then, a muzzle on his face, a dog collar around his neck, and handcuffed on his hands, we saw…

"Good Lord!" Roxanna cried out.

We saw a boy who was no older than eighteen. His body, covered only at the loins by a cloth, was stooping and studded with scars. The boy knelt before Mahler, who took out of his suit pocket a pair of white gloves and put them on slowly. He quickly patted the lowered head, felt with a cynical contentment the back and shoulder muscles of the boy. Then he grabbed him by the collar and took him for a "walk" around, laughing. They reached the edge, and he released the collar. He gave a slight kick to the boy, who stood up obediently and jumped into the pool, disappearing from view, just like the dog a little while ago, and we saw the man with the shaved head throw something after him, something that quickly flashed in the air.

It was the key to the handcuffs—we saw that when the other camera showed us the inside of the pool once again. Down there, the boy ran to the spot where the key landed, reached down, and took it with his right arm. He twisted his wrists so that he could unlock the handcuffs, while the dog was crawling toward him, yellow fangs bared. The boy released himself from the handcuffs and threw them at the dog, and it stood up on its legs. Its snarling, although soundless, seemed to echo between the bluish walls, its wide-open wolfish jaws dripping with frothing saliva. His muzzle taken off too, the boy was now ready to fight. He moved forward, baring teeth and snarling, but this only made the dog limp away, tail between its legs. The boy stopped, hesitating. He looked up...

Standing on the edge, Femke Mahler capriciously stamped his foot and pointed at the dog with inciting gestures. The boy at the bottom shook his head; he didn't want to attack a wounded animal. The other man joined their exchange—he was the uncle, of course. He shouted something from above, threatening with a stun baton. The boy—Valdo from the past—replied to him with another shake of the head. The dog had already reached one corner of the pool and was cowering and whimpering there, its ugly muzzle twisted by an eerily tragic expression. Pointing at it with a white-gloved hand, Mahler stamped his foot once more.

The boy suddenly jumped up, grabbed him by the ankle, and pulled him down, and Mahler fell into the pool. The uncle immediately sat down at the edge, carefully slid down, stepped on the bottom, and rushed toward them, still waving the stun baton. The boy broke Mahler's neck with a quick twist. He lunged at his uncle, bringing him down on the tiles; the baton flew away...

"I am so happy, so happy, so happy..." Roxanna whispered, clutching at Valdo's arm. "I am so happy that you've killed them!"

"You'll be even happier," Graziella told her right away, "*much* happier the moment you remember that you've killed the other three."

The fight between the boy and his uncle was a short one. The uncle was a bigger man, but the boy was possessed by a savage rage. It was not human but a beast, a rabid dog, tearing not only at the camouflage overalls but also at the bared neck. Teeth flashed: white before sinking into the dark skin, red afterward when the boy threw his head back, and then white again. For before each bite, he spit the blood out. Blood and bits of flesh.

"Enough!" Roxanna screamed. "Yes, yes, I killed them...I shot them dead..."

"Of course you did!" Graziella paused the horrific scene and stared at the tablet screen, which now showed only Roxanna's face. "And the gun, dear? Where did you hide it?"

"Where?" Roxanna closed her eyes and pressed her fingers against her eyelids. She pressed harder

and harder, as if trying to blind herself. "I cannot…
I cannot remember. I don't know."

"All right then!" Graziella hissed. "Open your
eyes!"

She waited, watching the image of Roxanna
in her hands, and when the eyes on the screen
opened, she reached for the tablet keyboard. She
was about to play the recording again when Valdo
stood up and turned to look at her. She withdrew
her finger from the key.

"Hey, buddy!" Sirius stood up too, hiding the
syringe behind his back.

Valdo pushed him aside and leaned toward
Graziella. His face was dark in the green twilight,
and his teeth were bared and as dark as his face.
Without taking her eyes off his, Graziella reached
for the small table nearby and grabbed the remote
control from there, and after a couple of awkward
attempts, she managed to lift the blinds, which
rolled up with a barely audible creaking. Daylight
filled the room, and then I saw it—I saw the blood
on Valdo's still-bared teeth. He had been watching
himself in that death-soaked scene from his past,
chewing on his lips…

"That's enough," he said. "We don't need to see
more of that video."

His voice wasn't threatening; actually, it lacked
any feeling whatsoever, and it was this flatness that

made me shiver. I wanted to be standing up too, but I remained on my seat—there was no need for more tension.

I glanced at the tablet screen—Roxanna had closed her eyes again, and a feeling of relief seemed to be smoothing out her face, bringing back its natural and gentle beauty. Alas, it was early to feel relief. From the corner of my eyes, I saw Sirius advancing in small steps toward Valdo. Graziella seemed to have noticed the same, because she did her best to draw Valdo's entire attention to herself, making unintelligible gestures at him. He looked at her, puzzled.

"We mustn't stop, Valdo," she began explaining, "not when Roxanna is about to remember it all…"

Sirius had reached his back by now. He raised his hand, syringe ready, brought it down in an attempt to drive it into his neck, but Valdo turned around sharply, raised a hand, and grabbed Sirius right above the wrist.

"You're underestimating me." Still in the same flat voice. "I warned you not to underestimate me."

He twisted the man's hand until he dropped the syringe.

"Valdo, let him go! Sit down, Valdo!" Graziella yelled the order and made a mistake.

It was a serious mistake. A roar erupted from his bloody mouth: The animal, the rabid dog, had come to life again. He brought Sirius down with an amazingly swift movement, and his teeth snapped shut less than an inch away from his throat. In less than a second, I was standing beside them and trying to pull Valdo back by the hair, but he grabbed me by the leg, and I fell, hitting my head on the table edge, and although I came to immediately, I was late. He had pressed Sirius down with his enormous body and was sinking his teeth into his throat.

"No, no! Please!" Roxanna wailed. "Please, don't!"

For a few moments, the savage scene here froze just like its counterpart on the huge plasma screen. Then Valdo slowly moved away from Sirius, crawled to the syringe, took it, and stuck the needle into his neck. He pressed the pump and then crawled to Roxanna and cowered at her feet. He fell asleep there or lost consciousness. And only then did Graziella stand up. She went to him and pulled the syringe from his neck. She went back to her seat and placed the tablet on her knees. Her lips were pressed tight in a straight line; her face looked as if made of marble, white and smooth.

"You're free to go. Go and clean yourself up," she said to Sirius. When he left the room, she tapped once on the tablet screen. She tapped the Back button on the video, made sure that Roxanna's eyes were open, and tapped another key.

Tearing not only at the camouflage overalls but at the bared neck also. Teeth flash: white before sinking into the dark skin, red afterward when the boy threw his head back, and then white again. For before each bite, he spit the blood out. Blood and bits of flesh…

"I threw it away." Roxanna's voice was shaking. "I threw the gun away."

"Where?" Graziella asked. "*Where?*"

"In the neighbor's well."

"Repeat that!" Graziella ordered, but she was not listening.

She was sliding down the chair, sliding toward Valdo, while the boy on the big screen was tearing at his uncle's throat…no longer spitting the pieces of meat out. Chewing.

CHAPTER TWENTY-FIVE

I climbed down to the gulf following a steep path of stairs carved in the rock and only then saw that there was an elevator nearby. I crossed the beach, stumbling in my shoes, and when I started to take my clothes off, I noticed that my hands were shaking. *It's from the headache,* I told myself, but I couldn't tell if my head hurt more from hitting it on the table or from the psycho tortures I had witnessed.

Now I had only my boxers on. I went into the cool water, but although I began swimming furiously, I couldn't stop thinking about the disgusting recording and the cruelty with which Graziella forced those two wretches to watch it. But why did she make me watch it too? Why was I given a part in that soap opera of hers? I slowed down, because I swallowed some salty water in my anger. I tried to go on swimming breaststroke but soon gave up and relaxed on my back. Right now my shape wouldn't make even an old man jealous.

I closed my eyes and started relaxing more when I heard someone whistle. I looked around. Maya was standing on the sand, waving something at me that at first I thought was a white flag, but that turned out to be just a bathrobe. I pulled myself together and swam toward her in a swift, effective front crawl. After all, I had to maintain the image of Merry Maker, who in her eyes was a great guy, a handsome athlete, and someone all-around cool.

My effort paid off. Maya greeted me with an enthusiastic smile. She ran to me and gently handed me the bathrobe.

"It's washed," she told me after I had put it on. "It was Kuber's."

It wasn't something I wanted to hear, but I nodded and walked with her to the colorful beach mat she had rolled out close to where I had left my clothes. I sat down, dressed in the dead man's bathrobe, and soon I was given a cup filled with coffee, because Maya had also brought a thermos.

"I'm sorry that I ruined your training," she apologized, "but we have to use the tension to have a quiet conversation."

Now I was worried. "What tension? Has Valdo come to?"

"No. He will sleep for many hours, but the rest of us are waiting. Of course, Graziella has contacted the cops right away, but will they find the gun? That's the question."

"They will," I said. "Roxanna was incapable of lying in those moments. How is she now?"

"Oh, much better. She even started crying."

"Hmm…I'm happy for her."

"Me too! The best way to let the poison out is through the tear ducts."

If I was in her place, I wouldn't have used the word "poison" either literally or figuratively, but she seemed to be above such subtlety.

"Speaking of poison," I began, "I wonder why you carried the vial in your pocket! Why didn't you throw it away?"

"I saw no point in doing it. I was thinking, *I'm about to die.*"

"Ah, Maya, Maya…so you're saying that you didn't eat a poisoned éclair by mistake?"

"Of course not. But first I took care of those things, the headmaster, and his deputy. I offered them the box in such a way that they took the poisoned éclairs!" She sat down next to me and rested her head on my shoulder in a friendly manner.

"Ah, Maya, Maya…" I mumbled again. "It's good that they managed to save you."

"It would've been even better if they had failed at saving the other five," she added.

I said nothing, only sipped the coffee slowly. I had to change the direction of our conversation to Kuber, but for some reason that escaped me; I felt that it would be more important to find out something more about Patrick Krenz, the medical student who, according to Maya, was murdered by Merry Maker in her name. But with every direct question, I risked revealing that I wasn't Merry Maker, and for now I couldn't think of a more roundabout way of asking her.

"I was a real freak back then," she said agitatedly. "And it will always be a mystery to me how you could have liked me as I was!"

I had to step into another full-of-murder soap opera:

"I liked you, Maya, because I realized that your soul was beautiful."

"Realized...only from the pictures?"

"From your eyes," I explained.

"My eye, you mean," she explained further. "The other one was under the lump."

"Yes, it *was*. Now there's not a trace of the lump."

"There's a scar, but it's a small one."

I was tactful enough not to stare at her face. I stared into the distance beyond the gulf, where the ocean was deceitfully flirting with the smooth sky.

"Well, aren't you going to tell me?" Maya suddenly urged me. "I want to know in detail how you decided to close that weasel's mouth forever!"

"You still haven't figured it out?" I added a twinge of disappointment to my voice. "And I thought that you at least had a version of…of what happened."

"I have. Of course I have! But I am not sure…"

"Tell me," I encouraged her, with a smile. "It's the only way to see if it fits what really happened. And if it does, we'll know that you could make a great detective!"

Although a murderer, Maya was still a child; she fell for the bait with a simpleheartedness that made me glad and feel like someone really mean at the same time.

"My version goes like this," she began. "After my release, you wanted to get to know me. You went to our house, and my grandmother told you I had gone away. That's all she knew, anyway, what with her not knowing anything about the experiment. So, while waiting for my return, you would call her regularly. Or even visited her?"

"I did visit, yes," I replied, without thinking.

"That's right! She was a bit hard of hearing; even if I had had the opportunity, I wouldn't have called her."

"You mean you haven't heard her voice since you came here five months ago?"

"Well, yes. But the truth is, from the beginning of the previous month, God has only been able to hear her."

"Of course!" I slapped my forehead. "My bad."

"That's good." Maya opened the thermos and poured me more coffee. "To be honest, I thought you had murdered her too, but she really must've died from a heart attack."

"And how did you learn about her death? From Graziella?"

"Yes, but isn't it strange that she died only a day before you murdered the weasel?"

"Strange or not, the fact is that I've nothing to do with this."

"You didn't make a mistake," Maya assured me. "There was no need to murder her. She would never have confessed that I had stolen not only the vial but also the poison from her. But I suppose Patrick went to her with some questions, and then she told you about his visit, and you...you got his address from the hospital, didn't you?"

"You're right! So far your version is perfect."

"Yes, yes!" She went on enthusiastically. "He told her that he was an intern there during the time I was in the intensive-care ward. He also most likely told her the lie that he and I had become friends?"

"That's true," I confirmed, without any hesitation, because for objective reasons neither the grandmother nor the student could disprove me. "He introduced himself as a friend of yours, but she didn't fall for that. And she scared after his questions…there was a slyness to the way he asked them: they were ambiguous, full of intimations, you understand."

"I do! So she died of fear. She was not only a hypochondriac but also paranoid, and Patrick scared her so much that her heart stopped. *Friend.* Yeah, right! I had no idea what his name was, and I wouldn't have recognized him on the picture if the article in the newspaper had not mentioned that he was studying medicine. I was under the influence of a lot of drugs when he tried to make me talk." Maya dug her fingers into her colorful hair and frowned, the tiny ring on her eyebrow flickering into my eyes. "I thought he had given up. But he turned out to be quite the determined and cunning person. If only he had believed me then, he could have been alive now!"

Her face twisted into an insincere grimace, which made me realize that she actually felt pity for the boy. My head began hurting even more. I drank the rest of my coffee and asked halfheartedly, "What didn't he believe you about?"

"That the vial wasn't mine and that I had found it in the box with the éclairs."

"Well, he wasn't the only one. No one believed you, at least in the beginning."

"Yes, but all the others were unable to step out of the vicious circle that went: 'a special mixture of poisons.' They were hoping that if they could find out what the ingredients of that mixture were, this would lead them to the place I got them from and, in the end, to more evidence against me. While Patrick was going in an entirely different direction. He was interested in the vial *itself*. What I still don't understand is why it kept his interest even after it… disappeared?" Maya looked at me quizzically. "Tell me! He must have been horrified before the end and confessed everything."

"No. Unfortunately, he confessed nothing."

"What? Nothing? You're saying you killed him without even giving him a chance to come clean?"

"That's how it happened, Maya," I mumbled guiltily. "He was my first victim, I had no experience, and I took it too far; I used too much laughing gas."

Her shock was so visible that I was shocked in turn.

"First victim," she said in a hoarse voice. "So it was you who…murdered the others? It was you, you *really* are Merry Maker?"

"Well…you knew that, didn't you?"

"No, I didn't! I thought you were pretending. Trying to fool Graziella and get to the money. I thought the other three were the victims of a copycat...I thought, I thought that you had murdered only Patrick...for me..."

She couldn't go on, and I was unable to respond to her words or to the sobbing with which she stood up and left. I only stared at her, blinking like an owl in the bright light.

CHAPTER TWENTY-SIX

As incredible as this might sound, I had fallen asleep. I awoke and found myself still lying on the motley mat, with the white robe tangled around me and the sun burning the left side of my face. I looked at my watch: 2:20 p.m. I had missed lunch, but I wasn't bothered by that. I pulled my socks and sneakers closer to me, put them on, and stood up effortlessly. I'm not one of those who wake up stiff and sore unless they've slept on a feather mattress. I threw my pants and shirt next to the thermos on the mat, made a bundle of it, and headed for the elevator. The cabin took me back up, and I set out through the empty space between the precipice and the back of the house.

The mirror windows made me feel like someone was watching me from inside, so I tried to look as casual as possible, swaying the bundle lazily in my hand like some tourist out for a stroll.

I ended up in front of the house and wondering whether to go in or continue to my bungalow, choosing neither option. From where I was standing, I heard someone scream in the distance and rushed in that direction. As I crossed the meadow, moments of silence punctuated the screams, making them sound even stranger: as if whoever had been screaming an instant ago was now singing and at the same time running—chased by someone? I threw the bundle, lifted the hem of the overlong bathrobe, and started running too. The voice sounded now male, now female, and then like a child's, and at times like an old man's. Or maybe it belonged to an old woman? I wouldn't be surprised if Fata's curses had reached the end of someone's patience.

I entered among the umbrellalike palms, where the screams came muffled and more like moans. I was now certain that they were coming from that hill with the half-mowed slope that I, Valdo, and Sirius had crossed yesterday after our visit with Fata. *So, it really is her*, I thought, but when I was in the open again, I saw Danko. He was by himself, climbing the hill, waving his hands and, as I soon realized, making that astonishing multitude of sounds.

I looked up at the sky and saw that a plane engine was contributing to the abundance of sounds. Probably the pilots were delivering the lawnmower that was ordered under dramatic circumstances. The plane lowered, and after it disappeared from my sight, I turned my attention back to Danko—he had now reached the top of the hill and was climbing down the other side, also disappearing from my sight. I climbed to the top, the sounds from the plane dying out completely in the meantime. Danko had also gone silent. I saw him rolling down the unmowed half of the slope, plucking flowers on his way and trying to stuff them in his mouth. I didn't have to have studied psychiatry to know that he had let go of his madness's reins and that the best way I could help would be to put him to sleep with a good blow of my fist.

"Hey!" I called, and he stopped rolling. He sat up, surrounded by flowers, and stared at me. A tiny bouquet stuck out of his mouth, as if he had been using it as a vase.

I walked closer to him and then stopped, hesitating. Although staring with eyes wide open, his expression was not that of a madman but only of someone in pain and despair.

"Easy," I told him. "Come on, take…the flowers out so we can talk."

He obeyed, but his first words were "Daddy, she's lying to you, lying, lying!"

"I understand," I lied too. "Your father must be a handsome man. Very handsome if he looks so much like me."

I laughed to show him that it would be good for him if he laughed too. I believe in that "Laughter is the best medicine" saying, and in his case the absence of a clear mind was obvious.

"You can kill me," he suggested.

"No," I declined the offer. "I won't kill you. And why did you kill Kuber?"

Unfortunately, he didn't fall in my trap. "You can kill me, but you cannot make me call her *mommy*!"

"That's OK," I told him. "Call her whatever you like."

"Stepmother." He pointed at me. "You're my stepmother, not my mother!"

I could see myself playing the father, but a stepmother? Father, stepmother, and Merry Maker at the same time?

"You're lying to me too!" There was no end to his accusations. He jumped to his feet and began swinging his fists wildly at the flower-covered half of the slope. "Notes are not flowers! Why are you lying to me, eh? Tell me, you godless woman!"

I grabbed him by the shoulders and shook him.

"Look at me! Look at me, and get a grip on yourself! That godless woman is not here!"

"I know." He snapped at me.

I shook him even harder. "Then why the hell speak all that nonsense?"

"Scumbag! You fooled me into thinking you were helping me when, in fact, you're distracting me!"

I peered into his eyes and again found no traces of madness in them. I let him go.

"I have no idea what's happening," I confessed, exhausted.

"Is that so?" He looked surprised. "No one told you I usually regress here?"

Now I remembered: 2:00 p.m. to 4:30 p.m.—that was one of the items of the daily program. In other words, Graziella had trained her patient so well that he was now able to apply regression analysis to himself. Childhood regression—self-service!

I caught myself smiling, but at the same moment, the truth slithered into my mind like a reptile: notes—Danko—Daniel? Daniel Menshov? It's him, of course! The murderer with the unique voice…and a singing that was uniquely out of tune. A sadist, known as the Jeweler because of his necklace made of human ears and tongues.

The tiny smile had frozen on my lips—it was way out of place. I turned my head to hide it, and at the same moment, I received a blow in my temple, after which the world went away—replaced by darkness.

CHAPTER TWENTY-SEVEN

The pain was slowly dragging me toward reality, but what finally brought me back was a gnawing question: How come my feet hurt more than my head? I tried to move and reached the answer. As it turned out, I was wrapped in the white bathrobe like a cocoon, and my ankles were tied so tightly that the center of my pain was now somewhere about them. My arms were pressed to my sides by a band of probably a belt. I was lying on my side in the flowers, unable to see anything further than a few inches away. I could see only the stalks of the flowers and the small insects crawling over them, but soon someone behind me signaled their presence by kicking me in the lower back.

"You're done!" I heard...Danko, of course. "I won't forgive you."

"Forgive me what?" I croaked.

"Grinning," he replied. "You made fun of my misery. You made fun of my mother's death!"

It was a misunderstanding of idiotic proportions. And so was his distrust, but that was only logical, what with him having to bear the brunt of so many jokes, most being about his mother's death. I, personally, had stumbled upon the following headline: *As a teenager, the Jeweler exterminated his own mother with a nonexistent mouse!* And that was probably one of the least vulgar ones.

I got embarrassed, although such delicate emotions were not a fitting answer to the situation. Teeth clenched, I started wiggling and managed to turn and lie on my back. What I saw above me was grotesque: the face of the psychopath, with the sky as its background, was haloed by a white cloud.

"That's a deviation from therapy," I reproached him, a psychiatrist's strict tone to my voice. "The daily program explicitly requires that you regress."

He pensively pulled his trousers up. He had used the bathrobe belt to tie my ankles, and his leather belt for my hands.

"You're clever!" he exclaimed an instant later. "You want me to regress because this would take me back to the time I was the victim. But today's session is going to be a different one, and you will be the victim!"

"Just like Kuber," I said. "Right?"

"I will cut you!" He made his threat more specific. "I will *mow* you *down!*"

He laughed and pointed at something I couldn't see from my position and then started walking toward it. *Let him be hallucinating!* I wished, but when, after more wiggling, I managed to sit up, I saw not only the promised lawn mower but also Sirius, who was standing next to it.

"I'm sorry!" He waved a hand at me and ran!

He ran to the magnolia grove nearby, chased by Danko. They disappeared among the trees. *That's more ridiculous than a dream!* I said to myself, and without hesitation I began sliding my hands out of the belt. It was an easy task because the profuse sweating had made both my skin and the leather of the belt slippery. Untying the robe belt around my ankles was the bigger challenge, but I went through it too. I wrapped the bathrobe around me like a cocoon again and waited, hoping that Sirius would not come to help me. I needed only Danko because I wanted to see how far his unorthodox therapy would take him. Were his threats only part of the game or real? Was he really going to mow me down for that stupid grin?

The latter seemed entirely plausible. I had no reason to expect logical behavior from someone who had strangled eight women because he *wanted* to strangle his stepmother. "They were all music teachers like her" was his explanation after he was arrested. And he got arrested when he showed up at some wedding, sporting a golden necklace with their ears and tongues strung on it. What an absolute freak! Nothing had changed, it seemed, after almost ten years of psychiatric treatment.

Shortly he appeared from the grove, singing in a loud voice, "Do...mi...fa...fa...re...do...ti," and so on. He marched lively, not even once looking at me. He reached the mower and started the engine as soon as he felt the driver's seat beneath him. He began mowing the flowers, turning random notes of his song into vengeful screams. Actually, *song* was an overstatement. His voice was truly beautiful and his range astonishing, but his inability to hit the right notes was also astonishing. All in all, if he wasn't a murderer, Danko would have been just... a wretched fool. Victim of circumstances and co-incidences that, although tragic for him, also had something comic about them.

The beginning of his murderous story was also tragicomic. He, the future Jeweler, was a thirteen-year-old kid when, in a moment of goofy spirits, he decided to play a joke on his mother. He cried, "A mouse, Mother, a mouse!" and she jumped with a scream on one of the chairs, lost balance, and fell on the kitchen knife in her hands.

And that was it. Since then, the joke was always on him. First, his father went through widowhood quickly—he married *that* music teacher. Second, about a year later, the family business collapsed. And third, the moment Danko's voice change ended, his stepmother had an "epiphany" and saw in him a chance for all of them to climb out of the pit of misery. She started tutoring him and made him attend various contests and participate in TV shows, and it wasn't long before he became a nationwide laughingstock...

I flinched—was I starting to pity this sadist too?

"Son of a bitch!" I yelled, only to remind him of my presence. Mowing that furiously, he would soon end up with no steam to let off, and I wanted him to be angry, affected, the same as he probably had been with Kuber. "Heeey, dumb, stupid freak!" I tried to outcry both him and the droning mower. "*Freak!*"

He heard me. This time he heard me. He took a turn and drove toward me. I remained unmoving, keeping alive the illusion that I was still tied up, and when the distance between us shrank to a mere ten steps, he hit the brakes and asked clearly in the newborn silence, "What did you just say? Repeat!"

I was glad that he had come nearer and that more clouds had appeared in the sky. Thus, in the soft, diffused light, I could see clearly the expression on his face.

"*Freak!*" I repeated, grinning.

His face was red from the screams, but now it was beginning to regain its ghoulish paleness, which made his unnaturally red lips and green eyes stand out even more. To my surprise, though, my teasing seemed to have calmed instead of infuriating him. He nodded at me or to himself and pressed a button, and the mower's rotation axis tilted upward, raising the blades on the same level as my chest.

"Yes, I am going to mow down your heart," he said, looking at me like someone who had seen a freshly served beefsteak after a long diet. "I'll have it in my hands in five minutes!"

"What about the experiment?" I reminded him. "It would fail if you killed me. And instead of winning the millions, you'd end up back in the psychiatric ward."

His hesitation lasted no longer than a couple of seconds. "Experiment-excrement," he said. "And I…well, I am the icing on it!"

"Meaning?" I asked.

"What could the icing on a shit cake mean? What other than camouflage?"

I did not entirely understand why he was thinking of himself as of the icing, but at least I found out that a favorable outcome of the experiment was not among his priorities. He had definitely decided to kill me—I could tell by the relaxed and even happy expression on his face. He had the look of someone who had overcome their restraints and was now free to follow their dreams.

"Sadistic dreams," I corrected myself aloud. "Just like with Kuber, am I right?"

"Kuber, Kuber, Kuber...say hi from me when you see him!"

He laughed and speeded up the blades and then slowly, very slowly, drove the mower toward me. Clearly, he was going to enjoy himself and not rush. I braced myself, ready to stand up and jump to the side the moment he came closer, although I continued lying unmoving—I wanted to be sure that he would not give up in the last moment. I fixed my eyes on the rotating blades and tried to summon a grimace of helplessness and horror.

Well, I failed at helplessness, and at horror. The features of my face refused to obey my will, and I knew that they were mirroring the euphoria that was raging inside me. Although at slow speed, the blades were coming toward me—coming for me!—and they looked beautiful, silver, clean. New. Able to kill but not killers. They were going to kill me, but they were not my enemies. I liked them; I really liked these blades. And they reminded me of the shark from yesterday. They reminded me of the tracks I would cross as a child right before the train would come through. They even reminded me of the tornado I faced not long ago, expecting to fly...or die.

Now what? *Time to react*, I said to myself, remaining still. The temptation to wait a bit longer... and longer and longer...was too big, was actually another burst of the hunger for adrenaline I had inherited from my mother and father. Yes, if I remained like that, I would be killed by my unknown parents, not by the psychopath riding the mower—that's what I realized at that moment. But I kept on waiting, although I could feel the breath of the swishing blades as they guillotined the taller flowers and threw their colorful heads at my face...

It looked like it was late for a jump to the side, yet I threw the bathrobe away and stood up. I met Danko's gaze, and a moment later the mower fell silent. His eyes became wider and wider, like a stepped-on toad's.

"You're insane," he said.

I did not object to that. I reached down for the robe, put it on, and walked up the hill.

CHAPTER TWENTY-EIGHT

J ust as I suspected, Sirius was on the top, observing from a comfortable position.

"Are you crazy?" He greeted me with outrage. "What if Danko had not stopped?"

"But he did," I replied.

"Yes, yes. But if he hadn't…dammit! It never occurred to me you had managed to untie yourself! You were lying like a mummy there!"

"While you were sitting here like a scoundrel."

"I had no choice, Miro. I'm not so dumb as to hand myself over to a karate-wielding sicko. He knows some deadly moves, man! You should be glad he chose only to play with you."

Now I was hurt. "That bastard hit me only because I didn't expect him to do it…"

"You didn't expect that? Ha! Where do you think you are? In an all-girls boarding school?" Swearing under his breath, Sirius placed a hand on his chest and bowed.

I traced his eyes just in time to see Fata reply to his bow with a waving fist. She was near the grove down from us, and I could feel the waves of hatred coming from her.

"She's angry." Sirius took a step back to be out of her field of vision. "Very angry! She was hoping to see you get murdered, but you survived."

"No thanks to you," I reassured him and also stepped out of Fata's field of vision by walking down the opposite, and much steeper, slope of the hill.

"If the pilots had not delivered the mower late," Sirius sighed behind my back, "everything would've gone well."

"You think so?" I said, unbelieving, and that seemed to be just what he was waiting for.

"No!" came his immediate answer. "Honestly, I don't think so. Graziella is a good psychotherapist, but in Danko's case, she made a dangerous mistake, which, I think, cost…one of us too much. Way too much!"

He caught up with me and looked at me knowingly. He was inviting me to ask the expected questions—"What mistake? Who was it who paid for it?

How?"—but I asked nothing. I was sure that he was hinting at Kuber, and that his silence wouldn't last long.

"You have to know," he began, "that when we gathered here on this island, Danko was not like that. Aggressive, I mean. But here Graziella unwisely raked up his past and even tricked him into admitting the shameful fact that he was actually obeying his stepmother not because there was no other option but because he wanted to. She was a cunning woman, Miro! She made him believe that if he worked hard enough, he would become a great singer, and he, naïve as he was, believed her and did his best to achieve…the unachievable."

Sirius shook his head bitterly. I could bet that he didn't care even a little bit about Danko's teenage torment, but why was he so bent on making me believe the opposite?

"And that is how, Miro, his stepmother achieved her goal. She started selling his lack of talent! People would pay her to have him in all sorts of reality TV shows. At first, he didn't realize he was being used for fun. What's worse is that when he finally did, he couldn't find the will to stop. He went on entertaining the masses with his curse of a luck to be so musically challenged but with a voice that is unique. However, the masses grew bored, and the money stopped, but instead of giving him a break, his stepmother included his father in her cruel game. She started lying to him that Danko was singing out of tune just to spite her!"

"I see," I said. "As far as I can tell from today, he's still not over it."

"Oh, he's not over lots of stuff, although it's been more than twenty years. You were just a kid back then, but I remember what he looked like and the way he sang. Such a sad thing to behold! She always dressed him like Elvis, that bitch…"

"Bitch…right, but why the hell did he murder all those women and leave her alive?"

"Because he didn't want his father to be a widower twice."

"Ah, yes." I nodded, as if such explanation made everything clear.

Sirius heaved another loud sigh.

"Still, we must not forget that Danko has had a long battle with himself. He left home after coming of legal age and began training in karate, hoping that that would keep his murderous impulses at bay. And keep them he did. Until he was twenty-five. But after that…"

Instead of with words, Sirius finished his sentence with a gesture mimicking the eight murders. We fell silent, although not out of respect for the dead—*that* would turn the island into the quietest place on Earth. We reached the base of the slope

and soon entered the shadows of the green umbrellalike palms. *It's good that the bungalow was built
here in the shadows*, I thought, *dying from the heat in
that damned bathrobe whose owner, by the way, was one
not to be envied either: a slab of ice in the middle of the
empty freezer room.*

"There it is again!" Sirius complained when the
drone of the mower came from the other slope
of the hill. "It's been like this every Tuesday for
the past two months. And instead of helping him
shake off all negativity, this wrongful therapy only
woke his aggressiveness. Aggressiveness that almost made him kill you today!"

He gave me another knowing look that cleared
more air for the questions I was expected to ask to hang.

"Listen, Sirius." I stepped in front of him and
stopped.

"Yes?" He stopped too and stared at me, waiting.

"I don't know if it's your way of picking guys up
or something else, but I don't like it," I said. "Look
at me. I'm as strong as a bull, yet you're comparing
me to a flower!"

I took pleasure in watching his countless freckles disappear as his face turned tomato red.

"Picking up guys...flower..." he stuttered in
shock.

"Didn't you just say that he almost killed me *too*?
Along with all the flowers I saw him kill today..."

"Oh, no! No! I didn't mean the flowers…" Then Sirius finally caught the drift of what was going on and laughed, although not heartily. "You're right. I guess I was too roundabout," he admitted.

He leaned his back against the trunk of the closest palm and slowly slid down to sit on the ground. It seemed like he was about to prolong our conversation, which meant more beating around the bush. Under different circumstances, I would have sat down next to him and began sifting through his words, looking for the wheat in all the chaff. My head still hurt from the bump on the table edge in the confession room, and my pulse beat madly in my temples after Danko's karate blow. And on top of that, napping on the beach had left its mark; the left half of my face was burning and itching.

I remained standing, looked down at Sirius, and crossed my arms over my chest.

"Dammit!" he fulminated. "I'll tell it to you straight: I no longer believe that Kuber fell down that cliff as a result of Fata's magic. Danko pushed him! I only suspected that until today, but now, after witnessing his aggression, I am almost sure!"

I showed him my surprise, careful not to make it look too eager, and then nodded pensively. "Yes, it's possible. If Kuber provoked him—"

"No! It wasn't Kuber's fault. Nor Danko's! Only Graziella is to blame. She was quick to realize that the mower therapy's not working but didn't dare to end it because Danko became addicted to it on the very first day. He's not always quite all there, Miro, and that's why his fantasies are like that."

"Like what?" I asked.

"Well...they're all kinds of fantasies. When he's on the mower, he somehow manages to convince himself that by destroying the flowers, he could get even with his stepmother. Back in the day, under the pretense of helping him out, she made him learn the notes by thinking of them as flowers. 'Just imagine that "do" is a peony, "re" is a freesia, that "mi" is a violet'...and so on. And he would melt at that nonsense...and at the sight of her. Something he still cannot forgive himself for."

"How stupid!" I said with compassion.

"Naïve, not stupid. He was only sixteen; he had no idea how duplicitous women are. He realized this only after she began lying to his father too. But all these traumatic memories were buried deep in his soul. Graziella, instead of leaving them rest there, *dug them up*! After which she decided to neutralize them with the so-called therapy of rebellion and...made a mistake. A grave mistake!"

"A grave mistake but only for Kuber. And only if it's true Danko murdered him. By the way, is she aware of your suspicions?"

"No! And she must never be!"

"Why?"

"What do you mean, why?" Sirius didn't bother to hide his vexation. "After all I've told you, you still haven't realized that no one here is more valuable than Danko? Isn't it clear that he would be the central figure during the trial? He has lost his marbles *on TV* many times, and the thousands of viewers found this entertaining! It's a kind of a *common guilt*, and Graziella is going to emphasize and use it. That is why even if we could prove to her that he had murdered Kuber, she wouldn't do anything. *Anything against him,* that is."

"Are you saying that in order to cover his guilt, she could do *something against us?*"

"My answer to this question, Miro, is as follows: It's easy to guess that before being granted an official permission to conduct the experiment, Graziella has faced and overcome many legal and bureaucratic obstacles. A special committee was appointed, before which she would have to report the condition of every participant in her experiment. I, however, have done my time and therefore am not under this committee's control, on whose list, by the way, you're not. So if the pilots—after getting handsomely paid, of course—told everyone that they took us both off the island, no one would come looking for us. And no one would suspect that our 'flight' was straight to the netherworld!"

Sirius raised his head and once again looked at me knowingly, and I, out of habit, once again disappointed him.

"All right," I said. "I have to go now. I have to find my clothes."

"God, man!" he burst out. "What are you calling 'right'? And what do you mean, *find* them? Where are you going to look for your clothes?"

"The hibiscus meadow," I answered. "They're there in a bundle."

CHAPTER TWENTY-NINE

I t was annoying that there was no hot water in the bungalow again, although I wouldn't have used it if there was. The only thing I could stand at the moment was a cold shower. At first, I had turned my back at the mirror while showering, but then I made myself look. What I saw exceeded my worst expectations. The left half of my face, the sunburned one, glowed red. The right sported a blue bruise close to the temple. My eyes were bloodshot and staring dumbly, my nose's aristo-cratic shape had disappeared under a swelling, my right ear looked bigger than the left...well, I'm not a vain person, but such change in appearance seemed too much. I came to the island only a day ago, and I had already turned into a clown.

I found a sunburn-lotion tube in the medicine cabinet. I applied some of it to the red half of my face and, after swallowing two aspirins, stepped out of the shower booth. I rolled out Maya's beach mat and, before putting my clothes for washing, went through the trouser pockets. I took the key for the bungalow out but did not find the flash drive with the police reports. I assumed that it had fallen out while I was still at the beach, so I put my jeans and a T-shirt on and rushed out.

I wanted to go around the house without being noticed, but that proved impossible. Everyone was at the entrance door, and everyone saw me. And by everyone I mean not only the six murderers and Graziella but also Fata. Standing in a warrior posture, she was waving a rolled-up newspaper and talking querulously, while the others just stood there and listened. But as soon as I neared them, she too fell silent. She minced energetically toward me and raised her bony index finger, pointing at something in the sky. I looked up, seeing only a few small clouds, and she slapped me with the newspaper across my face—across the burned half of it, that is.

"Wretch!" she lisped, through tightly clenched teeth. She turned around like an angry spinster and walked away across the meadow. Even the back of her tiny figure expressed outrage, her long braid moving like a grayish snake against it.

I reached to feel my burning cheek and then remembered the lotion. I couldn't say if it had soaked into the skin or was still visible. I dropped my hand and tried my best to summon an expression of condescension, an expression saying something like "Poor woman's gone totally senile," and turned to the silent group.

"What's with her?"

"Her?" Danko swayed as if my question had dealt a heavy blow to his dignity. "Nothing's wrong with her. I, however, am not well. Not well at all!"

"Are you? Why?"

"He was one step from killing you. That's why!" Maya said, with blame in her voice.

She had dyed her hair from predominantly green into entirely orange. Around her eyes, red from crying, were circles of Cleopatra-style heavy makeup that was not smeared. This meant that she must have cried before putting it on, and the reason for the tears was most likely our conversation at the beach and the painful (for her) revelation that I "truly" was Merry Maker.

"I'm sorry, Maya…" I had nothing else to say, so I only spread my arms.

"Ah! I think I understand," she replied. "But how could you choose such an unfair way to achieve it?"

"Achieve what?"

"The old hag told us everything," Sirius informed me.

My confusion grew bigger. "Told you everything… about what?"

"Oh, stop playing the fool!" Roxanna joined in the attack, looking surprisingly well, considering what she had to endure in the confession room this morning. "Yesterday you told me, 'I would happily kill myself. So that I could ask my victims for forgiveness.' Those were your exact, and quite insane, words!"

"Insane but also brave," Frant observed. "But to take advantage of Danko's vulnerability—"

Graziella stopped him by clapping her hands.

"Let's not judge him before we've heard him. Come on; we're going back! We'll talk to him, try to understand him."

Soon only I, Graziella, and Valdo, who, by the way, looked like someone had chewed him up and spit him out, were left standing there.

"Come on, Valdo! We'll go right after Merry Maker's explanation. I promise." She nudged him toward the house and shouted at me over her shoulder, "Hurry!" putting an end to my hesitation.

I shoved my thumbs into my jeans pockets and started walking along the house, whistling to myself so much out of tune that I could have accompanied one of Danko's performances. In fact, my lips were trembling, trembling with anger and, most of all, shame. They, the murderers, were right to despise me! They thought of me as a suicide, as a pathetic, vile guy who had decided to end his life by taking advantage of the crisis of a poor man who had spent ten years in the psychiatric ward—

"Stop!" Graziella caught up with me.

I did not, but I said, "All right, I will do...some explaining. All right. But afterward, you would have to take a walk with me. I have too many questions."

"Yes, yes." She nodded, walking beside me. "I'll answer all of them. But tomorrow. I promised Valdo that as soon as we're done with you, Sirius and I would take him to the isolation room. This cannot wait, Miro. He is absolutely crushed and can barely endure Roxanna's presence. He believes that he had disgraced himself fatally in front of her."

"And what are her thoughts on that? She looked pretty calm to me."

"Not calm, happy," Graziella corrected me. "Just before noon today, I got the confirmation from the prosecutor. They found the gun right where she said it must be. That's the end of her amnesia, Miro! And now that she can remember killing those who abused her, she has regained her self-esteem. But that recording we watched crushed Valdo. That is why I agreed to place him in the isolation room for at least a week to pull himself together."

"Where is this isolation room?" I asked.

"Well…it's far, and it's hard to get there. Come on!" Graziella took my hand and led me quickly back to the entrance of the house. "And don't worry. I'll help you justify your actions. I'll guide you… hey! You read the reports on the flash drive, didn't you?"

"No."

"No?" She froze. "But why?"

Her panic was as obvious as it was puzzling. What would it transform into if I told her that I had no idea where the drive was? *Let's go look for it at the beach, although it could be anywhere. Someone might have found it…*

"Why, Miro, why?"

"I didn't have time to," I answered. "I overslept…at the beach."

Looking up at my face, she wrinkled her nose as if she had just smelled something truly foul, and not the sunburn lotion. She shook her head and mumbled, "Dear Lord! Dear Lord!"—a comment that didn't sound religious despite being repeated twice.

CHAPTER THIRTY

At this moment, nothing showed that this was a veranda or that it was day outside. The French windows were covered by thick burgundy drapes, and the only light came from two lamps placed opposite each other at both ends of a long ebony table. The rest of the furniture was in a dusk, heavy with the fragrance of barely visible exotic plants.

I sat by myself at one side of the table, and right across from me was Danko's pale vampirelike face. On his left side were Graziella, Frant, and Roxanna. On his right side were Sirius, Maya, and Valdo. It didn't feel good to be the center of their attention. I've been subject to so many accusatory stares only once before: back in kindergarten when I let the canaries out of the cage without thinking that it was winter outside.

The silence went on for too long. Everyone was waiting for me to start explaining, but I seemed to be unable to come up with something other than to portray myself as a masochist who has reached the bottom, where he has discovered the irresistible desire to be cut into pieces by the blades of the mower. Yes, maybe if I gave prominence to the word "irresistible," they would believe me…and vindicate me.

"But why the hell do I have to explain myself!" I burst out. "That psycho hit me, tied me up—"

"Yet you managed to untie yourself," Maya interrupted me with reproach.

"So what? I remained where he left me to see how far he would go."

"I would've gone nowhere!" Danko snapped at me. "Nowhere. If you hadn't called me a freak! That's when I flipped, and you…why didn't you move away?"

I abandoned the masochist plan. I replied with arrogance. "I didn't move away because I was sure that I could stop you just with the power of my gaze. As it happened. You did stop!"

"Oh, no, no." Graziella shook her head. "That's not going to work. We're all open here, Miro. Be open like us. Confess to us, *and to yourself,* that your suicidal impulses are linked to your grandfather."

"That's ridiculous!" Roxanna said. "His grandfather is such a good and noble human being."

I saw every head nod in agreement and felt sick. They all knew him, of course, because he had "selected" them together with Graziella. He had spoken to each of them; had used his notorious charm of a kind, stately old man; and had won their sympathy and respect...

"Poor man!" Frant exclaimed. "Does he know that his grandson is the Merry Maker himself?"

"He does," Graziella confirmed. "But we won't be discussing now how or from whom he had found that out or what was his reaction." She stood up and pointed dramatically at me. "We've gathered here for him. And remember, today he is not Merry Maker. He is Miro! Don't think of the murders he has committed; only try to understand how he had become the madman who committed them. Give him a chance to open up about his pains, his suffering...about the wounds in his soul, just as each of you was given a chance to do the same! And you'll see that your fates are alike. You'll see that he too was a victim as a child—"

"Whose victim?" Sirius cut into her emotional speech. "His grandfather's? Excuse me, Graziella, but I too am going to say that that's ridiculous!

Before you made me part of the experiment, I had many one-on-one meetings with him, and he was always patient with me, understanding, and also *humane* in the greatest sense of the word."

"A man of exceptional greatness," Danko summarized and stared at me with his swamp-green eyes. "It's hard to believe you're his grandson!"

"Yes," Valdo rumbled somewhat timidly, "as Roxanna noted, he is a very good and noble human being."

I lost my temper.

"Human, humane, it's all you say! And he—" My voice dried out, I could barely breathe from the waves of acid emotions, the strongest one being jealousy, surging in me. "He was good and noble to you. To you, the murderers! But not to me! He was never patient with me, never understanding, and he was far from…humane."

Graziella was still standing up, watching me with a mixture of alarm and encouragement, and clearly trying to convey some sort of message to me with her eyes.

"I thought so," she said, after a short silence. "Your grandfather was cruel to you. He began tormenting you psychologically from the day you were born! But, Miro, apart from me, none of those who are present would believe that unless you tell…"

She fell silent, collapsing on her chair, and lowered her head, as if her fate now depended on my willingness to tell…what? What could I tell about? Would these murderers who grew up tortured be impressed by a story as simple as mine—how I believed my mother and father were dead when, in fact, they had left me right after my birth; how my grandfather had hit me with the news on my sixth birthday and had told me after that that I had inherited their stupidity because they both are idiots; how he would never forget to tell me that he's the one "raising" me; and he has always been niggardly with me, only with me! He was so stingy that he would make me wear his old shoes long before I was big enough to fill them, and he would never give me pocket money for school or to go to the cinema or to play a game. He let me go on a summer camp only once, but only after I promised that I would clean the rooms there to pay for my food. I never got his approval on anything, and he has always, always underestimated, oppressed, and traumatized me…and more and more such nonsense!

Here was Roxanna—turned into a prostitute at the age of only seven when her drug-addicted parents started selling her. Here was Valdo: "My brother died because I bit him. He got gangrene… he rotted alive before my eyes in our kennel of a room." And Frant: "My mother would stick needles

into me and put out her cigarettes on my butt."
And Maya: "I was a monster back then…because of
some terrible lipomas." And Danko—going mad
on TV while entertaining the viewers with his ill
luck to be someone with a unique voice and no
sense of tune. The only one about whose childhood suffering I didn't know was Sirius, but I was
sure that it had been greater than mine. I couldn't
tell them about anything, and this, in a strange
and irrational way, depressed me, made me feel
a lesser person than the people here who were
trying so hard to heal their wounds—to heal the
wound that was their childhood!—and continue
with their lives…so, *screw the other victims*, eh? No,
of course, not! But whose were the victims actually?
Victims of the victims…

I got tangled up in my thoughts like a fly in a
spider web—my head was buzzing in the absolute
silence.

"I had canaries," I said suddenly. "I would take
care of them, love them, but my grandfather…he
tore their heads off on my sixth birthday!"

Nobody reacted to this. All sat before me in almost identical positions: heads lowered, faces visible only as twisted reflections on the smooth black
surface of the table.

"And then, instead of cake, he served them," I
added. "He made me eat them…my own canaries!"

"Mhm," Sirius mumbled, "that must've been unpleasant."

"Unpleasant? It was terrible. A nightmare!"

"Did he serve them raw?" Maya asked.

"What? Ah, yes...raw, completely raw."

"What a horror!" Danko showed his support surprisingly. Then he added, "Your stomach must've hurt after that."

I couldn't tell if he was making fun of the story or simply following his insane logic, but in either case, my "confession" was coming across not as a tragic one but as a piece of black humor. Nevertheless, I decided to press on.

"My grandfather used to punish me by ordering me to go out in the garden and dig a grave. And then he would bury me in it. He would leave me with only a straw to breathe through. But sometimes he would spray...laughing gas through it, and I would laugh! I would laugh in my grave, my mouth filling with dirt."

Well, this time I got what I wanted: Now everyone, even Graziella, was staring at me, and I could tell from their eyes that they were impressed. I could tell they were ready to pour their questions over me, but I didn't give them the opportunity to do so. I pushed my chair back and stood up, and after looking down at them, I left the dusky veranda. I stepped back out in the colorful tropical day.

CHAPTER THIRTY-ONE

I could see the tinfoil that the flash drive was wrapped in glistening in the distance in the red sand. I picked up and put it in my pocket and walked along the beach. I wanted to go to the foot of the rock Kuber was pushed from but soon realized that I wouldn't be able to find it from here. The rocks looked as if they had merged into a single wall, covered with a chaotic web of cracks and jagged edges.

I sat down on the sand. There was no point in walking further, but I didn't want to go back. I looked at the birds darting with cries over the bay. From time to time, one of them would arrow straight into the calm waters, leaving behind only an ephemeral, foam-edged whirlpool, and then fly out, a fish flapping in its beak...

"They are insatiable," I heard Frant's voice behind my back.

I turned to look at him, and he nodded and sat down next to me. I felt as someone whose cup of patience was brimming over. I was surrounded by murderers, and I was allowing them to take me by surprise whenever they felt like it. And that was not all. I fell asleep for hours on the beach today and was later put to sleep by a karate blow.

"I'm glad that you've left your pruners," I said.

Frant laughed; I didn't.

"They are insatiable!" he repeated, and from the grimace on his face, I could tell he wasn't very fond of the birds. "If they catch one or two fish and perch on some rock, they'd have food for the entire day. But no, they're not stopping, hunting from dawn to dusk!"

"What do you want, Frant?" I asked him straight up.

"Don't you feel I've come in peace?"

"No. I cannot feel anything...anymore."

"I understand. It's a wonder you can feel anything at all after the burials you've been through. But let me tell you, only I believed you! The others think that you're ascribing to your grandfather some of your own...let's call them *deeds*."

"And to what do I owe your trust?"

"To my mother." He said "mother" with such hatred in his voice that he choked. "She's a chameleon, just like your grandfather. She would act like an angel around everyone, but as soon as the others were gone, she would let the demons out of her soul!"

We exchanged glances, and for a moment I thought that this tiny dandy of a murderer could be my friend...if he weren't a murderer. Or if I didn't know he was a murderer.

"That's a good comparison, Frant. We have that in common, having been raised by chameleons. But there's no point in talking about them now."

"I agree. We should be talking about Danko instead."

"Again?"

"Yes. Because he told me today you accused him of murdering Kuber!"

"Of course. After I realized he was intent on killing me..."

"You accused him before that. Even before he tied you up! And this morning you were asking me about Kuber's death too. I'm sorry, but you'll have to keep in mind that you're not a cop here!"

"But I'm also not a fool," I told him, with a confidence I didn't feel. "With six serial killers on the island, an incident can be a suspicious thing. That's my way of thinking."

"Well, it's not a good one," he concluded. "All of us are here for the money, Miro. For the enormous sum of five million! That's the reason no one would put the experiment in danger in any way, least of all by committing a murder."

"You may be right about the others. But not about Danko. Weren't you 'judging' me today for getting almost killed by him?"

"Yes, but that's because you provoked him."

"It's possible Kuber provoked him too."

"I don't think so. Kuber was a gentle and delicate man. And what makes you think that *your* murder would put the experiment in danger? Don't you see the difference between *your* position here and that of everyone else?" Frant waved a hand to show me he's not expecting an answer and explained patiently, "All of us, except you, are registered as participants in the experiment, and all of us are expected to make it to the end. Kuber is also going to make it, only in a frozen condition. You, however, are free, so…"

"So if you buried me somewhere on the island, the pilots would report my departure from here. Yes, I've been already informed about that option by Sirius. And it didn't come as a hint, mind you. He told me straight up that if Danko had murdered me, the blame would've been Graziella's, because his aggression is a result of her dangerous therapy with the mower."

"Dangerous, yes, but not wrong. If you ask me, Graziella is purposefully inflaming him through this therapy. She's gearing him up!"

Frant rose quickly and started for the elevator.

"Wait!" I tried stopping him. "Gearing him up? For what?"

"Not what. Whom," he shouted after the cabin began moving up the line. "*For whom!*"

CHAPTER THIRTY-TWO

I had lunch and dinner in one, although it was only 5:40 p.m., an hour unsuitable even for an afternoon snack. When I was done, I didn't bother with picking up the dishes, grabbed a beer from the fridge, and went to my cell to drink it and read the police reports on Merry Maker.

"Finally!" Roxanna was waiting for me outside. "You eat slow or too much?"

"Both," I replied. "But rarely."

"Hmm," she expressed her doubt and went on. "I told the others that I'm going to go to bed early because I have a headache. But you've already guessed that, haven't you?"

Well, no, I hadn't! It's been less than an hour since her fiancé was taken into isolation to suffer alone, and here she was…with an open invitation?

"You've waited in vain, Roxanna. You could have told me that…you're going to go to bed early in the kitchen."

"Yes, but I couldn't be sure that no one would hear us there. That's why I'm saying it to you here: Don't you dare follow me!"

I was confused. "Follow you…where? Your bed?"

"Bastard!" Her face flushed red. "You're lucky Valdo's not here!"

I had heard that same line before. And I knew that I was a bastard in her eyes.

"It might come as a surprise to you," I began with irony in my voice, "but my idea of luck does not include the absence of Valdo or even his presence…"

I stopped, pleasantly surprised by the kind smile that appeared on her face. I answered with a smile too and only then realized that hers was not meant for me. I turned around and saw the tabby cat, my acquaintance from last night, coming toward us. It moved closer and rubbed against my legs in a friendly manner. I reached down to pat it, but Roxanna rushed toward me, pushed my hand away, picked up the cat, and shielded it in her arms. She took a few steps back, put the cat down, and chased it away with a clap of her hands, a stomp of the foot, and several threatening interjections.

"Hey, are you insane?" I mumbled.

"Bastard!" She seemed to like the word. "Bear in mind that none of us has murdered animals in their childhood or later. And if something like this were to happen, we would know it was you!"

"No, no, it won't happen…I mean, I too haven't murdered…animals, I mean…"

"What about the canaries? It wasn't your grandfather, I am sure! It was you!"

I clutched my head; my mind was unable to deal with so much misunderstanding.

"Don't you dare come closer to the other animals either!" Roxanna warned me again. "Sirius made a mistake when he put you in charge of them. Maya and I are taking over. Understood?"

I nodded. *There is one benefit to all that,* I thought. *At least I won't have to work in the pens.* I felt relief, and that was the moment I realized what the meaning of her first warning was: I was the only one who knew about her secret visits with Fata.

"Don't worry," I said. "I won't follow you. I already know why you're headed to Fata's. You're in a hurry to brag how you no longer have amnesia, to share with her your 'wonderful' memories of the murders you've committed. Although I doubt that she'd be happy to hear about it…"

"I doubt it too," Roxanna admitted surprisingly. "She loves me…like her own daughter, probably because she is sure I hadn't killed anyone."

"Sure? On what ground?"

"My words are grounds enough. But now, after I tell her the truth…"

Obviously forgetting about the hostility between us, Roxanna looked up at me with her dark, uneasy eyes. She seemed to want me to help her in some way, to encourage her. I stood before her, feeling stupid and embarrassed because of the beer bottle in my hand, and once again falling under the spell of my sympathy for her—my sympathy for this young and tortured woman.

"Come on, go now," I urged her quietly. "I believe that Fata will understand. If you're so attached to her, she probably isn't the evil old hag she's pretending to be. You've seen her true, kind face…and you're going to see it again. Today and tomorrow…" I didn't know what else to say. "Come on, go now," I repeated.

I think I heard her say "Thank you" as she walked away, but I might have imagined it. I returned to the kitchen and took two more beers.

CHAPTER THIRTY-THREE

The police reports turned out to be only summaries of such or even summaries of the summaries. Also, there was no evidence whatsoever that they actually had been written by the police, and calling them "reports" seemed somewhat misleading, what with the absence of author names and dates of filing. The file consisted of a three-page document only, filled with short descriptions of the murders Merry Maker has committed and even shorter accounts of his victims. It seemed like Graziella has considered it unnecessary to flood me with information about the character she had insisted I play.

I opened the second bottle of beer and scrolled up to the top of the document. Patrick Krenz's murder was committed on the third of the previous month, and the next three toward the end of the same month, with a day between each. It was this increase in the frequency of the murders that started the media hysteria: MERRY MAKER UNLEASHED, THE SADISTIC INSOMNIAC, and others in the same vein. I had heard before of the message nailed to the chest of the second victim, Christian Deluc, aged forty, and now I had to read it:

"I made a mistake with the boy. But this sinner here will pay dearly. Laughter, laughter, laughter—through tears—that's all that waits for him. Ha-ha-ha is all that's gonna come from him!"

And indeed, the psycho did his best to "provide" the dying man with a mouth that's big enough—by cutting it out with a razor. He did the same to the next two, whose bodies, unlike that of Patrick's, also showed multiple lacerations, made, according to the investigation, while the victims were still alive. Examinations of the bodies showed that during the torture, the victims had breathed nitrous oxide, or laughing gas, whose anesthetic effect is accompanied by euphoria and bursts of uncontrollable laughter. In other words, the three victims were laughing as they watched their murderer cut them to pieces. And he was probably laughing with them.

I finished the second bottle of beer, but the third one had gone warm. I took it to the bathroom, where I put it under running cold water to cool. I returned to the laptop.

Nails were driven into the chest of the third and fourth victims—Eric Kotovich, fifty-six, and Philip Ramm, seventy-one—and the cops were right to interpret this as a sign by Merry Maker that they have to look for the respective messages. They found one in Kotovich's kitchen, hidden in a packet of salt: *Your jokes are not as sweet as mine! That's what he told me, dying.* And after going through everything in Ramm's house, they found the other, scrawled with the blood of the victim under the bathroom sink: *I washed my hands.*

Yes, Merry Maker was one messed-up bastard, and people here…and to think that people here instantly believed I was him! Couldn't they tell that I am not that insane?

I went to turn the water off, but before that I drank some water, which made me change my mind about the beer. I lay down on the bed, my thoughts focused only on Patrick Krenz. One could say that compared to the other three, he was lucky—he wasn't tortured because his death had come too soon as a result of too much nitrous oxide in his lungs. One could also say that by writing "I made a mistake with the boy," Merry Maker had meant precisely the dosage. But was Maya the real reason for Patrick's murder? He was an intern at the hospital, while she was in intensive care there, and tried to take advantage of the state she was in and elicit an interesting confession or two from her. Actually, this was the only fact upon which she had built her idyllic and at the same time sinister fantasies: how despite her being the "ugly one with the éclairs," Merry Maker fell for her so much that right after the trial he went to her place to introduce himself and, not finding her there, started paying visits to her grandmother instead, who complained to him about the perfidious medical student and his questions, thus sealing the fate of that student.

All right. Maya is a teenager; it's only normal for her to come up with all sorts of fantasies. But what if—due to some fantastic coincidence—those fantasies were in some way portraying reality? Would I have to take them into account over the course of my investigation here? The question seemed meaningless because Kuber's murder and the murders committed by Merry Maker had nothing in common. Yet my intuition seemed to see a hidden link between them...

CHAPTER THIRTY-FOUR

I didn't sleep well. I tossed and turned in the narrow bed, feeling as if my skin crawled with ants. And every time I drifted toward sleep, I would get the feeling that Kuber's fever dreams were coming toward me. The nightmares that had soaked into the fabric of the cheap mattress with the drops of his sweat.

Exhaustion threw me into deep sleep shortly before dawn, ruining my intention to watch the sun rise from that hill where I could plunge into the web in search of more valuable pieces of information about Merry Maker, Patrick, Kuber, Danko, Frant…and generally every single one of the living and the dead who were so aggressively struggling for a place in my mind.

I woke up a wreck and immediately headed for the mirror in the bathroom. The bruise on my temple had not faded, but at least stubble had covered the redness of my left cheek. My nose, though, was still red; the skin on my forehead was peeling off; and on top of it all, my whole face itched. I thought for a moment and then reconsidered and used neither the razor nor the lotion. I took a cold shower because there was no hot water, and I changed the Band-Aid over the healing wound on my waist.

I left the bungalow at about 9:00 a.m., when all I dreamed of was a cup of coffee. In no time I had left the shadows of the umbrellalike palms and was walking across the meadow with the hibiscus bushes.

"Did you read the reports?" I heard a whisper from a bush nearby.

"Yes," I replied automatically and stopped.

"Good!" Graziella peeked from the bush. "Give me back the flash drive!"

"I don't have it with me."

"Go get it!"

"Now?"

"Yes!" She took a step to the side and appeared before my eyes dressed in a baggy working overall, with a bouquet of hibiscus branches under her arm. "Come on! Hurry up, for God's sake, or I'll go crazy!"

"You already are," I mumbled but headed back for the bungalow.

When I returned with the flash drive, Graziella was still picking branches, this time from a bush that was closer to the house.

"Miro! Hey, Merry Maker!" she called, waving to greet me, probably to make the eventual watcher believe that this was our first meeting today. "Good morning! Come help me, please."

"Coming!" I shouted, even though less than thirty feet separated us.

As soon as I went closer, she thrust the bouquet into my hands, swiftly took the flash drive, and dropped it into one of the overall's pockets, and turning her back to me, she went back to picking branches.

"Aren't these enough?" I asked.

"More than enough. Had you spent one more hour in sweet dreams, you would've found me buried under these damned branches. I've been waiting for you to warn you that Sirius is suspecting us!"

"Of what?"

"Of you not being Merry Maker and of me bringing you here because I've hired you to investigate Kuber's death!" She was talking really fast and was soon out of breath. "Last night, after we left Valdo in the isolation room, he told me how he sold you the lie that according to him, Danko murdered Kuber, and how you, misled by his words, almost gave yourself away…"

"That's not true! I most certainly did not give myself away in that conversation."

"In which one, then?" She turned her face toward me only for a moment so that I could see the horror on her face. "To whom did you give yourself away?"

"To no one," I answered, albeit not entirely sincerely.

"Oh, Miro, Miro! I hired you to do your job, not to ruin mine!"

"You should've hired a telepath then, because I cannot do much without any information…"

"Go!" She piled the newly picked branches on top of the rest in my hands. "We shouldn't spend much time together. Give the bouquet to Maya or Roxanna, and get yourself together! It's crucial that you sound convincing during confession hour. Stick only to what you've read in the reports, and I'll support you by providing pertinent analyses."

"All right. But when are we going to have a talk about *my* job?"

"Today. After half past ten." She had turned her back to me again.

I walked across the meadow, clutching the fragrant bouquet, and really started getting myself together, although not with the forthcoming confession hour in mind. Sirius had once again taken the center stage in my thoughts. What game was he playing? And who the hell was he? So, he murdered "only three hookers," got life for that, and was released for good behavior. All right, but if that was true and if that was all, why would he hide his real name? Or more precisely, why would they—he and Graziella—hide it?

I stopped and looked over my shoulder. Graziella was walking away, entering the palm grove. She paced quickly and, it seemed, in the direction of my bungalow.

I resisted the temptation to follow her and continued toward the house.

CHAPTER THIRTY-FIVE

Roxanna met me in the vestibule, and I instantly knew that if not someone else, she had been watching us from inside.

"You were right!" she whispered as I gave her the bouquet, with relief. "I told her everything, but her feelings for me did not change. She said, 'Find a new amnesia for your past, and you'll have a real future.' She's so good! And so wise!"

"I'm happy for you." I smiled at her. "And I hope you follow her advice."

"Oh, I will! No matter how hard it is for me to do so!"

She also smiled. Her animosity toward me seemed to have disappeared along with every other bad and dark feeling. Her face glowed today as if her secret meeting with Fata had filled it with a magic light. That was something therapists like my grandfather and Graziella could never achieve. It's an impossible magic: to be able to give to someone what you don't have.

"Can I ask you a favor?" Roxanna said. "Tear that painting! Destroy it; burn it! Forget about it!"

That was embarrassing. I had forgotten about it, had not even looked at it. Noticing my embarrassment, Roxanna flustered too.

"I know, I know, now I know," she mumbled. "I must've been truly crazy. 'It was Death who was shooting, Death who was killing them'...how could I have believed in such madness? Believe for so long despite Graziella telling me over a hundred times how all this has gotten into my head."

"How?" I was curious.

"It was from that *Meet Joe Black* movie. I remember watching it with my aunt. And in this movie Death comes disguised as a man, and...it must've impressed me so much that something flipped into my brain. Ugh! Promise me you'll destroy it!"

"I promise. Only smoke and ashes will remain."

"Good!" Her face lit up again. "Now hurry if you want to have breakfast. Then come to the confession room. Confession hour is going to be only about you today!"

I mumbled a perfunctory "Oh, is it?" and continued toward the kitchen. I am not one of those who easily loses his appetite. Presently I was sitting at the table, with two large sandwiches and a big cup of coffee before me. I took my time, staring at the view behind the house.

I was surprised to see Graziella there and then got really worried when she started running toward the edge of one of the rocks—it looked like she was about to jump from there! The absurd thought that Fata might've bewitched her too crossed my mind. I opened the window to call her from here, to stop her somehow, but then I saw she was carrying something black and rectangular. I knew what it was: my laptop. I closed my mouth without making a sound. Then I closed the window.

When she got to the edge of the rock, Graziella sent it flying down the precipice with a shot-putter's throw. I didn't need to think much to realize that thrown from there, the laptop would land not on the sand but in the shallows overgrown with seaweed. I returned to my breakfast, still keeping an uninterested eye on Graziella as she walked back. I had nothing valuable on the laptop and wasn't even angry at her for what she had done. I also wasn't puzzled by it. She realized that I had copied the "reports" from the flash drive and decided to deal with this in such a primitive way. And it was no surprise that she had keys to each of the bungalows here.

I finished my coffee and left the kitchen. It occurred to me that I didn't have to confess anything to anyone, and still I headed for the confession room.

CHAPTER THIRTY-SIX

I told them everything I had read the previous night about Merry Maker, but although I spoke slowly and made long pauses, I couldn't stretch the story over more than ten minutes. Then I fell silent, depressed by the thought that I had to sit through this excruciatingly long confession hour devoted only to me and no one else. I sat facing my psychiatrist and the five murderers, all of them squeezed on the sofa. I did not like the furnishings here either—everything looked incongruously fresh and flowery because of the hibiscus branches stuffed in several vases around the room, and also the blinds were drawn up, exposing my burned and battered face to the merciless sunlight. The only pleasant thing around was the absence of Valdo, but it wasn't enough to compensate for the presence of the obnoxious six across from me.

Sirius was the first to say something, probably only to emphasize to Graziella that his suspicions were still high. "*Merry Maker,*" he announced skeptically, "there was almost nothing new in your story for us. We knew everything from the papers we get here every Friday. What we don't know, however, is what made you commit these…inexplicable murders."

"Why inexplicable?" Maya asked. "We all understood yesterday that his laughing-gas obsession began in his childhood years. As a result of the tortures, he was put through by his grandfather!"

"Ha-ha! So you believed him?" Sirius laughed.

"Why, yes, I thought about it, and I believe him."

"I didn't have to think at all." Frant was on my side.

"I too *believed* him," Graziella said, with aplomb. "But I have to tell you, I was fooled by his grandfather's refined *hypocrisy* until recently. I've been working with him for years, and only now am I beginning to see the monster hiding behind the mask!"

Obviously, she had enormous authority here, because Roxanna, Danko, and maybe even Sirius joined the group of the "believers." Their faces darkened as they accepted without objections her statement that the noble old man they admired and trusted was, in fact, a monster. "They renounced you in no time!" That's what I'm going to say to him at the first opportunity.

"Friends," Graziella resumed talking, "there is no doubt that Miro has suffered much before turning into Merry Maker, the man hated by most ordinary people. But you here are far from ordinary because you've also been through much and because you are also hated by all ordinary people. We shall use the event of the trial to open those people's eyes for the truth and to redirect their hatred toward those who are truly responsible for the murders and, of course, toward the state itself. But now it is important that you do Miro justice. You know from experience that in the beginning, it would be hard for him to be completely open not only with you but also with himself. This means that your questions must be delicate, stripped of any negative connotation."

"You're right," Sirius agreed and instantly attacked me with a "delicate" question: "What did you want to say with those messages of yours? I didn't get the deeper meaning."

"There wasn't any," I answered. "Only the obvious meaning."

"I forgot what your second message was," Graziella said, lying. "Could you please repeat it?"

"I had written that my jokes were not as sweet as his; that they were, in fact, *salty*; and that he had told me that himself, while dying."

"He? Who is *he*?" Sirius raised his voice.

"Enough!" Graziella reproached him. "You know well that in those particular moments, Miro was not seeing Eric...what was his surname?" She waited in vain for me to help her and then helped herself with it: "Kotovich. Notice how Miro could not answer! He struggled to remember the name of his victim and failed, precisely because while he was committing the murder—actually, while he was committing each of the murders with the exception of the first one—he would see only one face: his grandfather's! He would see it as it had been at the age of forty, because that was when the man had started to 'take care' of the helpless aban- doned baby. He would also see it at the age of over fifty when the cruelty toward him, toward his own grandson, was at its peak. And finally, he would see him the way he is now: an old man of seventy, who is still terrorizing him psychologically if not physically. That would explain why each victim is older than the previous one. His choice was dic- tated by his sick imagination!"

No one looked surprised, and no one com- mented on that psycho tirade of hers.

"All right. We have an explanation of the three murders." Maya darted me a sly look. "You were 'seeing' only your grandfather, I get that. But what about the first murder? The boy? You wrote it was a mistake?"

"I don't know why." I gave her my short reply.

"But I know why, Miro," Graziella said. "After your discharge, which was the factor that unlocked the traumas shut behind the door of your unconscious, the first person you turned against was you. Alas, it was so! In your mind, that boy was you…and by murdering him you made an attempt to satiate your desire for self-destruction. But you started to feel sorry with time, and so you wrote that 'I made a mistake with the boy' in your first message."

"Dammit!" Sirius cursed. "Those messages are so confusing. You nailed the first one to the victim's body; the second one you hid in a packet of salt in the kitchen of the third victim; and the third one…you scrawled on the wall in the bathroom of the fourth victim. Is that how it was, Merry Maker?"

I had made up my mind to answer no question, but he insisted. "Is that how it was? Tell me."

"Yes, dammit, yes!" I yelled. "I told you a minute ago…didn't I tell you how it was?"

"You said that you wrote something under the sink in that poor guy's bathroom. What was it?"

"'I washed my hands.' That's what I wrote. And I'll wash them again after I've smashed your snout!"

"Please," Graziella called upon us, "stay away from any animosity you might feel!"

"How?" Sirius exclaimed. "Only yesterday he wanted to kill himself using Danko as a weapon!"

"Water under the bridge," Danko said.

"Good, but have you thought what could've happened if you had not stopped the mower in time?" Sirius shot back.

"Guys, this is all in the past now," Graziella explained. "Let's focus on the present and, most of all, on the future."

"I'm focused exactly on the future!" Sirius exclaimed, even more dramatically now. "He *saw* himself in Patrick and decided to kill him. What if something inside him flipped and started *seeing* himself in one of us?"

"It's possible, yes," Frant mumbled. "I'm sorry, Graziella, but can you guarantee that he will remain stable in the future?"

"No, I can't. But I can hazard a guess that in the coming days he will surpass you all in his efforts to remain stable, because his struggle to come here has been much greater than yours." After saying this elaborate phrase, Graziella attempted a look of hesitation and then said, "I'm sorry, Miro. I will have to tell them the whole truth."

I was sure that she wasn't going to say anything even resembling the truth, so I waited with curiosity for the next piece of fiction.

"I must tell you that there is nothing accidental about Miro's coming here." She began with the practiced straightforwardness of an experienced liar. "He knew about the experiment from his grandfather; he also knew about the millions that each participant will make. And after overcoming the stress from his discharge and from the mistake he had made with Patrick, his mind started working on a truly insane but also clever plan. He decided both to take his revenge on his grandfather by 'murdering' him multiple times and to get rich by making me include him in the experiment as a serial murderer."

"Such vileness!" Sirius was quick to show his outrage. "Such calculating madness!"

"So calculating as to almost look feigned." Frant's remark was to the point.

Maya showed concern. "But, Graziella, how are you going to get him out of this if he makes full confession during the trial?"

"Oh, I will find a way," she replied. "I will get him out if he agrees to my conditions."

"And they are?" Roxanna asked. "And how did he make you include him—"

"We'll discuss this later," Graziella cut her off. "We'll discuss everything but not now. We must not exhaust him, friends. Whatever it is that you think of him, the truth is, he is one very tortured, very sick man."

She nodded at me and said a kindly, "Come on, Miro," and headed for the door. I followed her.

CHAPTER THIRTY-SEVEN

It is a well-known fact that women become prettier when they are happy. I personally have been the very reason for this phenomenon many times and hope for many more. But in this case, Graziella's becoming prettier meant only one thing: I was screwed. Or to be more precise, I had made her happy by giving her the opportunity to screw me over. I had a guess, but finding out if it was right was going to be a tough task, a really tough task. That woman's ability to juggle with lies and the truth would puzzle even minds that are way smarter than mine.

"That went well! Perfect even!" She revealed her joy the moment we closed the door of her office. "Did you see that? Sirius also believed you that you're Merry Maker. I put an end to his suspicions. You are now part of the group!"

"Yes, but you will have to also take me out of it. Doesn't that bother you?"

"No. I'll confess that everything has been a bluff at the trial, and by then you and I will be out of danger."

"You are out of danger here," I told her. "No one here is so insane as to lay a hand to the goose with the golden egg."

"I'm surprised by you, Miro. You think you can estimate the degree of everyone's madness here?"

Graziella sat behind her desk and invited me to sit on the psychoanalytic couch. I chose one of the chairs.

"Who is Sirius in reality?" I asked. "Why are you hiding his real name?"

"He did his time and has earned the privilege. Plus a few more."

"For example?"

"He can leave the island whenever he likes. He can choose not to participate in confession hour. He's been through a lot of terrible things during his childhood and prefers not to go back there. But he is going to reveal who he is and tell everything during the trial."

"Sounds convincing," I said.

"I don't care how it sounds; it's the truth. By the way, do you have…a favorite among the suspects? I mean, all six of them are suspects, right?"

"No," I answered and fastened my eyes on her. "There are seven suspects."

There wasn't even the slightest sign of anxiety on her face. Either she was able to control herself perfectly, or I was on the wrong path. But whatever the path I was on, it most certainly had reached thin ice, so I took a step to the side.

"I meant Fata," I lied. "We must not count her out of the circle of suspects."

"Miro! What are you talking about? Don't tell me you believe in Sirius's superstitions!"

"It has nothing to do with the superstitions but with certain physical actions from her side."

"You assume she could've pushed Kuber from the rock?"

"Why not? I'm only starting with the investigation, and I have to take every possibility into account. But to answer your earlier question, yes, I already have a favorite."

"And who is he? Or is it a she?"

"Sirius," I answered without hesitation, although I did not, in fact, suspect him. "I think that he's pretending to believe in Fata's magic abilities to divert any suspicion from himself."

Graziella wrinkled her brow to show me she was really considering this.

"Of course!" she exclaimed. "It's so close to mind that he is the most probable perpetrator! He pushed Kuber, and then when we went looking for him, he hid somewhere. He watched the body and waited. And bingo! He saw that I was the first to stumble upon it and move it closer to the rocks. He left me that message, and now he's waiting for the right moment to deal his crucial blow!"

"And what would that be?" I asked. "And how long is he going to wait?"

"He is going to wait until the trial, Miro. The trial in which he *will refuse* to take part!" She pressed her cheek with her hand as if she had just felt a sudden sharp pain in the tooth. "He will try to force me to pay him the millions without completing his part of the contract. Thus, he will compromise the entire experiment!"

I was unable to tell if her panic was just a simulation or real, which would have been absolutely justified if I had guessed right. If she had pushed Kuber and Sirius saw her, that is.

"Let's not jump to conclusions, Graziella. He could be innocent."

"I hope so!" she said, seemingly with all her heart.

"Why? What difference would it make if Kuber's murderer was not Sirius but someone else from the group?"

"None of the others would refuse to be in the trial, Miro. They all know that if they refused, they'll go back to prison or psychiatry. It's one of the fundamental clauses in our contract with the prosecutor's office, and I wouldn't be able to change it even if I was blackmailed. But Sirius is free and interested only in the money."

"I see." I nodded and went into a "cop of action" mode. "Show me the message."

"I don't have it here. I gave it to the pilots, in a sealed envelope, of course, to deliver it in person to a person I trust, a criminal lab technician. I was hoping he would find fingerprints on it, but there weren't any."

Her account sounded logical, provided she had received such message, and I doubted that. In fact, after I heard her logical—and psychiatrically founded—arguments explaining my transformation from Miro to Merry Maker, I began doubting every single word of hers. And I saw no reason to expect that the rest of our conversation could do anything but raise more suspicion.

"Miss," I began in an intentionally formal manner, "I'd ask you answer me one last question. Do you really believe that I would be able to find out who killed Kuber with *all the restrictions* of my role as Merry Maker?"

"Of course I do. That's why I hired you, after all. How are you going to do it? I have no idea. If it was an easy task, I wouldn't have offered you five million to carry it out."

"I say you offer me ten million not to carry it out," I said equivocally. "Both of us could benefit from that."

"Ha-ha-ha," she replied, with a deadpan face. "You're such a *merry maker*. Anything else?"

"Yes. Give me the key to the wine cellar. I'll use a moment when everyone is in the house to go there and take a look at the body."

"Oh, you don't need to go in the cold down there." She smiled. "I don't think you need *another* look at it."

CHAPTER THIRTY-EIGHT

Valdo or Maya? Which one of them told Graziella that I went to see the dead body? If it was Valdo, then good. He had the right to complain, because, according to him, I had rummaged around in his bungalow and had stolen his skeleton key. But if it was Maya, then it definitely was not good. Because this would mean that she is playing a double game with me. First, she asks me to take a careful look at the body and keep it a secret, only to spill the beans later to Graziella, who, allegedly, has never shared with anyone her suspicions that Kuber was actually murdered.

I did not go deeper into the hibiscus bushes. I chose to sit on a bench from which I could keep an eye on the house and be visible myself. I was sure that someone—most likely Maya—would come to have a talk or to continue dragging me into their game.

I assumed the relaxed posture of someone free of care and returned to the question: Was I being paranoid, or was there something truly reasonable in my latest version of how things went? If I had to think superficially about it, I would have gone with "being paranoid." Graziella hires me to find out who has murdered Kuber even though she is the actual murderer. Yes, it sounded absurd but not if one considered the facts more deeply.

Kuber was one of the four who were released from the psychiatric hospital by Graziella and my grandfather. But unlike Frant, Danko, and Roxanna, he would have frequent "fits of insanity," as Sirius put it. So, there was a real danger that fits such as those could occur during the trial and, of course, disprove her claims about the success of therapeutic sessions on the island. Something like this would ruin her authority as a psychiatrist and compromise the entire experiment. Would she allow anything of that kind to happen? My answer was *no*! The possibility of Kuber destroying her life's work by having a fits in front of everyone was motive enough for a fanatic like her.

From this point on, I did not need much mental effort to construct a hypothesis by following this scheme:

In Graziella's own words, she would inform my grandfather of everything that was going on, on the island, and both would discuss every problem that arose. And the most serious of these would be Kuber's fits of insanity. That is why when death came for him and not somebody else, my grandfather became instantly, and justly, possessed by suspicion. He insisted that an investigation be conducted, and Graziella had no choice—she agreed because a refusal on her side would have been equal to admitting she was the murderer. She quickly came up with some other "confession" to divert my grandfather's suspicions from her— something like "Yes, you are right; Kuber was murdered, and I made it look like an accident." And in the end, again on his insistence, hired as an investigator not one of her people but me. She did that because…

Well, simply because too much is at stake, and when push comes to shove, my grandfather would trust no one but me, no matter how lousy our relationship was. But I not only betrayed his trust but also allowed Graziella to screw me over in such a nasty way.

I took a few deep breaths to calm myself down and rushed back to the hope that my hypothesis could be completely erroneous, absolute nonsense. Still, I could not close my eyes to the fact that

Graziella made a considerable effort to obstruct the investigation. She put me on the Merry Maker ride, denying me the opportunity to carry out interrogations, to look for evidence, and generally do any investigative work. She also denied me the opportunity to have a normal conversation with my grandfather. If I were to call him now, what would I say to him? And if she had already told him everything, how would I justify my decision to portray him as a psychopath who, when I was a child, would bury me alive and make me laugh with gas, laughing gas…?

I stared at the house with the now-familiar feeling that someone or even everyone was looking at me from behind its mirror windows, exchanging vitriolic remarks about me. And if their psychiatrist was there with them, she was most probably giving her "professional" advice: "Don't judge him too harsh, dear friends. Don't forget that he's lost and confused and mentally ill."

CHAPTER THIRTY-NINE

Maya came out of the house just as I was standing up from the bench. I called her to bring me water and sat back down. A minute later, she handed me abottle of mineral water and sat next to me.

"I'm sorry," she said. "I realized only after you were gone that we would draw less suspicion if we talked in the open."

"You should be sorry for something else, Maya." I looked at her sternly. "You told Graziella about our supposedly secret visit with the dead man."

"That's not true! I didn't tell her! I'm not a snitch!"

"All right, all right. It was Valdo, then." I nodded and raised the bottle.

"And you're a nerd!" she said out of nowhere.

I put the cap back on and pressed the bottle against my forehead to cool it down.

"Neeerd!" she repeated. "In case you can't catch my drift, we all have laptops here."

"Except me," I sighed. "But I think I know what you mean. And can I just say, Maya, that you leave a really bad impression? Rummaging through other people's bungalows, rummaging through pockets that are not yours. Stealing skeleton keys and flash drives. Bad, really bad."

"Oh, and I guess it's OK to lie and lie and lie, and then fall asleep with a clear conscience and leave me crying?"

"Is it OK to rob a sleeping person? And then, instead of waking them, leave them to burn under the sun? Look at me!"

"You look better than yesterday." She grinned. "Your face was plastered with lotion like some diva's—"

"Maya!"

"And I didn't rob you. I gave you back the flash drive, didn't I? I knew you would go looking for it at the beach, so I left it there."

"What if someone else had stumbled upon it?"

"I didn't care. I was mad at you."

"And now I am mad at you." I knitted my brows. "You read the file without my permission. That's a theft of sorts. Theft of information."

"Are you saying that I should've asked Graziella for permission?"

"No. She has nothing to do with this."

"If that's so, why was the flash drive wrapped in foil from her favorite chocolate brand?"

"That doesn't prove anything. It could be my favorite brand too."

"What is it? Tell me the *name* of the brand," Maya cornered me.

"I don't remember," I answered. "I just ate the bar and wrapped the flash drive—"

"You're lying again." She stated the truth. "But I also lied! The foil was not from a candy bar. Yes, Miro, not that observant for a cop, are you?"

I wanted to say something in my defense but came up with nothing. The kid strutted her victory with a laugh, and continued.

"Let's not waste more time in lies. It's clear to me that Graziella gave you the flash drive so that you can cram every detail about the vile deeds of Merry Maker into your head in order to present them as your own. It's clear to me that you're here to find out who killed Kuber. And it's clear to me that this is the reason you agreed so easily that night to take a look at his corpse."

"Congratulations," I said, without enthusiasm. "Don't you get bored sometimes with so much clarity around you, Maya? Doesn't that sentence you to a life without mystery?"

"Miro, I can tell you're grumpy," she told me. "It's obvious you're struggling with the jokes, and you don't have to do this. Relax, man! I really am not a snitch. I won't tell on you. I want to help you. I want us to be partners!"

She invited me with a high-five gesture, and after sealing our contract with a clap, she said, "I wonder what made you take on the role of Merry Maker. And why Graziella has agreed to that? It doesn't make sense at all. And it's downright stupid."

"Actually it was the other way around. She insisted I play Merry Maker, and I agreed."

"That's even worse! This means it was not done on a whim and is no longer stupid. Graziella always has a plan, and in this particular case...that plan most likely won't be in your interest. Or something even worse than that."

"Just tell me what you think," I urged her. "No time to be careful. And to be clear, I now believe that I've been screwed over by a master in the game!"

"I believe so too."

"Well, all right then, but imagine I had arrived here with the following statement: 'Hello. Kuber's death is not an accident, and I am a cop come here to find out who did it.' What would your reaction be?"

"We would've been completely unperturbed," Maya answered. "All of us, including the murderer, would've reacted like this. For even if you did solve the crime, the 'accident' would forever remain an accident to the outside world. We know how to keep our mouths shut!"

"What about my mouth? How would you have kept it shut?"

"It is already taken care of, or will be, by Graziella. Otherwise she wouldn't have hired you."

"In other words, you're sure that the millions she's going to stuff your mouths with would be enough to keep mine shut too?"

Maya dug her fingers into her hair, threw me a look full of sympathy, and told me what I already knew: "Your mouth, Miro, could be kept shut by other means too."

"One of which being burying me six feet deep into the nourishing island soil."

"Probably, yes. Only it won't be six but three feet. No one here would bother with digging out more." She spread her arms in a gesture of apology. "I'm sorry, but you told me to say what I think."

"That's OK," I reassured her. "Three feet is OK."

"Another joke attempt." The sympathy in her eyes grew stronger. "Have you any ideas what Graziella is trying to achieve with this Merry Maker theater?"

I decided to restrain my urge to be sincere. "My guess is too vague. I just have the feeling that she doesn't want me to find out who killed Kuber, despite hiring me to do precisely that. Do you have a better one?"

"I do, actually. I think she purposefully made you look like the greedy and cunning man Merry Maker most likely isn't. We were all disgusted when she told us that you killed all those people only to get a place in the experiment. The others immediately hated you, as I would've too, if I hadn't found out the truth."

"But what use can your hatred for me have for Graziella?"

"Loosening our inhibitions. When you hate someone, it's easier to be...unrestrained toward them, isn't it?"

"*Unrestrained* sounds too general to me," I told her. "Could you be more specific?"

It was obvious that Maya had no desire whatsoever to be specific. After all, her sincerity had its boundaries too. I left it to her to decide if she would like to expand them, and after a short pause, she started talking, her voice thin and shaking.

"Graziella's great fear is that we're all going to be free after the trial and some of us could return to killing people. It's a known fact that once serial killers have started, they almost never stop. She's going to claim that this won't happen in our case, you know, although her fear that it might has been growing ever since Kuber's death..."

I had to give her some courage. "Just say it, Maya. Your guess is that Graziella's only purpose with this theater is to introduce me among you an experimental target, right?"

"Well…yes. If she had told us that she'd hired you as a cop to investigate Kuber's accident, our restraint would have been stronger. I'm not sure if it would be as strong when it comes to dealing with the hateful Merry Maker. And that is exactly what she wants to test. Moreover, if someone were to give in to the temptation…"

"All of you here can keep your mouths shut," I finished the sentence. "And my departure—my demise, I mean—would be a fact."

"Well…yes. I guess so…" Maya stood up, and if I hadn't grabbed her by the hand, she would've fled. "Let me go! I don't want to cry because of you again!"

"I don't want you to either," I assured her. "One cries over a grave, not for a living person."

"Stop it! Enough with the jokes. Dolt!"

I shook my head in reproach. "You're leaving another bad impression, Maya. You shouldn't be talking like that."

Well, I managed to lift her spirits—she went from teary to nervous and angry. I stood up, too, still holding her hand. I endured another "Dolt" from her, and then we both headed for the house.

CHAPTER FORTY

As most unstable people, Maya and I had soured our relationship in less than a second, and now, again in no time, we fixed it completely. We did this with another high-five right before entering the house, when she also gave me the following instructions:

"First, if they ask what took us so long, we'll tell them that you didn't want to come to the children's place. I had to persuade you to come. And second, once there, if you feel any curiosity about what the others are doing, don't show it. Just sit down in a corner with a book or a toy in your hands and immerse yourself in bitter memories."

We went into the house together with the cat, who was waiting and mewing at the door.

"I'll pour it some milk; you can go." Maya gave me directions to the place in question and, followed by the cat, headed for the kitchen.

I followed her directions, but as soon as I took a turn down the corridor, I saw Graziella.

"I was looking for you!" She seemed glad. "I forgot to tell you that I threw your laptop out. I assumed you had copied the reports from the flash drive, and I didn't want to risk someone seeing them…by accident. You're not mad at me, are you?"

"For now," I answered, staring at her curiously.

"I haven't had any, Miro. Not a single cosmetic-surgery procedure."

"I never thought you had…"

"Bullshit. That's the first thing you thought when you first saw me; admit it. Truth is, I've always been like this. I'm like my father. 'We are one of those people who would never fit into their skin,' he would say. Metaphorically, of course. But then, he was over seventy when he passed, and there wasn't a single wrinkle on his face."

"I see. He was young-looking…"

"Exactly the opposite. He was so thin, looking like a mummy with that tight skin on his face…" This seemed to upset her. She added quickly, "The pilots will bring you a new laptop on Friday," and turned away and left me staring at her back.

She walked toward the staircase and climbed up, two steps at a time. She was full of energy; that was undeniable. I remembered that hall filled with all sorts of electronic devices on the second floor— was she headed for there? To, say, have another video conversation with her colleague who, not co-incidentally, happened to be my grandfather?

Grandpa, Grandpa, who gave you the right to throw me into that shark's jaws?

I felt embarrassed before myself. As for the shark, I knew that comparison very well. The idea of the "jaws," though, didn't seem repulsive enough to me. Could it be possible that I found it attractive?

I put off the question "Should I sleep with my enemy?" for later. I walked over to the door where the sign, as if taken from another universe, said, Children's Place. I stormed inside. I already was the greedy and cunning Merry Maker; why not a complete oaf also?

"How are the kids today?" I shouted cheerfully. "Have you been good? Are you playing? Or fighting to total annihilation?"

The four faces that turned to look at me showed nothing more than light amusement. No animosity, no other signs of loosened restraints. Maybe if Valdo had been here, it would've gotten more exciting, but he was not. I had to accept the insulting indifference of these four who weren't even looking at me anymore. They had returned to their previous activities.

I moved toward Roxanna, who sat at the end of the long table, drawing something, but that was when Maya entered, and I, like a pupil caught doing something wrong, quickly took a seat at the other end of the table, where there was a pile of textbooks: *Ferro-Concrete Construction: A General Course; Earth Mechanics; Descriptive Geometry; Theory of Elasticity…*

"These are Valdo's." Roxanna raised her head. "He's going to become an engineer. A construction engineer!"

I nodded with respect, and although I had already grown bored with playing the oaf, I went around the table and peeked over her shoulder. She did not try to cover the drawing, probably because it was still at an early stage.

"Show him my portrait," Maya suggested, coming to us.

"It's not finished," she replied. "I'll show it to everyone when I'm done."

"But mine is finished," Frant called, leaving his electric-train set to join us. "Let him see it, please!"

Roxanna smiled coyly, leafed through the drawing pad, passing quickly over the faces of Valdo and Danko, and showed me…well, she showed me Frant's face, reproduced with such accuracy that for a moment I thought I was looking at Frant's reflection in a mirror.

"Ha! This is incredible!" I exclaimed, looking now at Frant and then at his portrait. "The likeness is…uncanny…"

The three of them laughed sincerely like children.

"You know what's even more incredible? I didn't pose!" Frant explained. "She drew me out of memory during one sleepless night."

"Out of her photographic memory!" Maya seemed proud of Roxanna's achievements. "She's amazing, isn't she?"

"You're exaggerating." Roxanna suddenly looked sad. "Talented painters have ideas, whereas I only copy reality."

She closed the drawing pad and asked us with a gesture to step back. Frant returned to his train set, and Maya went to the bookshelves to choose a book. I took advantage of their redirected attention and quietly stepped out of the room. Talented cops have ideas, also, and I was no exception! I hurried down the corridor and toward the entrance door, saying over and over to myself the words "photographic memory" and "copy reality" like a mantra. *Photographic memory, copy reality…*

CHAPTER FORTY-ONE

I didn't have to stare long at the portrait to decide where I should be taking it. I rolled it up and put it back into the polyethylene bag, and after taking my phone from under the bottom plank of the wardrobe, I left the bungalow.

It took me less than fifteen minutes, and I was at the door of Fata's tiny house. I knocked, not too loud but loud enough.

"I'm not deaf!" she yelled from inside. "Sit down and wait for me!"

I was just about to sit down on the nearest bench when I heard her yell again.

"The tree stump over there, not the bench! Or I'm not coming out!"

I walked to the tree stump that stood in the periphery of the magnolia-encircled meadow. It seemed like Fata wanted me to be as far away as possible when she opened the door, if at all. It crossed my mind that she was planning an escape through one of the windows on the back of the house, frightened by Merry Maker's visit.

"Don't be afraid!" I shouted. I took out the portrait and rolled it out. "I just wanted to show you this! You have to see it!"

I got no reply. I sat down on the uncomfortable tree stump, where I had to endure not only armies of crawling insects but also choirs of noisy birds. I turned my back to the overpopulated grove, and while waiting to see if I had come here for nothing, I took another look at the portrait. Its face perfectly white, the humanlike Death had the appearance of a geisha; it also looked like an Indian woman due to the red dot between the eyebrows, and with its eyelids painted in blue and lips in blood red, like a prostitute. An evenly beaten-up prostitute dressed for a funeral: a black headscarf and something that looked like a black robe but was so formless that it might as well have been just a large cloth wrapped around the body, which was drawn only from the waist up.

"Come!" Fata yelled again, stepping out of the tiny house. She sat on the bench there and mumbled something, probably her usual curses.

I rolled up the portrait and went to her.

"Don't waste your curses on me now," I said. "You should've done this yesterday instead of just sitting here and hoping that you would see me under the knives of the mower soon."

"Careful what you say! Unlike you, I am not a sadist to hope for such butchery!"

"Aren't you? Then what were you doing there?"

"I was watching. I saw you untie yourself. But I was surprised to see you just sitting there and waiting like a bull sent to the slaughterhouse."

Her eyes held a crushing contempt. No, this old lady was not afraid of me, and her sending me to sit on that stump over there was most likely a joke: a stump with a woodenhead on top, or something like that.

"Fata, I am not Merry Maker." I got straight to the point. "I'm a cop, and I'm here to investigate Kuber's death."

Her face showed neither surprise nor doubt. She seemed to believe me. She cackled demonically and raised her bony arms.

"I surrender! I confess: I put a spell on him, put a pin through him, cursed him—"

I cut her off, "Good, you've done a great job. Now we won't be talking about Kuber, though, but about Roxanna. I know that you have become really close. I also know that you meet in secret."

"And I know that you know. She told me everything. But if you think that this is going to make
me start putting up with you, you are wrong!"

"Fata, I have the knife you gave her. I'll give it to
Graziella as evidence that you've breached the contract between you, and she will have you off the island."

"Wrong again. Even if I were to arm her beloved murderers with automatic guns, Graziella
would never dare chase me off the island. My lawyers would sue her."

"Sue her and lose."

"Yes, but she will lose much more, because I
will tell not only the jury but also the media about
her dirty business here."

"Dirty? Any evidence?"

"I don't need evidence; I'll come up with something. I have to tell you, your threats only make
me laugh. I also laughed when I heard that that
pathetic being called Sirius has tried to get rid of
me with a recording."

"But Roxanna did not find that funny. And
came up with a complicated tale only to protect
you."

"Well, what's done is done. It's good for her to
believe that she has saved me. And now it's even
funnier because that wretch now lives in fear of
getting 'pierced' by one of my pins."

"By the way"—I tried to sound casual—"I understand that you consider him the lowest of the murderers around here for no particular reason."

"The reasons are not particular, only to those who don't know them. And you will never know about them either."

Fata waved to chase the insects swarming over her head, and from the look on her face, I was next on her list. I decided not to force my luck with more persistent questions regarding Sirius. I took a step forward and unrolled the portrait.

"Take that thing away from my eyes!" She moved back. "I'm not blind, you know. This...this idiot, who is she?"

"Who do you think she is?"

"How am I supposed to know? I've never met her."

"Good. Tell me what she looks like?"

"I told you already: an idiot."

"You're right. Actually, this is...Death. The way Roxanna *saw* her."

"Impossible! She describes her in a completely different manner."

"Her words are 'serious and stately.' That's how Death is in her delusional fantasies. But as soon as she started drawing, her hand was led by her photographic memory."

Fata produced a Marlboro pack from her cardigan pocket. I accepted the cigarette she offered me, even though I am not a smoker. I sat down next to her, and as we were smoking silently in the din coming from the grove, we somehow grew closer.

"Come on." She nudged me laconically, throwing her cigarette butt in the trash can nearby.

I did the same and after that told her how and why Roxanna had decided to "show" me Death. I didn't go into detail but made sure it was clear that it was by coincidence that I had visited her bungalow as she was finishing the portrait.

"She was drawing in a state of trance, and then she rolled it up and handed it to me saying that it would only work if I were 'alone with her,' meaning Death. *Fantasies of a mad woman* was my thought then. Now, though, I realize that after coming to from the trance, she *did not dare* look at the portrait, and that if she had, she would've experienced a true shock..."

"Because she would've realized that she had drawn her aunt!" Fata concluded.

"Have you seen her?" I asked. "In a photograph or another portrait?"

"I haven't, but who besides her aunt could it be? Roxanna had lived there for years. At the time of the murder, only the two of them were there. And look at the disguise. Clearly, this woman had quickly slapped some makeup on her face and covered her body with the nearest cloth."

"Yes, she improvised, which means that the first murder was not a planned one. For the next two, however, she would *consciously* recreate that look. That's how it was. And Roxanna has been telling the truth the whole time! Every time one of those nasty creeps would visit her room, she would become paralyzed. 'I would lie like a corpse and wait for Death. But she would come only for them.'"

"Well, yes, yes," Fata mumbled. "That's what she told me too."

"And yesterday, right before my eyes, Graziella put her in the same state! A psychogenic stupor that makes her mind distort reality, adding aural and visual hallucinations to it. Such was her explanation, and, naturally, it was followed by the lie that Roxanna would go into stupor not before but *after* each murder, later remembering nothing due to amnesia…"

"But is it a lie?" Fata asked, nervously pulling at her braid.

I ignored her affected skepticism. "Visual hallucinations, Fata! They made her see Death as serious and stately. Here!" I waved the portrait. "This is what she saw in reality."

Fata took another cigarette from the pack. She did not light it but rolled it around her fingers.

"The hypnotic…sessions," she said in fits and starts. "During one of those, Graziella had made her believe that she had thrown the gun in that well. And since yesterday the police really found it there and then…"

"Then Graziella had somehow taken hold of the confessions of the real murderer!" I stood up; I could no longer sit in one place. "Yes, the aunt had avenged her niece for everything those creeps had done to her through the years!"

"These are only assumptions," Fata said, with an unexpected coldness in her voice, and also stood up. "The facts are different. First, Roxanna has confessed that she personally had stolen the gun from the shooting range. Second, she has also confessed to burying the dead with her own hands."

"Good, but since you two are so close, she must've explained to you…"

"No. She has explained nothing to me. Neither about the theft nor about the burials."

"And what about her aunt? What has she told you about her?"

"Again, nothing. She didn't want to talk about her."

All of a sudden, Fata reached out, pulled the portrait from my hand, and ran toward the house-door. I could have caught up with her, but I let her go inside and lock herself in.

"Go away!" she screamed behind the door. "And leave your assumptions out of the girl's mind! Don't you dare tell her—"

"Of course, I'm not going to tell her anything without any evidence on my side. I repeat, I am not Merry Maker. I am not a sadist! But tell me, what does denying my request for help make *you*?"

So, that was it. We started this conversation in screams and ended it in the same fashion. I left, but as I was walking past the house, I heard a noise that made me look back. Fata had opened one of the back windows and was waving a newspaper. I went to her, and she handed it to me, and after I had dropped it into my bag, she stooped her head toward me and told me, "Sirius dyes his hair. It's one of the reasons I consider him the lowest of the murderers around."

She left me no time for questions. She shut the window and drew the curtain.

CHAPTER FORTY-TWO

I was back on the hill with the panoramic view of the ocean, keeping Kuber's murder at the bottom of my attention. Ever since I came to the island, I was doing everything else but not the work I was hired to do, and now I no longer knew what I was hired to do. Maybe indeed to serve as a practice target? Or simply a detail of the scenery?

I looked up at the sky but saw only fig leaves and unripe figs. I had been sitting under the tree for a long time now, browsing the Internet, staring at the low-resolution display of my smartphone. The photos of the aunt I was interested in were also low resolution. On one of them, though, there was a close-up of her face, and I was able to make the comparison. Well, the similarity between this and the heavily painted face was not easy to see, but certain details—like the slightly raised left brow and the specific indentation on the chin—left no doubt in me that she was the prototype of Death in the portrait.

I could not find any interviews with her, but I stumbled upon something Roxanna had said: "No! I do not blame my aunt for not wanting to be associated with me. I understand her completely. I love her, and I will be forever grateful to her, for by giving me shelter, she has saved me..."

She saved her, true, but after that she put the blame for three murders on her, I thought and immediately autocorrected myself. *But is now helping Graziella blame her for the crimes...or Graziella is helping the aunt clear her name...and maybe my grandfather too is part of that name clearing, I mean name-staining business... unless Roxanna is the murderer, although that seems unlikely...*

I was starting to feel as if someone had put a fan inside my head and turned it on. But enough! Teeth clenched, I found my grandfather's number and touched the Call button. "I'm waiting for an explanation from you, old man! Speak!"

The number was busy. I realized that I was up on my feet again. I sat back down. The phone in my hand looked like an insect about to start buzzing and pierce my brain with its sting. I began to sweat; my pulse quickened. Alas, that was the sad truth. Some people are afraid of spiders; others suffer phobias from snakes, enclosed or narrow spaces, heights, and I, at certain moments, experience irrational fear from my grandfather. I knew that it was important to talk to him about many things, but I wished I hadn't called him.

I had to clear my mind before he returned my call. I took Fata's newspaper out of the bag. Yesterday's issue, and on the first page—on the first page staring at me was my face!

"MERRY MAKER'S TRUE IDENTITY REVEALED" was the headline below my picture. And the subheading went further: "FRUSTRATED POLICE FAIL TO ARREST HIM." This was signed only with the initials "B. M.", and this is what followed in the article:

An anonymous tip on the whereabouts of the psychopath remained ignored for seven full hours! Our insider informed us that on Sunday, Merry Maker rented a room in a small hotel on the outskirts of the town X. He checked in under his own name—Miro Kazimirski—and paid in advance for the entire week. On Monday morning, however, when the police finally got to the place, there was not a single trace of him. Had someone warned him or did he slip out at some fortunate moment? That failed police effort has robbed us of the answer to that important question!

Despite the information blackout, we are in our right to make another significant fact known to the public:

On Monday afternoon, the head of the police department received on his e-mail address pictures that prove that Merry Maker is truly the man they had failed to catch in the same morning. "Had the pictures come earlier, we would have reacted to the anonymous message with a greater expediency," says our insider. What we are left with is the dubious hope that from here on, we are going to witness the aforementioned expediency. Otherwise, it would surprise no one if very soon the psychopath—who, by the way, used to be a cop until recently!—reminded us of himself by way of another "laughing" corpse.

Miro Kazimirski is the name to which years ago Merry Maker changed, through the court, his birth name, *Zomirovan Lavrovrodinski*. His argument, met with understanding by those in power, was that his parents left him right after he was born and that this act of change was his way of renouncing them as his parents. It seems we are once again under the blows of a person whose childhood traumas have led to horrifying psychological deformations. But we, the peaceful citizens, find the following circumstance no less horrifying: Only a month ago, this person was carrying a police badge and a gun with which he was able to "legally" murder! This, once again, brings to the fore the problem with the inadequacy of both the psychological screening for police officers and the regular psychological evaluation after that which seem to exist only on paper.

It has to be noted that Merry Maker would have remained an acting cop if he hadn't been stupid enough to hit his boss in the jaw. It was on accounts of battery, manifested in the aforementioned broken jaw, that he was fired on the first of the previous month, the discharge most likely being the factor that unlocked the following murder spree.

According to initial data, with the exception of Merry Maker's parents, whose whereabouts are unknown, his only relative is his maternal grandfather, Nathaniel Stralsky, who is...a psychotherapist! One with a long and successful career, at that. We shall do our best to get in contact with him and find out why he, the professional, could not see the symptoms foreshadowing the satanic metamorphosis that turned his grandson into a serial killer!

Look out for our next issue, which will feature more scandalous revelations.

"We will. Oh yeah, we will!" I said to the wind and looked down at my picture again.

I tried to figure out where the photo was taken, but the zoom and blurry background made it impossible to guess. I could, however, guess roughly how old the damn picture was. I cut my hair that short a week after I was fired—someone had photographed me last month. The month of all of Merry Maker's murders...

I started and quickly turned off the phone. Now I understood why my grandfather did not return my call. He has read, maybe even yesterday, what I had just read. He knows that they are after me and that they could easily find my current location by tracing the call. I wondered how he felt after reading this. Shocked, panicked, puzzled, outraged, and so on. He must have gone through and was probably still going through the entire spectrum of strong negative emotions, central among them being his blind rage at me...unless it was not completely blind and not directed at me solely.

Yes, it must be clear to him too that behind both the anonymous tip on my whereabouts and this absurd article stood some corrupted person Graziella has hired. "Childhood traumas," "psychological deformations," "discharge most likely being the factor that unlocked"—that "B. M." guy used mainly her words. But could the people on the yacht be corrupted also? No! None of them would take the risk of concealing a serial killer. If they are still unaware of the search for me, they soon will be, and the police will soon know that I was on the yacht. The crew will also provide the police with meticulous descriptions of Graziella, Sirius, and Valdo and will testify that in the end these three have taken me somewhere. A someone with the face and profile like Valdo's simply cannot remain unidentified. The cops will run his description through their database and find out who he is, and this will sooner or later lead them to Graziella and from her to the island.

"Sooner or later," I repeated to myself, although I should have said, "Too late."

The fact that I'd held my composure until now was due to either iron nerves or some brain paralysis. Now, though, I was starting to give in to panic. It even crossed my mind that it would be best if I called the police right away: "Hi, this is Miro Kazimirski. I'm on an island, but I have no idea where I am. Find me and come get me, because I am not Merry Maker."

Say they do come and get me. Then what? Of course, that part of the article saying that the chief of police has received pictures that prove that Merry Maker and I are the same person was a bluff. Although my "confessions" during that confession session have most likely been recorded by Graziella and were waiting to be used against me. They were the foundation of my trap. How could I refute my own words about the murders "I" have committed? And who is going to believe me that the series of murders has ended not because I am already under arrest but because the real Merry Maker has read the lying article and has decided to leave me behind bars until my final breath by simply changing his "style"?

I didn't call the police or my grandfather. I put the phone in my pocket and the bag with the paper in it into a hole in the ground by the fig tree. After so many "confessions," I could at least keep the impressions from the article only to myself.

CHAPTER FORTY-THREE

As I was unlocking the door, I saw Graziella, Danko, and Sirius file out from behind the bungalow.

"Your grandfather," Graziella began, "has asked me to tell you that he's not sending his regards to you."

"Thank you," I replied. "Tell him I'm not sending mine to him either."

"Good." She held out a hand. "Now give me your phone."

"Give it to her; give it to her," Sirius grunted, "and tell *me* whose phone did you throw from the yacht!"

He and Danko were now standing too close to me, breaching my personal space. I pushed them away, took the phone from the pocket, and handed it over to Graziella.

"It's more comfortable inside," she said and went into the bungalow.

We followed her. She took the chair, and Danko and Sirius sat on the bed. There was now no place for me to sit, but I preferred standing. Graziella switched on the phone.

"There's no connection here, right?" Sirius asked her nervously.

"Yes," she confirmed and then took her time with the phone's settings menu. "Thank God!" She sighed. "He hasn't talked to anyone during the two days he's been here. And tried to call no one except his grandfather."

"And no one has tried to call him?" Sirius wondered.

"Yes."

"What if he has deleted all calls, incoming or outgoing?" Danko asked.

"If he hasn't deleted the one to his grandfather, he hasn't deleted anything." Sirius guessed right and turned to Graziella. "Does it come with a pre-installed GPS?"

"No," she replied.

"Has he been using the Internet on it?" He was not stopping.

"I don't know." She shrugged. "The history setting is not on. Have you, Miro?"

I shrugged too. "If I told you that I haven't, would you believe me?"

"Actually, it doesn't matter." Sirius changed his mind. "Even if you have been online, they won't be able to find you, because that ancient thing you're using has no GPS."

"*Who*? *Who* won't be able to find me?" I raised my voice as if bewilderment had defeated my good manners. "Are you implying someone's looking for me?"

"We're not implying; we know," Graziella said to me. "It's the police, Miro! I told you about the hotel ambush when we were on the yacht. But don't worry. Your grandfather informed me immediately about your reckless attempt to get in contact with him, and I immediately ordered an associate of mine to take quick trace-erasing measures."

Associate or, in other words, some richly sponsored master hacker.

"How thoughtful of you," I said, apathetically.

"How? Very thoughtful, I must say. *Much* more than you can imagine."

"Miro," Sirius began, his excitement insincere, "you should know that a newspaper has run a very unflattering article on you. We didn't show it to you because we didn't want you to get upset. But it's time you realized that you are safe only here."

"Only here!" Graziella echoed him to add weight to his words and nodded at Danko, urging him, who stood up and took from the back pocket of his pants a newspaper page folded to the size of a napkin. He unfolded it and handed it to me in such a way that the first thing I saw was the crumpled picture of myself.

"Yesterday, when they delivered us the mower," he started explaining, "the pilots brought a couple of copies. But I am warning you: Maya must never see this article!"

"I am warning you too," Graziella backed him up. "Or she will start fantasizing that any moment now an entire army of cops could come here. And she's been having nightmares without such thoughts."

"I don't think it would be just a fantasy," I objected, after pretending to run my eyes over the article. "The people on the yacht's words would be enough for the cops to find the right direction in no time: Valdo and then you and then the island."

"Valdo and me, yes. But not the island."

"I don't think so. Your plane could easily be tracked down."

"Yes, but why would they? All documents say it belongs to a company that has nothing to do with me." She winked and went on. "I already told you how thoughtful I am. Now, I am going to support this with an example: Each and every connection I have from here to wherever, including to your grandfather, goes through a labyrinth filled with complex obstacles. The island's coordinates are almost impossible to locate, and the few people who know them would never risk divulging such information. I will announce to everyone the island's location in a month, after we're done with the experiment. But believe me, Miro, you will be as safe then as you are now!"

"That is, only if you're not causing trouble," Sirius specified, which in translation meant, "If you don't try to stop us causing trouble to you."

"Was that a threat?" I asked him.

"Of course it was," Graziella replied, instead of him. "Threats are a useful tool for mobilizing mind activity."

She put my phone into her purse, and accompanied by the two pests, she left the bungalow.

CHAPTER FORTY-FOUR

I moored myself to the bed and spent about half an hour there, wandering until exhaustion through all sorts of guesses, suspicions, and worries. I did not get far, and it only reminded me of my grandfather's offensive words: "It is high time my grandson took at least one intellectual risk." As if up to that day I'd stored my brain in a jar on some shelf.

I went to the bathroom. I drank water and then put my head under the strong water flow. After that, I shook the water off like a wet dog and, by association, decided that I had to also shake all thoughts that were not directly connected to Kuber's murder. After all, that murder was the reason I had found myself between the rock and the hard place that were my grandfather and Graziella. With that diabolical article, however, Graziella had just upped the game. Now the question was, Would she act in such an aggressive and complicated fashion if she weren't Kuber's murderer?

Of course, the correct answer was *I don't know.* But my hypothesis rises more convincing:

Kuber becomes more and more inconvenient for Graziella's needs because he could have one of his fits of insanity during the trial. So she decides to act more drastically. She pushes him from the rock and then moves the body to make it look like an accident. My grandfather, however, remains suspicious and insists on an investigation into the case. Graziella, having no other choice, agrees to that, and afterward it is her and not him who suggests they should hire me for the job. She brings me here as Merry Maker and thus achieves a double effect. First, she puts me into a situation that makes it impossible for me to do my job by doing X. And second, even if I were to find evidence that she had killed Kuber, her evidence against me, as the Merry Maker, would be enough to keep my mouth shut. I'll have to be as silent as a fish, because she has recorded me confessing to four sadistic murders. And the cherry on top of that foul-tasting cake is that these recordings have also my short but colorful accounts of how my grandfather used to torture and bury me alive when I was a child...

"I'll be damned!" I squeezed my head with both hands, wanting to crush it. "I'll be damned, damned...a fool!"

I thought I had reached rock bottom, but soon logic showed me I was wrong.

The current hostility between my grandfather and Graziella could not be a result only of Kuber's suspicious death. There must be other reasons, and whatever they were, Graziella now had the advantage. She was going to keep him on his knees with those recordings until his last day, and since he was too proud, this would not go for long.

Maybe I also would not last for long. If Graziella decided that it would be more convenient to her if I was dead, she could easily persuade someone from the group into carrying out the task. And later, to the cops, she would say, "My colleague's grandson made a full confession here, but this crushed his spirits. He ran from us, and when we found him...we could not put him back together. He had turned the mower on, and..."

I laughed. Why? Once again, the right answer was *I don't know.*

CHAPTER FORTY-FIVE

I was so glad to see Maya with the grazing animals. The field was where I could ask her more questions about Kuber, with no risk of someone eavesdropping on us. I walked to her, almost melting at the sight of her carefully brushing the bay stallion's mane.

"He's beautiful, isn't he?" She welcomed me with a smile. "Come on; grab that brush. Pretend that you're helping me!"

I picked up the brush from the grass and slid it down the smooth back of the stallion. Still brushing his mane, Maya looked at me.

"Now listen. I happened to overhear today a conversation between Sirius and Frant, and what they were saying was that there was an article on you as Merry Maker in some newspaper yesterday!"

"Well, since we're not the same person..." I didn't know what to say. "I mean, there's nothing to worry about," I finished, mumbling.

"There is, Miro! The reasons are many! The pilots brought two copies of the issue. Fata took one, and the other...I think Graziella's hiding it from me on purpose! Maybe there's something in it you're not supposed to read, and she suspects that if I read it, I'd tell you. She knows we're partners!"

"No, Maya. She gave me the article but warned me not to show it to you. She's worrying that you might start having even worse nightmares, because...because Merry Maker is described as a terrifying being there."

"Ugh!" She got angry. "Everyone here is still thinking of me as a child. A scared, teary-eyed child! But that's OK. It's better for us this way. With my help, you are going to find out who killed Kuber, and then Graziella will realize how unfairly she's been underestimating me."

"Exactly." I nodded, happy that our conversation was moving in the right direction. "But to do that, we must first focus on Kuber, the person. And more precisely, on his psychopathic outbursts. What were they like?"

"He was crying," Maya snapped at me. "Crying! But if you're implying that I have similar outbursts—"

"Come on! How could I imply something like that when I just found out what his were like?"

"That's true. I got confused," she admitted.

"That's OK," I said kindly. "No matter how confused you get, you will never be as confused as me. And Kuber...what was he crying for?"

"His mother. He was only four when she strangled his little sister. She thought that she was sleeping, but she was actually committing the crime before his eyes. He has spoken about this only with us, during one of the confession sessions here. It was here that he found out about his mother's motive, because Graziella arranged an exhumation of the body. The analysis showed that the father of the child was not her husband. That terrible woman had chosen to murder her baby instead of to live in constant fear that someday her unfaithfulness would be revealed."

"Such a horrific story," I murmured.

"Very. Just like everyone here's story. But Kuber cracked up for two reasons. First, he started asking himself if he had said to his mother that he had seen her, whether she would have murdered him too. And second, because he couldn't bear the fact that besides the murderer of her own baby, she was also a licentious woman. In his own way, he was an extremely moral man, Miro."

"Yeah, right! And if you ask Frant, he was also sentimental, 'full of love,' meek, delicate…"

"Why, yes!" Maya confirmed with excitement. "That's how he was!"

I could tell from her expression that she was about to start defending the deceased psycho with passion, so I hurried to stop her.

"But tell me, Maya, if he was so decent and sensitive, isn't suicide the most probable cause of his death?"

"No. That's out of the question! He had big plans for the future. He had decided to invest his five million in the construction of a one-of-a-kind asylum for abused children and animals. Also, he wouldn't have killed himself dressed like that: with nothing on but shorts. Out of the question!" she repeated, and the stallion snorted, telling us that that was enough brushing for today.

We let him move away from us and sat down on the grass. The two cows paid no attention to us, but the three sheep came and pushed their snouts into our faces. Maya took a packet with candies from her working-apron pocket and fed the sheep before offering one to me. I declined.

"By the way," she began, tucking the packet back in, "I started suspecting that he was murdered after

I saw how he was dressed. The murderer must've woken him up with the lie that something terrible was happening there, by the rocks, and that they must go immediately and help. Otherwise he wouldn't have gone out like that. He was very self-conscious of his body, Miro. He was ashamed of how hairy he was, and would always wear long pants and long-sleeved shirts."

"Aha," I said, "so that is why his bathrobe is so long."

"Yes. He didn't own a single short-sleeved T-shirt. And he would never go to the beach with us. He would swim by himself in the bay, late in the afternoon. But he thought that for a man, hair removal is a shameful procedure. What do you think?"

"Me? Well...I've never thought about that. But from what I saw of him in the freezer room, he really was quite...hirsute."

The moment I said "the freezer room," Maya flinched.

"He's so lonely there too! I feel so sorry for him. I want you to find out who murdered him!"

"Even if I did find out, what difference would it make? You told me this morning that to the rest of the world, the 'accident' will always remain an accident."

"Yes. But that doesn't mean that the murderer gets to walk away unpunished. Graziella will find a way to make him pay; be sure of that."

"Unless she is the murderer," I said, and Maya looked at me as if she had just realized she's been talking to a moron the whole time. "I meant, Kuber's psychopathic outbursts," I started explaining. "If Graziella was afraid he might have such during the trial…"

"Afraid? The opposite of that! She was hoping he would have one during the trial."

"But wasn't it her ambition to have healed everyone here with her psychotherapy by the end? To make everyone, including Kuber, normal? And if he…" I bit my lip. My version about Graziella's motive seemed worthless.

"Yes, what was expected of him was that he would start crying inconsolably," Maya assured me. "It would've been another proof that she had truly normalized him. Repentance, shock from what was done, sorrow for the victims, unbearable guilt, and so on. Everyone would have read his outburst as saying all those things, and they would've been right."

"Now I see," I sighed. "Kuber would have been the trump card of her therapeutic achievements."

"He will be, Miro. During the trial, Graziella will play the videos she has made of his outbursts and of everything he has confessed to us. Thus, although too late, his mother would be exposed. And it would become clear that she, not Kuber, is to blame for the murders committed by him, because by killing his little sister, she had driven him crazy in very early childhood. Oh yes, the terrible woman will go to jail at an old age! And will die there!"

Glancing at her watch, Maya quickly stood up. She nudged me. "Come on! It's almost half past four. Rehearsal time."

"Is it?" I raised my heavy head and looked at her. "But you didn't tell me…if you're sure it wasn't Graziella, who do you think has done it?"

"I suspect no one." She spread her arms. "Every time I start to think about someone, they seem innocent to me. But I have an idea, partner. I am going to help you by suggesting you as a prosecutor!"

"You are?" I asked without thinking, and one of the sheep came very close and peered into my eyes. "Prosecutor, you say…"

"Yes, yes!" The kid showed me an impish grin. She called, "Bye, Doro!" to the stallion and ran toward the house.

Looking at her now—a thin girl with orange hair and wearing a grass-green apron—I could not help but see a dandelion prancing on the green meadow, freed of its roots.

CHAPTER FORTY-SIX

Again, nothing showed that the place was a veranda or that it was still day outside. The thick wine-red curtains covered the French windows, and the only light came from the two weak lamps placed on both ends of the long ebony table.

"You should go to the wine cellar," I said. "It's a more suitable place for your vampire gatherings."

"We're not gathered here to party," Frant objected inadequately.

"I know, I know." I nodded at him. "You're here to rehearse once again your roles as the most innocent murderers the world has ever seen during the trial. But why that fear of daylight? What draws you to this artificial dusk?"

"I draw the curtains before each such gathering here," Graziella joined us. "But the room is wonderfully furnished—money was no object. The furniture is magnificent. The paintings are priceless. The plants are of the rarest kinds and brightest colors. In fact, the only black thing here is the table we're sitting at."

"So? What's the use of all that if it's drowning in dusk?"

"It's therapeutic, Miro. Life offers astonishing things only to those who are able to see them. And how is someone supposed to see them if their mind is tainted by dark memories, hatred, lack of faith...yes! Until you have cleared your minds, you will know that there are lovely things nearby, but to you, they will be but mere colorless silhouettes. And you would reach out in vain to grab them, as you sit...around the 'black table.' This is what the surroundings here symbolize."

"Quite pretentious." I laughed, and Maya quickly chimed in.

"You're bickering again! But I have an idea!" She turned at the others. "I say we use his potential for bickering and choose him for the role of the prosecutor!"

"That's a good idea," Graziella commended her.

"It is?" She grew more enthusiastic. "Come on, Miro! The nastier the questions you come up with, the greater the favor you would do us. Because it's going to be just like this at the trial."

"All right but no questions about Valdo," Roxanna said.

"Or Kuber," Sirius added.

"Yes," Graziella agreed. "Let's leave those who are not present in peace."

Maya could not hide her disappointment. It seemed she was truly hoping that by suggesting me as the prosecutor, she would help the investigation.

"You gave yourself away," Roxanna whispered. A moment later, she repeated with a scream, "You gave yourself awaaay!"

This surprised no one but me. And I was the only one who seemed to think she had meant Maya, while the rest turned their heads in the direction of Graziella.

"Do explain, dear," she urged her gently. "How did I give myself away?"

"*Let's leave those who are not present in peace.* You think so?" Roxanna tried to stand up, swayed, and slumped back into the chair. "To you, the absence of Valdo is the same as Kuber's! You're going to throw him to the crocodiles too!"

"What crocodiles?" I asked, and, of course, no one answered.

"You should be ashamed, Roxy!" Sirius looked outraged. "You know that Valdo is in the isolator by his own will. We took him there alive, and we're bringing him back from there alive!"

Roxanna stifled a sob and fell silent.

"What crocodiles?" I asked again.

"Large ones," Sirius replied. "Giant and gluttonous."

"But you told me there were no predators on the island."

"Well, there might be some for you especially." He smirked. "But if you ask me, the laguna is part of the ocean, not the island."

I nodded, and wasting no time for a pause, I provoked him with what I considered to be only a sarcastic fantasy on Fata's side: "You dye your hair. I wonder why."

Graziella flinched as if stung, while the others seemed merely amused.

"You've got a trained eye; I give you that," Sirius admitted. "You might fare better as a hair stylist than a prosecutor."

"Why do you dye your hair, *Sirius*?" I insisted. "Or is it a secret connected to your true name?"

"Nonsense! My hair got white too early. I don't like looking like an old man at thirty-four, so I started using hair dye."

"You should try some of Maya's," Frant suggested in jest. "The blue one, for example, will go perfectly well with your freckles."

That was followed by laughter from all sides, including Sirius's. It didn't take much to make these murderers laugh—this was not the first time I'd noticed that. But anyway. I was glad that Roxanna had calmed down, because I was hoping to disturb the healer, or maybe the pseudohealer, of her amnesia through her.

I began pompously. "Roxanna, I am asking you as a prosecutor, does the fact that you've finally overcome your amnesia mean that your statement that you'd stolen the gun only for self-defense is not true?"

"No. I still stand by my words. Ever since my childhood years, I've been living in constant fear. The gun under my pillow was helping me fight that fear."

"But your aunt's house is quite isolated. Wasn't it more reasonable for you to sleep on the second floor because of your fears?"

"For a long time, my bedroom was upstairs, next to my aunt's. I moved downstairs when her boyfriend started spending the night with her."

"Did she ask you to move downstairs?"

"Yes. Otherwise things could get awkward...you know."

"But otherwise the new arrangement was far from awkward and even convenient, for you didn't have to drag the dead bodies down the stairs, right?"

I saw that I had succeeded at making Graziella uncomfortable.

"I object!" she said, advocate-like.

"All right. We accept the statement that until yesterday Roxanna has had no memory of the murders. But how could she not remember how and when she got in touch with her torturers? Not remember what she has told them to lure them into her bedroom? Is such a thing possible?"

"Is such a thing possible?" echoed Roxanna.

"Yes, dear, it is absolutely possible." Graziella moved her chair closer to hers and embraced her shoulders. "Yesterday you remembered where you had thrown the gun only because I asked you the question while you were under stress. You were in *shock* after the video of Valdo. But everything else might remain buried deep into your mind. As I've explained to you before, dissociative amnesia is characterized by lasting loss of memories of events that have been particularly traumatic for the individual—"

"Enough," Danko said all of a sudden.

"You're right." Graziella smiled at him. "You've heard it all before. Come on, dear; go to my study and open the dictionary on *dissociative amnesia*. You might also want to read again the entry on *selective memory loss*."

There was no use objecting to this; Roxanna flew toward the door like a just-freed bird.

"And we can continue," I said, although I had no desire to. "Let me get this clear: During the trial, each one of you shall reveal their true story, just as it was in reality. Am I right?"

"Yes, you are," Frant replied. "We shall say only the truth and nothing but the truth. Hand on the Bible."

"You especially have already lied in the most malignant manner," I reminded him. "You blamed your father—your dead father—for sexually abusing you. So now you can even *sit* on the Bible if you want to, but that won't win you my trust."

"I don't think so," he objected. "I will win it easily...by showing you my butt, Mr. Prosecutor."

"Oh, how naughty you are," I said.

"Again, I disagree. I am serious. After leaving town, I sent my mother a letter: 'Pray to God the cops don't catch me! Because if they do, I'll show them the scars your cigarettes left on my butt!' And when I returned after ten years, I found out that she had kept the letter. I took it from her. I still keep it. The date on it proves that I was underage at that time, and the contents show clearly why she had decided not to inform the police about my disappearance, despite what the law says—"

"She's not going to get away with it!" Maya exclaimed. "She will have to confess that she left the scars, not his father."

"She told everyone in the neighborhood that I was with her parents." Frant sobbed. "But no one cared anyway. I was invisible, both at school and on the streets."

"Enough drama." I scowled. "It's simple logic. If the story you've been telling in the past is vastly different from the true story, then you weren't insane—"

"If I weren't insane, I wouldn't have wasted money and energy mummifying those old strangers. And if I hadn't met our neighbor on the Christmas night my mother threw me out barefoot and almost naked, I would have kept my sanity. I would have kept my sanity if *he* had not embraced me! If he hadn't taken me to his miserable home, if he had not given me warmth and love...yes, that's what makes my case unique, Mr. Prosecutor. Not evil—kindness made me lose my mind! It was like a bright light suddenly scorching the eyes of a blind man who has just started to see. A man born blind, darkness the only thing he has seen!"

"That's good for a fairy tale," I told him. "But the truth is that ten years have passed since your first meeting with *kindness*—your neighbor, I mean—and during all those years, you've never shown signs of madness."

"Yes, but only because I thought that *he* was alive. That I would go back to him and make him happy...and when I found out that he had been dead the whole time, his grave unmarked and lost

forever, something stretched so thin in my soul…
stretched and tore itself free!"

Frant looked around, squinting eyes against
the dusk enveloping us, as if hoping to find among
the colorless silhouettes and lovely things around
that lost piece of his soul. A tiny man. Dressed like
a dandy, perfectly coiffured, his goatee trimmed
pedantically…droll? Pitiful? Alas, he looked nothing like that.

"Oh, I've been crazy, believe me," he said, a
note of astonishment in his voice. "And I continued to be crazy after eight whole years of psychiatric treatment. It was only here that I healed. She,
Graziella, healed me. No neuroleptics, no antide-
pressants, no…no medicines at all. She healed me
by helping me bring my emotions to light. Bring
them before my own eyes! And I realized that
there is something good in me, too…but it's been
suppressed, crushed, smashed for so long, that it
had mutated into…I didn't want to murder the
old men; I only wanted to give them the gift of a
worthy death. They were so poor and alone in the
winter nights…"

"Which, Mr. Prosecutor," Graziella said, with
hate in her voice, "is the state's fault! It is to blame
for the abused children and for the old people
thrown on the *garbage heap* to rot! It is to blame for
these poor human beings here! It is to blame that

they, robbed of protection and human kindness, have become murderers. This is what we want to prove at this trial!"

"That's banal," I mumbled, staring as if hypnotized into her round and sparkling eyes. "It's always the state to blame for someone's troubles. That's a very banal generalization."

"It is banal because it is true!" Graziella rose, putting both hands on the table, and said, this time not to me but to some imaginary audience, "The greatest truths are always banal. Another such truth is that you, all of you, are the state…and you're all part of this terrifyingly soulless monster of a mass!"

CHAPTER FORTY-SEVEN

After failing to shine in my role as the prosecutor, I stepped back, and the rehearsal continued in my presence but without my participation. Actually, being there showed me nothing new. I learned nothing, although I listened carefully. Mostly, it was Graziella who talked, usually emphasizing the fact that during the trial—which she many times called the "megatrial"—no one can afford to say even the tiniest of lies. *Our weapon is going to be frankness. Painful, wounding frankness! Take your hearts out and let everyone see your suffering, dark and heavy like clots of blood!* And more words in the same key and coming from the same inexhaustive pit of pathos. I watched her, somewhat charmed. There was fire, but also ice, in this woman. And madness...probably larger than that of her patients.

I have to note that while all the others shared her pathos with words and gestures of agreement, Danko remained silent, glancing in boredom from time to time at his watch. In the end, he patted the face of the watch with a finger and announced that it was 6:00 p.m. sharp.

"Brother!" I know it sounds unbelievable, but he said this to me. "I choose you."

I was just about to ask, "For what?" but then remembered the compulsory walks in pairs from the schedule and only said, "Thank you."

"I commend you!" Frant clapped. "After the incident yesterday, the one with the mower, you are now acting like men of dignity. No hard feelings."

"I am proud of you!" Graziella was also lavish of praise, while Danko did nothing to hide his boredom.

We nodded at each other and hurried toward the door, accompanied by more clapping. It would have been funny if it wasn't so idiotic.

"There's not much to rehearse these days," Danko said, after we left the house and headed for...somewhere. "We've discussed every detail, and now we gather only to listen to such pompous speeches. Same as in confession hour. We repeat the same, yet we never stop being *emotional*, as if we're hearing it for the first time."

"Sounds dull," I said. "Where are we going now?"

"To the beach, but we'll take another path. I want to show you a spot. A spot of someone's death!"

I was so happy to hear that—finally, I was about to see where exactly was Kuber's body found. Yet I remained on my guard, and when we reached the path, I let Danko before me. I didn't want him to surprise me for a second time with his karate skills.

The path was getting steeper and rockier. I thought I knew why we had not chosen the shorter way—around the house and then down to the beach with the elevator. *He wants to show me the place secretly from the others*, I told myself, but when we got to the beach, he led me in the opposite direction from the foot of the rock from which Kuber had fallen.

Here, the rocks weren't much different from those at the other end of the bay, because they formed an almost symmetrical horseshoe around it. We walked past them for no more than twenty steps, with seagulls, cliff swallows, and geese flying and squawking above our heads.

"Wonderful!" Danko outyelled them. "It's still well lighted."

As it turned out, there was a recess in the rocks near the path, and this recess was our destination. It was shallow and low, sandy on the inside and with one big flat stone right in the center. Danko stooped and sneaked inside, kneeled before the stone, and started pointing it out to me, his face twisted by a grimace full of suggestion.

"What?" I asked him, peeking in his direction.

"This." He continued pointing at the stone. "He was bleeding more than a pig in a slaughterhouse."

"Here?" I mumbled in shock. "He died here?"

"Isn't it obvious?" Danko raised his eyebrows.

I walked stooping to him, and then, getting down on my knees, I stared at the stone. Now I could see that its surface was much darker than that of the reddish rocks and the reddish sand. I also saw that the sand around it was darker than anywhere else in the recess. Blood! Shed and dried up a long time ago.

"It rains frequently on the island," Danko said, "but here everything remains untouched. That's why he chose it. He wanted his blood to leave a trace—"

"Dammit! Are you talking about the Japanese guy?"

"Of course. No one else has committed suicide here, to my knowledge. For now."

"But why did you bring me here? Why are you showing me this place?"

"He was about sixty, short and thin," Danko mumbled. "But he was bleeding more than a pig!"

"You've already said that. So?"

"Soo…I expected more enthusiasm from you. Desire to think on the case together. I was hoping you would support me in this."

"Man, come to your senses!" I urged him. "How could I support you in something I know nothing about?"

"OK, listen. I think that the Japanese man had not slashed his wrists. He had committed hara-kiri!"

Still kneeling by the stone, Danko puffed his chest and began enacting the ritual suicide. He swung his imaginary sword, inflicted a "stab wound" on his stomach, and then made a cross section from left to right. He pulled out the "blade" and drove it back in, this time following it with a longitudinal section—downward. I watched his pantomime, thinking that it was coming to an end. But he got carried away: It seemed he had decided to mimic to the smallest detail the slow and painful death of the "samurai." His eyes rolled up, and their irises disappeared deep into their sockets; only the whites were visible now, two Ping-Pong balls below the eyebrows. His body shook in convulsions, and his mouth started foaming…

I reached a hand and squeezed his neck.

"Hey!" I yelled in his ear.

"What?" His irises returned to their place. "What did you say?"

"Nothing," I said and drew my hand from his neck.

"But you can draw so much blood only by disembowelment, right?"

I bent toward the stone again.

"Indeed," I mumbled, "a lot of blood must have poured over it to make it so dark in color."

"So you'll tell the others that you also don't believe Ichiro has slit his wrists? None of them wanted to come here with me to see for themselves. But you will corroborate that he had, in fact, committed hara-kiri here, right?"

My opinion was leaning toward something else, but that did not stop me from replying with a yes. After we'd stepped out of the recess, I clarified. "Yes, but only if you show me exactly where Kuber fell."

"No problem. See that piece of rock over there?" His arm stretched out, fingers closed, shaped like the head of a spear. "The one shaped like this? With the sharp point…you see?"

"Yes." I nodded after a moment.

"Well, that's where we found Kuber. If he had fallen just five or ten inches to the right, that thing would have skewered him like roast chicken."

This was followed by a cackle that made me speed up our parting.

"Tell me in a couple of words what was that nonsense about the crocodiles?"

"I will. Our plan is to defrost Kuber in the end and feed him to them."

I stopped his next cackle by kicking him in the ankle.

"Be careful!" I warned him. "One more cackle...and I'll slit your mouth from ear to ear!"

"Just like you did with the other four, eh, Merry Maker? Ear to ear?" He livened up even more. No wonder he had spent ten years in a mental hospital. I thought he should still be there.

"Where are the crocodiles, and why do you want to feed them...Kuber's defrosted body?"

"We have no other choice. How would Graziella explain keeping his death a secret and his body in the freezer room for two months? That's the only way, Merry Maker. We will lie that he was in the isolator but decided to leave it early, thus becoming part of the crocodiles' menu."

"Where is the isolator?" I asked, in utter bewilderment.

"It's in the laguna. Over there! There...there... there..." Danko lay down on the sand, looked up at the sky, and started singing: "Dear Lord, give me patience, give me, giiive—"

"Patience for what?" I leaned over him. "For what and until when?"

"Until tomorrow, Lord, until tomorrow evening! Although I don't know yet what fooor. Because, because…do, mi, fa, fa, re, do, ti…tiii, tiii…"

I left him like this without any compunction. He was sick, yes, very sick, but I wouldn't feel sorry for him if I saw him dead.

CHAPTER FORTY-EIGHT

I slowly walked around the large piece of rock but found nothing even hinting that Kuber had smashed his skull there. I wasn't expecting to find anything, actually. About forty days had passed since then; rains had fallen, washing everything away. But before all that, birds had been here, pecking at the chunks of brain tissue and blood clots among the stones.

I looked up and over at the many nests in the cracks of the rocks. Soon it would be sunset, but most of these were empty. The birds were still hunting about the bay. I could see them darting, mere dots above the open ocean in the distance. I could see those voracious, screaming birds everywhere, but in my imagination they were all converged at one point, right here, swallowing tiny morsels of brain, swallowing tiny bits of memory belonging to a serial murderer—and to a four-year-old child who was pretending to be asleep while watching his mother press against the face of his little sister with his own, bird-embroidered pillow.

I focused my attention to the rock he had been pushed from. He was walking along the edge, step by careful step, peeking down. Looking for something but what? And was that something, if it existed, on one of the jutting pieces of rock or down here where I was now? Maybe the murderer had taken it; maybe it was the reason for the murder. Upon seeing that Kuber was looking for it, the murderer panicked and pushed him over the edge impulsively...

My mind was sinking into fantasies, so I started thinking about Maya's much more logical assumption: *The murderer must've woken him up with the lie that something terrible was happening there, by the rocks, and that they must immediately go and help. Otherwise he wouldn't have gone out like that.* If that was true, then it wasn't an impulsive murder. It was premeditated; it had a motive. What could it be? And why had Roxanna seen only Kuber through her window? Where was the murderer at that time?

I headed for the elevator, digging my sneakers into the sand, tripping. My thoughts also tripped each other up, getting more and more entangled in the conviction that I had seen enough to know who the murderer was. And that this murderer was not Graziella and neither Danko nor any of the other "usual suspects."

CHAPTER FORTY-NINE

I took a seat opposite Sirius in the dining room on purpose, and as I ate my dinner, my eyes rarely strayed from his hair. It was blond with a red tinge and didn't look dyed.

"Masterfully done," I said at some point. "Have your eyebrows gone white too?"

"You can see they haven't," he mumbled and blushed—something typical for natural blondes.

"I see they have the same color as your hair," I said. "So I assumed you must be dying them too."

He clutched his fork, revealing his desire to stab me with it. His hand was covered in freckles, but they weren't as many as those adorning his face.

"Why aren't you using a sunscreen?" I went on, tactlessly. "Take example from Graziella. She's also a blonde, but she protects her face from the sun, and the result is clearly visible: no freckles on her face."

"Thank you for the compliment," Graziella hissed. "But don't you think you're going too far?"

"Not yet," I replied. "But before leaving this place, I'll make sure to go far."

No one seemed to like my promise, because it raised the question as to what shape exactly my going too far would take.

"Take it easy, Merry Maker," Frant mumbled.

"You think he's not taking it easy?" Maya came to my defense and then smiled widely at me. "It dawned on me that I haven't told you what I plan to do with my millions. Right after the end of the trial, while all eyes are still on us, I'll open a restaurant!"

"A super restaurant," Roxanna corrected her, with a smile.

"Two times super!" Maya took it to the extreme. "It's won't be a big place, but it's going to be shockingly expensive, because I will be the chef."

"That's a…bold idea," I said. "You have an impressive culinary talent, but your business most likely won't be successful unless you change your name."

"Ah, Miro, you don't get it! It doesn't matter if I have culinary talent or not. What matters is my name. At the Poisoner's—I'll call it that. Main dish on the menu? Éclairs."

"Hmm…I hope you're joking."

"No, man! I am absolutely serious."

"And you believe there will be clients?"

"Of course there will be," Graziella assured me energetically. "There are more empty-headed, bored rich people than you can imagine. It's why the restaurants that serve the fugu fish are always full despite the scandalous price."

"Fugu, fuguuu!" Danko started singing. "The poison of just one is enough to kill forty people. But that doesn't stop those maniacs. They eat it, gorge on it, knowing well that if the cook had not prepared it the right way, they might die at any bite."

"Now you see, right?" Maya reached and poured more wine into my glass. "The clients in my restaurant will know that they might die from my delicacies…if the one 'preparing' me now had made a mistake."

"Maya!" Graziella pretended to look offended. "You think I'm a cook?"

"Why not?" Roxanna said quietly. "I already feel like you've fried my brain…or stirred my soul into a stew!"

"Off topic!" Danko told them sharply. "We must finish the conversation about the fish. Fugu! Because…" He stared theatrically at me. "According to the ancient *Japanese* tradition, if a client dies from that dangerous delicacy, the cook is obliged to commit hara-kiri right away."

It was my time to pierce him with my eyes. "I can see where you're going, but as far as I know, the local Japanese man…"

"Dammit, Merry Maker! I'm not saying that Ichiro had something to do with fugu fish."

"What are you saying then?" I asked kindly.

"I'm saying…giving you a hint, helping you *remember* what you're supposed to say now."

"Oh, you want to talk hara-kiri again?"

Boredom covered every face in the room like ash. It seemed they had grown tired of that particular topic.

"Yes, yes!" Danko exclaimed and stretched out his arms imploringly. "Tell them how we went to the recess today and that you agree with me!"

"I am sorry, but I cannot agree with such nonsense," I replied. "I think the guy had simply slit his wrists."

"No! He had committed hara-kiri!"

"You're wrong. But what does it matter—"

"No, I'm not wrong! And it does matter; it matters *incredibly* much! How can you not see? The guy is dead, but the ancient tradition is alive! He has brought it to life with his death!"

His eyes grew clouded, but was it just tears or another fit of insanity? I had no intention to wait for the answer—I could see it in the silence and the tense expressions of the others.

I stood up, and Danko stretched his arms out to me, although there was nothing imploring about the gesture now.

"You saw the blood; you saw how much of it there is!" I could hear the threat gurgling and boiling in his throat. "And when you saw it, you promised me…"

I walked around the table. The least I could do was to fulfill my promise about going too far. I stopped behind Sirius's back, and while his eyes remained fixed on the ticking bomb that was Danko, I took a better look at his hair. It looked lighter in color and without the red tinge at the roots. It seemed it had really gone white prematurely. To be sure, however, I had to make the comparison under the brighter and natural light of the day outside. Tomorrow, when the sun would be at its highest.

I wound a lock of hair around my finger and pulled sharply, tearing it the moment Sirius jumped from his chair and turned around. His wide-open blue eyes held more fear than anger. I took a step to the side and then another one toward the table. I grabbed a napkin, wrapped the lock in it, and put it in my pocket.

"Good night," I said.

CHAPTER FIFTY

Shortly before sunrise, the weather was cloudy and chilly, and I—just like Kuber on that morning—was naked to the waist, dressed only in shorts, socks, and sneakers. To warm up, I ran the distance from mine to Roxanna's bungalow. I called her name, and a minute later she appeared behind the window bars. She looked sleepy, but my appearance quickly woke her up fully.

"Tell me," I began without a preamble, "was Kuber wearing a hat?"

She said nothing, only kept looking at me. I must note, though I know that's not the place for it, that for a woman who had just woken up, she looked gorgeous.

"Well?" I urged her.

"Yes!" she confirmed, surprised. "He was."

"What about down at the foot of the rock?"

"He wasn't with a hat there. It must have come off during his fall and the wind took it some-where…how did you know?"

Because of the feather in his hair and because he had fallen backward and because of the fact that he had no short-sleeved shirts.

I decided to give her the shorter answer. "I'm a cop, Roxanna. I'm used to building up stable, logical constructions using facts."

I waved good-bye at her before she had the chance to ask for a more meaningful answer and walked away quickly. I reached the house, walked around it, and headed for the rock Kuber fell from. I leaned over the precipice and soon realized why Kuber had had to change his point of view, taking step after step along the edge. From such height, the piece of rock down there that he most likely had used as a reference point was not as clearly outlined as it was when looked at from the beach. It was lost in the chaos of other pieces of rock, be-cause from here its specific shape of a spearhead was unrecognizable.

Well, I found it in the end, but as I peered down, my nerves jittered, and the bird's cries only made things worse. Clouds were gathering in the sky, be-coming thicker and darker at an alarming rate. I had to do it before the rain, or I could find myself in a most unfortunate situation: sticking like a fly to the almost vertical and now-slippery rock.

I lay down on my stomach and crawled forward, stopping after my chest reached the very end of the rock. I could see better from there, and what I saw was that this was a good spot for descending. I also realized that Kuber, despite being "full of love," was not a complete madman. The flat, peaklike ledge was less than six feet below me, and reaching it didn't seem like the risky undertaking I had thought it to be. There were plenty of jutting rocks that could serve as steps.

Still on my stomach, I started turning my body until my legs were hanging over the precipice. I began climbing down, my feet searching blindly to find purchase on the next jutting rock. I found a crack, not a shallow one, which I thought I could use. I shoved almost my entire foot in it. I made sure, pressing my foot against it, that it wasn't too crumbly and put all my weight on that leg. I climbed another three feet down in the same manner, and there I was, standing on the ledge, my arms not fully stretched yet still clutching the edge of the rock above with my hands. This meant that climbing up would not be a challenge.

Now, though, I had to loosen my grip and let go. I held my breath, and sliding palms over the grainy surface of the rock, I slowly leaned on my left knee while my right leg remained firmly planted on the ledge, although so bent that my knee touched my chin. I had to take an even more unnatural position: I arched my spine backward, tilting my head forward at the same time...

Yes! There was a nest in one of the cracks. And Kuber knew that it was there, although he couldn't have seen it from the foot of the rock because of the ledge. He knew because...*he would swim by himself in the bay, late in the afternoon.*

I changed back to the previous, slightly more natural, position. Two silvery seagulls circled and squawked high over my head. There was no doubt it was their nest, but since it was empty now, they probably wouldn't dare come closer to me. I smiled bitterly—I had found Kuber's murderers. I had discovered that about forty days ago, one merciful serial killer had met his death here, by this nest, which back then was teeming with life—the tiny, fluffy progeny of the seagulls.

He saw one of them fall off the nest on that afternoon, took it to his room, and on the next morning came back here to return it to its home. He wasn't wearing a short-sleeved T-shirt, but wearing a long-sleeved one here would've been more than uncomfortable. That's why he was naked to the waist. And the chick was in his hat because there was no other way for him to carry it while climbing down. Now I knew why his palm and knee were bruised. His body was in the same position when, scared for their small ones, the seagulls swooped down on him. He drew back, instinctively, the rough ledge bruising his knee, and then tried to remain balanced on its edge but failed and started sliding down, his right hand leaving some of its skin here. It was more than clear why he had fallen backward and why his mouth had remained open: It had frozen in his final scream.

I began standing up. The narrowness around, the heavy sky over, and the gaping abyss below had an almost therapeutic effect on me. There was no trace of my pathological hunger for adrenaline now.

"*Again?*" Graziella's laugh rained down on me, more unwanted than even a hailstorm. "Are you feeding your obsession for senseless risk again?"

I finished standing up and looked up. Graziella's hair was flowing toward me like a veil of thready fog in pale yellow.

"You're up early," I said, through clenched teeth.

"Not today. Actually, it was you who woke me up."

"Really? Forgive me, then, for singing you a serenade without being aware of it."

"You are forgiven." She laughed again. "Come on; hurry up. It's going to start raining soon."

By "hurry up" she probably meant that I reach out with my arms, grab the edge of the rock and, when my face was on the same level as her feet, get a kick in the head from her—accompanied by laughter, of course. A laughter that would fall together with me toward that piece of rock down there in the shape of a spear.

"You did not move Kuber's corpse," I said. "And you won't move mine, although this time it would truly be a murder, not just an accident."

"You speak in such a convoluted manner! It doesn't suit someone in your position," she said, with reproach. She grabbed her hair and lifted it, revealing not only her face but also her body.

Only now I saw that she stood at the very edge of the rock, and the way she was leaning forward could terrify any observer. Yes, this woman was as intrepid as she was insolent. I almost shouted at her, "Careful, you might fall!" or something like that. Pressing lips hard together, I tried to shake off the sudden—and quite inappropriate at that moment—erotic desire for her.

"Lady," I began in a ceremoniously polite fashion but then quickly shot out the question, "is there anything you didn't lie about?"

Her reply was even quicker. "No. There isn't."

I believed her. I didn't say anything, and she spread her arms, palms turned over, and mumbled, "Yes, it's raining now!" and stepping back, she disappeared from my view. I climbed to the top, nimble as a monkey. I thought that the perfidious psychiatrist was still up there, waiting to push me down, but I saw her walking away.

CHAPTER FIFTY-ONE

I was in Graziella's office, waiting for her to come.
She had told me that she would return in a minute, but ten had passed since then. I was becoming more and more exasperated and less patient.
I stood up and went to the window, the only view
from which was water. It was raining so hard that
all streams of rain merged into one river, as if God
had opened the floodgates of heaven. He had also
opened the floodgates of his wrath, sending it
down in the form of blue lightning and deafening
thunder.

"I'm here now," Graziella informed me. Her entrance had coincided with one of the thunders, it
seemed.

"Great!" I turned and faced her. "It's good that you and God make a good team."

She ignored my riddlelike comment. She put the laptop she was carrying on the desk, came to me, and handed me a checkered shirt with long sleeves. I put it on with reluctance, because I quickly figured out it had belonged to Kuber. I leaned against the wall by the window and crossed my arms.

"There are cameras set around the house," Graziella said, sitting behind her desk. "Any human presence activates them, and they record everything."

"They recorded Kuber walking to that rock and starting to climb down!"

"Exactly." She nodded.

"To put it straight: It's another setup from you, making me investigate a well-documented, unarguable accident as murder."

She nodded again. "Yes. The only way to lure you to the island was to lie to you that Kuber was murdered. And why lure you? I will find out soon from *here*"—she pointed at the laptop—"that no one in the group knows about the cameras. So when Kuber disappeared, I took part in the search, and only after Frant and Danko had found his body was I able to find some time alone to see the recorded material. Upon zooming, I saw that that dumb man was holding some chick in his hand, which later he covered with his hat, the brim of which he had cut so that it didn't obstruct his climbing down. Ugh!"

Her face twisted into a grimace full of contempt, which—like everything else—I did not like.

"The guy doesn't deserve your scorn," I told her. "He was trying to do something good."

"Oh, come on! 'Dumb' is the word you're looking for. The sky's full of birds. One more or less won't matter."

"Graziella, by that logic you could say that saving a child is a stupid thing to do. Because the world is full of people."

I thought I could sting her with my exaggeration, but she only shrugged.

"I had big plans for Kuber, and he ruined everything. Still, I will make some use of his death. I am going to play the video at the trial; I'll also upload it on the Internet. 'What you see is a man all of you have branded as a serial killer, who, after undergoing the *right* psychiatric treatment, has revealed his true, humane face! Look at the compassion he's capable of, at the gentle way he's holding the helpless bird!' And after the story has gathered enough speed, I'll arrange the funeral he deserves."

"What about the crocodiles?" I tried to look worried. "Danko is hoping you'll feed his defrosted corpse to them."

"Don't worry about Danko." She looked at me with spite. "I'll find a way to compensate him for the disappointment."

"But I'm also worried about you, Graziella. Your image is going to suffer when people find out that instead of informing the police about the death of one of the patients in your custody, you had treated him like a piece of pork meat."

Resting her hand on the laptop, she pierced me with her cold and glassy blue eyes.

"Soon the only thing you'll be worried about will be you, Miro. But let me finish." She waited for a roll of thunder to fade and began in a singsong voice, as if telling a fairy tale, "So, after Kuber had covered the chick with his hat and disappeared from the range of the camera, the camera stopped recording. And resumed recording two minutes later. This time because of Roxanna! She appeared in frame, running; looked down; and covering her mouth to suppress a scream, I guess, ran back to the house. That's how I knew how she'd come up with the story about Fata cursing Kuber to fall from somewhere high and so on. It's good that his hat had flown in some unknown direction; otherwise, everyone would've guessed why he had cut its periphery out and what had truly happened."

"Did you look for it later?" I asked.

"Yes. I found and hid it. It was convenient for me that Sirius believed in Fata's voodoo magic. Out of fear that she might *pin* him too one day, he finally stopped pestering me with pleas to chase her from the island. He even destroyed the recording of her cursing he had made. Ugh! He's a fool also, but—"

It seemed she had almost said something I was not supposed to hear.

"Mmm, yes," I mumbled teasingly, "you love recording each other, eh? But don't worry. I won't say anything about the cameras around the house, inside the house, inside the bungalows…"

"Alas, not in the bungalows. It's impossible to hide anything there, not even a pin. And I knew that as soon as they arrived, each one of the group would start looking for bugs in their room."

Each one except me, I thought, disgusted by my dilettante naïveté.

"Do you think he's going to rat you out for visiting the dead man?" Graziella asked out of the blue. I disappointed her by not showing any surprise, and in the end, she elaborated. "I'm just asking Maya's question. She asked you in the vestibule, meaning Valdo. You were both whispering there on the morning after your arrival."

"Another recording."

"Yes. And I'm glad that I listened to it before it was too late! That's how I found out that you had started investigating right away and even examined the body, *despite* my insistent advice to take on the role of Merry Maker and do nothing else for the first couple of days. That's why I set the camera that can 'see' the crime scene to signalize every time someone went there."

As she talked, her fingernails went from tapping at the laptop lid to slightly scratching it. Her intention to make me boil with tension and anxiety was obvious.

"Too bad," I sighed. "It was not my serenade but a signal from some camera that woke you today."

"Miro! Now is not the time for showing how witty you are. How can you not see—"

"Oh, I see. I see, for example, why the day before yesterday, when you saw me walking by the edge of the rock, you looked so panicked. If I had found out or at least suspected back then that Kuber had died by pure accident, your plan would've crumbled like a sandcastle. Because I would've dropped the mask of Merry Maker, making no confession whatsoever."

"That's true." Graziella flinched as if, although unfulfilled, the possibility still terrified her. "To me, it was of utmost importance to take your confession on record. And, thank God, I succeeded!"

Standing up, she took the laptop, came to me, and handed it to me.

"If you've got a weak stomach," she said, "you'd better skip breakfast. Go straight to your bungalow and open the file named *Merry Maker*. It will tell you why I lured you here."

CHAPTER FIFTY-TWO

I was finishing my breakfast when Maya came into the kitchen. She was wearing a raincoat in bright red-and-white rain boots, her orange hair sticking up as if electrified.

"Good! You're here," she exclaimed. She ran to one of the cupboards and got a candy packet. "The animals must be so stressed after the thunderstorm that just passed. Let's go and calm them down!"

I took the laptop and followed her. I had some important questions to ask her. Now that Kuber's murder had turned out to be a bluff, the shadowy figure of Merry Maker was becoming more and more distinct due to the fact that Patrick Krenz was his first victim. And this being a coincidence seemed more and more out of the question.

The rain had stopped, but the sky was still scowling. Heavy with raindrops, the hibiscus bushes looked sullen and identical, gray under the gray clouds. The silence was depressing too. Birds and insects hid silently in their damp shelters.

We walked across the waterlogged meadow. I didn't want to go to the pens, so as soon as we were at a safe distance from the house, I stopped. I made Maya turn and face me and began.

"The other day you told me that unlike the others, Patrick had shown interest not in the mixture of poisons but in the vial itself. Why? Was there something peculiar about it?"

"Nothing. It's a stupid story!"

"Is it? I wouldn't call it stupid if—I repeat—*if* it contains the motive for the murder of a twenty-two-year-old boy."

"So, you too believe that Merry Maker killed him because of me?" She livened up, and I could tell she was flattered.

"Dammit!" I threw her an indignant look. "I don't believe in anything. Just tell the story, Maya!"

I don't consider patience to be among my strengths, and she decided to test it even further by pouting and falling silent. I had to change my expression, so I edited it from indignant to kind, hoping this would loosen her tongue.

Actually, neither the weather nor the place welcomed waiting. Suffocating air, heavy with sticky vapors. Wet grass teeming with slugs and some frogs. I did not feel comfortable in my shorts, squelching sneakers, and the dead man's shirt. My soul was restless from discomfort too, torn between the sympathy for the kid and the desire to give her a couple of resonant slaps on the face.

"For as long as I can remember"—she started talking at last—"my grandmother would always buy the same perfume. I grew up surrounded by the scent of jasmine, which got stronger each year because she would spray more and more of it on herself, as her sense of smell started gradually to deteriorate. But that afternoon, while I was preparing the éclairs, she came into the kitchen and filled it with a completely different aroma. Of *melon*, can you imagine?"

"That's unfortunate," I said sincerely.

"I hate melons!" Maya continued, anger in her voice. "And she knew well that I hated them. But she never cared about my feelings. She told me that from now on, she would only use that essential oil instead of perfume. She read in an article on aromatherapy somewhere that the scent of melon strengthens the immune system of those with her zodiac sign. That's when, Miro, I realized that I could not take more of her...well, of her everything! So, I dropped two sleeping pills into her teacup, opened her medallion, took the sachet with the poisonous powder—"

"The mixture was actually a powder?"

"Yes, but I dissolved it into solution so that I could inject it into the éclairs. I used that small vial on purpose—after throwing the nasty melon oil away, of course."

"I understand." I nodded. "But who was your grandmother preparing that mixture for?"

"Not her; it was her mother. She kept the ingredients secret because she would make money from selling it. She came up with it to get rid of the moles infesting the village at that time. And her daughter—my grandmother, that is—simply stole a quantity of the mixture and since then, which is more than half a century, had been carrying it with her in the medallion. She was a hypochondriac from an early age, I think."

"I don't think hypochondria has anything to do with it," I said. "She wanted to use it on someone from the beginning."

"Ah yes, that's true. But she was that someone. She wanted to poison her own self! She imagined she had all sorts of diseases, mostly terrifying and incurable. And she was most afraid of the possibility of a slow and painful death. 'That's why the quick death is always with me, around my neck,' she told me once, letting her secret out."

Maya scowled and fell silent. I traced her eyes to where she was looking and saw two white herons not far from us. They wandered about the meadow as if it was a giant dish, slowly swallowing now slugs—now frogs, mainly slugs actually.

"I know this *family*," Maya said with disgust. "They fly here after the rain and eat so much that it's a wonder they are able to take off after that... ugh! They make me sick. Let's go!"

"Wait," I stopped her. "You were going to tell me about Patrick."

"Ugh!" she repeated. "I only know what he told me. And he told it to me only to prove that there's no use denying it, because he had found out about everything. So he Googled 'essential oil from melon,' and, when, among the thousands of results, he saw the link for an article titled 'Aromatherapy for your zodiac sign,' he didn't ignore it. Unlike the cops who probably didn't even noticed it, he clicked on it. He saw the name of the magazine that has published it. Then went to the post office, checked, and found out that my grandmother is a subscriber to that magazine, which meant that she had bought the vial shortly after the article was published. He found confirmation for his hypothesis when he matched the birthdate of my grandmother to the sign the article was recommending the melon oil to. He cut our pictures

from a newspaper and began asking every phar-
macist if they had sold melon essential oil to any of
us. Without success."

"What about the cops? They must've ques-
tioned the pharmacists the same way."

"Yes. Again, without success. Because, Miro, my
grandmother did not buy the vial. She stole it."

"Ha! How do you know?"

"She told this to my lawyer, although I would've
guessed by myself. She was always buying piles of
pills…I've seen her stealthily put small packages
into her pocket."

"Maya." I made her look me in the eyes. "The
vial was in a box, right?"

"Yes. So?"

"I'm wondering why it had only your fingerprints on it. If your grandmother had taken it out
of the box, as you're saying—"

"*If?*" Her voice trembled. "You don't believe
me, and we're supposed to be partners! But listen:
When I decided to poison myself too, I wiped all
the previous fingerprints from the vial. I wanted
everyone to know after my death that I *and no
one else* had poisoned those freaks! I wanted their
parents to realize that their children had died because they failed to raise them as…as human beings. That's all. And you…just leave me alone. Go
shoot yourself!"

She headed for the pens, zigzagging, probably because she didn't want to step on some slug, and I, zigzagging for the same reason, headed for my bungalow, where only a few minutes later I felt like following her advice.

CHAPTER FIFTY-THREE

"Miro, it was easy for me to lie to you, but telling you the truth is something I cannot bear. That is why I chose this way, so that I don't have to look you in the eyes." Such was the opening paragraph of the file called "Merry Maker," and Graziella was looking at me after all, only not exactly in the eyes.

She had recorded the video in high contrast, obviously with the idea of making a piece of art out of it. Washed in bright white light, her image stood out like a cutout against the black screen. The lighting had erased the lemon color of her tied-back hair, making it look like a silver halo around her forehead. Her earrings also looked silvery, as well as her lip gloss and the pearl necklace around her graceful white neck. The strange silvery tinge of the skin of her arms looked somewhat enhanced, and the white sleeveless shirt covered her torso like a second skin.

I could only assume that she was seated behind a black desk because its outlines merged with the black background, making her look like someone chest-deep in cosmic darkness. The most impressive thing, though, were her eyes, whose pale-blue color was lost to the white light. Large and round, now they resembled silver coins, carved into the eye sockets. There was something both shocking and arousing to those seemingly otherworldly eyes. But when Graziella started talking, the shock quickly took over the arousal.

"You are the Merry Maker, Miro," she said. "It is *really* you."

Her image disappeared from the screen, replaced by the following text:

A team of British scientists from King's College London, led by Simon Rinders, has put an end to the controversy surrounding the condition known as split personality. They announced that it is a real mental condition, dissociative identity disorder (DID).

Until recently, there was no consensus on whether split personality is a specific brain disorder or a result of active imagination in emotionally unstable persons. But now scientists have proven that DID is characterized by the coexistence of two or more personalities in one person. And since each personality comes with a self of its own, they take turns at controlling the person's behavior, completely unaware of each other. This distorted perception is accompanied by changes in the patient's mood and condition, which unconsciously aims to help the patient escape from him or herself and move into another personality, capable of realizing his or her suppressed desires. This explains why the DID personalities can be of varying age, gender, intellect, and even handwriting.

"You read it all, didn't you?" I heard Graziella's voice. "Of course, these are only the opening paragraphs, but they are enough to help you get the gist of the facts I'm about to show you."

My shock had dissipated, and I even felt like laughing. I prepared myself for some psychobabble—such were her "facts" usually.

"But first, Miro, I want you to calm down. Here, you truly are safe. You will be safe even after we've left the island, because by that time we and the prosecutors would've finalized the best deal for you."

Appearing again on the screen, she slid her silvery hand over her face, as if to wipe an imaginary redness from its surface.

"I'd like to say sorry not only for the lies. I also edited the police reports heavily, but I did it for your own good. Or else you would've guessed that you are Merry Maker and sink forever into his dark personality. Actually, the danger still exists, although it's not as big now, thanks to your smooth transition to the truth, which was made possible by me and my lies."

Her image became unfocused and transformed into a flickering white blur, from which emerged the face of a man of about forty I didn't know. Below it was written, "Christian Deluc, second victim."

"I shall explain why I don't begin with the first victim." Graziella started talking behind camera. "It so happened that your grandfather confided in me his worries about a week after your discharge from work. 'Jobless, my grandson will now start looking for even more extreme experiences,' he told me. 'I'm afraid that his desire for self-annihilation has gone out of control!' I decided to hire detectives to keep an eye on you. Yes, yes! It was me, not your grandfather. But Patrick Krenz's murder had been committed before I hired them, which is the reason I have no photographic evidence of it."

While I listened to her voice, the face of Christian Deluc was always before my eyes, looking more and more familiar with each second. I figured I had seen his picture in a newspaper or on TV, but the screen began showing me a sequence in which:

Me and Deluc are sitting on a table outside, drinking coffee.
We look at each other, smile at each other.
Deluc stands up, nods at me, and leaves.
I am alone but not for long; seconds later I rise too.
We are on the street. I am walking a few steps behind Deluc.
He crosses the street and walks into the yard of a shabby one-floor building.
I walk on, but my eyes are on him.
He unlocks the door of the house. Goes in…

"That's the moment you assumed that Deluc was living by himself," Graziella said, freezing the frame. "As you can see, the date is August twenty-fifth, at eighteen thirty-three. On August twenty-fifth again, between twenty-three hundred and midnight, Deluc met his death in his own home. You didn't break into the house; he opened the door for you. What did you tell him? On what pretext were you there? Many questions remain unanswered. I hope to make contact with Merry Maker during our therapeutic sessions and then maybe everything about this and the other three murders will become clear."

She stopped talking, and I kept staring at the slowly dissolving image of Christian Deluc. I now remembered him more clearly. I even recalled that brief assumption that the man was most likely a loner who has decided to go to the local café after work instead of heading straight back to his shabby house. Yes, but I also recalled that our paths met by coincidence and that only a few steps later he stopped existing for me—he was one of the thousands of strangers I would pass by every day on my wanderings about the city...

"Two weeks has passed since my detectives started following you," Graziella broke her silence. "They would send me video materials and reports on you on a regular basis, but since you weren't showing any disturbing signs, on August twentieth, I ordered them to start following you only during the day. That is why I have no evidence of your fatal midnight visit to Christian Deluc's home."

Another portrait appeared on the screen. Below it was written, "Erik Kotovich, third victim," but Graziella seemed to have more "revelations" about the second one:

"My nightmarish suspicions began plaguing me on the twenty-sixth at about noon when I saw on the Internet the news about Merry Maker's second murder and the photograph…the photograph of the same person my detectives had been following the previous day! Of course, I instantly ordered them to resume following you during the nights also, and the result, the terrifying result, Miro, was not long in coming!"

I was now sure that, unlike Deluc, Erik Kotovich was truly a stranger to me. It was a short-lived relief, though, for his portrait was replaced by a night-time picture of an apartment building I knew all too well. I had spent almost an entire night in one of the apartments there at the end of last month. I was waiting there for its owner because I had a bone to pick with him. I had spent hours in the stale darkness of his living room, washing down boredom with a bottle of cheap vodka, waiting for that weasel, and he had never come back home…

"Kotovich also lived alone," Graziella said as the screen showed me walking swiftly toward the building's entrance. "I assume you had chosen and researched him in the days before I had hired the detectives. That's when you had found out that there were no surveillance cameras around. But you're about to see that my man's camera did a good job."

Well, at least her last sentence was true. I saw myself disappearing into the black entrance, leaving the lights off, and a moment later I saw myself passing by the window of the staircase between the ground and first floor in the form of a shadow. Then disappearing and appearing again at the window between the first and second floor, after which disappearing completely.

"Kotovich's apartment is on the second floor," Graziella said.

"But I was on the fourth!" I objected in vain to the screen, in whose lower corner I could clearly see not only the hour, 22:18, but also the date, "08.26.2017."

Then the clock started changing quickly, and the windows on the second floor, on which the camera was focused, went dark, one after another.

"I don't know why you waited that long" came Graziella's voice. "Maybe you were waiting at the door, listening through it to make sure that Kotovich was by himself. Or maybe you were hesitating, torn between the subconscious conflict between the cop and the serial killer in you. I don't know, I don't…but you did nothing for an hour, after which you rang the door, woke the guy…"

The camera clock returned to its normal speed, showing 23:25, and at the same moment, one of the second-floor windows was lit. It remained lit until the end—that is, until the next rapid change of the clock slowed down, showing 03:12. Then the camera changed its point of view to catch me coming out of the entrance, swaying like the drunkard I was after hours of waiting in vain and drinking poor-quality vodka.

"The lit window is that of his bedroom." Graziella decided I needed to know this. "But you murdered him in the kitchen, the window of which was on the other side of the building. You tortured him for a long time, having *fun*, first gagging his mouth because of the neighbors and then ungagging it, only to cut in its place *this smile...*"

The faces of Deluc and Kotovich appeared, smiling widely, thanks to the psychopath's razor, and below them, on a white background with red words, was written, "If at this moment you are Merry Maker, then there is nothing I can say to you. But if you are still Miro, don't be confused if you don't remember any of what you are seeing. It is important that you understand that this is not a case of amnesia. You...and I mean *both of you*, are two different persons. It's impossible for you to have a memory of his experiences, just as you cannot have of mine."

The pictures and the text lingered on the screen for too long. I wanted to close my eyes, but I was like hypnotized. I could not find the will to tear my eyes away from them.

"I don't have a recent portrait of the fourth victim." Graziella's voice was coming from somewhere far. "He, that poor *old man* Philip Ramm, had not taken pictures of himself for the past twenty years. I also don't have a camera recording of you breaking into his tiny house on the night between the twenty-seventh and the twenty-eighth, when you murdered him. It was my detectives' fault this time. You escaped them. But thanks to a psychological trick I used, yesterday you confirmed my diagnosis."

The bloody smiles finally disappeared from the screen. An epistolary scream appeared: "LOOK AT WHAT YOU'VE READ IN THE REPORTS!" And below it, the following excerpt: "...a message was found in Philip Ramm's house, written in his blood under the toilet sink: *Hygiene is important...*"

NOW HEAR YOUR WORDS FROM YESTERDAY! another scream across the screen, followed by the sound of Sirius's words:

"You said that you wrote something under the sink in that poor guy's bathroom. What was it?"

Followed by my answer:

"'I washed my hands'! That's what I wrote. And I'll wash them again after I've smashed your snout!"

Those silver coins—the otherworldly eyes of Graziella—stared at me from the cosmic darkness, from the black screen. Her white face was swaying, floating there, now just an oval with no neck, no shoulders below it, no arms...just a face with a silvery halo above the forehead and with silvery lips that barely moved when they said through a whisper:

"The real message was kept in secret from the media. Only four people knew about it, one of them me. I changed it to the false, 'Hygiene is important,' in the reports, but as I expected, yesterday in confession hour, you involuntarily said the real one. Or more precisely, it was said by the one who wrote it after committing the gruesome murder: 'I washed my hands.'"

CHAPTER FIFTY-FOUR

Of course, the file named "Merry Maker" gave me reasons for a plethora of bad feelings, the most torturous of which was shame. Panicky shame of what my grandfather would think about me if Graziella sent him the file. I couldn't even tell if I would be more humiliated if he believed her "diagnosis" or if he simply stated the fact that I had let her catch me in her net like a fish.

But in a moment the paralysis that had petrified my brain began to wane. I stood up. I took the knife from where I had hidden it in the wardrobe and tucked it under my jeans belt. I needed it for self-defense, although I didn't expect that the concentrated psychological attack would be followed by a physical one—or at least not so soon. I put my jacket on, took the laptop, and went outside. I went to Maya's bungalow and knocked. I was glad she didn't answer; I was glad she had forgotten to lock the door—otherwise I would've had to break in. I went in and turned her laptop on. It was filled with RPGs and romantic movies, but that didn't slow me down. I quickly found the file I needed and opened it, as it wasn't password protected. Maya didn't seem to care much about the importance of the so-called police reports. I was lucky because now, in possession of what I really had read, I could easily prove that...

"Hygiene is important."

"What the..." I gaped at the just-appeared text.

"...a message was found in Philip Ramm's house, written in his blood under the toilet sink: *Hygiene is important...*'

I lost my sight for a moment, it was as if someone had stuck their fingers into my eyes, and when I was able to see again, I saw the same nonsense about the hygiene instead of "I washed my hands" as it was written—as it definitely was written—in that file.

I realized I was gnashing my teeth in rage and helplessness. I took a hold of myself. I switched Maya's laptop off, tucked Graziella's under my arm, and left the bungalow. The sky was dark with clouds again, no spots of blue anywhere in sight.

Maybe another storm was coming. Not that this could make me more worried than I already was, but I preferred not to play the role of a walking lightning rod also.

Because of the squishy ground beneath my feet and the lack of positive stimuli, it took me more time to reach Fata's house than yesterday. I approached it from the side wall, the one with no windows. I stooped and walked to the front side, silently sneaking beneath the windows there. I stopped at the door and stood there for two minutes. I could hear noises coming from inside but no talking. I was disappointed.

I knocked, and as soon as Fata appeared at the door, I put my hands on her shoulders. I gently moved her to the side and went in, stepping into a small but well-furnished kitchen.

"Cognac or whiskey?" Fata hissed. "Just song or song and dance? How do you want me to welcome you?"

I searched her expression for signs of fear but found none. She was looking at me with the perfectly normal expression for the situation: outrage. I decided that there was no need to check the other rooms.

"You've got a nice freezer," I said, sitting down on one of the chairs by the table. "But Roxanna tells me you're frequently left with no electricity.

And products usually go bad until Valdo has managed to fix the generator."

"They go," she said nonchalantly.

"So you throw them out?"

"No! I use them as decoration."

"Where? Where do you throw them?"

"Why? Are you hungry?" She cackled. "I throw them in the woods, but don't go looking for them. Birds and rodents eat everything."

"That's too bad," I replied to her cackle, with a meek smile. "But following Graziella's orders, the pilots always bring you new stuff, right?"

"What do you want?" She bristled up. "Why have you come?"

"To borrow your phone," I told her right away. "I'll bring it back—"

"I don't have a phone."

"Really?"

"Yes. I call my nephews from the hall in the house. Graziella connects me to them through a computer after a lot of…tinkering."

As much as I hated to do it, I had to press her now.

"I went to that recess in the rocks, Fata. My opinion is that all of you had gone a bit too far. So much blood. Maybe a pig?"

"How dare you?" she yelled. "How dare you make fun of my brother's death!"

"Are you implying that his ghost might start haunting me for that?"

She flinched and began to say something, but I cut her off.

"I was wondering why yesterday you made me wait on that stump. But when I later saw the *spill* in the recess, I stopped wondering. You helped your brother sneak out of here through one of the back windows."

"How dare you?" she repeated mechanically. "My brother is dead; he committed suicide."

"But he seems to have a healthy appetite for a dead man," I said, thinking that if I was making a mistake with this, then I had just descended to the level of the truly most vulgar fools. Yet I continued, "You two put the generator out of order on purpose. Or you wouldn't be able to justify your long list of groceries."

As I talked, Fata watched me with growing attention. I remembered that my face still showed the defects of the bad sunburn and felt embarrassed.

"You're blushing." She nodded in approval, sat opposite me, and began in a low voice, "If I deny that my brother is alive, you wouldn't believe me. No need trying to convince you that if I had a phone, I would have given it to you either. But it's bad, very bad for you that you still haven't realized what Graziella is."

"Oh, I have," I mumbled.

"No, you have not." She shook her head worriedly. "You haven't if you still think it is possible for me and my brother to exchange messages on the phone while he is hiding somewhere on the island."

"You think Graziella has tapped the lines?"

"She personally? No, of course. But she has experts for every occasion."

And that's when it dawned on me: experts who yesterday had told her about my attempt to call my grandfather! And she told me—actually, she lied to me—that he had informed her about it. My head was dizzy with relief—he hadn't betrayed me! At least now that was the more plausible version...

"Come on; go home," Fata urged me timidly. I may have failed to scare her with my words, but my smile now seemed to have done the job.

"Don't be afraid," I told her. "You're safe with me. But Graziella isn't, and she should be terrified. Only, she doesn't know it yet."

"It's obvious she doesn't. You're still alive." After that convincing argument, the old woman pointed at the door with a more insistent gesture.

I looked at her reproachingly. "I was hoping you would help me, Fata."

"I helped you enough yesterday."

"If you mean the newspaper—"

"Yes, the newspaper itself, not what's written in it."

This time Fata did not seem content with just pointing me in the direction of the door. She stood up, walked toward it, and opened it wide. She waited for me to step outside and immediately shut it behind my back.

CHAPTER FIFTY-FIVE

I t didn't start to rain, but a fog fell and in no time grew so thick that when I raised a hand before my eyes, I couldn't see it. I was at the foot of the hill where everything now looked like a swamp as a result of the water flowing down after the rain. I went blindly ahead, sinking ankle-deep in the mud, and when I started to climb up, the terrain became slippery, even slimy, as if I was treading in the wake of thousands of slugs. Reaching the top without falling or dropping Graziella's laptop seemed almost impossible, but I did it. I groped for the fig tree, found it, sat on the damp leaves under it, relaxed, and the expression "deadly silence" suddenly became meaningful to me. I listened for any sounds from the ocean but heard nothing. As if the ocean itself with all its infinite greatness had ceased to exist—either missing or dead. A colossal corpse under a heavy shroud of the fog.

I'm used to my fantasies, which often step beyond the boundaries of the ordinary, but this time fear had tightened its grip around my throat. I felt as if I was disappearing, as if my personality was dissolving into the inner fog of my soul. And since I was still alive, and someone alive cannot remain for long without a personality, the empty space left by the *dissolved* one would be taken by another one that is stronger, more aggressive, sadistic…

The silence was no longer deadly. I could hear my shallow breathing and my quickened heartbeat. A pain, starting from my fingers, shot through my hands, and I realized that I had been clutching the laptop while imagining how I was strangling Graziella's white neck.

"I am not Merry Maker, but I will probably kill her," I said to myself, mad with anger from her cruel and convoluted lies.

Unnecessary complications, though, often lead to mistakes, so I had a chance of finding a truth or two that went unnoticed among Graziella's lies. She was using too many ornaments, trying to be too artistic—it was her weakness, and it was clearly visible in the Merry Maker file. But there were also facts there whose sources—the detectives' recordings—plus my "confessions" would be enough for her to put me in an isolated cell for the rest of my life.

But why? Why would she do this? Why the hell did she need me? The version that she was aiming for my grandfather now seemed too elementary. I was her target, and through her vast arsenal of carefully crafted psychological manipulations, she was really trying to convince me that the ex-cop Miro Kazimirski and the serial killer Merry Maker take turns in using my body, like two paupers sharing a suit.

Yes, I am going to reveal these manipulations when I'm in court. I am going to reveal to everyone the maniac that psychiatrist was: the silvery halo, the coinlike eyes, everything. I am going to call for an expert appraisal of the file to tell why the sequence showing that I had not stopped on the second floor, where Kotovich's apartment was, but had continued up is missing. Whether it was done on purpose or due to the camera's range.

Whether—or, it didn't matter. Whatever the truth, I needed to have everything in the file analyzed by an expert. From which followed another paradox: that was my best plan—to somehow reach the courthouse. Because the alternative was to never leave the island, dead or alive.

The fog was beginning to clear. I couldn't wait for it to become so thin that I would be able to dig out the bag with the newspaper and take a look at it in the light. After hearing Fata's words, I had come up with another hypothesis, and confirming it could be very helpful in revealing Graziella's manic nature. For now, though, I closed my eyes and immersed myself into the sea of, unfortunately, unarguable facts:

The detectives were following me for two whole weeks without me noticing anything. All right, that wasn't surprising. Back then boredom and confusion had turned me into a careless scatterbrain. And how could I know that I had to be careful? What for? I wasn't doing anything special with my life.

So they follow me and take pictures of me drinking coffee on a table with a stranger and then leaving right after him and in his direction. And only a few hours later, he is found dead! On the next evening, I somehow decide to break into the apartment of that enemy of mine and spend the whole night there, waiting for him, while at the same time and in the same building and entrance, only two floors down from me, the same psychopath is committing murder! Is such *harmonious* arrangement of coincidences possible? And is it also a coincidence that the first victim of the psychopath is none other than Patrick Krenz, the student who poked his curious nose into Maya's business and thus into Graziella's? The answer is clear: No, it isn't possible. It's absurd. Which means that, in broader strokes, the closest to the truth must be this:

The one who had to die was Patrick Krenz. The next three were murdered only to confuse the investigators, setting me as their murderer before that. In other words, Graziella hires detectives who, in fact, are assassins and gives them the following instructions: "The student is the main target, but besides him, I want three more victims for cover; one must be an old man, and the other two must be in some way connected, with video footage to prove it to this fool here." And she shows them a picture of me. She gives the orders to torture the victims in the same "style," using laughing gas and then writing the messages she has come up with on spots chosen by her. That is how she first created her monstrous child—the psychopath called Merry Maker—then convinced me, without much effort, to play his role...

And here I was. Dreaming of getting to the courthouse.

I am not a vulgar person, but I put a minute of my time aside to curse. Then I cleared the place I had buried the bag from foliage and dug the bag out, and wiping my hands on my pants, I took the newspaper out. I hadn't opened it yesterday because my picture was on the front page. But now I noticed that the font of the article is slightly different of that of the pieces on the following pages. It seemed that the newspaper pages printed on this sheet—second page and the last two pages—have been copied from the original, and the real leading article had been replaced by Graziella's forged one: MERRY MAKER'S TRUE IDENTITY REVEALED, and so on.

"Yes, she's crazy." I nodded to myself. "She is tirelessly crazy!"

So, this article was never published, and the police were not after me—a fact that now could bring me neither joy nor comfort. I put the newspaper back in the bag, together with the laptop. I buried them deeper this time, put some litter on top, and imagined time flying—years, decades, centuries passing—while these two lay in the ground, disintegrating into the resilient unecological bag. Forgotten by all…because somewhere around, maybe somewhere very near to here, also forgotten and decomposing, I will be lying in the ground.

CHAPTER FIFTY-SIX

The fog had lifted completely, and the sun was at its zenith. Quite a lot of crocodiles were out of the water, enjoying the sun. Idling in the most natural way on the rocky strip between the lagoon and the forest, one of them lay insolently right in front of the boat I needed to get to the isolator.

I thought of the lock I tore from Sirius's hair—now, in this light, was the best time to take a look at it. I pulled the napkin out of my pocket, unwrapped it, and started staring. The hairs were red blond, the roots—not exactly white or gray. Actually, the lower one tenth of an inch were yellow in color. Maybe Sirius has lied about his premature graying. So what?

I went back to the forest, where I found a branch the storm had brought down. I cleaned and sharpened it with the knife and made a stake out of it. I grabbed it in my hand and headed for the boat, but when I walked out of the forest, I stopped to take a better look at the landscape. After the heavy rain, the lagoon looked like a lake, although in dry weather, it probably looked like a swamp, because between it and the ocean, there was a line of rocks rising above water cut at one only place by a narrow channel. It wasn't too narrow to stop the crocodiles from preying in the rich-in-fish shallow waters. Unfortunately, these reptiles did not eat only fish, which made me a welcome visitor here.

The isolator, a large anchored raft with a tent on it, was almost in the center of the lagoon, which meant that it was about three hundred feet from the forest in one direction and the closest reef in the other. The raft was edged with a three-foot-high fence of metal rods, their sharp ends blinking like blades in the sun, and the tent looked slanted to one side but still usable. Either the reefs had weakened the storm here or Valdo had taken measures before it started.

I was about to whistle to check if he really was on the raft—in the tent or behind it—when I remembered what I had to do next and decided not to announce my presence. I had no desire to

entertain him while wandering among the crocodiles in the shape of a two-legged steak. I walked
toward the water, keeping an eye on the beasts.
Not a single one of them moved, not even the one
in front of the boat. It lay there, head raised and
mouth open in the direction of the sun. Busy with
taking in more heat, the bastard didn't care if it
was in my way or not. I looked at it with curiosity. I
would estimate its size as impressive—as long as a
pickup truck, as wide as…let's say that it would be
difficult for me to hug it in case we became friends.
Its fangs could make even a metal-cutting saw envious; a game of bridge could easily be played on its
head; the ridges on its back, each one a spike, were
a categorical proof of its kinship to dinosaurs—

"Hey, dumbass!" came from the raft.

Impatient to give me his "compliment," Valdo
stood facing me, waving his arms. Instead of replying, I waved with the stake.

"No!" he cried. "Behind you! *Behind* you, dumbass!"

I turned around. Another smaller but faster crocodile was quickly moving toward me. I
stepped before it and only hit it on the head with
the stake, although I could've driven the sharp
end into its eye. That worked, and the animal
abandoned its plan. The big croc, however, had
woken up and was coming in my direction, moving its massive webbed feet with amazing agility,

its mouth still wide open, only this time not toward the sun. I moved out of its way so that it could see its smaller colleague, and that was a clever move. The good old competition for food did the rest. Leaning on their tails, the reptiles rose against each other and started making unpleasant hissing sounds. Finally, the small one stepped back, just as I should've done. But I was unable to fight the temptation.

I stepped behind the big croc and tried to drive him forward using the stake like a cowherd tending cattle. Surprisingly flexible, its thick tail arched and slapped me on the leg. I fell to the ground and dropped the stake. I reached out to grab it, and the foul breath of the crocodile ruffled my hair. Its snout was now only five inches from my face. I groped for a stone and found one and then hit the beast in the snout. I rolled to the side, jumped up to my feet, grabbed another stone and threw it, this time aiming for its mouth. It was wide open, impossible to miss. The crocodile instinctively shut its jaws, with the stone between them. I used the moment to pull the stake from beneath its belly and again try to drive it away, now keeping an eye on its tail and keeping in mind that I was dealing with a ferocious beast whose character was probably far from dovelike. I looked around for other crocodiles in dangerous proximity to me. There were several. The commotion had stirred almost every one of them.

I somehow broke free from the grip of the adrenaline-fueled euphoria. I leaped over big croc's body and bolted for the boat. It wasn't tied to anything, but someone, probably Sirius, had made sure to drag it at least twelve feet away from the water. I dropped the stake in it and started pushing it. The rocks were making everything much harder, and the crocodiles were approaching. Twice I had to jump into the boat and chase them away, leaning over the boat's board, stake in one hand and paddle in the other. From time to time, I could see Valdo's silhouette in my peripheral vision, now sitting and then standing, like a cheering fan's. Which team was he supporting, though—mine or the crocodiles'? I was about to find out.

CHAPTER FIFTY-SEVEN

When I reached the raft, I tied the boat to one of the metal pickets of the fence, and Valdo opened the small door, which was made of the same sharp pickets. I stepped on the raft.

"Sharks, reptiles…" He shook his head. "You like them, eh? Something's wrong with your brain."

"I think you might be right," I replied. "But now let's focus on the fact that I'm also a great cop. A killer one!"

I sat down by the fence, facing the crocodiles that had followed me. The raft was low, almost at the same level as their ridged backs. *Yes, "isolator" is a good word*, I thought, *but "insanator" might be a better one.* One more place on the island where

Graziella has let her psychotherapeutic imagination run free.

"Come on!" Valdo urged me. "Go on. I know that you're a killer, but I don't care what kind of cop you are."

"You will care soon," I assured him, "because that's important to Roxanna."

"Did she send you here? She's leaving me, isn't she?"

"No. And no."

"What then?" Valdo sat down next to me.

There was no need for a detailed account of the portrait of Death. I also didn't want to involve Fata. I said loftily, "What? For example, the fact that applying the complex combination of both the deductive and inductive methods, I have come up with a concept showing the objective reality of her innocence. In simpler words, for you, I think that Roxanna has not murdered those three."

"But yesterday she remembered where she had thrown the gun! That's what I know."

"I think that Graziella has *planted* through hypnosis that particular memory after Roxanna's aunt confessed to her that she is the murderer and that she had thrown the gun in the neighbor's well."

Valdo did not look surprised. "Yes, there were moments when I also suspected the aunt. But we can never be sure."

"We can if I find her confession in one of Graziella's computers. That's why I want to break into that hall. But I'm going to need your skeleton key for that."

"How do you know I have it with me? Have you been through my stuff in the bungalow again?"

"No. And I'm not here only for the skeleton key. I don't know Roxanna very well, and I cannot say if by telling her that her aunt and not she is the murderer, I would help her or harm her. The choice she will have to make will be a tough one, even for someone with a stronger mind than hers. Tell on her aunt during the trial and thus wash the stigma of the serial killer off herself, or corroborate the story about the 'breach in her amnesia' and win the five million? And also—will she, no longer a murderer, want to marry one…"

"Or and also will…" Valdo began in a singsong voice. "Shall I knock your teeth out, or tear your ears off?"

"I will start with your ears," I promised him. "I don't like them. They look like flip-flops. But you'll need them to hear what I have to say."

"Don't bother. I know your game. You want to get your hands on the aunt's confession, if there is such a thing, and blackmail Graziella. You're just pretending that you care about Roxanna!"

"I don't want to cause any harm to her, that's all," I said. "Although I admit that I care mostly about me at the moment. Graziella has my 'confession' too, but I doubt she keeps the file only on her computer. She certainly has sent it to her lawyer also. But if I find the aunt's confession, I will send it to a lawyer too. And then Graziella will find herself in a corner: *If you show them my 'confession,' I will show them the aunt's, and you will have to stand trial too. If meanwhile I disappear, my lawyer will do it.* Am I clear so far, Valdo?"

"No," he snarled. "With or without the confession, you are busted. The cops are after you, and really, your only chance is to disappear. And this could happen only if you make Graziella put you on a plane to some unknown destination and give you enough money to get a fake ID and pay a plastic surgeon for a fake face."

"Sounds good, but I like my face," I told him. I waited for him to say, "Soon you won't be so fond of it." And when he did, although not with words but with a glance, I continued, "You would've been right if the cops were really after me."

I felt that someone else was also expressing their bad intentions toward me using only their eyes. I looked down and wasn't surprised to see a crocodile staring at me. Yellow, unblinking, and cut in two by long black pupils, its eyes were so close that I could touch them just by reaching out…

Valdo shoved his hand between the pickets of the fence and slapped the flat snout of the crocodile. The animal reacted instantly, but Valdo was prepared: He drew his hand even quicker, clenching it into a fist at the same time to protect his fingers. The jaws of the crocodile closed only an inch from his fist.

"They are after you, Merry Maker; believe me." He returned to our conversation, throwing me a look that was not just severe but humiliatingly severe. Full of contempt! "How petty and pathetic you must be to hope that I would agree to help you!"

I stood up.

"I can do it without your help," I told him nonchalantly. "And you'd better think of a way to help your fiancée. Or maybe you wouldn't want to help her too? Because—just an example—if she found out that she's not a murderer, she'd immediately break up with you, especially after…" I pierced him with my eyes. "After seeing you in that little *dog* movie!"

I never thought that a dark-skinned man could turn pale and red, but now I witnessed both. First, Valdo's face turned gray, the scars standing out like cracks, and then it took on a deep mahogany hue, which made the cracks look as if swollen with blood. I was already sorry for my words. I should've challenged him in a more delicate manner. With a kick or a slap in the face.

Still sitting, he put his palms on his knees and started talking quietly, almost intimately. "I wanted to kill you even before I met you. It's been more than a month since I read how you'd made that boy 'laugh' in his dying agony. That's the moment I felt that desire for the first time, and I'll be damned if I don't fulfill it now."

"Just try," I challenged him. "But since you might succeed, I have to tell you right now that I didn't kill the boy, and I haven't killed anyone ever. For now."

"Are you suffering from a sudden memory loss? How pathetic you are—"

I cut his speech with a kick in the ankle, and he jumped to his feet. Again, the Cape-buffalo comparison worked best, not least because his eyes were bloodshot. Although I knew it quite well, the fact that he excelled me in height, mass, and muscle drove me mad. I wasn't used to such proportions. I ducked his blow by squatting, which made me even madder. What followed was something resembling a dance on the swaying raft. Each of us made several attempts to smash the opponent's nose; neither succeeded. Then Valdo aimed for my chin, his fist whizzing in the air like a flying black cannonball. I evaded it by the skin of my teeth, realizing that if he had hit me, I would've flown out and landed on the blades of the fence—or on the other side of it, where the crocodiles waited. These two possibilities brought my common sense back, and I saw that I had a 99 percent chance of losing both the fight and my life.

I pulled the knife from under my belt and threw it aside. The way things were going, the temptation to use it could easily stun and silence my sense of dignity…

"What?" Valdo froze, and I could not stop the swing of my arm in time and hit him under the chin.

He swayed toward the fence. I grabbed him by the shirt and stopped his falling or at least helped him find balance, his shirt tearing at his back with a drawn-out sound, which at one point mixed with the hissing of one of the nearby crocodiles.

"What?" Valdo repeated dumbly. "Why did you throw it?"

"Try to guess," I replied.

He grew pensive and then walked to the knife, picked it up, handed it to me, and told me, "I won't give you the skeleton key. But I will take you to the shore with the boat and then come back. I'll meet you by the house at midnight."

CHAPTER FIFTY-EIGHT

Even though the island was small, the distance from the isolator to my bungalow was about five miles. Or at least that's how it seemed to me, because I took the wrong direction a couple of times. The wild area, covered here by trees and there by bushes, was a challenge to my sense of direction and slowed me down. I wasn't in a hurry anyway. My meeting with Valdo was in several hours, and I had no plans until then, except—maybe—to find Sirius and shave his head and spare him the burden of dying his hair. I liked the idea; it made me laugh. Despite being pressed down by fate, I saw no reason to keep a constant long face.

I went into the bungalow grinning and—*bam*! There she was—Graziella. She was in her work overalls again, looking worried. "Thank God you're back!" she said. "When I didn't find you here, I thought that after the shocking revelations about you, you might've tried to take your own life. But thank God, here you are! Alive!"

"Let's leave God out of this," I suggested. "We both know we're in Satan's territory."

We exchanged playful looks. It was hard to believe, but we were starting to flirt! I went into the shower booth, drank some water, and looked at myself in the black-framed mirror. I didn't look like an idiot, despite the wide grin. I splashed my face with water, used my wet hands to smooth down my hair, and went back to the cell. Graziella was sitting on the bed. I sat on the chair by the table.

"You hid the laptop," she said, with no reproach in her voice. She rubbed her forehead with the back of her hand and added, "I'm tired. I spent all night working on the video."

"Yes, it must've been tiring. Especially when you had a web of other lies to work on too."

"I told you already—"

"I know, I know. You wanted to introduce me to the truth, carefully using lies. But sometimes you outdo yourself, Graziella. Take the newspaper article, for example."

"Oh, that was easy since I own the newspaper. I just sent the text and the picture to the editor and asked him to put them in a couple of copies and give these to the pilots. But how did you know that the article is fake?"

I did not violate the way we were communicating by being too honest. I lied. "There's a factual mistake."

"What mistake?"

"I'll leave that for you to find out. But while we're on the topic of mistakes, I'll tell you about another one: that Maya had copied the file from the flash drive in two directories, and you have deleted only one."

"I assume you're bluffing, but I won't deny that. I saw Maya throwing the flash drive on the beach and figured out what she had done while you were sleeping there. I decided to replace the file on her laptop with another, in which Merry Maker's message is different from the real one. And I see that I've done the right thing!"

Now I was really bewildered.

"I'm telling you that I know about two of your most blatant lies, and you seem to be OK with that."

"Of course I am! Because by doing so you've confirmed my diagnosis. I had a suspicion that you might be suffering only from amnesia, but if such stress factors as the articles and the faked message have not stirred the dormant memories in you, then split personality is the most likely hypothesis."

I laughed. Her desire to convince me that besides being myself, I was also a psychopath was reaching comical proportions.

"You still don't believe me," she said, with sadness in her voice. "But, Miro, I was trying to be gentle in that video. That's why I left out something very important, which I am about to reveal to you now, when I am here to support you."

"Go on!" I urged her. "Support me. And in case I faint, could you please carry me to the bed?"

I wanted to make her smile, but instead, her eyes teared up, and she asked me an unexpected question: "When was the last time you met your grandfather?"

"Why are you asking?"

"*When?*"

"Last month, in the beginning."

"More precisely, you were fired on Monday, August first, and on Wednesday, August third, he called you to his study and kept you there for more than an hour."

"Yes, he took the opportunity and used a lot of *I told you*s. But you seem to know that. Why ask?"

"To see if you remember at least that," she replied.

I was getting bored.

"I remember everything, Graziella. But you've forgotten that my memory loss is an invention of yours."

"Very good. And what did your grandfather tell you about Patrick?"

"Nothing. He's never said anything about Patrick or the experiment."

Nodding her head tiredly, she mumbled, "I'm sorry, Miro." Then she took out a phone from the pocket of her overalls. She handed it to me. "Call and ask him. Go to the meadow; you can get a signal there."

I took the phone and stepped out of the bungalow. Graziella stayed inside. I headed for the meadow, walking slowly and stiffly like a zombie. I had no idea what was happening. I seemed to have lost connection with my brain. *And I surely will hear "No connection" when I try to call,* I thought. *She has taken care of that. She's lying, lying again…*

I tripped in the roots of the palm tree I was passing by. I stopped and leaned my back on its trunk. What if I call and he answers? *Hey, Grandpa. I'd like to ask you something—have you ever told me anything about Patrick…because if you had, then it wasn't back in your study; it was him, Merry Maker…*

"No!" I said to myself. "*No.*"

I calmed down a bit, and a new suspicion crossed my mind. I went back to the bungalow to use it immediately on Graziella. "You want to convince him I'm crazy! That's why you're sending me out there to ask him crazy, stupid questions."

She reached out her hand in silence. I gave her back the phone, but after doing something to it, she handed it back to me.

"You're right," someone sighed—in my hand.

I looked at the screen. And my grandfather looked at me! I instantly froze his image and muted him.

"I've had enough!" My voice was so high that I could barely recognize it. "I've had enough," I repeated in my usual baritone. Bass-baritone: "When are you going to stop with the recordings?"

"If you had called him, there would've been no need for this last one," Graziella said.

I collapsed in the chair. My grandfather's proud image was waiting for me on my palm. The face of an ascetic with high cheekbones, the piercing gray eyes below the thick gray eyebrows, the thick gray hair, the brow of a nobleman, the chiseled nose of a statue by a sculptor from Ancient Greece...damn him! I put the phone on the table, because my hand was trembling. Graziella was looking at me mirthlessly. With compassion. And understanding.

I tapped on a button. The lips, until now frozen into a rigid straight line, moved:

"Both of us were devastated back then. He because he was fired; I because of Patrick's threats. That's why I was tempted to believe him."

"I'm not blaming you, Nathaniel." Graziella's words sounded somewhat muted. "Did you notice anything strange about his behavior?"

"No. Probably because he *usually* was strange. Like his mother and father."

"Yes, yes, I know…by the way, I am now recording this, so you can speak to him also. Is there something in that Patrick story you've left out?"

The gray eyes shot through both time and the screen. They pierced mine, also gray and, on ordinary days, penetrating, which now did nothing but blink in the darkness of absent reason.

"No, I left nothing out, Miro. I told you everything. I pushed you to murder him, but I didn't know that until it was too late."

CHAPTER FIFTY-NINE

The silence between us was growing deafening. Someone had to break it.

"All right, tell me..." I whispered because I had no strength for more. "Tell me...what he has told me."

This gave me two or three precious minutes to help me regain control of myself while Graziella repeated the story about Patrick's interest in the vial of melon essential oil.

"So in the end," she went on, "one of the pharmacists told him that the day before Maya served the poisoned éclairs, her grandmother had purchased various items from him, but melon oil was not among them. He also told him that following the cops' orders, he had checked if one of the vials was missing, but they were the right number."

"The right number?" I asked, without thinking.

"Yes. Luckily, on her first meeting with Maya's lawyer, the frightened old hypochondriac lady confessed to him that she had stolen the vial. And the lawyer, of course, was one of my men. I hired him the morning after the tragedy at the school, because for the experiment I need a *victim* who had turned into a murderer. Like everyone else here, Miro…including you."

Her eyes teared up again. She made an angry gesture and continued, "I went to the pharmacy before the cops and put on the shelf a vial of melon oil bought from another store. I was in disguise—a wig, makeup, glasses…" Tears continued to sparkle in her eyes, but now she laughed. "You should've seen me that day! Even you wouldn't have recognized me, despite your keen eye for detail."

The compliment together with her tears and childlike smile stirred in me not only the erotic desire I was already aware of but also a deeper and more complex emotion. Nothing seemed more ridiculous now than falling in love with her! But ridiculous and absurd things have always been part of my life—why not another one?

"A bit later," she resumed after the pause, "I also arranged the disappearance of the vial carrying Maya's fingerprints. That was one more obstruction for the prosecutor, who was after that annihilated by the defense lawyer's speech. Maya was acquitted on lack of evidence. I took her to a great surgeon, who fixed her face. I comforted her, helped her, brought her here. And for four months everything was fine. But after that…"

"After that came Patrick," I said bitterly.

"Unfortunately. As it turned out, he had been busy with internship and studying during those months. And as soon as these were over, he jumped into his clunker and…drove all the way to the village of the grandmother! He started asking, and a couple of old men told him that once, about fifty years ago, her mother had helped the village get rid of the moles. That she used to sell poison, they said to him. A very effective *poison*, you see?"

"I see," I confirmed. "And then?"

"The worst happened," Graziella replied. "Patrick returned to the city and went straight to the old lady's house. He pressed her with the fact about the poison she got or stole from her mother and blamed her of poisoning the éclairs, and that weasel of a woman blamed her granddaughter for everything. And when Patrick left, she called the lawyer and told him what she'd done, and he called me, and we both made a conference call to your grandfather, who also panicked…"

"Hey! Panicked? Why? Maya's going to confess that she's the poisoner, right?"

"Miro! Hasn't anything stayed in your head since you came on the island?" Her disappointment made me regret my pointless remark. "Yes, Maya, like everyone else of the group, is going to confess everything, *but at the trial*! And she's going to do this at her *own* will and after signing an agreement with the prosecutor that in the end she would be acquitted on grounds of some pathological effect at the moment of the crime or...I still haven't decided what exactly. What's important is that if things go this way, she won't be sent to prison *or* a mental hospital. But if Patrick had told the police, everything would've been over! The prosecutor would've asked for resumption of court proceedings, and the cops would've come here to arrest her."

"I see. Yet you were afraid not only for Maya's fate but also for your experiment. The prosecutor could have asked for its termination."

"Not 'could.' He most definitely would've asked for that. That is why your grandfather and I found Patrick's address and sent our lawyer to offer him a substantial amount of money in return for his silence. Patrick promised to think until Friday, but we will never know what his decision was because... on Wednesday evening your grandfather told you about this, and on the very same night you—"

"No!" I clenched my fists. "He's told me nothing. He's lying! Lying!"

I couldn't bear the compassion in her eyes anymore, but her words were even harder to take. They carried irrefutable truth. "You've always wanted to do something unique for your grandfather, something he would be grateful for. And you have always loved him as well as hated him. You've been *torn* between those two opposite feelings since you were a child. You know that, don't you?"

"Yes, but—"

"Torn right until that fatal night when your personality couldn't take it anymore and...*split* in two!"

"Has it?" I croaked in an attempt at irony. "And did we divide the feelings between us two? Who of us hates him and who loves him now?"

"Again, only you." Something resembling a smile flickered on her lips. "Merry Maker is dead now. That's what I think, based on observing some of your unconscious reactions."

"You think, but you are not sure?"

"No, I'm not!" she groaned. "I'm not sure even about whether...your grandfather has really told you about Patrick or..."

"Or?" I looked at her, startled by the unexpected turn. "Or what?"

"I don't know. But if you're right that he's lying, then he must have a motive. Why would he lie?"

*Why, why…*that's what I was asking myself too, getting ugly speculations instead of real answers.

I looked down. I wanted to hide my face because I could feel the nervous tics with which it reacted to the situation. I heard Graziella stand up but did not look at her. Then I heard her quietly slip out of the bungalow.

CHAPTER SIXTY

As it turned out, Graziella had left me not out of tactfulness but because she had heard the sound of the approaching plane. Now I heard it too. From the window I saw her walk away, almost run actually, and impulsively followed her. I knew that regular flights to the island were on Friday, so it must've been urgent that they came here on a Thursday afternoon. What was that urgency?

At first, I wasn't sure if I was secretly following Graziella or simply walking after her, but when we came closer to the house, I hid behind one of the hibiscus bushes. Opposite me, standing before the closed door of the garage, Sirius and Danko were gesturing at each other. Sirius was saying, "No, no!" and Danko was saying, "Yes, yes!" while grinning.

Or was he crying? Well, I couldn't say, but his condition seemed serious, because now Graziella was not running lightly but speeding in their direction.

Upon reaching them, she pulled the remote control from Sirius's hands and opened the garage door despite his attempt to stop her. I moved to another, closer bush.

"Without him! You promised me!" Sirius wasn't happy. "You have no right!"

"She has! She has all the rights!" Danko announced victoriously, and Graziella grabbed his arm and led him to the garage, smiling kindly.

A moment later from inside came the rumble of a car engine, and soon she was out in the pickup truck. Danko was sitting next to her, but since the driver's cabin was open, I noticed that he looked different. His head was drooping, and he was rubbing at his neck, babbling.

"Why, why, why…you stung me…what…"

"Come help me!" Graziella called, driving in reverse gear and taking the pickup truck back to the garage.

Sirius disappeared inside with quick steps, and a minute later I saw him in Danko's seat. The remote was back in his hand, and he used it to close the garage door while Graziella drove the car on the road to the landing strip at full speed.

Soon I found out that the garage door was not only closed but also locked.

"Hey, Danko!" I yelled. "What's going on?"

"Do, mi, fa, fa, re, ti, dooo…I'm the one meeting youuu…" he replied.

"OK, but…why did they lock you up inside?"

I couldn't make a single word out of his babbling, but at least I managed to understand that Graziella had really injected something into him. She was carrying a syringe with a sleeping drug in her overall, which unsurprisingly was her clothing of choice here. Only the devil knew how many of these "tamers" waited in those big pockets.

"Danko, Danko!" I banged with a fist several times on the door. "Don't fall asleep! Not before telling me—"

I heard him snoring. I went back into hiding behind the closest bush, sat down on the grass, and waited. Whatever the delivery that spurred this flight, Graziella and Sirius should be back in the house in half an hour. I looked at my watch—4:12 p.m.—and corrected my estimation: in less than half an hour, because they would be in a hurry for the meeting at 4:30 p.m.

The airstrip was not more than a mile from here. I could hear the pickup truck driving away, and I heard it stop. Ten minutes passed in silence—what were they loading on it?—then I heard the sounds of the plane taking off, and a moment later I saw it in the sky. I also saw the pickup truck, with Sirius behind the wheel now, coming down the road, stopping in front of the house to leave Graziella, and driving away again. It continued across the meadow, maneuvering among the bushes. I rose to my feet and watched it drive around the acacia grove. It disappeared on the other side and stopped almost immediately after that. I was unable to see what was in its storage slot, because a tarpaulin covered it.

The sound of approaching footsteps made me turn around. Roxanna was coming toward me. I greeted her with a nod and asked, "Is there anything else beyond that grove beside the pens?"

"Yes, there's a pavilion there. Danko and Sirius put it up last week."

"What for?"

"I have no idea. Let's go! But promise to ask for me for your compulsory walk companion after the rehearsal!"

"I'll skip the rehearsal, Roxanna. I don't belong to your 'theater' group. But if you insist on the walk—"

"I insist. Meet me at six on the beach, because… I really insist!"

We parted without saying more. She continued toward the house; I headed for the grove. I took the shortcut through the trees, and as soon as I stepped out, I saw the pavilion—domelike, covered with colorful shapes…of clowns. It was a circus pavilion. I smiled. Compared to the isolator and its crocodile guardians, this whim of Graziella at least looked funny.

The pickup truck was parked at the entrance of the pavilion, and the sagging tarpaulin and the lowered ramp told me that part of the cargo was no longer in the storage slot. I walked toward the pavilion, and the paintings of the clowns became clearer, revealing more details, none of them funny actually. I circled the pavilion, looking at them. They were painted in different postures, different clothes, with different grimaces and different make-up, so at first I didn't realize that the prototype for all of them was one person: Danko. I recognized him only when I focused my attention to the eyes. The painter had painted them with astonishing accuracy: swampy green and sparkling with madness.

I walked into the pavilion, which on the inside was just a round arena covered with a thick layer of dry grass. To one side of the entrance, there were several folding chairs, a rake, and a three-pronged pitchfork, and across the room there was a two-winged screen with full-length portraits of clowns on each wing. The resemblance of these two to Danko was emphasized by his characteristic half smirk and knitted eyebrows.

I assumed that Sirius was in the space behind the screen, so I took a few steps forward, but then I noticed that the thick layer of dry grass I was wading through consisted of mainly dry wild flowers. It seemed that after cutting them with the mower, Danko had brought them here. *Another therapeutic method*, I said to myself and went ahead. I got to the screen, but just when I was about to reach out and pull it, its wings slid open, and Sirius appeared between the two clowns. He was naked to the waist, breathing heavily and with an angry expression on his face that instantly changed into a startled one.

"Miro!"

Without turning, he stretched his arms behind him and closed the screen. I noticed that his chest was absolutely hairless, as if waxed, and that there were no tattoos on it or on his arms. That was unusual for a man who had spent fourteen years in prison. The absence of scars on his pumped-up-with-steroids body was also an unusual sight.

"What are you unloading?" I asked him.

"Danko's pathological whims, is what," he snorted.

"Meaning?"

"Well…I just brought here a chest…full of music instruments. And a piano in a box is waiting in the pickup. Dammit! I'm going to be really late!"

Sirius walked around me and headed for the exit with quick steps. I followed him, and by the time I went outside, he had jumped on the storage slot. He threw the tarpaulin aside, pulled the big box toward the ramp, and dragged it down, taking step after step backward. I stared at his back, suddenly convinced that I was staring at something important, without knowing what exactly. Just like in a hidden-picture puzzle, it was before my eyes, yet I was unable to see it.

By the way, though blond, Sirius had a nicely tanned body, and that was obvious when compared to the strip of pale skin around his waist that appeared when he bent down...yes! *This strip of skin is the important thing,* I thought. I stepped toward him and pulled down his bermudas. He dropped the box, turned around, and looked at me with eyes wide with puzzlement. He swung his hand to hit me, but I jumped to the side, and a moment before he pulled his pants back up, I saw the silvery white color of his hip.

"How curious," I said mockingly.

"Son of a bitch! You pulled my hair yesterday, now you—"

"The color of your hair is also curious. I bet that your natural color is that of a sick lemon too."

"Son of a bitch."

"Are you brother and sister?"

"Bastard!" He widened his repertoire. Then he added with sincerity, "No. We're cousins. Our fathers are twins."

"And you've never been in prison, have you?"

"No, I haven't. I am not a murderer, Miro. I became part of the group only to help Graziella."

"Of course," I said through clenched teeth. "You helped her a lot for my 'confession,' for example."

"Yes. I tricked you into confessing more convincingly by creating tension. And at first, I didn't believe you were Merry Maker—"

"At first? Scoundrel! You knew from the beginning that I am not him."

"I neither know nor don't know. And I don't care," he mumbled, grabbing the box with the piano again. He started dragging it toward the entrance of the pavilion, but after a few seconds, he stopped and turned to me. "Will you help me?"

"Of course," I told him.

I went to the pickup truck and slid the loading ramp back into the storage slot. Next, I sat behind the wheel, picked up with two fingers the shirt he had left on the other seat, and threw it out. Then I stepped on the gas.

CHAPTER SIXTY-ONE

I had plenty of time until six. I undressed down to my swim briefs and waded into the bay. Although many hours had passed since the storm, the water was still troubled, cold and murky yet clear enough for me to see the jellyfish the tide had brought in. They were exactly what I needed now: If I had to avoid their poisonous and pulpy bodies, I wouldn't be able to think of my grandfather and his wicked lie.

Less than ten minutes had passed when I noticed with surprise that Roxanna had already arrived at the beach.

"You're early," I said, after ending my slow swim to the shore.

"Graziella cut the meeting short. Sirius came, whispered something in her ear, and she let us go."

I grinned gloatingly: He had whispered to her that I'd discovered they're relatives.

"Did she look worried?" I asked. "Or worried and angry?"

"No. Neither."

After the disappointing reply, Roxanna sat on the nearest rock, and I made myself comfortable on the sand. I would've preferred to remain standing and dry up quickly, but our conversation would go nowhere if I continued looking at her from above.

"Miro," she began, "I believe now that Graziella has lured you into making false confessions. That's why I want to explain to you why instead of helping you, I am going to warn her about your plan to escape her trap."

I shrugged, meaning, *If you want to, feel free to explain*, and she continued:

"I went to Fata's last evening. I complained to her that I am feeling again as if I hadn't killed anyone, and she showed me the portrait I gave you. Thank you for not destroying it! Because this time I realized *whom* I had really painted while I imagined…someone else completely. Then Fata told me that you think that my memory of the place I had thrown the gun into might not be real, and this morning Graziella told me everything!"

"What do you mean by 'everything'?" I asked.

"Everything connected to the murders, my aunt, and my delusions. I was surprised she gave in so easily. I lied to her that I had suddenly remembered how during the hypnotic sessions she would try to plant false memories of the gun, and she looked so glad. 'This proves that your therapy has been successful, and you are ready for the truth,' she told me and took me to the hall, where she played a video of my aunt's confessions…which you are planning to use to neutralize your own."

"I see. So, Valdo had another visit to the isolator this afternoon."

"Yes. I had to tell him that I finally know the truth, but that my feelings for him have not changed. And now I am telling you that I still feel the same for my aunt. That's why I am going to tell on you. Of course, the chance of you finding the video is close to zero, but still…I cannot take even the slightest risk because the woman who has sacrificed five years of her life could go to jail. She was only twenty-six when she took me home. I almost destroyed her with my phobias, panic attacks, hallucinations, anxieties—"

I cut her off gently, "I understand, Roxanna, but you also have to accept the fact that this woman blamed you for the murders she has committed."

"She didn't want to blame me, and in the beginning, she didn't want to kill. She wanted *me* to kill. She saw me hiding the stolen gun under my pillow, but even before that, she had realized that only the death of at least one of the three men could bring me back to life. She got in touch with the nastiest of them, the one who would give me the worst nightmares, lured him to come visit us as…as a client, and led him into my bedroom. She thought that the moment I saw him, I'd pull the gun out and shoot him…"

Looking down, Roxanna repeated several times, "She overestimated me, she overestimated me," and then she embarked on a confusing account filled with pauses, which, in short, went like this:

Upon seeing her "client," she not only didn't shoot but also sank into the stupor familiar from her childhood. He went out into the corridor to her aunt and told her that he knew this condition very well and would wait for Roxanna to come out of it. He ordered her to bring him some liquor to "get him started" and went back into the bedroom.

Angry, the aunt decided to shoot him herself. She quickly put some disguise on—the "funeral" veil—and stepped into the bedroom, where she lied to the client that she had managed to bring Roxanna back using the same shocking disguise before. She leaned over and pulled the gun from under the pillow. She kept it hidden under the veil, hesitated for a while, but then the client decided to leave, telling her that the twenty-year-old Roxanna was too old for his taste…

Well, it's not hard to imagine what the aunt's answer to that was.

However, after she fired the gun, she succumbed to panic. She rushed into the bathroom, hysterically cleaned up her face, and gulped down a solid dose of sedatives. An hour passed before she could return to Roxanna's room, where she found neither her nor the dead man.

"Graziella thinks that I had known at that moment that my aunt was the murderer, and that's why I had buried the guy, as well as the next two she lured and shot, this time on purpose, later." Roxanna met my eyes and suddenly smiled. "It was something like waltzing in the dark. Each of us making our own dancing moves, never discussing any of it. But we both started to feel better. Until the moment her boyfriend's dog dug out one of the corpses, that is…"

We stopped talking, because we saw Graziella approaching. She nodded from afar and waved her hand.

"Yes, it was the sight of the rotting corpse that led to your amnesia!" she yelled. Then she came closer, taking her time, and continued, "Retrograde amnesia, which is a loss of memory for events from the past, like the three murders in your case. And the strong fear that your aunt might be found out became the engine for your delusions. That personified Death was born inside your mind as a sort of reality surrogate."

Stepping closer to Roxanna, she shoved two fingers under her collar and pulled something the size of a green pea from there—a microphone, of course, which she dropped into the upper pocket of her overall.

"Hypocrite!" Roxanna exclaimed. "That's why you hugged me at the end of the meeting! That's how you managed to attach the microphone without being noticed."

"Yes." Graziella seemed unmoved. "I've known from this morning that you never had a 'sudden memory of the false memory.' I saw Miro's long shadow in this story too, so I took some measures to tape your conversation in case you chose him for the walk. By the way, congratulations, Miro; you're right. I did plant the memory of her throwing the gun into the well in her mind. I thought that this way I could make her 'recall' the exact spot, but that didn't happen. I had to torture her a bit with Valdo's video for that."

"I'm not surprised," I said. "I know from experience what you're ready to go through when you want to convince someone that he's a murderer. But your sincerity is something new."

"New? Nonsense. You should've realized by now that I stick to my lies only for as long as they are of use."

"Of use to whom?"

"My patients, Miro, you being one of them. As for Roxanna, I decided today that truth would work better for her than any lie. We all saw that she never fully believed that she had murdered the men, which only increased the disagreement between her mind and her emotions. But now she is much more stable, and she will be like that during the trial where, careful not to reveal the truth about her aunt, she will act more responsibly."

"You mean, once she's convinced that she is not a murderer, she would be more convincing as a serial murderer?"

"Exactly!" Roxanna joined the conversation in a sharp tone. "I will not tell on my aunt, even if it's a lie that she wanted to blame me."

"No, it's not a lie," Graziella assured her and turned to me. "I was informed of the three dead bodies on the day of their discovery, so I immediately sent for a lawyer for Roxanna. He went to their house, and her aunt told him that she was the murderer. She told him she was ready to confess to the police, but he advised her to talk to me first. We met, and I explained to her why I need a victim-murderer like her niece for the experiment I was about to start conducting. I convinced her that they wouldn't send Roxanna to jail for these murders because she was unanswerable for the actions. I also told her that she would get five million dollars..."

"I will give them to her. To the last cent," Roxanna added. "I decided today."

"That's a good thing to do, although I don't think she'll accept." Graziella gently put a hand on her shoulder. "Your aunt is a brave, proud woman. And it really wasn't me but her who insisted I record her confessions. She wanted you to have a choice in case your amnesia went away. So…" Her eyes pierced mine again. "This is how, Miro, one can achieve a higher form of justice through lying. If the truth had 'won,' her aunt would've gotten the death penalty or a life sentence for cleaning the world of those disgusting pedophiles. And now…"

Graziella left as suddenly as she had appeared. We watched her walk away, and then, as if pulled by some invisible force, we followed her. We caught up with her, and she laughed.

CHAPTER SIXTY-TWO

I was hungrier than I was tired, so it came as a surprise to me that I felt sleepy halfway through the dinner. Then I remembered Danko, who did not show up in the dining room, and made a connection between my sleepiness and his snoring in the garage. I also remembered how, when we sat by the table tonight, the two bottles of wine were already open. And how Graziella had filled my glass and those of Maya, Roxanna, and Frant with wine from one bottle but took the other to pour into hers and Sirius's, although there was still wine left in the first bottle.

Now Maya's and Roxanna's glasses were almost full, and mine and Frant's—half-empty. I read Frant's frequent blinking as another sign that

Graziella had been quite generous with the sleeping pills today and used the first opportunity to pour the remaining wine on the carpet, which soaked it up immediately. I continued eating and asked in passing, "Where's Danko? Is he sick or something?"

"Your guess is right," Sirius replied. "He's sick with impatience. He has a…concert tonight, but he wanted to start it in the afternoon hours."

"Yes. That's why I put him to sleep and locked him in the garage." Graziella surprised me with her straightforwardness.

"And nooow"—Frant yawned—"you're putting us to sleep."

"Yes," she confirmed, adding insolence to the straightforwardness. She raised her glass and ordered: "Drink! Everyone. To the last drop!"

Noticing that my glass was empty, Sirius made to fill it with the remaining wine from the first bottle, but in the end he poured it down his throat.

"I decided to sleep too!" He grinned and threw a defiant look at Graziella.

Maya, Roxanna, and Frant also grinned, and then with clearly visible pleasure, and drained their glasses. I couldn't take this anymore.

"What's wrong with you people? She's intoxicating us, right before our eyes, and you seem happy!"

"We are," Roxanna said. "In one way or another, each of us suffers from insomnia, but until now she's always refused to give us sleeping pills."

"I wouldn't have given you them now either," Graziella said. "I did this for Danko. He wants to be sure that only I will go to the pavilion tonight."

"What about Sirius?" I asked her. "If he had not joined our small party of anesthetized souls, how would he have gone there? In secret? Or by the privilege of being your..." I paused to make her uneasy that I might say in a loud voice the revealing "your cousin." I went with "Of your bodyguard?" in the end.

"In secret, because he is not privileged." She smiled at me. "Not privileged at all, although...it's no secret that besides my bodyguard he is also my cousin."

My eyes slid over the faces of Maya, Roxanna, and Frant. None of them looked puzzled.

"Since when it is not a secret?" I asked, puzzled.

"Since about an hour ago," Sirius replied. "You were hoping to hold us at bay with the threat that you would reveal how we are related, weren't you?"

"Whatever it is he was hoping for, he has made a mistake," Graziella concluded. "And that's all for the evening. Go back to your bungalows now, or you'll end up sleeping here or somewhere on the meadow."

We walked out, a group of dizzy and staggering people. I patted Sirius on the shoulder and asked in a seemingly kind manner, "Why all the complications? Why didn't you tell me that you're relatives in the beginning?"

"They've done the right thing," Frant joined in. "Back then, we wouldn't have trusted someone who was both not a murderer and a relative to the boss. But now we know him, and we've forgiven him everything, even his spying on us."

"Danko and Valdo might not forgive him," Maya chimed in. "They don't know yet…" Yawning, she mumbled out a "Bye" and headed for her bungalow.

Frant's and Sirius's bungalows were in the same directions, so Roxanna and I soon parted ways with them too. That was what I wanted: to have some time alone with her before the pills started working.

I jumped straight to the question. "Roxanna, when was the first time Fata accused Sirius of being the lowest of the murderers here? Please, remember!"

"The moment they met. About five months ago."

That was disappointing. If she had answered with an "About a month ago" or "Recently," my version would've made sense: Following his cousin's orders, Sirius murders Patrick and then the other three; Fata, somehow, discovers about this and—

"She accused him, but she never explained why," Roxanna said listlessly.

I could tell from a look at her eyes that the sleeping pill had started to hit her, and she walked with a tottering gait now.

"Roxanna?" I grabbed her by the elbow. "Answer me one more question! Here it is: Has Sirius left the island at the beginning and then at the end of last month?"

"No…but why—"

"He hasn't, right?"

"Yes, but—"

"Are you sure?"

Vexation brought her back for a moment. "Yes, I am sure, Miro. None of us has left the island until last Monday when Valdo, Sirius, and Graziella went to get you. Now leave me!"

I didn't, because I had to carry her. Luckily, we were not far from her bungalow—even though I had swallowed only half a dose, I too could feel the sleeping pill starting to work. I staggered, overcome with physical weakness, and my mind was also beginning to betray me. I had this insistent, itchy feeling that I had just heard something important without being able to process it.

I put Roxanna on her bed, took off her shoes, covered her with a blanket, and straggled toward my bungalow. *Following his cousin's orders, Sirius murders Patrick and then the other three.* Too bad I had to abandon that version. Considering his character of a true scoundrel and his closeness to Graziella, Sirius fit perfectly my idea of the so-called Merry Maker, but since he was already here when the murders started, it probably wasn't him. I stopped, rubbed my temples, and concentrated. *No, it's not him…but why couldn't it be her?*

I went back to Roxanna. I woke her up by shaking her persistently, calling out her name, and splashing cold water on her face.

"What? What?" she screamed.

"Has Graziella also not left the island until this Monday?" I asked. "Or by 'none of us' you meant no one from the group?"

"By none of us…I meant no one, period."

"Including Graziella?"

"Yes, including her. No one, Miro. No one."

"OK, go to sleep now," I mumbled.

I left and went straight to my bungalow, not giving a single thought to any new versions or speculations.

CHAPTER SIXTY-THREE

I remained under the cold shower until my skin turned blue, and when I stopped the water, I could hear my teeth chatter like castanets in the hands of a drunken dancer. At least I wasn't sleepy anymore. I put on my camouflage pants and a plain brown T-shirt, went out of the bungalow, and did not head straight for the pavilion, because I heard a car horn. I walked to the palm tree, from behind which I could see what was happening in front of the house. The pickup truck was parked at the door, and Graziella was walking around it, reaching out a hand from time to time to hit the horn. I couldn't see any details from that distance, so I couldn't tell if she was angry or simply impatient.

A couple of long and boring minutes later, Danko came from his bungalow. He was wearing black pants, a white shirt, and a dress coat, and in his hand he was holding a top hat. Combed back, his black hair was shining like a helmet. I thought that both would get in the car and drive away for the "concert," but they went inside the house instead. I welcomed the opportunity to reach the pavilion before them. Thus, I would be able to look around without having to hurry and find a hiding place with a view at the stage or, more precisely, the arena.

I took a longer path, diminishing to zero the possibility of being seen from the house. According to the clock, it was evening—it was almost eight—but outside was still light as day. As far as I could tell, it would be sunset in less than an hour. I imagined Maya, Roxanna, Sirius, and Frant sleeping soundly in their bungalows. A sight as unnatural as their willingness to be put to sleep. As if they wanted to be sure that not even the faintest echo from Danko's concert would brush their ears.

Sirius had left the box with the piano at the entrance of the pavilion. I walked around it, and once I was in, I saw the two clowns, drawn in full size, staring at me from the wings of the screen. I walked across the arena toward them, ankle-deep in dry wild flowers. Unlike his cousin, Sirius was not good at improvising when lying; his reply that he'd been unloading "Danko's pathological whims" over there somehow did not match the fact that the whims in question were actually musical instruments. That emergency flight was for some entirely different delivery, and I had to find what it was and use it to my advantage.

I slid open the wings of the screen and looked around. The room beyond it was in the shape of a half sphere, and the only object in it was…a coffin. A large, polished, black coffin set up straight before me. I took a step forward and realized that Fata was also here, standing only two feet away from me. She was wearing a flower shirt and baggy pants, and she had her hands in the pockets. As usual, neither the clothes nor the posture looked suitable for her age, least of all her attitude.

"Where are you going?" she hissed.

I turned my head in the direction of the coffin. "Over there."

"Why?"

"What do you mean 'why'? I just want to take a look at it."

"You can also try it," she suggested. "Looks like the right size for you."

Her cackle grated on my ears, but I was glad that I met her here.

"I was going to pay you a visit tomorrow—"

"Again?"

"Yes, Fata, again. But I'd prefer it if you answered me now: Why did you have to say that thing about the dyed hair? Why not simply tell me that Sirius and Graziella are cousins?"

"I wanted you to find it out on your own. You're always saying you're a detective."

"Ah, you're not getting away that easy! If we winnow your words and take a look at the important stuff you've said, it turns out that to you Sirius is the lowest of the murderers here...because he's Graziella's cousin!"

"Yes. That's right...oooh..." She swayed, summoned a martyr's look on her face, and moaned, "I feel sick. Help me get out of here!"

She wasn't good at acting, and there was no need for her to pretend. I knew that her goal was to get *me* out of there before I could reach the coffin. Of course, under normal circumstances, there would have been only two possibilities: it being empty or being occupied by a dead body. But these were not normal circumstances.

I went closer to the coffin, and after taking a quick look alongside it, I found that I wouldn't be able to see what's inside, because it was locked with a padlock. It occurred to me that maybe Fata wanted me out of there before I'd seen what was behind the coffin, not inside, and it was the right guess: A rotund Japanese man showed up, spreading arms apologetically, and said, "Hello, mister."

He was about sixty, with a pleasant face and salt-and-pepper hair tied at the back and a black, perfectly trimmed moustache. He was wearing camouflage pants just like mine and a shirt of the same material, and there was a compact camera hanging from his neck.

"My name is Ichiro. Ichiro Ashikawa," he introduced himself after I said nothing.

"My brother," Fata explained, although she didn't have to. Then she added the obvious: "I'm older than him, and we're not from the same mother."

While saying this, she was pulling the end of my sleeve, and now she started pushing me toward the screen. Ichiro was already walking in that direction.

"Hurry up!" he urged us over his shoulder. "We cannot hide here."

We filed out between the two wings of the screen, and Fata slid them shut. Something about her behavior and also that of her brother made me return to my earlier guess. "You actually don't want me to find out what's in the coffin, do you?"

"Nonsense!" Fata snapped at me. "Didn't you see the padlock?"

"I did, but I guess you've—"

"Mister, there's no time for guessing, lying, or even twisting information. So I'll be honest with you. Yes, we know what's inside the coffin, despite the padlock. You will know too, when the psychiatrist and the madman come here and unlock it."

"Why not tell me now?"

"Because we fear that you might try to stop what's about to happen, and we want to film it."

"I see!" I didn't hide my enthusiasm. "You're expecting to witness something illegal so that you can use it against Graziella later. Very good! I won't bother you or stand in your way but only on one condition: You have to give me a copy of the recording."

"Deal." Ichiro nodded. "You'll have it tonight. I know which one your bungalow is, but you must be alone when I come."

We parted ways. Fata left, and I and her brother took positions opposite each other but with an equally good view of the arena in the pavilion. We covered ourselves with the abundance of dry wild flowers and waited for the psychiatrist and the madman to come and do their illegal business, whatever that was.

CHAPTER SIXTY-FOUR

I heard a voice and then realized it was my own. I opened my eyes. I was in a heap of dry grass, cursing and shaking my head.

"Don't worry. These are just common earwigs," Graziella said, leaning over me.

I stood up. The nasty bugs were all over me. It took me a while to get rid of them. Her arms crossed, Graziella was looking at me with resentment, which seemed to be directed both at the insects and me.

"What a shame!" she let out her outrage. "Did you have to sleep here?"

"What did you expect me to do?" I responded in the same tone. "Not sleep after taking a sleeping pill?"

"No, I didn't expect anything...I mean, I expected but in your bed..." She realized there was no need for elaboration and stopped.

I noticed a movement on the opposite side of the pavilion. Behind Graziella's back, the Japanese man who had "committed suicide" was begging me with gestures. I was so dizzy that I almost yelled at him, "Don't worry. I won't tell her you're here!"

"Everything's fine," I said in a loud voice, seemingly to reassure Graziella up.

He heard me and hid in his pile of dry grass, but Graziella, of course, was not reassured up.

"Go away!" She stomped her foot. "Leave!"

I shook my head and looked at her in silence. She had finally taken off that working overall and was dressed in something that could pass for formal clothing: a white suit, pants and jacket, with thin dark-blue stripes, a silk shirt in light blue, and low-heel closed-toe shoes in white. Her hair was put up in something like a bun, black circled her eyes, blue was on her eyelids, and deep pink on her lips. And on top of that, rouge, so much rouge on her cheekbones that it made her pale face look even paler. I didn't like her like that. She didn't look good, and she looked out of place here, as did the now-unboxed piano, which was in the center of the dry-grass-covered arena.

"Where's the pianist?" I asked. "I came for his concert, after all."

Her involuntary glance at the screen told me that Danko was behind it, in the room with the coffin.

"You have to go!" she insisted. "No one invited you here."

The growing tension inside her was almost visible, and I didn't think I was the only reason for it. I walked toward the folding chairs by the entrance, and this time I noticed that it was dark outside and that the light inside came from two powerful accumulator lanterns.

"I saw you in front of the house more than an hour and a half ago," I said, unfolding one of the chairs. "So. What took you so long?"

"You were sleeping, and you didn't hear us. We've been here for quite a long time. The piano slowed us down."

She lied to me, and I pretended to believe. It was our way of communicating with each other: standing face-to-face, "honestly" throwing dust into each other's eyes.

I unfolded another chair and invited her to sit down, but she clutched at my arm and started pulling me toward the screen. When we got there, she let go of my arm to open the wings, and then with a nervous gesture, she showed me Danko, who stood motionless by the coffin. A long silence followed, during which he didn't move. He looked petrified. So much so that Graziella had to go to him and shake him. He blinked and looked at her, she pointed at me, and he saw me. He saw me only now, even though during the long silent pause, he was "watching" me.

"You can stay," he said to me. "You can, because I will never play or sing again. Never again!"

"OK." Graziella nodded at him. "We're waiting."

We left him there and returned to the chairs. We moved them closer to the piano and took our seats. We had not shut the screen, so we were able to witness from there the whole weird scene: the coffin, set up straight for no clear reason, black and smooth like a mirror reflecting the image of Danko dressed in a white shirt and black dress coat. The top hat was not on his head but on the coffin, a sinister miniature pillar. For the first time, it crossed my mind that there might be a real dead body inside.

I turned to Graziella. She looked reconciled with my presence.

"It's not easy for him," she whispered confidentially. "It is a peak moment for him. Peak for me also, because I am about to see the proof that he is finally cured. Yes, yes! I am sure that everything will end well."

"Your cousin didn't look so sure, though. That's why he preferred the sleeping pill to coming here with you."

"Damn him! He's a coward. He thinks that Danko is dangerous."

"I think the same," I said. "A sadistic karate master, cured by his psychiatrist's crazy form of therapy, which includes using a grass mower."

I did not express my opinion in a low-enough voice. Danko heard it and—which was worse—liked it. He stretched his lips into his usual red lined-with-tiny-white-teeth smile. He put the top hat on and stepped behind the coffin. He grabbed the handles on both sides, tilted it toward him, and, pushing it, moved in our direction. As it turned out, the coffin was on wheels, like a giant suitcase, and before Danko put it up before us, I saw that its bottom end was covered with holes, as if someone had shot at it with a machine gun.

My puzzlement was only momentary. Yes, there was somebody in the coffin, but he or she was not dead but breathing—hoarsely and quickly. So, that is why Fata and Ichiro had made their best to take me far from the coffin. They didn't want me to hear what they had heard. They knew that I would try to do something for the carefully packaged "delivery."

Graziella took a key from her suit pocket and gave it to Danko, and he unlocked the padlock. Then he put his forehead against the lid and began in a singsong voice, "Do you know, do you know that cicadas sing with their wings? Rubbing wing against wing, they sing and sing...but I have no wings."

He stepped to the side, and screaming, "I have no wings!" he kicked the coffin, sending its lid to the floor with a bang. Inside, clutching at two metal clamps screwed into the wood was a woman. She was middle-aged, of medium height and weight, and with hair of medium length. She was dressed in a plain gray dress and was wearing flat black shoes. Unable to take his eyes off her, Danko seemed at a loss for words. His mouth opened and closed, but nothing came out. The woman in the coffin was silent too. She looked frightened but not terrified. Danko was the terrified one.

"I've been deceived." He found a few words at last. "You...you are not her! Not that...stepmother."

"It's been twenty years," Graziella told him in a gentle voice. "She was young and beautiful then. Then, but not now, when she's grown old."

"But her treachery is still young. And her greed and cruelty also...right?" Danko stretched out his arms toward Graziella like a beggar.

"Everything ages." She disappointed him. "Your desire for vengeance has aged too."

Following her command, the woman stepped out of the coffin. Her movements were stiff from the long stay inside, but she was also trying to give them the air of the weakness of old age by slumping her shoulders and pressing a palm against her lower back.

"Sit at the piano, Cornelia," Graziella told her. "Your stepson has ordered it especially for you."

I noticed the conspiratorial looks the two of them exchanged, but even before seeing them, I had figured out that there was some arrangement between them. Otherwise the stepmother wouldn't have stayed so docilely in the coffin. Now, pretending to suppress her moans, she dropped onto the chair at the piano. Danko stood by her.

"These are also especially for you." He pointed at the clowns painted on the screen wings. "Look at them! Do you recognize me in them? Answer me!"

"Yes," the woman whimpered.

"I'm on the outside too," he added, with delusional cordiality. "This circus pavilion carries tens of images...of me. Especially for you. So that you can recall how you used to turn me into a laughing stock. Into a clown. And how you would sell me as such! And here are the notes." He dug his foot into the dry wild flowers. "I've been collecting them especially for you, so that you can remember how you used to lie and deceive and humiliate me...but look at them now! They are rotting. Because they are not notes, you godless woman! They were beautiful, colorful flowers; they were alive, but I would murder them. So that I could kill you among them. Get up!"

Raising her head, the woman glanced at Graziella, who again encouraged her with a gesture and what looked like a wink. I was disgusted by both of them.

"Come on; get up!" Danko repeated. "Take that hayfork and start turning them over...the notes, the rotting musical notes; turn them over..."

This time the woman obeyed. She shuffled her feet toward the hayfork. Danko was looking at her with increasing disappointment. It seemed like she—diminished by old age—was not suited to carry out his fantasies. He had worked on that specific ambiance for nothing.

"You deceived me also!" he screamed at Graziella. "This is the end! I'm not taking part in the trial, in that megatriaaal. The deal is off!"

"The deal is off if you tell me how have I deceived you," she responded to him and paused a long time, during which she watched him with eyebrows raised questioningly. "You can't!" she said in the end. "You can't say anything. Because I did my part of the deal: I paid dearly for your stepmother to be found, and here she is now, at your disposal. You can do whatever you want with her...if there's still anything you'd like to do with her."

She unbuttoned her jacket, and a moment later, her hand was holding a dagger in a leather sheath. She threw it at Danko; he caught it in the air and resumed staring at his stepmother, who bared her teeth and raised the three-pronged hayfork at him.

Laughing, he stepped closer to her. He took the hayfork from her with a single, lightning-fast movement and threw it at her feet. Then he left the pavilion. Seconds later, we heard the pickup-truck engine.

The woman—the stepmother Cornelia—rolled her eyes at the ceiling and puffed with relief.

"Poor Danny," she said, arranging her hair coquettishly. "They would always call for an encore at his concerts. Especially when I dressed him up like Elvis or in a dress coat and top hat."

She smirked, and Graziella stood up and walked to her.

"It took you too long," the woman reprimanded her. "I almost died in there. I think you'll have to pay me for that too."

"I will pay. I'll pay you for everything!" Graziella promised her. She bent down, picked up the hayfork, swung it…

And drove it into the woman's chest!

I jumped up, but by the time I got to Graziella, she had stabbed the woman two or three times more. I heard smacking sounds. The feet in the black shoes were kicking, digging into the dried flowers.

Graziella turned to me. She looked surprised.

"I didn't expect this to...I didn't want to...I acted on an impulse..." Her face twisted, went pale.

But her face was pale from a shock that had nothing to do with the just-committed murder. "I know where Danko's going!" she groaned.

CHAPTER SIXTY-FIVE

Valdo was lying facedown on the cement landing in front of Roxanna's bungalow. The pool
of blood underneath him was not large, but it was
growing. I took ahold of him carefully and turned
him on his back with some help from Graziella.
He was fully conscious, and I felt sorry for him because I just realized what had befallen him.

"Danko...he paralyzed me...he's with her." I
could barely hear his voice.

I could see that he was making inhuman efforts to move only in his eyes; they were bulged,
almost out of their sockets. I wouldn't wish such
nightmare even on my worst enemy: to lie paralyzed, a living corpse, while only a few feet from

him a raging psychopath was probably murdering his fiancée. Or maybe he had already murdered her?

The bungalow door was open, but nothing came out except for monotonous yellow light. Graziella took a step forward and stopped. She couldn't summon the courage to look in. I had never seen her like that—no self-control and on the verge of collapse.

"I made a mistake; I failed," she whimpered shakily. "And now…if she's dead, how will I live with that? How, God?"

"You won't," Valdo replied, although the question was not directed at him.

"I can hear you." Danko's howl came from the bungalow, followed by the songlike "Do you know, do you know that cicadas sing with their wings?"

I heaved a sigh of relief.

"Don't worry." I leaned over Valdo. "Nothing has happened yet. He's only now beginning with his ritual."

I pulled up his T-shirt, and Graziella turned on her flashlight so that we could take a better look at his wound. It was in the area between the right armpit and the chest. A serious wound, though not a lethal one. But it was not the reason for his paralysis. It seemed that Danko had neutralized him using his karate skills.

"He surprised me…first with the knife." Valdo looked at me somewhat guiltily. "I wanted to see her before coming to you, but he…"

"Of course he surprised you. After five months of friendship!" I touched his shoulder soothingly, stood up, and said to Graziella, "Stay here. Don't come in, no matter what you hear. Is that clear?"

She nodded and kneeled by Valdo. "I'm sorry, so sorry," she whispered to him, and from the bungalow came the words of the madman: "Do you know, do you know…"

"Yes, I know!" I yelled and moved stealthily to the door.

I stood in the doorway and saw that he was sitting on the chair by the bed. Although he looked at me, I don't think he saw me. His eyes were aimlessly roaming the place, and his confused face told me that I had stopped his ritual just in time. He was unable to go on; he needed to start all over again. But his hand still held the dagger and looked ready to use it any moment now, and Valdo's blood covered the entire length of the seven-inch blade.

Roxanna was sleeping. Just as I had left her hours ago—lying on her back, covered to the waist with the thin blanket, dressed in her dress from the evening. She was breathing deeply, evenly in the grip of the narcotic mixture of wine and soporific. Maybe that was the reason she was still alive.

If the singing and howling of Danko had woken her up, he would've continued…to the next step—the torture he used to inflict years ago on those eight women, young and beautiful like his stepmother then, young and beautiful like Roxanna now.

"No, you don't know." His eyes finally focused on me. "You don't know, and she's lying to you. She's lying to you, Daddy!"

"Hey, come to your senses, will you?" I told him jokingly, as if simply replying to his teasing in a game. "I am not your father, and she is not your stepmother. Go back to the pavilion, pal. The godless woman is still there, although her soul has left for hell."

Tilting his head to the side, he gaped at me, intrigued. I thought that I had found the right approach, but the moment I tried to take a step forward, he waved the dagger in the air and stopped his hand only an inch from Roxanna's throat.

"If you come closer," he said, "I will kill her."

I raised my hands peacefully. There was no chance I could reach him before he carried out his threat, although in this prison cell of a room, the distance between us was no more than eight feet.

"I will cut her throat in a blink of an eye." He proved my guess right. "But if you stay where you are, I will spare her. I will spare her but not her ears and her tongue. Not them!"

He shook with soundless laughter, mouth frothing. What was so funny? The memory that he had cut the ears and tongues of his other victims? The idea of doing the same to Roxanna...while I stay where I am, like a stuffed animal in the doorway?

It was a stalemate, and I could do nothing else but use the word-attack strategy to distract the sadist. Slowly lowering my hands, I began.

"It's not true that you strangled those women because you thought they were your stepmother. You wanted them to be conscious while you tortured and mutilated them, and that is why you had to kill them in the end." I clenched my teeth and went on with a hissing whisper. "You were taking out witnesses, not her. Not the wife of your father, *who you were in love with!*"

Danko wiped with his sleeve a string of froth down his chin.

"You're making up...funny stories," he said. "Actually, she was in love with me."

"Well, that is one true joke!" I whispered. "By the way, I am sure that she, *the love of your life*, was very disappointed when they put you in the loony bin instead of frying you on the chair."

"All right." He switched gears easily. "She was disappointed, yes, but she was more scared. She knew that as soon as I was released, she would be the first on my list. That's why she divorced my father and went hiding in another country under another name."

"Hiding for a good reason, I think. She, that poor naïve lady, found out only today that nothing in you has changed. Sucker!"

I stopped, waiting for his reaction, but his attention was again on Roxanna.

"Do you know, do you know…" he went on.

"Frankly, Danko," I told him, "I lied to you. Cornelia is alive and well. Now go to her in the pavilion and do everything to her you've dreamed of!"

"I want her to be deaf and mute. But why go there when she's here?"

He ran his free hand over Roxanna's forehead, grabbed her by the hair, and pulled so strongly that she sat up before even waking up. Then her eyes opened, and the first thing they focused on was the bloody dagger. I hoped that the shock from this sight would plunge her into the familiar childhood stupor, but what I saw was something else entirely: Her eyes became clearer, and the fear in her…seemed to be about something other than her own life.

"Valdo!"

"He's OK; he's safe," I hurried to say. "How are you, *Roxanna*?"

"Don't try too hard," Danko advised me, with a surprisingly normal expression on his face. "I see she's Roxanna. So what? I like her, not that old bag of a woman."

He let go of her hair, put his hand in his dress-coat pocket, and took out two elongated metal plates. He gave these to the fully woken-up Roxanna.

"I prepared them especially for this special evening. Put them in your mouth!"

She looked at me with horror in her eyes, and Danko immediately put the dagger to her throat.

"Stay where you are!" he warned me, and then he warned Roxanna. "Be careful! Valdo is lying facedown outside, but he's still alive. His life depends on you. Understand?"

"Yes," Roxanna said in a clear voice. "What do you want?"

"I want, I want, first I want to…to cut your tongue out! I need you to put these plates on both sides of your tongue so that your mouth stays open. Wide open. Say ahhh!"

This time Roxanna obeyed, and seconds later her face took on a painfully deformed expression. There was no time to waste; I had to risk not only my life but also hers. I cursed myself for forgetting to take Fata's knife after the cold shower. I could've made good use of its flying blade now.

I put my hands together as if for a prayer and unclasped the chain of my wristwatch with a stealthy movement of my thumb.

"Hey, Daniel!" I called. "Do you know, do you know that cicadas sing with their *feet*?"

He gaped at me, his seeming sanity dissolving into a grimace of idiotic bewilderment. I shook my hand, and the watch slid down, falling into my palm. I went on with pathos.

"Not with their wings, man, but with their feet! They rub their bellies and—"

A screaming "Noooo!" flew out of his mouth, louder than a fire truck's siren. I waited until it stopped, and then, when the room was silent again, I took advantage of the moment when he was blinking to throw the watch at the wall behind his back. The knocking sound made him turn his head, which was when I leaped toward him and grabbed him by the wrist of the dagger-clutching hand. I twisted it sharply, and he was forced to drop the dagger. It fell at our feet.

"Let's stop here!" he asked me all of a sudden.

He looked up at me and smiled. And then he shot his free fist toward my diaphragm. I blocked the blow with a knee, bent down over him, and grabbed him into something like an embrace. We both fell down on the floor. Now the dagger was under us. We rolled to the side and reached out for it simultaneously, but at the same time some-one's foot in a white shoe sent it with a kick under the bed. I squeezed Danko into another "embrace" and looked up. Armed with her favorite weapon, a syringe, Graziella was extending her arm toward us. I moved slightly to the side to make way for the needle, trying to keep the psychopath from tossing and turning too much. I could barely restrain him.

"Hurry up!" I yelled at her.

And she yelled in reply, "Calm down, Merry Maker!"

And she stuck the needle into my neck!

I knew that it had taken me a long time just to get up on my feet when I saw Danko sitting on the floor in the corner by the door. His had buried his face in his knees, and this way—with his black hair and black clothes—he looked like a headless raven. He shook in soundless crying, and Roxanna was kneeling next to him, holding his hand and soothing him with gentle words.

Standing next to them, Graziella was watching me tensely. I walked past her, stepped outside, and crossed the landing, where Valdo still lay paralyzed.

"Everything is fine," I told him on my way, rubbing the bump on my neck.

Pain, puzzlement, astonishment, rage, helplessness—these were my companions while I staggered down the path to my bungalow. To my cell, actually.

CHAPTER SIXTY-SIX

Waking up was like crawling out of a swamp—a slow, torturous, and somewhat dirty business. I dozed off a couple of times, dreams sucking me back into their sticky abysses, before I finally opened up my eyes. Through the barred window came enough light to know that it was day outside. But was it morning, noon, or afternoon? The palm trees outside provided no answer to that question, and the watch was not on my wrist. I remembered where it was only when I saw that I was still in my brown T-shirt and camouflage pants. That was when the fog inside my head lifted, and I could see some memories from last night. And among them stood out the demonic image of Graziella.

I remained lying, my body stiff, my eyes staring at the ceiling, where, as if on a movie-theater screen, I saw her driving the three-pronged hayfork into the chest of that woman...then driving the needle into my neck...then watching from the first row the death-sentence needle piercing my skin: *Calm down forever, Merry Maker!*

I felt like laughing, and this startled me and helped me clear my thoughts. No, there won't be a death-sentence needle, and there won't be a room for me in a mental hospital either. Those two possibilities have turned into impossibilities since last night. Because by committing a murder before my eyes, Graziella had predetermined my murder-"suicide" as well as, of course, the place of my execution: here, on this island, sold to her by the widower Ichiro... who had broken his promise. He didn't bring me a copy of the discrediting video. I was sure that he had managed to film everything from his hiding place in the pavilion, including the ending, which surprised even Graziella. So now he was in possession of a video recording with which he could blackmail her for millions. No wonder he had decided not to share it with me. My only chance now was to acquire it by force and get into the computer hall and send it to my lawyer. Graziella will lose the game, and my "confession" will never see the light of day, and I will soon be on my way out of here on a plane.

But if I don't get that precious copy, I will most certainly become, just like Kuber, a posthumous participant in the megatrial where she, the master psychiatrist, will tell everyone how she had caught and psychoanalyzed me, which led her to the revelation that, as a result of my childhood traumas and my recent discharge from the police, the psychopath in me was set free. And how, once free, I had started murdering, seeing the face of my sadistic grandfather in every one of my victims but not in the student Patrick Krenz, because in him I saw my own face.

What sick imagination could come up with so much nonsense and weave it into such a delusional account? And wasn't it more logical...that she didn't make it up?

"Enough!" I said in a strangely hoarse voice.

My throat felt like sandpaper, and when I sat up in the bed, I felt as if my body had been dismantled and now I had to put all the parts back together. I had no idea what Graziella had used to "calm me down," but judging by my condition now, I could tell that she was probably happy with the result. Anyway, I somehow put myself together and reached out for my sneakers. But I didn't get them. I stopped, staring at the linoleum. It was unpleasantly mouse gray in color, and over there, close to the door, was a darker spot from which a wide trace of dragging *something* led to the bed. There were also a couple of footprints in the same direction...

My hair stood on end. I picked up one of the sneakers, and when I saw its sole, my heart sank with the truth: Last night, coming here, I had stepped into that spot, which then was not a spot but a puddle. Of blood. And then...I had taken my sneakers off and had fallen asleep. And have slept for hours with him under the bed. Who? Ichiro?

Ichiro's corpse.

I didn't want to touch it, so I dragged the bed. I switched on the lamp, and the strong light showed me a frighteningly familiar "smile." Cut out probably by the same knife—Fata's knife—which now stuck out of her brother's chest. Weeks ago she had given it in secret to Roxanna to protect herself from the local murderers, but then it had found its way into my hands, and now its blade was there, deep into that stiff body on the floor.

Even without the razor and the laughing gas, Merry Maker had tried his best to leave his typical mark on the victim. But how could he be here? *How*, when he had committed the other four murders during the previous month and no one here had left the island until this Monday...and no one new, except me, had arrived?

CHAPTER SIXTY-SEVEN

Graziella met me on the path through the palm trees. This time she wasn't wearing her working overall but a medical coat, and a medical bag hung on her shoulder.

"If you're coming for my autopsy, you're early," I told her. "I'm not ready yet." My "joke" did not impress her.

"I changed Valdo's bandages and decided to stop by your place." She took my watch out of her pocket and handed it to me. "It's still working, but if you throw it against a wall again, it might stop."

"Are you criticizing me, Graziella?" I asked her, once again astonished by her brazenness. "Or straight up accusing me of something?"

"No, no. On the contrary. I want to apologize to you. I was confused last night. I wanted to neutralize Danko, but then I saw him growing calmer while you…I thought it was not you there. I thought I was neutralizing Merry Maker—"

I stopped her.

"Where is Danko now?"

"I don't know, but he was with us during the night. He is really sorry, Miro. He helped us carry Valdo to Roxanna's bed and then brought from the house everything we needed to clean and dress the wound. And he is as worried about him as we are. He is almost sure that the paralysis will go no later than this evening, but he admits that sometimes such a blow can inflict serious and lasting damage."

"So, you think Danko is an angel again?"

Graziella laughed. "Well, no. But I believe that no demon would lay a hand on him in the future."

"After your spectacular missteps last night, I don't think that what you believe in matters much," I said, putting the watch on my wrist. "Ah, it's only eight…"

I fell silent. Her eyes wider than usual, Graziella was staring at my hand.

"What…what is this?" she asked.

She touched with trembling fingers the sleeve of my T-shirt. Then she bent down to take a better look at my pants, walked around me, and rushed down the path to the bungalow.

Only now, after her reactions, I realized that the end of my sleeve was darker in color and crusty from the dried blood. I also didn't have to look too long at my pants to see the spots of blood among the camouflage colors.

I hurried after Graziella and saw her storm into my bungalow. Then came her piercing scream.

"Stay away from me!" she cried, jumping out. She ran among the palm trees like a sprinter, screaming, "Murderer!"

CHAPTER SIXTY-EIGHT

Sirius was not in his bungalow. *If he's not sleeping, then he must be eating,* I said to myself. I headed for the house in quick steps, and three minutes later I was in the kitchen. He was sitting at the table, head bowed over a large plate with spaghetti.

"Are you OK?" I asked him.

"Why wouldn't I be?" he asked me.

"What do you mean 'why'?"

I pulled the plate from under his nose and turned it over his head. The sound he made with his pasta-filled mouth resembled grunting. I stepped back and gave him time to shake the spaghetti off, and just as he was about to say something, I shut his mouth with a blow under his chin.

Making more hoglike sounds, he waved his arms and made several unsuccessful attempts to hit me.

"Don't make me laugh," I told him. "You steroid scarecrow."

I saw that my message had gone across, because he switched from meaningless attack to meaningless defense. I jammed my knee into his stomach, and while he was gasping for air, I grabbed a napkin from the table, wrapped it around my fist, and hit his nose as soon as he looked up.

"But why…" he snuffled.

"What do you mean 'why'?" I hit him again and threw the dirty napkin away. "I am Merry Maker, right? I'm preparing you for a *smile*, of course. For one final and wide and deep smile!"

He ran to the door. I let him reach it before catching up with him. I was in the mood for a couple more blows, but I figured that he wouldn't be able to talk after that, and I needed him to tell me a lot.

Kick after kick, I drove him back to the table, where I dropped him on a chair and asked him the main question: "Why did you kill him?"

"Who?" He pretended to look perplexed, which won him another loud slap in the face.

"Don't waste my time," I said. "I know that you killed him, but I want you to tell me why. Was he a threat? Was he an obstacle to you guys?"

"Who?"

Covering cheeks with his palms, Sirius compressed his lips as if he wanted to glue them together. I took this as a good sign. If he had started talking right away, the only logical conclusion would've been that he had ruled me out as a possible witness or, in other words, that he was sure that I had zero chance of leaving the island. I hesitated for a second whether I should stop or continue with the interrogation, although the latter would most certainly bring me closer to the aforementioned zero. I decided on something in between: I went on but this time following a different strategy, whose aim was to open up a chasm between the cousins.

"Too bad," I said, "such a pity that you and Graziella look alike only on the surface. On the deeper, intellectual, level, nature has denied you a lot."

"Where's that nonsense coming from?" He bristled up.

I replied readily, "Before you even came to the island, Graziella had ordered cameras to be set up around the house. Secret surveillance cameras she never told you about. She also didn't tell you that there's a video recording that shows that Kuber had fallen from the rock while trying to return a chick to its nest. She let you believe up until *last night* in the bullshit that he had been pushed down by Fata's voodoo magic. Watching you shake like a leaf before a harmless old woman amused her."

The "ungluing" of his lips came earlier than I expected.

"No! She wasn't amused; she was worried about me. She suspected that the damned Japanese man had not killed himself and was hiding somewhere on the island. That's why she wanted me to fear Fata and stay away from her. Otherwise I could've stumbled upon her brother, and one of us could've... gotten hurt."

"But *last night* both of you got hurt." I looked at him with compassion. "Alas, it was she, your own cousin, who's responsible for this."

I went to the coffee machine and chose a double espresso with cream and no sugar. Sirius was watching me more and more intensely, and when I leaned nonchalantly by the window and sipped from my coffee, his nerves couldn't handle it anymore.

"What do you mean 'both'? How did I get hurt?"

I smiled slightly. The time to use Graziella's maxim that the best lies are those that are dipped in a plentitude of truths had come.

"A little while ago," I began, taking my time, "you didn't even ask me how I knew that it was you who killed him."

"I didn't ask because it is not true that I killed him."

Although the napkin box was right in front of him, he again wiped the blood from his nose with a sleeve.

"Behave yourself," I warned him. "And use your brain. If I had said 'I assume,' 'I suspect,' or something like that, maybe there would've been use in denying. But I said, 'I know.' I know you killed him. See the difference? Yes or no?"

I took a step forward, and he mumbled a quick yes.

"Good," I commended him. "Now listen carefully, because there will be an exam in the end. But you will have to guess how you got hurt. And how you will get even more hurt in the near future. Much more hurt!"

I sat opposite him and continued playing on his nerves, infusing my story with unnecessary pomposity. "As you already know, here I was able to demonstrate my talent as a genius cop by revealing that the case your cousin had deceitfully presented as a murder case was, in fact, an unfortunate accident. Thus, I earned her admiration, and she, gripped by uncontrollable sexual desire for me, opened her heart and confessed. Of course, I'm not going to tell you what most of these confessions were, but I shall shed some light on a certain fact: After my arrival here, she changed the settings of the camera that's within range of the 'crime scene' spot to *signal* her every time someone appeared there. She was worried I might solve the case before she had time to arrange my 'confessions' and set me up."

I finished my coffee and asked in a stern tone, "Are you following this?"

"Yes," he confirmed, with a trace of contempt in his voice. He looked calmer now.

"Your stupidity has so far shielded you from the bitter truth," I said. "But this will end now when I tell you how Graziella described to me the events of last night and what she showed me in the end."

I got another coffee from the machine, returned to my seat, and embarked on a retelling of "Graziella's account." I was at a stage in my investigation where I could combine facts and guesses without risking a major mistake.

"Of course, there were working cameras in the pavilion also, and their purpose was to gather evidence for the megatrial that Danko is completely cured. Indeed, he did not murder his stepmother, even though Graziella had given him everything he needed for his ritual."

"His psycho ritual," Sirius said, with malice. "He's been pestering us with his pretensions for months, and I was the one who had to build that pavilion."

"So," I went on, "Graziella, being careful as usual, set the cameras in the pavilion to signal her if someone sneaked inside uninvited..." I spread my arms and sighed. "Well, we sneaked in. First Fata and her brother and then me. He promised me to record the 'performance' and give me a copy in the night. Hearing this, Graziella put Danko's pathological impatience on another test. She locked him in the house, ran to your bungalow, and injected you with a stimulant that neutralizes the effect of the sleeping pills, and when you woke up, you both went to my bungalow to look for something suitable for cutting the trademark 'Merry Maker' smile. You were so happy when you saw the knife—"

"Stop! Stop, that's enough!" Sirius screamed. "Yes, following Graziella's orders, I really did wait for Ichiro there but only to take the camera from him—"

"Shut up! You son of a bitch! That knife, with my fingerprints on it, was a bonus for you. But even without it, you would've discovered another way to murder the poor man and incriminate me. By the way, last night Graziella found a reason to 'calm me down' and put me to sleep so that you could carry out your task, even if I went back to my bungalow first and Ichiro came after that. But he went straight to my bungalow while we headed for Roxanna's. And you—"

"I saw you murder him!"

"And you murdered him, imitating Merry Maker's style, and then hid the body under the bed and waited for me to come back and fall asleep so that you could smear some of his blood on my sleeve and pants."

"Hey, are you deaf? I repeat: *I saw you murder him!*"

"No. It's the opposite. Because this morning Graziella showed me the video."

"What video?"

"Video of you murdering Ichiro. Dumbass! I told you that she has a habit of documenting everything. Everything everywhere, not just the confession room. Yet you still don't get it—she put cameras in my bungalow too. Such a dumbass."

"Let's say there really is a video...why would she show it to you?"

"Ask her. And answer me this: Why was Ichiro a threat to you?"

"He wasn't."

I jumped to my feet and kicked him off the chair.

"I will give you another chance." I leaned over him and grabbed him by the neck. "Here it is. I am asking you again: Why was Ichiro a threat to you? Why would Graziella think that if the two of you met, one would certainly get hurt? And what is the connection between this and Fata's statement that you are the lowest of the murderers here?"

He looked up at me, and his eyes told me that he would not answer these questions. I had reached a limit beyond which kicks and blows didn't work. I stepped back, let him stand up, and he rushed for the door.

"Wait!" I stopped him. "Have you at least figured out why Graziella needs to have a video of you murdering someone in such a sadistic manner?"

He mumbled out a tormented no.

"She's going to use it to get rid of you!" I informed him dramatically. "'I'm sick of that parasite,' she told me. 'I'll get rid of him without paying him even a cent.'"

After his face went from pale to red to pale again, Sirius suddenly burst out in laughter, sincere laughter. That was unpleasant. But before leaving, he made the mistake of explaining his reaction: "The Japanese's camera is still with me! I have a video of her murdering that woman. Ah. We'll see who'll laugh last…"

CHAPTER SIXTY-NINE

I left the kitchen immediately after Sirius. I had no doubt that he had left Ichiro's camera in his bungalow and was now on his way to get it and hide it somewhere safe. Well, that was my intention too: Get the camera from his bungalow and hide it somewhere safe.

"Just a moment, gentlemen!" Graziella called at us from the stairs.

We stopped halfway through the vestibule and looked at her stupidly. Still in her medical coat, she was climbing down the staircase, camera in hand. Ichiro's camera. She came to us and threw the device at Sirius. It fell with a muted thud on the carpet, and he said, "The video. You've deleted it."

"Yes," she confirmed. "I deleted it in the bungalow while you were sleeping...like a stone! You saw what's on it; you saw me. Then you left the camera on the table and slept..."

"Like a stone," I gave her a hint.

"What if I had not deleted it?" She ignored me. "It would've ended up in his hands."

"No," he said angrily, "it wouldn't have."

"Really? And how were you going to stop him? Look at yourself! You're such a dumbass, indeed."

"You've eavesdropped on us!" he realized only now. "You've placed hidden cameras even in the kitchen! Without telling me!"

"Telling you? You! You're nothing more than a hired hand...a servant!"

"Excuse me," I said. "As much as I enjoy listening to you, you will have to postpone your fight for later."

I clutched Graziella by the elbow and led her toward the staircase. Just as I expected, the cousin or bodyguard didn't dare to do anything. On the contrary he rushed out of the house, shutting the door with a bang.

On the second floor, we stopped at the computer-hall door.

"Open it!" I ordered her, and she unlocked it.

We went in. I pointed at a table by the door. "Empty your pockets there."

She took off her medical coat and threw it on the table. She was wearing jeans and a short-sleeved blouse under it.

"That's OK too," I said.

I pushed her slightly toward the computer, the screen showing the kitchen, and told her to sit down to its side. I took the seat from which she was watching Sirius and me only a few minutes ago. I checked if she had recorded anything. She had. I decided to send it to my lawyer immediately, but I needed a password to use the Internet. The phone, placed negligently by the keyboard, also was locked with a password and therefore of no use to me. I wasn't discouraged, though. I opened the desk drawer, found a sealed box with flash drives, and took two out. On one I copied the video and then put it in my pocket. The other I plugged to the computer's USB port, set the computer's camera to recording mode, and looked at Graziella, who showed no signs of fear or even anxiety whatsoever.

I glanced at my watch—it was almost nine.

"The plane arrives at about noon, right?"

"Yes." She nodded. "Like every Friday. Why?"

"Why? I bet you know why."

"I know only how you imagine things will go: You take me as a hostage, force the pilots to fly us to some bigger city, hand me over to the local police, show them the flash drive with my cousin's confessions and maybe another one with the confessions you're about to try wrench from me…" She waved her hand resignedly. "But you don't have to resort to 'wrenching,' Miro. I'll tell you anything you want, and I'll let you tape it."

"You're telling me to prepare for another set of lies, aren't you?"

"No. I will stick only to the truth from now on, because my lies are useless now."

"But until now you were happy with how useful they were, right? You accused me falsely, and with help from me, alas, of four murders, and last night you added a fifth one to the list. Or two, if your plan was to blame me for the stepmother's murder also."

"No. That murder wasn't planned. She was just… so incredibly repulsive!"

"What about the Japanese man? Why him…"

"I had to. You will soon know why. Now I'm asking you for an honest answer: Was there a moment, no matter how brief, when you believed or at least assumed that you really are Merry Maker?"

"No, no such moment," I replied, maybe not with whole honesty. "All your efforts have been in vain."

"That's a pity. That old maxim, 'The road to hell is paved with good intentions,' kind of describes me very well."

"Lady," I said coldly, "enough with the empty talk."

"Empty words and especially *empty* actions are a trademark of yours," she retorted. "I told you in the beginning, on the yacht, you're seeking out extreme experiences because without them you feel hollow. And now I am telling you that you really are hollow! Unlike me. Because I have a cause! And I've given—and will continue to give—everything I can to turn it into reality. All of your extreme experiences pale in comparison with what I've been through...*more than a hundred times*. Yes, yes, Miro! Before choosing these six participants in the trial, I met and *got close with* a hundred and eleven serial killers. My soul will never recover from the horrors, the vileness, the perversions, and sadisms I had to listen about for months and months. You cannot even imagine how hard it is to find a sympathetic serial killer, not to mention six such!"

"Oh no, I can. But, Graziella, at the trial it will quickly become clear that you've made a manipulative selection."

"I won't deny that. But I will stress the fact that both the sympathetic murderers and the other ones, the truly disgusting ones, are, in fact, tormented people. Victims. That over each one of them hovers the shadow of some seemingly normal...freak. Dammit! It's a fact, for example, that among those one hundred and eleven murderers, there wasn't a single one who was born with physical disabilities, brain anomalies, damage, or anything of that sort. They had only psychological damages from the nightmare that was their childhood. And these damages were inflicted on them by the 'normal' freaks."

Graziella was walking around the hall, knitting eyebrows, clenching fists.

"But do you know what the scariest part of this fright fest is?" She stopped before me, arms akimbo. "That it's such a banal fright fest. That's the scariest and the nastiest thing about it! Because everyone knows about that, but no one ever tries to change it. Only small corrections in this or that law from time to time. Fundamental change is needed."

After another hectic walk about the hall, Graziella dropped in her seat.

"But, Miro, don't get me wrong. I too am convinced that most of the serial killers should be... well, they should be removed like tumors from our lives, our society. Psychiatric wards, prisons, death sentences—there are no other ways to save ourselves from them. But that is so only because no one has ever protected the children those murderers used to be. And we all know that children are still being molested, raped, humiliated, destroyed.

And those children could become murderers unless we help them on time, unless we protect them. But how? How can we protect them when the state has armed us with such *toothless legislation?*"

Her energy was rising again, her eyes burning with the flame of madness. "Oh yes! At the megatrial I personally will stand against the state. And I will sue it on behalf of both serial killers and their victims!"

This is where I cut in. "And who are you going to sue on behalf of your victims? Me? Or the state again?"

She not only didn't get what I was saying but also got mad at me. "Miro! I am talking to you about the *cause*, and the only thing you can think of is the stepmother and that Japanese guy!"

"It's a good cause—"

"It's a great one!"

"But you're too small for it. And I wasn't talking about the stepmother and the Japanese guy; I meant Patrick and the other three who were tortured and murdered on your order."

"You're wrong! I never wanted them to be tortured." She anticipated my objection and said, "And as for Patrick, it hadn't even crossed my mind to order his murder. I sent one of my…agents to introduce himself as someone from the prosecutor's office to him and ask him some questions. I had to find out if he had shared his discovery about the poisonous mixture with someone other than Maya's grandmother. But the agent went too far. He decided to take some laughing gas with him to loosen the boy's tongue, but the boy had asthma and...did not survive the interrogation."

"Another lie," I said. "You wanted him to kill not only the boy but also everyone the boy had shared his—"

"No! It wasn't like that! We only wanted to kidnap them and keep them here, on the island, until the start of the trial. Later, after Maya would've confessed everything, Patrick's discoveries wouldn't have mattered. And his death...his death actually threatened to destroy the entire project, because, while investigating, the cops had discovered that he was working as an intern at the hospital Maya was taken to at the same time when she was in the intensive-care ward there. I also got information that one of their versions was about a possible connection between the mass murder in Maya's school and Patrick's murder..."

Silence followed, sprinkled with sighs and teary blinking. This woman seemed addicted to the stage. I went on instead of her.

"So, in order to lead the cops away from the right version, twenty days after Patrick's murder, you ordered your agent to imitate a serial killer and kill, in a short period of time, three more people, using laughing gas. You also ordered him to nail to the second victim's chest a message saying that the boy was the first victim only by mistake."

"No, it's not like that," she mumbled. "That terrible thing with the nail was again his own initiative. I repeat: I never wanted him to torture anyone!"

"But you did want him to choose only victims for whose death you could blame on me, the grandson of your psychotherapist colleague. Or you're going to deny this too now?"

She ran her palm over her forehead as if removing a spider web. She closed her eyes and went silent again. I stood up from the chair.

"Come on," I urged her. "We'll find some isolated place until the plane comes."

I reached for the plugged-in flash drive, but she clutched at my arm.

"Listen to me, please! Only if you understand me will you be able to make the right decision."

I didn't want to fan the fire of her panic with more meaningless bluffing. "I already made my decision, Graziella. We'll leave together, but after that I'll let you return here. I only need you as a hostage until I get off the island, and I need the flash drive with your confessions only as a guarantee that you won't use my 'confessions.'" I looked down on her while she still clutched at my arm, pulling me slightly back toward the chair. "Well, of course," I said, "I'd be happy to see you in jail for-ever, but I'd be happier to see your cause become reality. I believe that if it does, your victims' deaths would not be meaningless."

"What about your grandfather?" She dug nails into my hand. "You have to have the truth about him too on that flash drive. The truth about his claim that he told you everything about Patrick!"

She hit me right in the weak spot. I knew that that was the reason she was keeping me here, yet I slumped back into the chair. She talked fast.

"I overstated your grandfather's contribution to the preparations for the experiment so that I could convince you more easily to come to the is-land. In fact, he did not take part in my criminal 'activities' or in the selection of the people here. I chose the six of them. The only thing he did was support my choice before the committee by provid-ing an expert evaluation after having a few sessions with each of them—"

"Graziella, make it short. Just tell me when and how you fooled him into saying those lies on your phone!"

"In the beginning, I lied to him too that I was hiring you to investigate Kuber's death. But yester-day I called him and played your confessions to—"

"Dammit!"

"Yes, he reacted the same way." Graziella nodded at me as if she and I were discussing some everyday topic. "So I gave him an ultimatum: 'You have to choose, Nathaniel! Either I send your grandson on his way to the electric chair with the help of his confessions and the photo evidence that I've collected, or we both play that he's not answerable for his crimes because he suffers from split-personality game.' And of course, Miro, he chose option number two and agreed to record on the phone the words I gave him to say—how he told you everything about Patrick."

I stood up, unplugged the flash drive, dropped it in the pocket where the other one was, stepped toward Graziella, and forced her to stand up too. Then I pushed her toward the door.

CHAPTER SEVENTY

While we climbed down the stairs, we heard someone crying on the first floor. We hurried down and soon recognized Maya's voice, although we were unable to understand what she was saying, because her words drowned in sobs. Then we heard the sharp sound of a door opening, followed by a screaming "Help!" and a wail: "No, Danko! Please, don't!"

We exchanged glances, horrified by the same guess, and rushed down the corridor and to the closed verandah from whence came a familiar deranged singing: "Do, re, mi, a, fa, re, do, ti…"

I reminded myself that without Graziella as a hostage, leaving the island with the priceless flash drives would be just another dream, but the moment I saw Maya, my careful plans and calculations vanished. I left Graziella behind my back, and three leaps later I was with them. It was then that I saw that Maya was actually clutching at Danko, and he was trying to break loose in a very gentle manner. It seemed that he didn't want to hurt her. They were at the threshold of the open door, Maya pulling him toward the corridor and he pulling back at the verandah. The curtains were drawn this morning, with the only light coming from the two lamps on the ebony table.

"Maya, let go of him!" Graziella called. She came running to us, and instead of stopping, she rushed right into the murky room.

"Let me go, let me go!" Danko sang out of tune.

He was naked to the waist and barefoot. He was wearing only a pair of black leggings and black gloves.

"What the hell is going on?" I raised voice. "Maya?"

"Help! Help him!" she screamed, and collapsing on the floor, she clutched at his ankles. "He wants to kill himself! Stop him, stop…"

Dragging her along, Danko moved slowly toward the table, behind which now stood Graziella. There was a dagger on top of it—it looked the same as the one the raging Danko held in his hand last night. Yes, it was the same, and Graziella didn't seem to see it, even though it was right before her eyes. *That's all the better,* I said to myself and swiftly walked to the table. I reached for the dagger, and Graziella reached a hand to me, and I saw that she was holding a flashlight. I didn't have time to even think where it came from, but I instantly knew that it was an electric-shock flashlight, because she didn't hesitate before putting it against my temple. My head exploded in multicolored fireworks before my eyes.

The pain was indescribable. I lurched forward and hit my jaw in the opposite edge of the table, my face hanging over the open drawer from which Graziella was taking a pair of handcuffs. I was unable to move. She grabbed my hair, said "I'm sorry," and lifted my head. Then she pressed with her thumb the electronic lock of the drawer, sliding it smoothly shut.

I don't know what made me lose consciousness: the pain or the humiliation. The painfully humiliating fact that this woman had fooled me again. And again...

When I came to, I was handcuffed, and Danko and Graziella were dragging me toward the sofa nearby. They dropped me on it, and she took the flash drives out of my pocket. She put them on the floor, pulled one of the chairs closer, and used its leg as a hammer to crush them. She heaved a sigh of relief and finally found the time to ask me, "Are you OK?"

What was I supposed to say? Nothing, of course.

Maya came running with a carafe of water. She made to pour it over my head but saw that I was conscious and let me take a few sips instead, before asking me if I was OK.

"He is, he is!" Danko sang in response and went to the table.

He climbed on top of it, kneeled in the center, the two lamps flanking him, and took the dagger. Maya tried to follow him, but Graziella stopped her. She forced her to sit on one of the chairs and stepped behind, placing her hands on the girl's shoulders.

"Leave him!" she ordered her.

"Leave him?" Maya's face twisted in puzzlement. "You seem to agree with his desire to kill himself!"

"She does, she does." Danko nodded. "You will too."

"No! Never!" Maya was unable to stand up, because Graziella was pushing her down with all her strength. "Danko," she whimpered, "whatever it is that has happened, I can help you. We're friends!"

"Friends," he repeated sarcastically. "I thought I was Roxanna's friend too, and Valdo's, but last night...last night I stabbed him with this dagger and then paralyzed him so that I could mutilate his fiancée without him interrupting me. If it wasn't for Miro, I would've cut her tongue and ears out. I wanted to cut them out!"

Maya was listening to him with a gaping mouth and an expression that seemed torn between terror and disgust.

"If this is a joke…it's a very sick one," she mumbled. She looked at me and then up at Graziella. She saw enough to answer herself. "No, it's not a joke. But why! We were sure you were cured…"

"I am." Danko now spoke in a frighteningly calm voice. "I am cured to the highest possible extent, the one where only one truth remains: that people like me can never be cured. I should never be free in the world, Maya, because sooner or later I would murder again. Last night taught me that."

"Even if that's so…you can be under constant supervision."

"In a mental institution? For the rest of my days?" Danko shook his head. "No! I'm not going back there. I'm not going to the trial either, where I will be nothing more than a laughing stock, my insanity proven again and again by recordings of my…singing, singing…Do, mi, fa, fa, re, do, tiiii…"

Crosslit by the two lamps, kneeling on the table in his black leggings, he looked as if his body ended at the waist: one half of a man gleaming white on top of the dead body of an ebony tree.

"Hara-kiri, hara-kiri, hara-kiri…" His black-gloved hand rose up, ready for the ritual cut.

"Stop!" I cried.

"Leave him," Graziella said, and when I looked at her, I saw tears flowing down her cheeks. "Understand him."

I turned to Danko again, who was swinging the dagger closer and closer to his stomach.

"Stop! You scoundrel!"

His hand froze in the air. Puzzlement froze on his face. "Scoundrel?"

"Yes, yes." I started nodding. "Because you don't care that this girl here will keep forever the memory of your…half-baked hara-kiri. The memory of you disemboweled on this table!"

"Maya, Maya, forgive me, Maya," he said, in a singsong voice, and then started singing out of tune: "Forgive me and understand and please get out, get out, get out!"

Nudged by Graziella, Maya stood and walked across the dim room. And Danko, barely waiting for her to shut the door behind her back, swung the dagger again…but this was not hara-kiri.

The dagger went straight to his heart.

CHAPTER SEVENTY-ONE

After ascertaining and announcing Danko's death, Graziella switched off the recording devices, sat on the sofa next to me, and collapsed into a state of hysteria. She was crying and wailing, writhing and trembling with pain, suffocating. Of course, I too was upset by the suicide we had just witnessed. I knew what she was going through. For a moment, I even felt like comforting her, but I didn't want to look to compassionate, especially when my head still throbbed with pain from the electric shock administered by her, and I could not feel my hands because they were numb from the handcuffs she put me in.

I went on watching her in silence. Bending down, she grabbed the carafe from the floor. She tried to take a sip but couldn't, her teeth hitting the glass a couple of times, and she sent the carafe flying to the wall. Fingers buried in her hair, she wailed, "I failed! He is dead because of me! I made a mistake! I misjudged him…"

Unfortunately, I too had misjudged him. I thought that he would only wound himself lightly, trying to perform the hara-kiri on himself. But recalling certain details from Graziella's behavior, I realized that she was lying again—lying to herself.

"Shut up!" I exclaimed. "You knew he was capable of committing suicide. And you *wanted* him to."

"No, I didn't want to, but I had to," she replied through tears. "Because how else was I going to explain to the prosecutor that our deal is off because I have a patient who…once released, would most certainly commit another murder? Such a statement would make everyone else in the group suspicious. The entire trial would look suspicious!"

"And how are you going to explain his suicide?"

"He will do the explaining. I will play the video, and everyone will see that the best ending for him is…this ending…"

I decided not to raise any objections. It wasn't appropriate to discuss Danko here, only a few steps away from the table on which his pale corpse still kneeled. Graziella leaned on my shoulder and rose. She headed for the door, and I followed her. Both of us staggered but for different reasons.

We were at the door when Sirius opened it and almost bumped into Graziella. He was holding a gun. His nose was red and swollen; his hair was wet and parted crookedly. White three-quarter trousers, white canvas shoes, and a colorful Hawaiian shirt completed his image as a man who was quite unpleasant. His grin did not make things better.

"There you are! I looked for you upstairs in the hall and the office. But, of course, I checked the *bedroom* first—oh!" He didn't even stop grinning after seeing Danko. "Another dead body, eh? How many now? Three for half a day?"

His vulgarity helped Graziella's sorrow transform into relieving rage.

"You sadist!" she screamed and rushed at him. She pushed him into the corridor. "There is no other sadist on the island. You are the only one!"

Startled by her own words, she looked at me as if to check whether I believed her or not.

"You're right." I nodded. "He's a sadist. That's why he was so good at imitating Merry Maker's style on Ichiro."

"Speaking of Ichiro..." Sirius seemed unperturbed. "The witch who is also his sister is waiting for us in the confession room."

"You're late because of her?" Graziella pushed him once again, unable to control herself.

"You were waiting for him to come with the gun?" I said bitterly. "That's why you were so willing to talk upstairs in the hall. You were stalling me."

"That's not entirely true," she said. "I would've told you the truth no matter what."

"Yet you even agreed to be recorded only to keep me there until your cousin came 'flying…'"

"Yes, but he didn't come flying. He crawled here. That reptile!"

"Watch your words." Sirius finally looked offended. "And I'm not late because of Fata. She came here by herself. I just had to take a shower. Because your beloved Miro poured an entire bowl of spaghetti over my head!"

Their rude exchange continued in the corridor, and when we entered the confession room, Fata joined them.

"Monsters! Dirty, ignoble murderers! Why is he with you?" She pointed at me with a wave of her hand. "Get him out of here. I want to talk only with you two!"

"Do you think I care what you want?" Graziella asked tiredly. "I am exhausted from your—"

"Murderer!" Fata jumped on her, but Sirius grabbed her braided hair and pulled her back.

"Hey, easy!" I said, breathless with helplessness. "Let her go!"

"Yes, let her go!" Graziella told him and then turned to me. "I'm sorry, but I cannot free you now."

"That's right!" Still holding Fata by the hair, Sirius waved the gun. "If you take his handcuffs off, I'll shoot him."

"I know." Graziella sighed. "Coward. You'll shoot him and ruin everything."

"That's interesting," I said. "What else do you need me alive for?"

I didn't expect an answer, but I got one. From Fata. "They need you to kill me."

"She's telling the truth," Graziella confirmed. Turning toward the sofa, she said, "Come. Let's sit there, calm down, and talk."

"Calm down?" Fata turned and shot two fingers at Sirius's eyes, which he barely escaped. "I went looking for my brother," she moaned, looking at me. "I looked for him and found him in your bungalow, but I know that it wasn't you who killed him. It was that excuse for a human being." She pointed at Sirius. "And he murdered him following orders from this lowlife here!" Her index finger poked at Graziella. "And last year they did the same to my sister-in-law—"

"That's not true!" Graziella dropped on the sofa and hid her face in her palms. "I never ordered him to murder your sister-in-law. It was his own idea."

"It wasn't an idea but a carefully thought-out decision," Sirius corrected her. "A decision in the direction of which I was pushed by no other than you, because you complained at least ten times to me how you could not find another suitable island and how that Japanese man was not willing to sell it because of his wife's sentiments. I learned from you that she would go swimming in the bay every morning. She loved greeting the rising sun from there. Well, I made sure she said both hi and farewell in the same morning!" Sirius laughed at his own vulgar joke. He made himself comfortable in one of the armchairs and elaborated especially for me. "I wanted the experiment to start sooner so that I could get my millions sooner. I helped Graziella buy the island she needed. I arrived here by boat one night, anchored it behind the rocks, and waited for the sun to rise. I geared up and dove underwater, where I waited for the Japanese woman to come swimming by. Then I grabbed her by the ankles. And she drowned like a kitten!"

He threw these last words at Fata. It was his revenge for the time spent in fear of her "voodoo magic."

"Well, now you know why he's the lowest among the murderers here, don't you?" she asked me. She looked more composed now, but I could see from the stiffness of her face that it was taking her a lot of effort. "The others are sick people, poor souls, but this one here, he does it for money. A murderer for money."

"A *lot* of money." Sirius made a flagrant remark.

"Monster!" Graziella burst out.

"Easy for you to say, cousin. Your father was a millionaire, and mine gambled everything before I was even born. Actually…" He drew her attention to the gun with a gesture. "I'm not going to wait for this experiment to end. I want my money today, after we're done with these two pieces of garbage."

The "pieces of garbage" were, of course, Fata and me. We exchanged glances, brought together by the same unenviable fate, and I saw her lips moving silently: "Run!" As if I had somewhere to run to with my handcuffs and that idiot's gun aimed at me. I shrugged and took a seat next to Graziella. She had the key to the handcuffs and also had the look of someone in deep hesitation.

"I wonder, Fata," she began meekly, "how your brother found out that Sirius had drowned his wife."

"He didn't have to find out," Fata replied. "He saw him. His wife was late, and he got worried, went out to take a look at the bay, and did not find her but saw a boat farther in the ocean. He thought that he wife had been kidnapped and ran back to the house for his binoculars. So he was able to see the boatman and his lemon-colored hair, which gave him away as your relative. And later, when my sister-in-law's body was washed up on the beach, there were black-and-blue impressions of finger-prints on the skin of her ankles…"

"Dammit!" Sirius cursed.

"Good-for-nothing," Graziella said, in a tired voice, and turned to Fata again. "So, your brother knew from the beginning that she didn't drown by accident. And was sure the whole time that I had ordered her murder."

Fata walked to the window on the other end of the room and leaned on the glass.

"Yes, he was sure. He was also sure that you were going to make him another offer to buy the island, even though he had refused many times. That's why, instead of calling the police, he decided to revenge his wife's death alone. He agreed to a contract that allowed me to stay on the island so that he could have food and shelter. Then we staged his suicide and waited for you to arrive with the group. He immediately recognized the murderer among them."

"He recognized me but didn't have the courage to kill me," Sirius grunted in contempt.

"He didn't want to kill you anymore," Fata said quietly and looked out the window. "He had given up on revenge."

"Why?" Graziella flinched. "What do you mean?"

"His initial intention was to destroy everyone, because he thought, and I agreed with him, that not only you and Sirius but the other six also deserved death. Serial killers! But it so happened that I got too close with Roxanna, and she told me everyone's story. I told these stories to my brother and…that was it. They were no longer freaks and psychopaths; they'd become hurt, tortured, suffering human beings. And when we realized that, we started to see the meaning of the experiment. And the meaning of your fight for the children—"

"*Cause.*" Sirius injected a new dose of contempt into his tone. "Use the word *cause*, and she will love you forever. And will start practicing self-flagellation for murdering your brother 'by mistake.' But I want to ask you something. If he had given up on revenge, why would he film the creepy theater in the pavilion? To blackmail, right?"

"Of course not!" Fata looked offended. "But we needed some evidence just in case—"

"But it didn't work," Sirius said firmly. "And it's time for you to pay your brother a visit. Maybe with a wide 'smile' on your face, eh, Merry Maker?"

"Why don't you try keeping silent for a change?" Graziella offered him, her voice heavy with hatred. Then she started feverishly explaining to me: "I began suspecting that Ichiro had not killed himself only a month ago, and a quick check in the funeral registry confirmed my suspicion. Then I realized that he had figured out what had happened to his wife and had remained on the island, with the knowledge of his family, to revenge her. I didn't think he would kill anyone, because it'd been four months without him doing anything, but...I just couldn't risk him and his sister coming to the trial and destroying—"

"Oh, no!" Sirius chimed in. "I'm not gonna put up with your guilt trip. The truth, Miro, is that she brought you here to carry out as Merry Maker the murders of these two. Otherwise the investigation would've turned to her patients, bringing the experiment to an end. Am I right, cousin?"

"You are, but—"

"No *buts*! It was like that." Standing up, Sirius came closer to me and poked me in the ribs in a seemingly friendly manner. "Well, buddy, you've already taken care of Ichiro. The blood on your clothes, your fingerprints on the knife, and most importantly the *style* you told us about during confession hour will show that. Unfortunately, now you'll have to get rid of the old hag too. Why 'unfortunately'? Because I was hoping to do it myself, again on your behalf, of course. After which you would've 'killed' yourself in, say, a 'fit of psychopathic remorse.' Such was our plan, but Graziella grew softer in the last couple of days. Now she doesn't want you dead anymore."

"Yes!" she confirmed and looked closely into my eyes. "You saw, Miro, that I've spared no efforts. I did everything I could to make you believe you are Merry Maker—"

"Because"—Sirius did not let her finish—"if you had believed in that, we would've kept you alive and not made you murder the witch. As I've already said, I would've done it on your behalf. And you with your confessions would've simply taken part in the trial as a symbol of our psychiatrist's professional prowess."

"On the contrary," I objected. "My confessions would've discredited her. According to her diagnosis, the Merry Maker and I are two separate persons, which means that there is no way I could remember anything he does, no matter how gruesome it is."

"You underestimate me," Graziella reproached me. "Of course, I'm not going to introduce you at the trial as someone with such diagnosis. We'll think of another psychosis; we'll prove, with the help of my trusted experts, that you're certifiable, and after a six-month treatment, you'll be free and very rich. But we want—"

Sirius took over impatiently. "We want to make a video of you murdering Fata. With evidence as 'eloquent' as this, even if during the trial you start hearing the voices of compunction and start denying that you're Merry Maker, no one would believe you. But now, if you refuse—"

"He's not going to refuse," Fata said suddenly. "Come on, Miro; let's go. It's time for you to kill me."

CHAPTER SEVENTY-TWO

B efore leaving the confession room, I listened patiently to Sirius's instructions, according to which I was supposed to murder Fata behind the house, about three feet from the edge of the precipice and 'facing the window with the sharpshooter,' whatever this meant. I was allowed to commit the murder as I 'liked'—with bare hands, a stone, anything—but in the end I *had to* throw the body in the precipice because this would explain the absence of the characteristic 'smile' on the victim's face—a spontaneous and impulsive affair, the result of pathological effect provoked by the old hag's discovery that I had killed her brother.

Maybe it was the effect of having a gun in his hand, but Sirius was much more talkative than usual, while his cousin was exactly the opposite. Actually, she only cut his instructions twice. The first time to tell me straight that Fata would end up dead, no matter what, and that I had two options—be murdered too or stay alive and find meaning in my life through her cause. And the second time was to express the emotions that seemed to suffocate her.

"My cause is grand, but I hired a tiny helper!" she said through clenched teeth, staring at Sirius with eyes bulging with hatred. "Vile, cruel, greedy dwarf! If it wasn't for you...I would've found another island for the experiment, and these innocent people would've continued living their lives here, happy among their children and grandchildren and...and hibiscus bushes. You've bloodied my purest and brightest deed!"

"Yeah, right! It's always me who's the devil and you who's the saint. A delusional saint who thinks that only because she has inherited millions, she has the right to play with and risk other people's lives. Screw you, cousin. You truly believe you're larger than life, as your dad used to say. And you're about to burst with your manic ambition to 'fight the state.'"

"Anything else to share?" I asked them.

"Because," Fata said with impressive composure, "if you're done, you can now follow me to my killing spot."

She headed proudly for the door, and the three of us followed her, making the whole situation look even more absurd. We continued down the corridor, Fata still leading us. This meant that she probably would be the first to step out of the house, and then I could give her a chance to escape. She had told me that Graziella had arranged for her to receive a call from her nephews once a week, from which followed that if she stopped calling them, they would get worried and come here. If she managed to escape now, she could wait for them, hiding in one of her brother's secret places. He must've had such in order to remain undiscovered on the island for four months.

Shortly before reaching the door, Sirius stopped and stepped in Graziella's way. "You stop here," he told her. "Go back!"

Handing the keys to the handcuffs over to him, she looked at me guiltily or maybe simply to say good-bye. Then she turned her back to us and walked across the vestibule.

"And don't forget!" Sirius called after her. "You must turn the cameras on after I've come back to you. No earlier!"

Without looking back, Graziella raised her hand to show that she heard him.

"Is that a yes or a no?" he yelled.

In the meantime, Fata left the house. I rushed to the door, kicked it shut, and leaned my back against it, handcuffs cutting painfully into my skin. By that time Sirius had moved right in front of me and hit me with the handle of the gun. He swung his foot, aiming a blow that could easily leave me without offspring, but I turned aside and stopped the kick with my hip. I could tell from his groan that the canvas shoe had not protected his toes from twisting or—as I hoped—breaking. Limping, he stepped forward again, his angular face wrinkled by a frown.

"You're lucky you have to be in one piece for the video," he said through clenched teeth.

I sat down on the floor, still blocking the door, and while he was kicking and pushing me in an attempt to move me to the side, I hoped I had given Fata a long start.

But she was waiting for us outside.

"Ah, Fata, Fata," I mumbled bitterly.

"I saw you were trying to help, but I don't want to live anymore," she explained. "Not after my brother's death."

I exchanged some insults with Sirius, and just as we started walking around the house, Roxanna and Valdo came out from the inside. With his slumped shoulders, swollen face, and bloodshot, dim eyes, he didn't look like himself at all. The wound from the dagger was in such a place between the armpit and the chest that now most of his torso was bandaged, and he was unable to move his right hand. There was a red stain on the white bandage.

"He was not supposed to move," Roxanna stated the obvious and continued with her futile attempt to sling his left arm over her shoulders, which only exhausted him more because he stubbornly refused to lean on her. Considering the drastic difference in their height and weight, he was the one acting reasonably and she the uncooperative one. "We heard you and came back," she explained, breathing heavily. "We were going to the veranda, because...how's Danko? Maya told us that he wanted to—"

"He's fine," Sirius lied.

He was hiding the gun behind his back, and I was standing so that Roxanna and Valdo couldn't see the handcuffs. I had no doubt that if they find out what was about to happen, they would try to help us and end up getting hurt too.

"Maya!" Fata suddenly exclaimed. "Maya and that other one, the tiny one...Frant. Are they in the house?"

"No, no." Roxanna looked at her in bewilderment. "They're in my bungalow. Maya was very upset, and he stayed with her, and we came to see—"

"Go back to them," Sirius urged them. "Tell them not to worry and that Danko is fine, and change that bandage. Come on, go!"

"Go, go," I urged them too, and as I watched them slowly walk away, I felt a sense of guilt. If yesterday I had not visited Valdo in the isolator, now he still would've been there, healthy and surrounded by crocodiles. Last night he came because we had arranged to meet and now—"Wait!" I yelled. My whole body was shaking. "Valdo!"

He stopped and looked at me over his shoulder.

"Valdo!" I repeated, almost dizzy with what had just occurred to me. "Has anyone else been sent to the isolator since you all came to the island?"

"Only Sirius," he replied. "But what—"

"Only Sirius. Only him but twice! Right?"

"Yes."

"Yes, yes!" I took a deep breath and went on. "The first time he was sent there was at the beginning of last month, and only for a day or two. And the second was at the end of the same month, when he stayed there for almost a week. Right?"

"Yes," Sirius said. "I wasn't feeling well in the head, and I needed some isolation. But you seem to know. Why are you asking?"

"I'm asking…for fun," I said, and Roxanna and Valdo kept walking across the meadow, not saying a word. They seemed to have gotten used to my out-of-the-blue outbursts. I waited for them to move farther away before turning to Sirius. "You weren't in the isolator. You weren't even on the island during those days. You would leave by boat, the one anchored behind the rocks, and return in the same way."

"So?"

"So, I thought that you, just like the rest of the group, were here, on the island, at the time Merry Maker was committing the murders. That's why I made a mistake in thinking that you had only imitated his style when killing Ichiro. But the truth is that in reality *you are Merry Maker! You! You and no one else!*"

"You don't say!" He laughed in my face. "I had given up hoping that you would arrive at the conclusion. I'd only like to make one small correction: It wasn't a boat; it was a yacht, brought here for me by two of Graziella's highly paid pawns. And yes, I did eliminate that snot-nosed guy Patrick, but I didn't mean to. He died because of his asthma, and that's why I had to go back there at the end of the month on the yacht the saint-psychiatrist hired for me. She sent to my tablet the video information her detectives had been sending her in real time so that I could choose three more suitable victims for you—"

Fata reached out in a sudden movement and slapped him across his grinning face.

"Scoundrel!" she said to him, and he glared red-faced at her. "The fact that I'm going to die soon doesn't mean that I have to put up with you. Come on, Miro!"

She grabbed me by the sleeve and led me around the house. Sirius followed us, quickly getting back his good spirits.

"There were other 'candidates' to be murdered by Merry Maker—by you, I mean. Fired from work and unhappy, you were wandering about the city all day long, so I could choose between the many people who crossed your path. But eventually, Deluc, Kotovich, and Ramm turned out to be the best victims. You see, we needed loners of different ages so that they could fit into your profile of a psychopath who is obsessed by the fantasy that he is killing his grandfather in different periods of his life. Kotovich was the easiest target because you stayed in that apartment building for hours, and he not only lived alone but was also extremely gullible. He let me into his apartment to wait there for the ambulance because I was 'having a heart attack'—"

Fata tried slapping him again, but he was prepared this time and jumped back.

"What's going on?" We heard Graziella's voice.

We looked up, and since we were behind the house now, we realized that when Sirius had said "the window with the sharpshooter," he wasn't talking metaphorically. One of the confession-room windows was open, and Graziella was leaning on the sill, with a sniper rifle in her hands.

"Thank God!" Fata said, her voice touched by inexplicable relief, and I laughed with an even more inexplicable sense of humor.

"Idiots." Sirius looked offended.

He gestured at us to move in the direction of the so-called killing spot, and we obeyed, which, as was clearly visible, offended him too. He was probably hoping that we would start pulling away and begging for mercy and thus give him another reason to push and ridicule us.

"I advise you to jump without thinking much," Fata said to him when we stopped there, only three feet from the edge of the precipice. "It would be less painful."

Her words had an ominous sound to them, and this made him even madder. Cursing under his breath, still red-nosed, he gave her the key to the handcuffs, and while she was unlocking them, he started moving backward, his gun aimed at me. His cousin also had her rifle aimed at me.

"Just a kind reminder," he said, stopping about ten steps away from me. "You will live only if you kill her. No other chance for you. If you run, Graziella will shoot you 'in a *failed* attempt to save the poor old lady from Merry Maker.' Yes, she is going to shoot you, even though she will cry and suffer afterward. It's what she is. A fanatic. Her dream of the megatrial has driven her mad. We used to be close, she and I; we grew up together, took care of each other, believed in each other, and now—"

"Is there a problem?" Graziella called.

"Yes," Fata yelled. "A problem for both of you."

"I'm coming!" Sirius joined in the calling and then resumed the instructions. "I need a cast-iron alibi, so you have to wait for me to give you a signal from up there. The confession-room cameras are going to be on too, and later everyone will see that I was with Graziella when you were murdering the old woman. And watch it! If you do it before the signal, I will shoot you myself."

"If we're going to continue with the sweet talk, why not sit down?" I offered, rubbing my wrists energetically.

Seeing me without handcuffs seemed to re-mind him of my love for extreme risk, and he fi-nally rushed to the house. Now we were unable to see him from our vantage point.

"You know that I'm not going to kill you, right?" I whispered to Fata, and after she nodded, I went on. "But I don't know how to get out of this."

"I do," she said. "That's why I said 'Thank God' a little while ago when I saw Graziella aiming at us from the confession room. By the way, if they hadn't come there with you, they would've been dead by now. Me too. Your presence stopped me—"

"Fata, do you think I understand what you're talking about?"

"No, I don't think so. But I am sure that you will know soon." She smiled shakily. "I told you a lot of things up there, but I didn't tell you that my brother planned to eliminate everyone…*at the same time*. He was prepared for it even before the group arrived here. But unfortunately, he was a good man. He gave up on his plan and paid with his life for this."

We fell silent, staring at Sirius, who was standing next to Graziella now, gesturing at us—yes, it was Merry Maker on that window, giving me the signal to kill.

"Well, that's it," Fata sighed. "I too was a good person like my brother. I was. Now I am not."

She took something from her pocket…a miniature remote control. I glanced at its tiny display and saw the digits "2:00," and then I understood; I understood what she meant and reached out to her, but it was too late. She pushed the button and threw the remote in the precipice.

"Get out of there," I screamed at Graziella. "It's a bomb! It's going to *explode!*"

"Ha-ha-ha!" Sirius's laughter thundered. "How clever you are!"

Graziella was still aiming at me.

"Don't move!" she warned me, with a scream.

But I ran toward the house.

"Stop! I'll shoot!"

I did not stop. She did not shoot.

When I stormed into the confession room, they were still by the window. Sirius was trying to wrench the rifle from her, but she was not letting it go, even though he had smashed her mouth and was now kicking her in the stomach with a knee. They both saw me at the same time, and both let go of the rifle at the same time. Sirius pulled the gun from under his belt and aimed it at me, Graziella dug her teeth into his arm, I leaped toward them, the gun fired, Sirius dropped it, and I caught it in the air and threw it out the window.

"There's a bomb here! A real bomb!" I said, out of breath.

By my estimation—and it was an optimistic one—we had no more than ten seconds until the explosion. I grabbed Graziella in my arms, and she started twisting and turning, pulling at my hair at the same time. A moment before heading for the door with her in my arms, I saw in my peripheral vision that Sirius had picked up the rifle and was aiming it at us. The next moment came, and I no longer could see anything. I felt the wave of the explosion picking us up and throwing us through the door. We landed on the corridor tiles, and I covered Graziella with my body, bracing myself for the heavy objects that might come flying in our direction. Luckily, nothing hit us.

I only felt a pat on the shoulder. It was Sirius's hand, still clutching the handle of the rifle.

EPILOGUE

Autumn was at its height, and the day was windy. Graziella walked toward me, leaves of all colors swarming around her. Yellow and orange and red, they fluttered like exotic butterflies in the air. When she came near me, she stopped, stripped her hospital gown, and threw it aside. And she seemed to turn into a butterfly herself! Her dress, sheer and multishaded, flickered over her body, its wide sleeves sliding down her arms that were now raised toward the sky as if for flight...or prayer.

I watched her in puzzlement, my lips stretched into an artificial smile. It'd been more than a year since we last met, and less than a few hours ago, I was thinking that I would be happy if I never saw her again. But now I felt an all-too-familiar confusion tearing my mind in two. I felt as attracted to that woman as I was repelled by her, and once again she looked as gorgeous as her theatrical gestures looked grotesque.

"I bought it especially for our meeting," she said, pointing at her dress. "I knew that the weather would be like this, sunny with a strong wind."

"You also knew that I would come," I added grimly. "That I would waste no time."

I was hoping that she would deny it out of courtesy at least, but she nodded in agreement and sat next to me. I felt offended by her and angry with myself. She sent me a one-word message—a single "Come!"—and here I was, dammit. Here, in the dilapidated yard of the mental hospital where she was "interned following an expert's recommendation for psychiatric treatment."

I went to pick up her hospital gown—it looked cheap and worn thin with use. I beat out the leaves stuck to it and put it over her shoulders. She laughed. She waited for me to sit back on the bench and began in a serious voice,"I'm broke, Miro. Intentionally driven to bankruptcy and robbed by the person I had trusted my property with. But I kept my promise. Yes, although there was no trial, now the four of them are rich and unconditionally free. Maya is going to invest her money into a school for handicapped children—"

I tried to make a joke. "So, that super restaurant, At the Poisoner's, is not happening?"

"Yes," Graziella confirmed, still serious. "Frant is well too. He's working on a project for the orphanage Kuber dreamed of building. Valdo and Roxanna are husband and wife now. He's studying to be a construction engineer, and she's preparing her paintings for her first exhibition."

"I'm happy for them," I said. "It was high time something good and positive happened after so much misfortune. But you didn't call me here to tell me this, didn't you?"

"Of course, not. I could've written you a letter if it was only this. I could've expressed my gratitude in written form, you know. I was surprised when I found out you had not testified against me."

"And I was surprised that Fata has not testified either. It's her you should be thankful to."

"Well, let's not forget that she has five nephews, and each of them is the father of several children."

"You threatened her?"

"My lawyer did that. It was his initiative. I have nothing to do with it. But I did call her here yesterday, and I thanked her, and she even calmed down." Graziella evaded my question by quickly adding, "I'll explain everything, but first tell me, do you think I deserve to be locked here?"

I looked away from her eyes. I still remembered, would probably never forget, the state her cousin's excruciating agony brought her to. She called for an air ambulance not from one but three of the cities closest to the island. She wanted to make sure he had the minutes of life the fastest helicopter would secure for him. And after that, as we waited, she cradled his severed arm, talking to him, telling him incoherent stories from their childhood, promising him that she would double—no, triple!—his payment. And she would constantly urge him to take a look and see that his arm is "intact and could be sewn back on," as if she was consciously ignoring the fact that even if he were able to hear her despite his pain, he was unable to see anything, because his eyes…they had leaked out…

"That's too bad," she sighed. "It seems like you too believe I've gone mad."

"No, Graziella," I replied. "I think you've always carried that madness within you. It so happened that on that day you let it out for everyone to see."

She grew pensive.

"Maybe," she said in the end, "but it's back inside, that's important. I'm scheduled for an evaluation by the committee, and this time I shall give them no reason to not let me out. And the moment I'm out, I'll go to the court with a large group of journalists and publicly bring accusations against myself. Against my own self, Miro! Oh yes, there will be a trial, a *megatrial*, during which I'll tell the truth about everything…except for one thing: that you and Fata have committed perjury. I assured her yesterday, and I am assuring you now, I won't tell on you just as you did not tell on me. I will tell that you truly had no idea about my part in the murders committed by my cousin."

Graziella stared at me expectantly, and as I was wondering how to reply to that, her face lit up with an expression of ecstasy I knew well.

"I've planned even the tiniest details in my accusations!" she stated fervently. "First, I'll emphasize the fact that my cousin is guilty only of murdering the Japanese woman—I forgot her name—and of the accidental killing of Patrick. Then I will confess that he had murdered Deluc, Kotovich, Ramm, and also Ichiro following my orders. And finally, I will play them the video recording where it's clear that I am murdering Danko's stepmother!"

"But why?" I asked, confused. "That sounds like the shortest way to spending the rest of your life in prison."

"Exactly! Although I intend to insist on getting a death sentence. It's by way of such scandalous pleas that I am going to draw the entire world's attention to me, after which I will present all materials I've gathered during my five-month stay on the island. I'll also upload some of these materials on the Internet so that millions of people will be able to see Kuber saving that bird's life and Danko killing himself...only to stop himself from killing again. They would also be able to see that old recording in which Valdo is refusing to attack the wounded dog..."

Tears were flowing down her cheeks, but the wind was quick to dry them up—as if it was drinking them up.

"And the entire net will 'hear' Frant's words also: 'Not evil, good drove me crazy. It was like a bright light suddenly hitting the eyes of a previously blind man'...I will also upload a picture of the seven-year-old Roxanna—that beautiful girl with eyes plagued by horror. And two pictures of Maya: the first one showing her face disfigured by lipomas, and the second one, that of a homely teenager. 'The surgery was quite simple,' I am going to caption them. 'It took less than an hour and cost less than a pair of sneakers. The price of its delay, though? Eleven lives!' Yes, Miro, that's what I'm going to do. But I don't know, I still don't know, if I'll be able to find the strength to publish this too..."

After a brief moment of hesitation, Graziella took a postcard out of her hospital-gown pocket, gave it to me, her hand trembling, and I took it mechanically. I glanced at it, and my hand immediately began trembling too.

I saw a child. A boy, no older than eight. Stark naked, shockingly thin. A crown of thorns on his head. Crucified. The spikes of the thorns piercing his forehead, his blood flowing down his face like tears. Blood covering his palms too—and there were nails driven through them! His eyes so blood-shot that there was no white, only darkness, the dark of a pit. His mouth also looked like a pit, from which only endless, eternal moans seemed to come out.

"This is a frame from a video recording," Graziella said. "Fifteen years ago I ordered this picture to be put on postcards, and I've been sending one such to the parents every Easter ever since… but no, no!" She waved her hands before me. "Don't be so quick to accuse me of cruelty! The cruel ones, actually…the unspeakably, unforgivably cruel ones were the mother and the father of that tortured child."

I felt as if the postcard was burning the skin of my fingers. I gave it back to her, and she shoved it back into the pocket with a hurried gesture. More than a minute passed before she started talking again.

"His name was Mark. His parents were members of a religious sect. Fanatic followers of Satan, they decided to show their unreserved devotion to him by sacrificing their own son. According to the sect's rules, the ritual included all sorts of tortures and had to take place between two full moons, and if the victim survived until the second one, this meant that Satan had spared him or her.

Well, Mark survived. His physical wounds gradually healed but not the ones in his soul, because about a decade later, he ambushed the sect leader and murdered him. After that, he sent to Satan another three of his most "diligent" torturers in the ritual, and finally, he tied up his parents with the intention of murdering them too, but unfortunately his strength took him only so far. He gave up. And he probably would have been sentenced for life if they hadn't found a terrifying video collection at the house of the leader containing the recording I told you about. After seeing it at court, not even one of the members of the jury hesitated before voting in favor of *non compos mentis* and psychiatric treatment. And indeed, when I started working here, Mark was in a very, very sorry state...

Noticing my puzzled expression, Graziella smiled somewhat apologetically.

"I forgot to mention that I am here, in this clinic, because I explicitly asked for it. It was important for me to come back here where it all started, the place that determined not only my destiny but also the destinies of many other people. Sorrow, rage, obsession, cause, madness...every name we put to it will ring true. As true as the fact that in the beginning it was...it was only love and nothing else." She gently touched the pocket with the postcard.

"When we first met, Mark was already twenty-three years old. Same age as me. I had just finished an internship, and there were many possibilities before me, but since I was mainly interested in forensic psychiatry, I chose to start work here, in the same clinic. This is how Mark became one of my first patients. And my first love. My first and only, and most likely last love."

Standing up, she shrugged the hospital gown off her shoulders, wiped her tears once again, and went on talking, a peculiar pride in her voice.

"He was a true mess, despite the four-year-long treatment. In the following two years, though, he recovered completely. Not because I was a great psychiatrist. No! Our love healed him. Pure, beautiful, platonic love. And when he was discharged from the hospital, we decided to leave for someplace far, far away from here. And we were happy, so happy, that Mark went to see his parents and tell them that he had forgiven them. But his father thought he was coming for revenge and...shot him. Straight in the heart, Miro!"

We remained silent for a long time. She stood on the path, her gaze wandering somewhere in the distance as if looking for the shadows of the past there, the shadows cast by her only beloved. I could only see her face in profile. It was very pale, looked even ethereal against the lush autumnal beauty surrounding us. In a sense, she also was a shadow now.

I felt the ridiculous desire to call her, "Come, come back to me!" but then we heard someone whistling from the clinic. We looked in the direction of the sound—there was a nurse at the entrance, dressed in green overalls, looking serious and gesturing at us. The visiting hour was over, it seemed.

Graziella replied to the nurse with an untypically servile nod of her head. Then she looked down at me.

"I'm sorry," she said, blushing, or so it seemed. "I wish you could stay longer, but…I mustn't annoy anyone before the meeting with the committee. Plus, there isn't anything else I could tell you, is there? I know that there's no excuse for what I've done."

"There isn't," I replied, gloomily. "'The end justifies the means' is a hollow phrase. Especially when the 'means' are actually orders for the murders of innocent people."

"You're right; you're right," she repeated it like an echo. "Still…now that you've heard what I had to say, I feel much better. Thank you!"

The nurse whistled again. I rose, and at the same moment, Graziella put her arm around me, her lips touching mine. It was a quick and hot kiss, like a spark that, had the circumstances been different, could have started a fire. But I stepped back. She did the same. People say that the eyes are windows to the soul, but as I peered into her strange and glass-blue eyes, the only thing I saw were my two reflections on their smooth surface.